"You came he~~~~
we're going to b~~~ 2019

"I came here to tell you th~~ ~~~~ ~~~~ said. "I'm respecting the fact that you're ~~rn up abou~ everything that's happened and that's why you're avoiding me. I don't want to make things more diffi-cult, especially with our best friends getting mar-ried."

Chelsea opened her mouth, then closed it.

"Speechless?" he asked with a slight grin. "That wasn't the reaction I expected."

"What did you expect?"

"Well, you didn't slam the door in my face, so I'm already a step above where I thought I'd be."

She bit the inside of her cheek to keep from smiling, but failed.

"And a sexy grin? Hell, I better leave while I'm ahead."

Chelsea took a step back. As much as her body want-ed to invite him in, she also had to be smart.

No one had ever tempted her the way Gabe Walsh had.

* * *

Best Man Under the Mistletoe
is part ~~ ~~~ ~~~~~ ~~~~~ ~~~~~~~~~ ~~

BEST MAN UNDER
THE MISTLETOE

BY
JULES BENNETT

MILLS
BOON

First Published in Great Britain 2017
By Mills & Boon, an imprint of HarperCollins*Publishers*
1 London Bridge Street, London, SE1 9GF

© 2017 Harlequin Books S.A.

Special thanks and acknowledgement are given to Jules Bennett for her contribution to the Texas Cattleman's Club: Blackmail series.

ISBN: 978-0-263-92847-1

51-1217

MIX
Paper from
responsible sources
FSC™ C007454

Printed and bound in Spain
by CPI, Barcelona

National bestselling author **Jules Bennett** has penned over forty contemporary romance novels. She lives in the Midwest with her high-school-sweetheart husband and their two kids. Jules can often be found on Twitter chatting with readers, and you can also connect with her via her website, www.julesbennett.com.

To the Harlequin Desire team:
Stacy, Charles & Tahra.
They say it takes a village to raise a child...
The same is true for books.

One

"This investigation has really been a community effort. Thanks to the diligence of so many in Royal, the final piece of the puzzle has been put into place. Maverick has been identified as Royal's own Dale, a.k.a. Dusty, Walsh."

Gabe Walsh muted the TV and tossed the remote onto the leather sofa. He didn't want to hear any more about his late uncle's betrayal. The old bastard had passed away last week from a brain tumor and now the mess he'd caused to so many in the town of Royal, Texas, would have a ripple effect on Gabe's security firm. He would undoubtedly have a hell of a mess to clean up.

He still couldn't believe it. His uncle Dusty was Maverick, the cyber criminal who had terrorized members of the Texas Cattleman's Club for months now, revealing their secrets online and often resorting to blackmail.

Perhaps worst of all, he'd leaked nude photos of Chelsea Hunt, taken without her knowledge in the locker room at her gym.

According to Gabe's law-enforcement sources, all evidence pointed to Dusty working alone, except when it came to the locker room photos. There was now another person of interest in that particular crime. A woman, the police claimed. They were still studying months of surveillance-camera footage from the public areas of the gym to figure out who could have planted the camera.

Who the hell had aided his uncle? And was that the only instance when Dusty had taken on an accomplice? The man had been dying. There was no way Dusty could've done so much on his own. The man had been too feeble, too weak.

Though not so weak that he couldn't plot to destroy lives. Luckily, the citizens of Royal—Chelsea Hunt included—had risen above his attempts to take them down. Investigators had also seen through his elaborate attempt to pin the crimes on someone else.

Gabe raked a hand through his hair and glared at the screen as Sheriff Nate Battle continued his press conference. A picture of Gabe's once robust, smiling uncle filled the top right corner of the TV screen while the sheriff spoke.

How and why Uncle Dusty had pulled off such a grand scheme of blackmail and betrayal were open questions, but one thing was undeniable. He'd managed to put a big dark cloud over the family security firm, the Walsh Group—Gabe's new baby. As if taking over a company wasn't difficult and risky enough, now he was forced to deal with the backlash of questions from clients, both old and new, because of his relationship with Dusty.

How the hell was he supposed to dodge all of this bad press? The business's reputation was on the line. Sure, finances were the least of his concern. He'd busted his ass from the start of his career, saved every dollar, invested wisely and had worked his way up to be the best in the industry. He could close up shop and never work another day in his life, but he valued his reputation and family loyalty. Ironic now, wasn't it?

Gabe once again thought of Chelsea Hunt and it had him seeing red. His uncle had gotten his hands on compromising photos and proceeded to put them out for the town to see. And why? Yes, Chelsea had played an important role in the Maverick investigation, bringing in computer-security experts from out of town to help. But the leak was part of a bigger pattern: Maverick had been especially vicious when targeting women. One theory was that Maverick acted this way because the Texas Cattleman's Club had begun admitting women a few years back. By contrast, Dusty had been passed over for membership, one of the things that incurred his wrath.

Gabe's uncle had certainly been hidebound in his views of women—but going so far as to leak nude photos like that? What had been wrong with the man? Chelsea hadn't deserved the embarrassment and scandal that had been brought upon her by his uncle and some unknown accomplice.

Gabe cursed as he spun away from the television. He had been careful not to look at the photos when they'd been released for all the world to see. He hadn't wanted to be totally disrespectful or to violate her privacy. Plus, where Chelsea was concerned, he had problems of his own to deal with.

Replaying that kiss he and Chelsea had shared last week, it was a wonder he hadn't lost his damn mind.

Gabe and Chelsea had started spending a lot of time together when their best friends, Shane Delgado and

Brandee Lawson, had asked them to be best man and maid of honor in their wedding. Brandee had wanted Gabe and Chelsea to be very hands-on in the process. Gabe had known full well when they'd started working together that they'd be spending quite a bit of time alone.

But the other night, something had shifted. They'd been making name cards for the reception, which had triggered an argument, which had his last ounce of control snapping.

Gabe had grabbed the gold ribbon from Chelsea and tossed it aside, gripping her face and taking what he'd wanted for months.

Raking a hand through his hair, Gabe tried like hell to forget how she'd tasted, how she'd felt against him. But the scene replayed over and over in his head.

He could use a stiff drink and the company of a good woman between the sheets. But right at the moment neither would solve his problems…and the only woman he wanted between his sheets was the very one he needed to forget.

To top it all off on this hellish day, he had to meet Chelsea for some wedding planning nonsense later. How was she handling the news that his late uncle had been Maverick? Would she blame Gabe simply by association?

It was bad enough that he'd been roped into the wedding planning. He may as well have given up his man card for all the flowers and candles he'd been sniffing lately. If Shane and Brandee hadn't specifically asked Gabe and Chelsea to help with the planning, Gabe would've given this project the middle finger. But Shane was as close as family and, even though Gabe didn't believe in happily-ever-after, he was glad to see his best friends so in love.

Gabe just wished Chelsea wasn't the maid of honor because until the Christmas nuptials rolled around, dodging her wasn't an option. Nearly every single day he'd be spending hours looking at seating charts, passing on the bride's playlist to the band, finalizing the caterers and florists...and all of that time would only lead to one more thing. Another kiss.

Why the hell did it have to be this woman who intrigued him? At first he'd wondered if he'd just felt bad for all the negative attention she'd been getting, but he'd quickly squelched that notion. He wasn't one to take pity and turn it into lust.

But there was something about her strength and the fact she wasn't letting this scandal break her when it very well should. He admired anyone who could rise above adversity and still remain in control.

And then there was just plain, old-fashioned, sexual desire.

She was hot, and he was a man with breath in his lungs. He would have been a fool not to be attracted.

That kiss had upped the stakes and now all he could think of was getting another taste. Given everything that had transpired today, was that wrong? Should he even allow himself to crave the woman his uncle had publicly humiliated?

Muttering a curse, Gabe turned the television off and grabbed his keys. He might as well get this little meeting with Chelsea over with and then go back to doing damage control at the Walsh Group. Not only would the clients be pouring in with questions, his employees would, too. The sheriff had told Gabe about his findings before the press conference—and cleared him of any wrongdoing, for that matter—so Gabe had already given a heads-up to his assistants that this was coming and instructed them on how to handle the expected calls.

The people in Royal knew him, knew that he wouldn't

partake in something so heinous. But there were clients who didn't know him and those were the ones he'd be personally calling and meeting face-to-face. He wasn't looking forward to doing damage control, but he'd worked too hard for his impeccable reputation and he'd be damned if he let anyone tarnish it…especially family.

That was business. He knew how to handle all of that, but he had no clue how to approach Chelsea. No doubt she'd heard on the news or directly from Sheriff Battle the identity of her blackmailer and Gabe would be the perfect target for her to take out her frustrations. And then there was the unacknowledged-but-hard-to-ignore attraction between them.

But she was in a vulnerable position and only a complete jerk would take advantage of that. She may put on a strong front, something he commended her for, but no doubt she still hurt. All he could do at this point was to show her he wasn't like his uncle, that he was completely innocent, and he was there for her if she needed him.

The screwdriver hurtled past Gabe's head and Chelsea cursed herself for missing. She was still shaken up by the news, that was all. If she'd been fully on her game, she would've nailed the target. The sexy, arrogant, infuriating target.

She didn't condone violence, but this man had stepped into her bad mood at the wrong time. She'd only just learned of the Maverick's true identity and Gabe Walsh was guilty by association. For all she knew, Gabe had helped cover his uncle's tracks. He was a sneaky PI, after all. Even though the sheriff had assured her there was no evidence Gabe had any involvement whatsoever, she was furious and needed to lash out.

"Is that any way to treat someone who's come to help

you build this archway for the ceremony?" Gabe asked, slowly making his way toward her.

Chelsea grabbed the hammer. "I don't need, nor did I ask for your help."

Gabe cocked his head and kicked up his wicked smile. Gabe had that whole don't-give-a-damn attitude down pat; nothing ever bothered him. He seduced and charmed everyone in his path...but not her. And she wasn't going to think of that kiss, either. She *wasn't*.

"Brandee texted me and asked me to come help you with the arch for the ceremony," he informed her.

Chelsea glanced at the piles of wood, flowers, tulle and wire all spread out in the old barn at Hope Springs, Brandee's ranch. Brandee could've hired a company to take over the decorating and organizing of the big day, but Chelsea had wanted to make things special for her friend. She'd wanted to be hands-on since she knew Brandee better than any stranger would.

But Chelsea would rather have worked her fingers to the bone than ask Gabe for any help. Now that the Maverick had been revealed as his uncle, Chelsea felt utterly betrayed.

"I wasn't sure how Dusty managed to get those images of me and splash them around, but now it's pretty clear he had help." Chelsea continued to stare at the man who was too sexy to be legal. The tattoos, the scruff along his jawline, the arrogant stance. "You were his errand boy."

"What?" Gabe said, jerking back. "I—"

"Anything for the family," she went on, dropping the hammer to the concrete floor at her side instead of hurling it at his head next. "You were trained to take over the family business. Taking orders from your dying uncle just came naturally."

"You have no idea what you're talking about," Gabe

countered, an edge to his voice. "You might want to have evidence before making such claims—evidence you will never find because I had nothing to do with the pictures or the blackmail."

He may have been a former special agent, he may have put the fear of God in many suspects in his time, but Chelsea wasn't afraid. The only thing she worried about was how he managed to infuriate and turn her on at the same time. She hated how her body responded to just the sight of him when her mind told her she knew better. Why did lust have to cloud her judgment?

"I'm not arguing." She turned her attention back to the mess before her. "I have too much to do here. If Brandee doesn't see some progress, she'll worry it won't be done in time, and I won't have my best friend stressed for her special day."

"Then it sounds like you need an extra pair of hands."

Chelsea shuddered. Gabe had used those hands to grip her shoulders and haul her against his hard body as he'd kissed her so fast, so fierce—

"I say we call a truce."

Chelsea swallowed and finally nodded. He was right. They had to work together and she had to believe the sheriff when he'd said Gabe was in the clear. She just wanted someone to blame, someone to take her anger out on.

"A truce," she said. "I think I can handle that."

Gabe flashed that smile again. "So what are we doing here?"

"Brandee wants a large arch for her and Shane to stand beneath to exchange their vows. She wants it to be elegant and Christmassy, not tacky. Everything will be done in whites and golds and clear lights. She told me to order one, but I wanted to make it so she had something special and meaningful."

Chelsea couldn't help but feel a twinge of jealousy at her friend's upcoming nuptials. Chelsea may be hard, she may be independent and run the tech side of Hunt & Co. like a boss, but she was still a woman with dreams. She didn't want a man to take care of her, but she certainly wouldn't mind a man to hold her at night, to appreciate her Italian-lace lingerie collection, to laugh with her and share stories about their days. Was it too much to ask to meet just one man who wasn't a jerk?

"Is there a blueprint for this or are we just winging it?" Gabe asked.

Chelsea came to her feet, dusting her hands against her holey jeans. "No blueprint, but Shane had everything cut and ready to assemble once I told him my ideas. I told Brandee I'd take care of it since it's my idea. I have a picture on my phone of what it should look like. But it's just a mock-up of the picture in my head."

She slid her phone from her pocket and pulled up the image.

Gabe came to stand beside her, having the nerve to brush his shoulder against hers.

She shouldn't be attracted to such a…a…wolfish man. He was a hell of a kisser, but he was also related to the enemy. That was reason enough for her to be leery. Wasn't it? There was only so far a hot bod and toe-curling kiss could take Gabe Walsh. So what if she'd had vivid, detailed dreams of the infamous kiss and all the delicious things her mind conjured up without her permission?

"Subtle," she said as she took a half step to the side. "Don't try using this opportunity to kiss or seduce me or whatever else you're thinking."

Gabe came around and stood directly in front of her. She still held her phone out, her hands frozen in the narrow space between them. His deep eyes held her in place, and Chelsea trembled as if he'd touched her bare skin.

"Darlin', when you were kissing me, you weren't exactly shy about it."

Chelsea opened her mouth to object, but Gabe leaned forward, coming to within a breath of her lips.

"So don't try to deny that you're attracted to me," he murmured. "And I won't deny it, either. But right now, we have more pressing things to do than worry about who is seducing whom."

Keeping his eyes on hers, he eased back and slid the phone from her grip. Damn the man for making her entire body heat up like he'd lit a match from within. The broad shoulders, the scruff along his jawline, the ink peeking from beneath his fitted T-shirt…and the way he'd drawled out "darlin'" had her ready to ignore those red flags and kiss him again. Maybe it hadn't been that good and she'd remembered all wrong. Had her toes actually curled? Had her body tightened with arousal?

Stifling a groan, Chelsea stepped over the supplies and went to the pile of wood. As much as she liked to think she could do everything on her own, she was going to need Gabe's help here.

"This is some setup they're wanting," Gabe said behind her. "I guess we better get started. The wedding is only a couple weeks away and this isn't our only task."

Gabe again came up beside her, this time not touching, and handed over her phone. "Tell me we've decided on the florist. I really don't want to look at one more plant or bloom or branch or anything else that I know nothing about."

"The florist has been nailed down and contacted. Now, we need to finalize the appetizers and beer and wine list for the combined bachelor/bachelorette party," she told him. "I have the final numbers for those who sent in their RSVP."

Gabe blew out a sigh. "I'll handle all the menus if you promise I don't have to pick out tablecloths or do little calligraphy place cards."

Chelsea crossed her arms and turned to fully face him. "Well, Gabriel Walsh, I'm disappointed in your knowledge of contemporary weddings. Calligraphy cards are definitely a thing of the past. I actually already ordered name cards in the same design and font as Brandee's invitations. You really should update your wedding magazine subscriptions if you're ever going to do this yourself."

"If I ever lose my mind and marry, I'll let my bride handle everything." He raked a hand over his stubbled jaw. "Food and alcohol are easy. Especially since we're having the party at the TCC. What else do you want me to do that doesn't involve something frilly or flowery?"

"Someone is grouchy," she muttered. "Is it because I threw the screwdriver at your head or because I'm not throwing myself at you after the kiss?"

Gabe shoved his hands in his pockets and tipped his head sideways to look her in the eyes. "Are we going to be able to get along to get through this together?"

Chelsea shrugged. "Depends. You keep your hands and lips to yourself and we might just. And just so you know, I tend to believe you when you say you didn't know what your uncle was up to. Shane and Brandee wouldn't put their trust in you if you were involved. But you better hope like hell there isn't a connection, because if I find out there is, I won't miss the next time I throw a screwdriver at your head."

Two

"This doesn't look right. Is it leaning a little?"

Gabe stood back and stared at the arch he and Chelsea had been grunting over for the better part of the day. They'd gotten along surprisingly well, as long as they'd kept the topic of conversation on the wedding...or when they weren't talking at all.

When the silence stretched between them, though, his mind started conjuring up all sorts of naughty thoughts and each one starred the woman at his side. The way she wore her holey jeans low on her hips and that fitted tank, she didn't look like an expert hacker and CTO of the most prestigious chain of steakhouses in the South.

She could drive any man out of his mind, even if she was spitting in his face and smarting off with that sweet mouth. It was one of the many reasons he couldn't help but admire her. She didn't take crap from anyone and was her own hero, saving herself from the evils in her own world. Damn if that wasn't sexy as hell.

It didn't go unnoticed how she'd kept glancing his way. The attraction simmering just below that steel barrier she kept around her was going to explode…and he damn well would be the man to experience her passion. He'd had just enough of a taste to crave more, and she could deny all she wanted with her words, her body told a whole different story.

He gave the arch a slight push. "Did that help?"

Chelsea stepped back, angling her head. "That did it."

Gabe's cell vibrated in his pocket. He pulled it out and glanced at the text from one of his assistants. After a quick response, he slid the phone back in.

"Late for a lunch date with your girlfriend?" Chelsea asked as she gathered the tools and put them off to the side.

"If you want to know if I'm seeing anyone, just ask."

She tucked her shoulder-length, honey-blond hair behind one ear and quirked a brow. "I didn't ask."

"I'm not seeing anyone," he informed her, taking long strides to close the distance between them. "A fact you should know before you kiss me again."

Chelsea crossed her arms beneath her chest and it was all he could do to keep his eyes on hers. "You're arrogant enough to think that's going to happen?"

"Arrogant? Perhaps, though I'm positive it's only a matter of time." Whistling, he turned to head from the barn out to his car. Any second he expected a tool to hit the back of his head or go whirling by his ear. But nothing happened. He was proud she showed such restraint. Obviously he was growing on her.

But he'd be lying if he claimed he wasn't irritated by the fact she thought he had something to do with those leaked pictures. What on earth would his motive be? There was no reason for him to go around with his uncle terrorizing the people of this town. Gabe actually liked those who had been affected by his uncle's activities and would never want to see any of them harmed. Shane and Brandee had even been targeted, for pity's sake. Dusty's antics were absolutely inconceivable.

As Gabe slid behind the wheel and started the engine, Chelsea came strutting out of the barn straight toward him. He rolled his window down.

"I knew you'd chase after me."

Rolling her eyes, she propped her hands on her hips. "Brandee just texted me and asked if we'd run to Natalie Valentine's bridal shop so I can get my last fitting."

"As much as I'd love to help you with a fitting, I'm afraid I have work to do. My uncle, as you know, is ruining my name even in his death and I have too many clients to coddle during this sensitive time. Besides, how could you ever bring yourself to trust me at a fitting?"

Chelsea's lips thinned and she gritted her teeth before saying, "Brandee wants us to stop at Priceless to pick up her wedding present to Shane. She bought a table and chairs for their dining room, says it's just like the one his grandmother used to have, and she wants to surprise him. The dress fitting just makes sense because we'll already be there."

Gabe dropped his head back against the headrest and groaned. "You know, I do have a company to run."

"Yes, and here I am with nothing to do. Or maybe you've forgotten I have a demanding position, as well."

"That's not what I meant," he argued. Blowing out a sigh, he glanced back up at her. "Get in. We'll swing by my place and pick up my truck so we can go get this furniture."

"I'll drive myself."

"There's no reason we can't ride together. I have to

take the truck anyway to pick up the table. Unless you're afraid to be alone with me."

Chelsea narrowed her eyes. "I hate your inflated ego."

"Duly noted. Now, get in."

He couldn't help but smile as she rounded the hood of his car. He didn't know why he wanted to provoke her, but he couldn't help himself. In actuality, he wanted to spend more time with her. Seducing her was something he wanted to pursue, sure, but more importantly he wanted her to know that he would never, ever, treat a woman the way she'd been treated by his uncle. Above all else, he needed her to know that. And she wouldn't just take his word for it. She needed to see that he wasn't some jerk that got off on blackmailing people and ruining reputations.

As soon as she got into the car, he put it in gear and set off toward his downtown loft.

He kept his truck in the second bay of his garage, for which he paid a hefty monthly fee to have parking beneath his downtown loft apartment. But a man couldn't live in Texas and not own a truck. It was practically against the law.

"You know—" he began once they'd switched to the truck and were back on the road.

"We don't need to talk."

Well, apparently this was going to be more difficult than he'd thought. Gabe tightened his grip on the wheel.

"Yes, we do," he countered. "As I was saying, you know there are many people in this town who know me and know I would never side with my uncle. I wouldn't have covered up such maliciousness."

"I know you were cleared of any wrongdoing. The sheriff told me he's positive you had nothing to do with the scandal. But at the same time, he was your only family member. How did you not know what he was up to? He was old and feeble. Someone had to know something about what he was doing."

There was bite to her voice, but beneath that gruff exterior there was pain. Gabe hated what she'd gone through, the humiliation and embarrassment. The fact that so many had suffered at the hands of his uncle didn't sit well with him, but he was especially upset about Chelsea. Her betrayal had taken on a darker, more personal feel than the others.

No matter how much anger she projected toward him, he was hell-bent on proving to her that he understood, that he totally agreed with her, that they were on the same page. He knew his uncle was a bastard, but just because Gabe's last name was Walsh didn't mean he knew what had been taking place in the months leading up to his uncle's death.

"I can't imagine how difficult this has been," he started, hoping she let him finish. "I know you're angry, but I swear I didn't know about those photos until they were leaked. I never even looked at them."

Chelsea snorted and shot him a glare. "If you think for a second I believe that lie, you're more of a fool than I thought. You're a guy. You looked."

"We could argue this till we're both blue in the face, you still wouldn't believe me," he growled. "But you'll see. Once the truth is revealed and they catch whoever this accomplice is, you'll realize that I truly knew nothing. You think I'd actually keep information like this to myself? Dusty self-destructed and that has nothing to do with me. I have a reputation, a multibillion-dollar security business to look after. The last thing I want to be involved in is a scandal."

Gabe had to believe she'd eventually come to see that

he wasn't lying. He prided himself on honesty, and liked to think he was a man of integrity. Sure, he could be hard when it came to work, but when it came to his personal life, he could admit he was a bit softer when it was necessary. And this situation called for delicate measures unlike anything he'd ever known.

As he pulled into the Courtyard Shops, Gabe figured that even though he'd rather do anything else than wait on Chelsea to try on her dress, at least this forced time together was giving him the prime opportunity he needed to win her over. Which was important to him, even though he had big problems to deal with at his business right now.

"You can go on into Priceless while I try on the dress."

Gabe hopped out of the truck and shot her a wink. "If it's all the same, I'll just stick with you. You won't be long and then you can help me load the table next door."

Chelsea groaned as she jerked on her door handle. Normally, Gabe would get the door for a woman—he was raised in the South by a well-mannered mother—but he also had a feeling if he tried to get the door for Chelsea, he'd just be taking a step in the wrong direction.

But the moment he stepped inside Natalie's shop, Gabe started to reconsider his ploy to stick close to Chelsea. There were dresses everywhere. Fluffy, lacy, silky dresses, and the place smelled…pink. If a smell could have a color, this place was definitely pink.

The peppy little shop attendant greeted Chelsea and promptly went to get the dress from the back. Gabe spotted a lounge area in that direction and made his way to a white sofa in front of the wall of mirrors. He could catch up on a few emails that needed his attention and check in on his right-hand man doing some security work in Dallas for the next few weeks.

Nothing was as important as his business, especially during this crucial time. He'd already reached out to some of his closest clients and assured them that Dusty's scandal had nothing to do with the Walsh Group. He'd also made sure they knew they could come to him personally with questions or concerns.

The unfortunate, untimely setback wouldn't change the way Gabe handled his business. But it sure did complicate matters. If ole Dusty weren't already dead, Gabe would have no problem driving out to his mansion and beating the ever loving sh—

Every single thought vanished when Chelsea stepped from the dressing room and came to stand in front of the three-way mirror. The fitted gold gown shouldn't have looked so damn sexy, seeing as how it was long, with full sleeves, and a high neck. But the material hugged every single curve and dip on Chelsea's luscious body, mocking him. He'd seen her in jeans, even in little flowy sundresses, but nothing like this, all sultry and glamorous.

She smoothed the dress over her flat stomach and turned from side to side. The innocent gesture shouldn't have gripped his attention, but this woman had him in a total trance.

Emails and damage control forgotten, Gabe set aside his phone. He had nothing else to be doing right this second except for admiring her as she watched her reflection.

Hell. This wasn't the time or the place to be getting uncomfortable in his jeans. Just who the hell was seducing whom here? But from the unsure look on her face—her brows were drawn, her mouth turned down in a frown—it seemed she had doubts about how damn perfect and sexy she looked.

"It's fine," he growled after what seemed like an hour of pure torture. "Can we wrap it up here?"

Hands on her hips, Chelsea glared at him from her reflection in the mirror. "I need to make sure I can breathe and sit without busting a seam, if you don't mind. It seems tight."

Actually he did mind, and it was damn tight…the dress and his pants. He should've gone to the antique store because this was pure hell. Then again, at least he had a heads-up for how she'd look when he had to escort her down the aisle. He'd hate to be all mouth agape and drooling in front of Shane and Brandee's friends and families.

The idea of Chelsea and him walking down the aisle shouldn't have made him feel awkward, yet it did. Weddings in general made him twitchy. That whole happily-ever-after wasn't for everyone; he'd even managed to dodge being in any type of wedding party his entire life. But there was no way he could say no to Shane, his very best friend.

The more Chelsea shifted and turned and smoothed her hands over those luscious curves, the more uncomfortable Gabe became.

Commotion behind him had him tearing his gaze from the mirror and glancing over his shoulder. A slew of teenage girls came in the door, chattering and giggling about homecoming and needing perfect dresses. He could not get out of there fast enough. Between the lace, the satin and the chatter in such high octaves, this place was sucking the testosterone right out of his body.

"This will just have to work because I don't have the time to do more measurements," Chelsea muttered as she stepped off the platform and headed back into her dressing room. "Give me two minutes and we'll be out of here."

Gabe came to his feet, more than ready to get the hell out. As he shoved his hands in his pockets and rocked back on his heels, he heard Chelsea mumbling and cursing from inside the dressing room. Seconds later, the door eased open just a crack.

"Um… I'm stuck."

He eyed the narrow strip of her face showing through the door. "'Scuse me?"

"The zipper," she whispered through gritted teeth. "The damn thing is stuck. Get the salesclerk to come help me."

Gabe glanced over his shoulder at the mayhem of teens and fluffy dresses. The two workers were running in all directions accommodating parents and demanding girls.

He could do this. How hard would it be to get a zipper unstuck? Pulling in a deep breath, Gabe pushed open the dressing room door and offered up his assistance.

Three

"Gabe. What—?"

She backed up and stared as he shut and locked the door behind him. The narrow space seemed to shrink even more with his broad frame filling the area.

"You said you needed help."

Chelsea crossed her arms over her chest. "I said to get the salesclerk."

"Well, darlin', there's about a dozen teenage girls out there and only two staff that I saw. That's not a great ratio, so if you want out of this dress anytime in the next few hours, I'm it."

That gleam in his eye was just about the naughtiest, sexiest thing she'd ever seen. Which was one of the many reasons she shouldn't be closed in with him, and definitely why he shouldn't help unzip her dress. Being half-naked and in close proximity with Gabe would only lead to…

She couldn't even let her mind wander down that path.

"I'll do it myself," she claimed, though she'd already tried that. "Go on to the antique store and I'll be right over."

Gabe took one step and was right against her. "We both have other things to do today, so you might as well let me help you out."

"You seem to be enjoying this a little too much."

His hand skimmed up her side where the zipper was carefully hidden. "I'll be enjoying this even more if you'd let me work this zipper down."

The image that immediately popped into her head had Chelsea thinking for a half second of lifting her arm and letting him have a go. But then she remembered who he was...or rather who his uncle had been.

"This isn't a good idea," she told him. Surely he saw that...didn't he? He knew her feelings and knew full well she didn't trust him.

"What's not a good idea?" he asked, his eyes traveling over her face, landing on her lips. "Us in this confined space alone or the fact that you're attracted to me?"

Chelsea fisted her hands at her sides—to keep from hitting him or grabbing his face and kissing him, she wasn't sure. Her attraction wouldn't be such an issue if Gabe wasn't a Walsh. If his uncle hadn't tried to destroy so many lives, hers included. The guilt by association was enough to have her emotionally pulling back.

But the sizzling attraction didn't let up, no matter how much she tried to shove it aside.

Chelsea's body trembled, betraying her vow to keep him at a distance. When his fingers skimmed over her again, he quirked a half smile as he brought his eyes back up to meet hers.

"Is this the part where you deny your attraction?" he

asked, still using those clever hands. His fingertips circled around to where the dress exposed her back.

Chelsea sucked in a breath and cursed every single goose bump that popped up along her skin. They were both fully clothed, yet his fingertips on her bare back was something too akin to a lover's touch. And it had been too damn long since she'd taken a lover; she was clearly letting this affect her more than it should.

She'd not made the best choices in men. When she'd been younger, she confused attention with attraction. Then as she'd gotten older she'd distanced herself because she didn't trust her judgment. The scandal had her more than hesitant at getting close to any man. Now, here she was attracted to a man who was the next of kin to the bastard who'd humiliated her.

"Turn around," he whispered in her ear.

Without thinking, she turned to face the mirror. Gabe stood directly behind her, his body practically plastered against hers and those fingers still roaming over her heated skin. His eyes met hers in the mirror as he raised his other hand to the top of the zipper. Just the brush of his knuckles on the underside of her arm had her shivering even though the thick material served as a barrier.

Chelsea closed her eyes, hoping that if she didn't have to look at their reflection she could ignore this entire moment.

"Look at me," he demanded.

She gave in way too easily as her gaze met his once again. "Stop," she muttered.

"Stop what exactly?" He gave the zipper the slightest tug. "Stop helping you out of this dress or stop tormenting us both?"

She'd never been one to think of having sex in a public place, but right at this moment, she'd give just about anything to alleviate this ache caused by a man she shouldn't want.

"You had to know when we kissed that there would be more," he whispered. Though he didn't need to keep his voice down. The chaos of teen girls on the other side of that locked door drowned out anything they were saying…or doing.

"There can't be more."

The zipper gave way just as he brushed his lips along the side of her neck. Chelsea's body betrayed her…much as it had ever since Gabe had stepped foot into this tiny room. Closing her eyes, she dropped her head against his shoulder. Maybe she just wanted to take this moment, maybe she wanted to ignore everything and let him pleasure her. He was doing a damn fine job already.

Why did she have to be so torn? Why did he have to be such a mystery?

The hand on her back came around to her throat, tipping her head just enough for him to trail his lips over her exposed skin. He continued to work on her zipper just as expertly as he heated her up. She was about one strategically placed kiss away from moaning.

"Don't lie to me again and tell me you don't want me," he murmured in her ear. "You're shaking in my arms and I haven't even gotten you out of this dress yet."

He cupped her jaw and turned her head toward him. As his mouth crashed onto hers, Chelsea turned in his arms, threading her fingers through his hair and taking what he so freely gave.

Just for a minute. That was all. Then she'd go back to loathing him and believing he was a liar. But right now, common sense and reality had no place here.

Nothing lied about his lips or the hands that roamed

all over her body. He wanted her just as fiercely as she wanted him.

Gabe backed her against the wall and gripped her hips, pulling her toward him. His arousal was obvious.

If he lit her up this quickly, this intensely, what would happen once they were skin to skin? Would he take his time and savor the moment? Would he—?

"Excuse me?" A knock came on the door. "We have several girls who need to try some things on."

Gabe eased back slightly and muttered under his breath. Chelsea wanted the floor to open up and swallow her whole. First, there'd been the naked pictures and now she'd been pretty much caught getting it on in the dressing room of the only bridal shop in town. Could she provide more fodder for the gossip mill? Maybe she should parade down the main street of Royal in the buff.

"My zipper was stuck," she called out, realizing how lame that sounded. "Be right out."

Chelsea pushed Gabe back, but he couldn't go far considering the narrow space. "Either help me with the rest of this zipper or get out."

His dark eyes were heavy with arousal, the bulge in his jeans an added reminder of what they'd nearly done. Heat crept up her neck and flushed her face. She reached to the side of her dress and found that he'd actually gotten the zipper all the way down. When had that happened? Likely somewhere between that first touch and when he'd nearly kissed her to orgasm.

"Your work here is done," she told him, more than ready to get out of this dress and back into her jeans and boots.

Gabe took one step toward her, framed her face in his hands and leaned to within a breath of her mouth. "My work with you hasn't even started."

Releasing her, he stepped from the room and out the door just as casual as you please. Chelsea sank onto the tiny accent chair in the corner and took a deep breath. Right now the least of her worries was the people on the other side of that door when she walked out.

No, her greatest concern was the man who'd just left her aching even more than before. Nobody had ever gotten her so worked up, and here she was still trembling and in desperate need for him to finish the job.

Damn it. How was she going to keep her distance while they worked on this wedding, and not fall into bed with Gabe Walsh?

Four

Gabe shut down his laptop and came to his feet. It had been two days since his close encounter with Chelsea at the bridal shop and he was no closer to finding relief than he was then.

The damn woman had gotten to him. Perhaps it was her sassy mouth, or maybe it was the fact she hadn't initially believed him when he'd said he was in no way involved in leaking those nude photos. Maybe it was the way she wore jeans and tanks like they were made for her. Hell, he didn't know. All Gabe knew was that Chelsea Hunt was an enigma that he simply couldn't solve.

He'd been a damn special agent and still he couldn't figure out how someone as smart-mouthed and difficult as Chelsea had gotten under his skin. He could find any woman to scratch his itch, but he wasn't that guy anymore. In his twenties, he'd been selfish, falling into the bed of any willing woman. He was more particular now, definitely busier with work. And no one had pulled at him like Chelsea Hunt. So, no. No other woman would do.

But right now he had a few other pressing matters. Several of his clients had questioned him about his connection to his uncle. He'd already spoken with quite a few of them and he wasn't done yet. Gabe planned to spend the rest of his day running interference and hopefully smoothing ruffled feathers.

He grabbed his hat and headed out the door of his loft apartment. He loved the prime location in downtown Royal. There were shops, restaurants, and it wasn't too far from the Texas Cattleman's Club. He planned to head over later to get some riding in. Getting on the back of a horse and taking off into the fresh air always calmed him and helped to clear his mind.

The only drawback to living in a loft in town was that he couldn't have his own horses. Growing up outside Dallas on a working farm had been every little boy's dream, and riding had been a staple in his life. At least being a member of the Texas Cattleman's Club offered him anything he could want, including access to the club's stables. So he had the best of both worlds right now.

Gabe's cell vibrated in his pocket as he headed to the garage beneath his loft apartment. Pulling it out, he glanced at the screen and swiped to answer.

"Shane. What's up?"

"Just checking in on you, man. How are you holding up with all the fallout from your uncle?"

Gabe tightened his grip on the phone and resisted the urge to groan. "It's been a bit of a nightmare, but nothing I can't handle."

"Brandee and I are here for you, whatever you need. We know you'd never have a hand in anything this scandalous and cruel."

Gabe slid his sunglasses from the top of his head and settled them in place. "I'm doing damage control with the company. There's not much else anyone can do. I appreciate the offer."

"Of course. I hate how all this is happening on top of the wedding details," Shane added.

"Not a big deal. Like I said, nothing I can't handle."

"Speaking of wedding details, my fiancée is not happy."

Gabe laughed as he settled in behind the wheel of his truck. "Sounds like your problem, not mine."

"Oh, it's every bit your problem," Shane corrected. "Were you in the dressing room at the bridal shop with Chelsea? Wait, I know the answer to that. What the hell were you thinking, man?"

Blowing out a sigh, Gabe started the engine. "Does it matter? Nothing happened. Her zipper was stuck, that's all."

Well, that was all he'd own up to. Whatever was brewing between Chelsea and him was their business. As much as he'd like to claim there was more, things hadn't progressed near to where he wanted them. This was the slowest form of torture and foreplay he'd ever experienced in his life.

"Listen, whatever you do with anyone else is fine."

"Glad I have permission, Dad."

"But," Shane went on, "Chelsea is different. After what she's been through and with her being Brandee's best friend, this is a little more delicate than you just messing around with any other woman."

"I'm well aware of how vulnerable Chelsea is." Anger simmered as Gabe clenched the steering wheel. "And we're not messing around. How the hell did you find out anyway?"

Because he knew for a fact Chelsea wouldn't have run to Brandee and spilled. Even though this was perfect girly gossip, Gabe liked to think he knew Chelsea pretty well and this wasn't the type of chatter she'd take part in.

"You think a shop full of teens and their mothers didn't know you or Chelsea?" Shane asked in disbelief. "This town isn't that big, man. And if I know about it, you don't think Daniel hasn't heard by now?"

Daniel Hunt, Chelsea's brother. Chelsea's older, over-protective brother. He and Chelsea had been through so much with the loss of their parents. Everyone knew their mother had run out on them and their father had passed a year later, some said from a broken heart. Was it any wonder Chelsea was so closed off, so leery and untrusting? Add in the scandal over the photos and she'd had quite a bit thrown at her. More than most people should endure. And other than Daniel and Brandee, who did she have to lean on?

"I'm not worried about Daniel," Gabe said as he put his truck in gear. "As much as I'd love to continue this cheery conversation, I have other things to get done. Even in death, my uncle is ruining my reputation."

Shane blew out a sigh. "Sorry, man. I wasn't thinking."

"No reason to be sorry. You and Brandee were victims, as well."

Hell, there was hardly a member of the TCC who hadn't been affected somehow by his uncle. Gabe still had no clue as to his motives, but he knew Dusty Walsh had been denied membership to the exclusive club three times over the years. And when women had been admitted, it had only made Dusty's grudge worsen.

Perhaps this was his uncle's way of getting back at the club because of the board's decision. Who knew? All Gabe did know was that it would continue to impact his reputation for some time and he'd have to stay on top of things to keep his security business running.

"Just try to calm down with the public displays," Shane warned. "Chelsea is dealing with enough and I'd really like this wedding to go off without drama."

Gabe knew exactly what Chelsea was dealing with and he cursed himself for putting her in such a position. But, damn it, when he was around her, all logical thinking just vanished.

"Your wedding will be drama-free," Gabe assured his best friend. "Go kiss your fiancée and let her know Chels and I have everything under control."

He disconnected the call before Shane could question him further. As much as Gabe wanted to concentrate on Chelsea, on the memory of her sweet body pressed against his and her zipper parting beneath his touch, he had a high-dollar client to see.

Business first. Business always came first. Then he'd check up on his girl.

"I'll make sure they're delivered here if you don't mind being on hand to put everything away in the freezer. They'll come packaged with instructions for how long they need to sit out to thaw and the exact way they should be marinated and cooked."

Chelsea was going over the to-do list for the joint bachelor/bachelorette party with Rose, her contact in the TCC kitchen. Rose smiled and nodded as Chelsea ticked the items in her head off on her fingers.

"I'm sorry," Chelsea said. "I'm sure you know how to cook a steak and this isn't the first party you've done, but this is my company and my best friend we're talking about."

Chelsea may have been the CTO of Hunt & Co., dealing with the computers and the technical end of the business, but she knew how to handle steaks, as well. There were good steaks and then there were Hunt steaks. Chelsea wanted absolutely the best for her friends and that could only come from her family's company.

Rose patted Chelsea's arm. "It's quite all right, dear. I understand."

Chelsea smiled. "Thanks. I promise I'm only neurotic because I want this to be perfect for them."

"And it will be," Rose assured her. "I'll take care of everything."

Chelsea headed from the kitchen area. Since her workday was essentially done, she figured she'd take advantage of her club membership and go riding. She needed the break from reality and being on the back of a horse was always so freeing. It helped to clear her head.

She definitely needed her head cleared because for the past two days she hadn't been able to focus on anything other than Gabe Walsh. The stubborn man wouldn't leave her mind. He took up entirely too much real estate in her thoughts. She'd tried throwing herself further into the wedding planning. She'd tried reading books. She'd even resorted to her old hacking skills and messed with her brother's social media accounts for fun. But nothing had taken away the memory of the dressing room.

The Dressing Room.

It was like the title of an epic romance she couldn't put down. For one, she'd never had a public make-out session. Two, she hadn't allowed any man to wrap her up so tight she feared she'd spring any minute. And for another, damn it…she just wanted to hate the man. Was that too much to ask? He was egotistical, arrogant…and too damn sexy for his own good.

But she couldn't bring herself to hate the way he

kissed, the way he'd touched her. How was it even possible that he had this hold on her? How could one man invoke so many emotions?

Chelsea headed toward the stables. The fresh winter air filled her lungs. She couldn't wait to spend the next few hours just relaxing and enjoying her ride.

When her cell vibrated in her pocket, she ignored it. Nothing was going to get in the way of this much needed alone time. Whoever wanted her could leave a message. If it was Daniel again, she'd get back to him. Any Hunt business could wait since it was after hours. And there was nothing pressing for the wedding at the moment.

In no time, Chelsea had chosen a gorgeous chestnut mare and was on her way. Getting back in the saddle felt so good. It had been too long since she'd taken advantage of the amenities TCC had to offer. Maybe she should schedule a massage and some sauna time after the wedding and holidays were over. She could use a good day of pampering.

Chelsea was just thankful they'd started allowing women to join a few years ago. There was a time when only men were members, but everything had changed when they'd opened the doors and their minds to the ladies.

Chelsea had jumped at the chance to join such an elite club. Who wouldn't want to be part of all of this? The clubhouse sat on gorgeous acreage, the amenities were absolutely perfect and everyone worth anything in this town was a member. Perhaps that's why Dusty was never admitted. Chelsea didn't know him personally, but his actions before his death had proved the guy to be a grade-A bastard.

Settling into an easy rhythm with her horse, Chelsea found a trail and rode off, thankful that with evening falling, there were no other riders. The stables closed at nine, so she had a couple hours to enjoy the open air, the peaceful evening, and to start figuring out her Christmas shopping list because she still had a few people she hadn't bought for. Online shopping was going to be her best friend in these last days leading up to Christmas.

With all the wedding planning, she'd dropped the ball on—

"And here I thought I'd be all alone."

Chelsea cringed at the familiar voice, her grip tightening on the reins. "Then take another path."

Gabe's laughter floated around her as he came up beside her horse. "Now, what fun would that be?"

His thigh brushed hers as he kept a steady gait. Chelsea didn't want any part of his body touching hers. Okay, that was a lie, but if she kept repeating it over and over, maybe the words would penetrate her stubborn heart.

"I came out here to think and be alone," she told him, refusing to look his way. She knew what he looked like— all brooding and sexy—without tormenting herself any further.

"Then by all means, think," he stated. "You won't even know I'm here."

"Are you kidding me?"

She pulled her horse to a stop, not at all surprised when he did the same. Now, she did glance his way. Yup. Just as sexy as two days ago when he'd been wrapped all around her, driving her out of her mind. His black hat shielded his eyes, but not enough that she didn't see that sexy gleam.

"You think I can have a peaceful moment when you're right next to me?"

"Well, darlin', I'll take that as a compliment."

Chelsea narrowed her eyes. "Why won't you go away?"

He rested his forearm on the saddle horn and shrugged. "I haven't seen you for two days. I went by Hope Springs and worked more on the arch, thinking you'd show up and lend a hand, but you never did. I'd say you've had plenty of space."

"Not enough," she muttered.

"You can't hide from me forever, Chelsea. We've got work to do and this tension between us isn't going anywhere."

Why did he have to be so blunt and just lay their attraction right on the table like that? It wasn't often she was speechless, but the man was bound and determined to throw her off her game, and damn it, it was working.

"You seem angry." He offered her a killer smile. "I'd say this fresh air will do you some good. Come on. Ride with me and we'll talk. Not about the dressing room or the fact you want me, and don't deny it. We'll do small talk. We can do that, right? The weather is always a good topic, but so predictable. Maybe we could discuss if you've put your Christmas tree up yet. I haven't."

Was he seriously turning into some chatterbox? She wasn't going to ride along beside him and talk like he was some girlfriend she was comfortable with. Gabe Walsh made her anything but comfortable.

"I don't want to engage in small talk with you." Chelsea pulled the reins and turned her horse back toward the trail. "I can't stop you from riding, but shut up."

Again, his laughter swept over her as he came to an easy trot next to her. Chelsea concentrated on the rocking of the horse, the smell of the fresh air, and not the man a mere foot from her.

"There's something I've been curious about."

She never knew where his thoughts were headed, but it was obvious he was going to keep going no matter what she said, so she just remained quiet.

"Why computers?"

Chelsea turned toward him. "Excuse me?"

"Just wondering why you got into computers."

She should've known he wouldn't honor her wish for silence. But work she could discuss. That was one topic where he wouldn't make her a stuttering, turned-on mess of emotions.

"I've always been interested in how things work," she told him. "When I was little, I tried picking locks. I actually got quite good at it by the time I was seven, but then I grew bored. Dad was always talking business, so I knew we were being raised to take over. When I wasn't learning fast enough, I tried getting into his computer when he was asleep one night. By the time I figured out his password, I'd gotten a little thrill and decided to see what else I could do."

"How old were you then?"

"Ten."

Gabe swore under his breath. "And here I've pissed you off. Are my bank accounts safe?"

Chelsea couldn't stop the smile from spreading across her lips. "For now."

"Did your father know you'd gotten into his system?"

"Of course. I was sloppy, as all beginner hackers are." Chelsea brushed her hair back from her face, wishing she'd thought to put on a headband. "You know, I really don't like that term. It makes me feel… I don't know… illegal."

Gabe tossed her a look with one arched brow. "It pretty much is illegal."

With a shrug, Chelsea forced her attention to the

smooth path in front of her. "Maybe, but I've never done anything terrible with my knowledge. I more do things to see how far I can get and to educate myself."

"So you've never done anything risky or wrong?" he asked.

Chclsca pursed her lips. "I may have changed a couple grades when I was in high school."

"And?" he prompted.

She swallowed. Was she really going to get into this with him?

"I might have hacked into one bank account to add some funds."

"You think hacking into a bank isn't illegal or bad?" he asked, obviously shocked at her admission.

"I admit it was wrong, but hindsight won't change the past."

Silence settled between them and Chelsea figured she shouldn't have told him. It was years ago and nobody had ever figured out what she had done. It had been her first real victory and, illegal or not, she wasn't sorry she'd done it. In fact, she was rather proud of herself.

"Are you going to finish the story or leave me hanging?"

Chelsea came to a stop and glanced toward a nearby cypress grove. Restless energy had her dismounting and tying the reins around a sturdy tree trunk. Gabe did the same and when he propped his hands on his hips and continued to stare at her, she figured she may as well tell him everything.

Five

Sweet, innocent-looking Chelsea had shocked him, but he was more than ready to hear what she had to say. If she claimed her hacking was for good reason, he believed her. He'd built the foundation of his career on reading people and was pretty confident she wasn't vindictive. And he wanted to continue spending time with her. She was opening up. Apparently when they weren't discussing the scandal that had rocked the town, she let her guard slip. He only hoped he could wipe his uncle's actions out of the picture for good.

"There was a husband and wife who worked for Hunt back when I was a teen." Chelsea tucked a stray strand of hair behind her ear and turned to rest against a tree away from the horses. "He had a gambling problem. She was pregnant with their first child, but tried to stick by him despite his addiction. I know my father offered to pay for help if the guy would just go. But, in the end, life became too much and he left her. She couldn't make the mortgage payments on her own and lost her house."

Gabe heard the compassion in Chelsea's tone. This was a whole new side to her he hadn't seen and it only made him want to uncover even more. He'd always figured she was giving, caring, selfless. His instincts hadn't proved him wrong before and they were dead-on now.

"She had her own income, but considering she was pregnant with no home, I couldn't stand it anymore." Chelsea's mouth twisted into a half grin. "I may have hacked into his private account and removed funds. And those funds *may* have found their way into her account."

Gabe honestly didn't know what to say. The woman was constantly a doer. She cared for others and wanted to see everyone around her happy. But he'd never thought once that she'd use her skills for something like this.

"Had you gotten caught—"

Her eyes met his. "At the time, I felt it was worth the risk. Now that I look back, I know it wasn't right to do that, but I got caught up in the moment and acted with my heart instead of my head."

She gave a slight shrug before she continued. "I just thought, what was he going to do? Tell the authorities? Most of his money was obtained illegally, because I uncovered that he was betting on cock fighting. He wouldn't want to open that can of worms and be subjected to proving where his income came from."

Chelsea's eyes misted. "All of that happened around the time when we'd just lost Mom. Actually, she ran off, but she may as well be dead because I haven't seen or heard from her since. I knew what that felt like, what being abandoned does to your soul. I couldn't stand it, Gabe."

Why did she have to have such a vulnerable side that

made resisting her impossible? He'd promised himself when he'd seen her riding up ahead that he'd keep his hands off, but the sorrow lacing her words only had him closing the gap between them.

"You shouldn't touch me. I'm emotional already and if you touch me…"

Her words were barely a whisper and he saw tears swimming in her eyes.

"This is just one friend consoling another," he explained.

Gabe wrapped his arms around her and she instantly returned the gesture. "We're not friends," she argued.

Smiling, he rested his chin on top of her head. "Maybe not, but we're something. I don't think they've created a label for us yet."

When she continued to just be still and let him hold her, Gabe figured she must be gathering her strength. She just needed a minute and he was all too willing to comfort her. As much as he wanted to get her into his bed, he could be patient. Chelsea would be worth the wait.

Hell, his job was based on patience and taking his time, being methodical. And he knew she was much more important than a job. Damn it. When had he let that happen?

Chelsea eased back and glanced up at him. "I'm not sure I can trust you."

Gabe smoothed her hair back and framed her face. "You will."

"Are you always so arrogant?"

Gabe smiled because her tone was light, but her question was genuine. "Confident," he corrected. "I know I did nothing wrong where you're concerned and, in time, you'll realize that, too."

Her eyes darted to his lips and he knew he'd just

knocked another brick off that barrier she kept around herself. She still clung to him and Gabe's last shred of control snapped.

He eased closer, keeping his eyes on hers as he lowered his head. "You plan on stopping me?" he whispered against her mouth.

"Not yet."

The second he covered her mouth, she melted against him. There was no other way to describe the way she simply let go and let him take the lead. But he wasn't naïve. Chelsea held all the power here. As much as he wanted her and was more than ready to seduce her up against this tree, she would ultimately have to give the green light.

Gabe rested one hand on her hip and thrust the other through her hair as he shifted his head and dove back in for more. More was the theme where Chelsea was concerned. He wanted as much as she would give…then he wanted even more.

She arched against him, groaning into his mouth. Gabe trailed his lips across her jaw and down the column of her throat. The neckline of her tank top mocked him, tempted him. So much exposed skin to explore… and still not enough. But he had to tread lightly. Chelsea wasn't just any woman, and their situation was extremely delicate.

"Gabe, please."

Easing back slightly, he took in her flushed cheeks and decided he couldn't leave her hanging. He was a gentleman, after all, and as gently as he needed to treat her, he also planned on giving in to her every desire.

"You don't have to ask twice."

Sliding his hand beneath the hem of her tank, Gabe kept his eyes locked on hers. If she showed the slightest bit of hesitation, he'd stop. But the way she bit on her lower lip and kept her eyes shut, he had to believe he was doing everything right.

He flicked the closure on her jeans, pleased when her hips surged forward. Glancing over his shoulder, he made sure no one was taking a late ride. But they were hidden behind the horses and around the side of a large cypress.

Gabe slid his hand inside the waistband of her panties and kicked her feet apart with the toe of his boot. He rested his forearm alongside her head, against the tree, and dipped his fingers into her heat. The moment she cried out, he covered her mouth with his.

Yes. Finally, this. He had wanted to see her come apart, had wanted to experience every bit of it, and now she was seconds away. He didn't want to just feel it, he wanted to taste it.

Chelsea's fingertips dug into his shoulders as she jerked her body against his. Then she exploded. There was no other way to describe it. She tore away from the kiss and tipped her head back, her mouth open in a perfect O as she clung to him.

Chelsea Hunt was letting every single guard down and giving in to her desires, and it was absolutely the most erotic thing he'd ever seen. He wished he could watch her forever, but he quickly pushed the idea aside. Forever wasn't in his vocabulary.

As she came down and her trembling ceased, Gabe knew for certain that he needed her in his bed. His entire body was wound so damn tight, but he'd have to wait. This was about Chelsea, about her needs and getting her to see that he was serious about this all-consuming need to have her.

But most of all, he wanted her to realize that he wasn't a liar and had never done anything to hurt her or to tarnish her reputation.

The horses shifted behind him and Gabe started to lean forward to kiss her, but she pushed against his shoulders. Her bold green eyes lifted to his and he instantly saw regret.

They'd made too much progress for her to have those walls come back up. Little by little, he was going to make sure she pushed beyond her fears. Why did she have to start letting her doubts and reality sink back in?

He removed his hand and stepped back, giving her a chance to right her clothes.

"I'm not going to apologize."

Her hands froze on the snap of her jeans as she glared up at him. "I didn't ask you to."

"You're angry."

"With myself. Not you."

Well, that was something. But he didn't want her in any way angry about this situation.

"Are you upset because you let yourself feel or because you hate me?"

She finished straightening her clothes and shoved her hair behind her ears. That defiant chin lifted an extra notch as she squared her shoulders and focused solely on him.

"I don't hate you," she retorted. "I just don't make a habit of getting involved with people I'm still on the fence about."

Raking a hand through his hair, he turned away and headed back to his stallion.

"You're not going to say anything?" she called after him.

Gabe tugged at the reins and freed his horse from the tree before glancing back over his shoulder. "You want to fight? You'll have to look elsewhere. A beautiful woman just came apart in my arms. I'm not feeling much like arguing. I want to be here for you, Chelsea. Not because my uncle tried to ruin you and so many others, but because I can't ignore this pull between us or what just happened."

He mounted the horse and turned him toward the stables, but held tight on the reins to keep him in place. "You riding back with me or alone?"

Still flushed and sexy as hell, Chelsea stared up at him. "Unless there's wedding business to attend to, we're better off returning separately."

He had a feeling she'd say something like that. It was expected, but that didn't lessen his frustration any.

Gabe rested his elbow on his knee and leaned down. "You can push me away, but that won't stop what's happening."

A rumble of thunder had him glancing toward the sky then back down to her. "Better get back. Storm's comin'."

He just hoped like hell they could weather it.

Chelsea dropped her keys onto the accent table inside her doorway and wiped her damp hair away from her face. The pop-up storm matched her mood—fierce and full of rage.

The lightning flashed, illuminating her open floor plan as she made her way inside. No sense in turning on the lights. They were set on a timer, anyway, and apparently her electricity had gone out because nothing was on in the entire place.

Perfect. Her phone needed to be charged and she'd wanted to take a hot bath and ignore the world…and the throb between her legs. Because as much as she tried to ignore what had just happened, it was impossible. Gabe was impossible. The stupid man was making her feel things, making her body hum and come alive like never before—all while they were still fully dressed. Her body still sizzled from the orgasm against the tree.

Chelsea made her way to her bedroom using what little battery she had left on her phone to light the way.

First, the man had tried to get it on with her in a dressing room and then he'd pleasured her at the damn club. He was slick, seductive and she'd loved every single minute of both experiences.

Well, she'd loved the way he'd physically made her feel, but the mental side…

Why did he have to keep messing with her head?

Everything circled back to Dusty and how he'd been so meticulous in planting evidence to ruin lives and pointing the finger of blame in so many different directions. The scandal had rocked the entire town and Chelsea wasn't sure she'd ever recover, if she were being honest.

It was humiliating to walk down the street and wonder if passersby had seen the photos of her naked.

Tears filled her eyes once again. She'd shed too many tears caused by a whole gamut of emotions. She'd cried from anger, from frustration, from hurt and resentment… so many things. And she'd had to do it all in private because her very best friend wanted and deserved the wedding of the year and there was no way Chelsea would ruin this monumental moment for her.

Chelsea's cell vibrated in her hand just as she hit her bedroom. When she glanced at the screen, she saw a text from her brother and a missed call from him earlier. With only an eight percent charge left on her battery, she opted to ignore it all. Not that she wouldn't have, anyway.

She definitely wasn't in the mood to talk to Daniel. She loved him and his fiancée, Erin, but right now she just wanted to get into pajamas and lie in bed. With the lightning flashing outside, soaking in her garden tub wasn't the smartest idea. It wasn't late, but late enough, and with the electricity gone, she could at least lie down and read on her electronic reader.

But as she sank to the edge of her bed, all she could think of was how amazing Gabe had made her feel. The man was so, so giving. All the focus had been on her and then, when she'd wanted to battle it out because she'd had no clue what to do with all her emotions, he'd walked away. Some might have said that was cowardly, but she saw it as gentlemanly. He hadn't wanted to make things more difficult than they already were.

Either that, or he'd just wanted to seduce her and that was all.

Unfortunately, she didn't think that was the case. She truly believed he wanted her. That he wanted to get closer to her, and not just for the sex. Yes, Gabe was often seen as a man of mystery, but she was starting to see him for so much more.

All of those reasons were precisely why she was so angry. She'd been furious with him back at the club. No, she'd been furious with herself. It wasn't his fault that when he touched her she went off like a rocket. It wasn't his fault that she'd never had a lover like him before.

Wait. Lover? No. They weren't going to have sex. They *couldn't* have sex. That would go against everything she'd vowed to herself. She wasn't even fully convinced of his innocence in his uncle's controversy, which was all the more reason she needed to keep her distance.

But how could she?

Six

The scream echoed through the barn and made his ears ring. Gabe spun around and spotted Brandee in the doorway, the sunlight illuminating her.

"That is going to be so gorgeous," she squealed as she raced across the open space.

Gabe glanced back at the arch, which he'd just finished. Well, he'd finished the framing and the structure. He'd texted Chelsea to come by later to do the actual decorating because that was not part of his skill set.

"You guys are really going above and beyond," Brandee exclaimed, getting misty-eyed as she came to stand beside him. Her eyes fixed on the arch before her.

Gabe wrapped an arm around her shoulders and pulled her in for a friendly hug. "It's no trouble at all. I'm just glad you've made my best friend so happy."

Disgustingly happy. These two were absolutely perfect for each other. Gabe hadn't believed people could be so in love; he hadn't actually believed in that emotion at all, but if it existed, Brandee and Shane were wrapped up tight with it.

"Where's Chelsea?" Brandee asked, easing back.

It had been three days since he'd seen her and he was getting rather twitchy—not something he wanted to explain to her best friend. He could barely explain his feelings to himself. He wanted Chelsea, but the fierce need that continued to grow inside him was something new. He'd wanted women before, but not like this. The strength she displayed, her loyalty to her friends and her intelligence were all huge turn-ons. There was nothing about her he didn't find mesmerizing.

Originally he'd wondered if it was because he felt sorry for her because of Dusty's actions. But Gabe had quickly discovered that he didn't feel sorry for Chelsea. He admired her. She had a strength he couldn't help but find attractive. She had a take-charge attitude and then, on top of that, with her sexy-as-hell looks, he couldn't help but be drawn.

"I'm sure she's working," he replied. "I told her this would be ready to go today for the flowers or whatever it is you want to decorate it with. I just needed to get the base sturdy enough."

Brandee stepped forward and ran her hand over the oak grain. "This is far more than I'd envisioned and it's not even done. I can't wait for my wedding day."

Gabe hooked his thumbs through his belt loops and rocked back on his heels. "I'm sure Chelsea will be by soon. I texted her earlier."

Brandee tossed him a grin and raised her brows. "You two taking shifts on the wedding preparations? Is that because of the whole dressing room issue?"

On the one hand, he wasn't surprised at all that she'd brought up the incident. On the other hand, he was sure as hell glad she didn't know about their session at the Texas Cattleman's Club. Gabe wanted to keep the stolen moments with Chelsea to himself. They were private and, until he could figure out what the hell they were doing, he wanted to keep things that way.

"I doubt it," he answered with a slight laugh. "She doesn't seem like the type to run over something like that. But I think this attraction has her being extra cautious."

"Attraction?" Brandee said, her brows shooting up and a smile spreading across her face. "Well, she needs something to keep her mind off the bad press caused by those photos. I think it's great you two are working together."

Oh, he did, too. Because when he and Chelsea were together, he couldn't keep his hands to himself and, for the most part, Chelsea wasn't complaining, at least until she started letting her mind take over.

Damn it. He wanted the hell out of her and she still wanted to keep him at a distance. Someone was going to lose this fight...and he'd never lost yet.

"She's still unsure about trusting me," Gabe went on. "She's learning, but given my last name and all, her hesitancy is more than justified."

"You were cleared of any wrongdoing," Brandee said. "Besides, anyone who knows you would never believe for a second you had anything to do with releasing those photos. Shane and I couldn't believe when your name was even mentioned."

"I appreciate that. I would never do something so vile," he declared. "I'm just as disgusted by my uncle's actions as anyone. He's gone and now I'm the one carrying his family name and trying to keep my reputation as far removed from his as possible."

"You're a victim, too," she stated.

Yeah. He was. If only Chelsea could see things from

that angle. But he wasn't one to play the pity card. He didn't want her pity—he wanted her in his bed.

"I'm glad you're here, actually." He was happy to change the subject, he legitimately had something he needed to tell her. "Your wedding present will be arriving tomorrow. It isn't exactly something I could've brought to the reception."

Brandee tipped her head and smiled. "You know you didn't have to get us anything. You and Chels are doing so much already. The load you have lifted from Shane and me is immeasurable."

Gabe shrugged. "Trust me when I say you will want this."

Besides, his uncle had caused so many problems for Brandee and Shane months ago. Their relationship almost hadn't made it at all, let alone to the altar. Gabe was all too happy to give them this extravagant present. They were his friends and Brandee had such a huge heart, giving back so much to the community.

Brandee ran a camp for teens in need. She used her time and her own funding to keep the place on her ranch open for impressionable teens, and it was time she didn't have to carry so much of the load on her own.

"What's that smile for?" she asked.

"Just anxious for a little surprise I have planned," he replied. "Now, if you'll excuse me, I have some business to attend to. Chelsea may be here later."

As he started to head out of the barn, Brandee called out to him, "She's more vulnerable than you think."

Gabe stilled. He knew how fragile Chelsea was, but hearing her best friend confirm it made him wonder what hurt Chelsea kept inside.

He threw a glance over his shoulder. "She's also stronger than you think."

And he wanted her to trust him. Whether she liked it or not, he would protect her. She was done doing everything alone.

Chelsea leaned back in her desk chair in her home office and stared at the bright screen of her laptop. She'd kept tabs on her mother for a year or so now. She'd made sure not to do anything illegal, but some simple investigative work by someone of her skill level…well, it hadn't been too difficult to turn up Shonda Hunt. Or rather, Shonda Patton, since she remarried.

Bitterness burned like acid in Chelsea's gut. She hated that her mother had run out on them. Chelsea had never fully known the reason why and it wasn't a topic she had ever brought up to her father before he'd passed. The poor man had been devastated after his wife left, so much so, he'd died a year later of a heart attack. Chelsea had always figured he'd been so crushed he'd lost his will to go on.

She continued staring at the image she'd uncovered of Shonda and her husband. It was a random photo from a newspaper in Kansas. They were on a park bench attending a town festival or something. There her mother was, enjoying the life she wanted.

Trust didn't come easy to Chelsea and staring back at her was the very reason why. When a foundation was shaken and everything you ever knew turned out to be a lie, it was difficult to see another way, let alone try to rebuild on uneven ground.

The spiral Chelsea spun into after her mother had left had been a cry for help, but her actions, no matter how troubled, had ultimately led her to become the woman she was today. She was damn good at her job and refused to let anyone have control over her life ever again.

That included Gabe Walsh. He'd been smart to keep their interaction to texts these past few days, but part of her really wanted to get into that verbal sparring match she was gearing up for. He had texted earlier that he wanted to talk, but he hadn't said when and he hadn't said why.

How could one man turn her on and infuriate her at the same time?

Closing out her screen, Chelsea came to her feet and secured the knot on her robe. She was done spying on Shonda. Chelsea refused to call her *mother*, because that woman didn't exist. Chelsea knew she needed to let it go and move forward. She had a lucrative career that she loved and she was planning her best friend's wedding. She didn't need anything more.

Right?

Unfortunately, there was that young girl living inside her that wanted answers. That impressionable girl needed to know what she could do to ever fill the void of abandonment.

Chelsea had just stepped into her living room when the doorbell rang. She glanced at the large clock on her mantel and wondered who would be dropping by unannounced at nine at night.

She smoothed her hands down her robe and pulled the lapels a little tighter to her chest. A quick glance out the sidelight caused Chelsea's heart rate to kick up. She pulled in a deep breath and flicked the lock.

When she swung the door wide, she expected Gabe to just walk on in. Instead he gave her a head-to-toe appraisal and propped his arm on the door frame. It caused his bicep to tighten, which only drew her attention to his excellent muscle tone.

"I do like how you greet your guests."

"A heads-up text would've been considerate," she stated, crossing her arms.

The corner of his mouth kicked up. "I texted earlier and said I wanted to talk."

She couldn't help but laugh. "Specifics would've been nice."

"I'll remember that for next time."

He pushed off the frame, but continued to stand in the light of the porch. "But I'm here now and I want you to understand there's no reason to be afraid of what's going on between us. I know you've been dealt a bad hand lately and I also know you're strong. I'd never push you, but I also won't let you run."

Chelsea opened her mouth but Gabe held his hand up to stop her. "I get that you're still reeling from what Dusty did. I even understand that trusting me at first was difficult, but we're past that, aren't we?"

"You confuse me," she whispered. "I can't get into this right now, Gabe. I need to think."

She started to shut the door but he was quicker. His fingers curled around the edge and held it open.

"I want you so much," he replied, stepping in closer until she had to tip her head back to look into those mesmerizing eyes. "Which is why I'm putting the next step on you."

Confused, Chelsea jerked back. "What?"

"There's nothing I want more than to cross this threshold and peel you out of that robe, but I want you to take control. I want you to ache just as much as I do. Because when we finally make it to a bedroom, it will be your decision."

Chelsea swallowed. Her body stirred at his words and his boldness. "Is that why you came here?" she asked, shocked her voice sounded strong at all. "To tell me that we're going to have sex?"

Gabe raked a hand over his face and blew out a breath. "I came here to tell you that I'm not going to coddle you. You're a strong woman and you don't want pity over what happened. I get that you want to be respected, and I respect you. So if anything happens from here on out, it's your call."

Chelsea opened her mouth then closed it.

"Speechless?" he asked with a slight grin. "That wasn't the reaction I expected."

"What did you expect?"

"Well, you didn't slam the door in my face, so I'm already a step above where I thought I'd be."

She bit the inside of her cheek to keep from smiling, but failed.

"And a sexy grin? Hell, I better leave while I'm ahead."

Chelsea tucked her hair behind her ears and took a step back. As much as she wanted to invite him in and take him up on what he was offering, she also had to be smart. She'd never been a woman to just sleep with someone for the sake of getting it out of her system. Then again, no one had ever tempted her the way Gabe Walsh had.

"Do you want me to do anything for the wedding?" he asked, his tone softer as he stared into her eyes. "I have a few hours free tomorrow if you need anything."

"Well, I'm almost done with the arch. I've planned for the steaks to be delivered the day before the bachelor/bachelorette party, so if you want to call and make sure the club has all of the staffing covered for that night, that would help. I just don't want them to be understaffed, because we're expecting quite a few people. The bartenders need to be the best, too. Make sure Tanner and Ellen are on the list to serve."

Gabe nodded. "I can do that. Didn't you message me about some chair covers you wanted picked up?"

Chair covers, yes. She'd forgotten all about those. Maybe it had something to do with the man who stood before her because the past couple of weeks he'd been consuming so much of her time, both in person and in her thoughts. But they needed chair covers for the party. Something elegant, yet something that would fit in at the club with all its dark wood and trophies.

"I can pick them up," she told him. Silence stretched between them and the tension stirred deep within her. "Is that all?"

He flashed her a devilish grin. "Unless you're ready to invite me in now and let me unwrap you."

Oh, she wanted to be unwrapped. Gabe could tempt a saint into stripping and doing naughty deeds.

Chelsea laughed and poked at his chest until he stepped back. "Good night, Gabe."

When he leaned in, Chelsea stilled. His lips feathered across her cheek. "Good night, Chels."

He turned and walked away, bounding down the steps and heading toward his truck. Chelsea closed the door, turning the dead bolt back into place, and rested her forehead against the wood.

What was she going to do about that man? He purposely kept her on her toes and tied up in knots. Part of her loved this catch-and-release game they were playing, but the other part didn't want to play games anymore. She wanted to know for sure that she could trust him. But how? How could she be certain?

Chelsea flicked off the light and headed for bed, knowing full well she wouldn't be getting any sleep tonight.

Seven

"What do you think?"

Chelsea stood back and stared at the archway that was covered in sheer, pale gold material, twinkling clear lights and delicate white flowers.

She then glanced over at her friend, who stood there staring and silent. Okay, maybe it didn't look as great as Chelsea had thought. This wasn't exactly her area of expertise, but she'd like to think it wasn't horrendous.

"It will look better at night for the ceremony when you can see the lights better," Chelsea rushed to say when the silence became too much. "I mean, I can change whatever you want. I'm not really a decorator, but I can look up other ideas—"

"It's perfect."

Chelsea breathed a sigh of relief. She'd honestly had to look at so many wedding planning websites, at images of elegant arches and Christmas-themed weddings just to piece together everything her friend would want.

The expression on Brandee's face made all of that digging worth it.

Because Chelsea had hated every second of searching through blissful pictures of couples deliriously in love. Not that she wasn't happy for Brandee and Shane, but part of her truly didn't believe in the hype of marriage or love. All of that had to be built on trust. But trusting someone with your whole life? No. That just wasn't going to happen. Not for her. And she was okay with living alone.

Chelsea ignored the niggling ache in her heart. Okay, maybe it would be nice to find someone to share her secrets with, to lie with at night and talk about absolutely nothing, to go on trips with and see the world. But all that would require her to fully open up and expose a part of herself she'd shut off far too long ago.

The sound of approaching vehicles had both women turning toward the large entrance to the barn. Brandee headed toward it and Chelsea followed.

As soon as she stepped outside, Chelsea's mouth dropped. There were six, brand-new, shiny white vans and three large pickup trucks sitting in the drive of the Hope Springs Ranch. The driver of the first van got out and crossed the yard toward Brandee.

"I'm looking for Ms. Lawson."

Brandee shielded her eyes from the sun. "That's me."

The middle-aged man held out a clipboard and pen. "I just need you to sign for the shipment of vehicles and let me know where you'd like them all parked. Do you want the keys left in the ignition or brought to you?"

"Excuse me?" she asked. "I didn't… I'm not sure…"

"Oh, I'm sorry," he said with a smile. "These are all paid in full from a Mr. Walsh. He said this was your wedding gift."

What in the world had Gabe done? All of this? He'd paid for every single vehicle here? They were brand-new, not a speck of dirt on any of them, and they were all for Brandee.

Chelsea's heart flipped.

"He said he had something being delivered, but…" Brandee trailed off as she stared at the fleet of new vehicles. "I can't believe he did this."

Chelsea was absolutely stunned. She couldn't take in everything at once. This was a…a *wedding gift*? Weren't you just supposed to get the bride and groom toasters and towels? This went so far above the items on any wedding registry, Chelsea didn't even know what to think.

Gabe had done all of this without fanfare and without mentioning a word to her. He hadn't wanted the recognition or the praise. The man had legitimately wanted to help out with Brandee's work with the teens. How could Chelsea sustain her anger toward him when he kept proving over and over how selfless he was?

Chelsea took in each vehicle as Brandee pointed to where they could be parked. The dollar signs were scrolling through her head. She'd known Gabe was wealthy—from his expensive loft apartment to his luxury cars to his expensive taste in bourbon—but she'd never thought for a second he could do something like this.

"Can you believe this?" Brandee asked when she came back to stand beside Chelsea. "He told me he was having something delivered. I thought maybe it was… I don't know, a horse."

Brandee laughed and raked her hand through her long hair. "I don't even know what to say. A thank-you card isn't even enough. These vehicles will make a huge difference in the camp for my teens. We'll be able to take in more kids."

Brandee's voice broke as she dissolved into tears. "Sorry," she said as she wiped her cheeks. "I'm an emotional mess with the wedding."

Chelsea turned to her friend and pulled her into a hug. "It's understandable. This is a big step in your life. You're entitled to a meltdown. And Gabe's gift was a bit unexpected."

Brandee eased back and smiled. "He's such a great guy, Chels. I spoke with him yesterday and he seemed..."

Chelsea stilled. "What?"

"I don't think it's a stretch to say he's interested in you."

Her friend's misty eyes met Chelsea's. She truly didn't want to have this conversation with anyone, let alone the woman standing there with cupid silhouettes practically bulging out of her eyes.

"He's a guy and I'm single." Chelsea figured shrugging it off would be safest at this point. "But, to answer your veiled question, we're just friends."

Friends who made out like teens in a dressing room. Why didn't she have a friend like him before?

Oh, right. She hadn't trusted him before.

The barrier she'd kept around her soul where Gabe was concerned cracked a little. Okay, more than a little. The very foundation shook. She wanted to give him the benefit of the doubt, and had actually started to.

"You're interested in him, too," Brandee murmured. "Don't bother denying it. This is more than a friendship."

Chelsea jerked her attention back to the moment. "You have too much love and wedding bliss on the mind to think clearly."

But her friend was absolutely correct. Whatever Chelsea and Gabe had going on, it was so much more than friendship. When he'd said there hadn't been a label created for them yet, he'd been accurate. Because they weren't really friends. She didn't trust him. Did she?

Chelsea said farewell to Brandee and headed out to her car. At this point she didn't *not* trust Gabe. The mental sparring match she continued to have with herself was exhausting.

As she drove toward downtown Royal, she realized she was tired of something else, too.

Fighting her needs.

Gabe's doorman had let Chelsea up nearly fifteen minutes ago. He stood at the floor-to-ceiling window, watching as the sun cast a bright orange glow across the horizon as he waited for her. People were starting to really fill the street. Couples were strolling hand-in-hand, heading into restaurants for dinner dates. The little town came alive at night—especially on a Friday.

He watched as people posed in front of the giant Christmas tree in the town square just a block away. The tree stood tall and proud, decorated with what seemed like a million clear lights. There would be an annual candlelight and caroling evening in less than two weeks. He loved this town, loved the traditions it upheld.

Before the doorman had called to announce Chelsea's surprise visit, Gabe had actually been getting ready to head out and grab a drink at the TCC to see who was spending their evening there. Though there likely weren't many people hanging out in the club's bar tonight. These days, nearly everyone was either married, engaged, caring for or expecting a baby.

So much had happened over the past year, both good and bad. Weddings, babies—all of that had brought families together. But the Maverick scandal still left a dark cloud over the club and the town.

Just this afternoon, he'd been in contact with the sheriff to see if there were any updates regarding Dusty's accomplice in planting the camera in the locker room. There had to have been someone and Gabe wanted to know who it was. Until that person was brought to justice, this nightmare wouldn't fully be over.

At least he had been cleared of any involvement early on in the investigation. And even more importantly, Chelsea had started trusting him more and more.

Something had changed Chelsea's mind about him, otherwise she wouldn't have come of her own accord to his loft.

Which made him wonder why she hadn't knocked on his door yet. Gabe had given the doorman a small list of guests who didn't need an okay from him before they were automatically rung up. Chelsea had been at the top of the list for over a month now. But the doorman had called Gabe fifteen minutes ago to tell him she was on her way up.

Yet his unexpected guest hadn't made her presence known to him. She was most likely hesitating out in the hallway, wondering why she'd come. He knew exactly why she'd come.

Gabe shoved his hands in his pockets and smiled. He'd put the proverbial ball in her court and it had been excruciating waiting on her to come to the conclusion that they needed to get this out of their system. Those two make-out sessions hadn't even come close to alleviating his ache.

Turning from the window, Gabe crossed his loft and went to the door. If she'd come this far, the least he could do was give her a hand and help her the rest of the way.

Gabe opened the door wide and spotted Chelsea leaning against the wall directly across from him. Clearly startled, she jerked and clutched her purse in front of her…as if trying to use something to shield her from the big bad wolf. Didn't she know? There was nothing he couldn't knock down to get what he wanted.

"How long were you going to wait before you knocked?" he asked.

Squaring her shoulders and tipping her chin, she cleared her throat. "I wasn't sure I was going to knock. I was thinking of leaving."

"No, you weren't."

Chelsea blinked, opened her mouth then closed it and continued to stare.

"Are we going to do this in the hallway or are you coming in?"

"Do what?" she asked.

"Whatever brought you here." He stepped back and gestured her in. "Don't look so worried, Chels. I only bite when I'm asked to."

Her eyes widened for a fraction of a second before she blinked and stepped forward, turning sideways to pass without actually touching him. Gabe bit back a grin as he closed the door, securing it with a click of the lock. He had the entire top floor to himself, and knew they wouldn't be bothered, but he still wanted that extra layer of privacy between the outside world and his Chelsea.

No. She wasn't his. Gabe needed to stop thinking along those lines. He wanted her. That was all. Once, not so long ago, he'd let emotions over a woman cloud his judgment and it had resulted in his partner being killed. He'd let his need override his job, thinking he could handle an attraction to a woman and still think clearly out in the field. He'd been wrong and his partner had paid the ultimate price.

He couldn't forget the promise he'd made to himself

after that to stay focused on work. Any extracurricular activities had to remain strictly physical, which was more than fine with him. Especially where a certain computer hacker and CTO was concerned.

After the hell that she'd been through, she deserved respect. She may keep that steely front in place, but he knew there was an underlying vulnerability after the leak of those photos.

Gabe appreciated Chelsea enough to place the control in her hands. And now she'd risen above her vulnerability and had come to him.

Damn, she smelled amazing. That familiar jasmine scent he'd come to associate with her surrounded him. Gabe crossed his arms and watched as she did a slow circle, taking in his space.

He'd imagined her in his bed many times, but never had he imagined her in his living room for a casual visit. That would have been too personal.

"You're sneaky," she muttered. "I mean vans and trucks, Gabe."

She turned to face him and raised her brows as if waiting for him to answer, but he'd missed the actual question.

"I take it the fleet arrived at Hope Springs."

Her eyes narrowed. "Your wedding gift was incredible. A fleet of expensive vans and trucks. I was buying them the china set they registered for and you go and spend…well, more than the cost of the entire wedding, reception, and honeymoon combined."

Clearly he was on shaky ground here, so he dropped his arms to his sides and crossed to her. "I can't tell if you're angry or shocked. Regardless, I wanted to help Brandee with the camp. It seemed like the logical thing to do."

"Logical." She lifted her head to hold his gaze and those green eyes definitely pinned him in place. "You're not a logical man. You're reckless, unpredictable, maddening, but never logical."

"Well, darlin', I think you just gave me a compliment."

Chelsea rolled her eyes and threw her hands out as she turned to head toward the wall of windows. Gabe remained where he was, waiting on her to say something.

"Only you would find those words to be flattering." With her back still to him, she tucked her hair behind her ears and blew out a sigh. "I want to hate you. I want to keep not trusting you, but then you go and do this. It's so unselfish and giving and...damn it."

One step after another, Gabe closed the distance between them and came to stand directly behind her. As the sun started to set and the evening grew dim, their reflections were easy to make out in the window. He saw the uncertainty on her face, the passion in her eyes. She had come to his door for one reason and one reason only.

"You're frustrated," he murmured against her ear, still holding on to his amazing restraint by not touching her. "Tell me the real reason you're here. It's not to pat me on the back for giving the best wedding gift."

"Part of it is." She met his gaze in their reflection. "I was standing there watching as one truck after another pulled onto the ranch. And I realized, maybe you're not a jerk."

Gabe smiled and smoothed her hair away from her neck. "What else did you realize?"

She trembled beneath his lips and he gave up all restraint. Trailing his fingertips up her arms and back down, he took a half step to bring his chest against her back.

"That I want you. I want this."

Finally.

"I'm done fighting," she went on as he continued gliding his fingers over her silky skin. "I never take what I want."

"And you want me."

"Yes," she whispered.

He hadn't asked, but hearing her repeat her affirmation had arousal consuming him. He'd put her at the helm and she was going after what she wanted. Him.

"If I'd known it was going to get you to my door, I would've bought the fleet a month ago," he joked, figuring she needed the tense moment to ease her nerves.

She smiled, which was exactly his intent. Her body relaxed against his and he reached around, flattening one palm against her stomach. His fingers splayed across the fabric of her tank top, pulling her back against him. Chelsea continued to watch in the window.

Gabe curled his pinky finger beneath the hem of her tank and slid it just inside the waistband of her jeans. Her swift intake of breath had him nipping at her ear. He wanted her as off balance as possible, because he'd been that way for weeks now. He wanted her so achy and needy that she begged him, that she came apart in his arms and cried out his name.

Gabe began to pull her shirt up over her head but Chelsea gasped and attempted to cover herself.

"The windows—"

"Are mirrored on the other side," he stated. "Nobody can see you and I want you right here, right now."

"But—"

"You came to me," he reminded her, turning her so she could face him. "We're playing by my rules now."

Chelsea relaxed a little as he finished taking off her shirt and tossed it over his shoulder. Then he crushed his mouth to hers and was instantly rewarded with a groan.

This time, nothing would stop them. They weren't in public anymore and he was damn well going to take his time. Later. This first round was going to be quick and fierce because he'd waited long enough.

Gabe pressed her back against the glass and started working on the button on her jeans. In no time she was wiggling those hips and helping him remove the unwanted garment. Now that she was only clad in lacy panties and a matching bra that would bring any man to his knees, Gabe lifted her by her waist and nipped at her swollen lips.

"You knew exactly why you were coming here."

Chelsea bit down on her lip and met his gaze.

"Say it," he commanded. "Tell me exactly why you're here."

He wanted her begging, pleading.

Gabe ground his hips against hers as she locked her ankles behind his back.

"Tell me, Chels."

Eight

"You," she ground out. "I want to be with you in every way. Now, Gabe."

He knew full well just how to get her begging and, for once, she was all too anxious to give up control. She needed him, needed this. Trust issues, worrying who was exactly behind what would come later. She couldn't think of one time in her life she'd done something rash, for purely selfish reasons, without analyzing it to death.

Gabe Walsh was the perfect reason to be selfish. He was also the perfect man to prove that she was still in control after the scandal. She wanted to be here. She wanted him. And she was going to have him.

"Damn right you do."

He released her, easing her legs back to the floor, but only long enough to perform the quickest strip she'd ever seen. By the time he was completely bare and he'd procured protection from his wallet and covered himself,

Chelsea's body was aching in ways she'd never known. She continued to stare into his gray eyes as he rid her of the last pieces of lace. Then he was on her.

Once again, he lifted her and she wrapped her legs around his waist. He slid into her like they were made for each other. Chelsea tipped her head back against the glass as a groan escaped her.

"Look at me," he murmured.

The fact they were doing this against the window had a shiver of excitement coursing through her. Still, she was thankful for the mirrored glass on the other side.

Chelsea locked her eyes on Gabe and smiled. "You're bossy," she panted.

He smacked her backside as he jerked his hips faster. "You wouldn't have it any other way. You're enjoying this just as much as I am."

She was. Oh, mercy, she was. This experience with this man made her feel so much more in control of her body, of how a man looked at her. How did Gabe make her feel so treasured and so erotic at the same time? She didn't know she would be this comfortable with intimacy so soon after the Maverick scandal, but Gabe made her feel alive and sexy.

When she opened her mouth to speak, he reached between them and touched her in just the right spot to have her eyes rolling back and a groan escaping her. Her entire body tightened as she clutched his shoulders and let him do whatever he wanted…because he clearly knew her body better than she did.

"Chels," he strained to say as his own body trembled. His grip on her hips tightened.

She remained wrapped all around him, taking in every bit of his release. Feeling all of that taut skin beneath her hands, having such a powerful man at her mercy right now was absolutely incredible. Gabe Walsh was doing things to her mind and body that she wasn't ready for, but she'd started this roller coaster and it was too late to jump off now.

He was perfect, and had come along at the perfect time—when she didn't even realize she needed someone. But she did. She needed him to show her she was a passionate woman and not defined by those photos.

Their bodies ceased trembling, but she wasn't ready to let go. Not quite yet.

"Stay here tonight," he whispered in her ear.

The warm breath tickling her skin had her fisting her hands on his shoulders. There was nothing more she wanted than to stay and do this all over again, maybe in a bed this time, but she couldn't let her post-coital feelings dominate her common sense. She still had questions and she still had concerns.

"You're thinking too hard." He turned from the window, still holding on to her, and headed toward the hallway leading deeper into the loft. "Apparently, I didn't do my job if you're still able to have coherent thoughts."

"My thoughts are jumbled, if that counts."

He tightened his hold on her and Chelsea had to suppress a moan of pleasure. Being skin-to-skin after sex was even more intimate than the act itself. This moment was... Chelsea suddenly realized she couldn't do this. Not with a man she was still so unsure about.

Gabe turned into a bedroom—his bedroom. The dark navy and rich wood tones screamed masculine dominance. She'd just voluntarily come to the lion's den.

"Gabe, I can't—"

"You can."

Her arms and legs were still draped around him. He held their bodies together so tight, she just knew when he let go she would feel cold, alone. But this was fun while it lasted, right? She hadn't come here for a sleepover or to do anything other than what had just happened.

"No," she told him, pressing against his shoulders. "I can't."

He studied her face for just a moment before easing her down to stand on her own. But he kept his hands on her hips.

"I don't want a relationship, Gabe."

"Is that right?" he asked, gliding his hands up the dip in her waist and back down.

The way he continued to stare at her made her feel foolish for making assumptions, but he had to see her side. "I came here for sex. That's all. Staying overnight implies more."

She'd wanted him, plain and simple. She'd also wanted this man to help her get over the feeling that she'd been tarnished somehow. The things he did to her, with her, had helped Chelsea realize she was still in control despite the scandal that followed her.

The corners of Gabe's mouth twitched as he continued that maddening feathering of his fingertips over her heated skin. Her heartbeat had yet to slow down from the moment she'd walked through his door. She was seriously out of her element here and, judging from the relaxed manner of the frustrating man in front of her, he'd clearly been in this position of power before.

"So now what?" he asked. "You're going to get dressed and leave?"

Honestly, she hadn't thought all of this through. The man was wearing her down and she couldn't even think straight.

"This isn't something I do," she admitted. "So, yeah. I guess I'll, um, I should just get dressed and go."

Gabe towered over her, leaning forward until she sank back onto the bed. His hands dipped into the mattress on either side of her hips as he came within a breath of her mouth.

"Don't be ashamed that you're here, that you took what you wanted." His eyes seemed a darker gray now, desire filling them. "This doesn't have to be awkward or complicated."

"I'm not ashamed," she stated, trying to seem strong and in control when her bare butt was on his duvet and he was a breath away from getting her flat on her back and having his way again. "I just don't know what to do from here."

That naughty grin kicked up a second before he nipped at her lips. "I'll show you exactly what we're going to do from here and then you can decide if you want to stay the night or leave."

Chelsea wanted to protest, she really should stick to her guns, but the only thing she could think as Gabe's weight settled over hers and she lay back was, *Finally.* They'd finally made it to the bed.

"Missed again, Walsh."

Gabe muttered a curse. "I didn't miss."

"But you didn't hit the bull's-eye," Shane countered. "What's up, man?"

Playing darts and drinking a beer with his buddies at TCC usually calmed Gabe. Not today.

He headed back to the bar and grabbed his beer, taking a hearty swig. What the hell was wrong with him? He'd thought once he got Chelsea in his bed, he'd be over this need. If anything, though, he was achier than ever and, damn, if he wasn't pissed about it.

"Nothing," Gabe replied, setting his bottle back on

the glossy bar top. "Getting ready for the big day? Did you get your vows all written?"

Shane's smile widened, as it always did when his fiancée was mentioned. The two were so obviously in love and Gabe couldn't be happier for them. After all Dusty had done to try to ruin Brandee, she deserved a happy ending.

Gabe just hated that there were so many amazing people, *innocent* people, who were still recovering from being the Maverick's victim. Since discovering Dusty had been at the helm of the scandal that shook Royal, Gabe had personally reached out to each of the victims. Apologies were just words, but he hoped they understood his sincerity.

With the exception of Chelsea—and even she seemed to have come around to believe his innocence—nobody had blamed him or accused him of guilt by association. He'd been a victim, as well, considering the impact on his reputation and on the business that carried Dusty's last name. But Gabe could take care of himself—he was taking care of himself. He'd been more concerned with making things right for the Maverick's true victims.

The majority had moved on with their lives. And the strange thing was, for some of them, their experiences with Maverick had led to positive outcomes. They'd married, had children, settled deeper roots in Royal. Gabe was just thankful the repercussions Dusty's dark, twisted games hadn't been worse.

"My vows are done," Shane replied, pulling Gabe's attention back to the conversation. "Brandee is a little stressed."

Shane sank onto a bar stool and ordered another bourbon. "I told her so long as the minister shows up, nothing else matters. That was the wrong thing to say."

Gabe laughed as he leaned his elbow on the bar. "Chelsea and I have everything covered. You two just show up and worry about remembering those vows you're preparing."

Shane's brows shot up. "How is Chelsea? Brandee said she wasn't too talkative over the past couple days. Her texts are to the point and only about wedding details. Would you have any idea what's up?"

"Not a clue."

Shane took the tumbler from the bartender and swirled the amber liquid around. "You're a terrible liar."

"Actually, I'm an exceptional liar and my bank account proves it."

Being in the security field occasionally had him going undercover in disguise. He was a remarkable actor, if he did say so himself. But there were just some aspects of his life he wasn't ready to share and Chelsea was one of them.

Shane tipped back the bourbon and finished it in one long gulp before setting his glass down and motioning for another. "Fine. But you can't lie to me, and I know something is up with the two of you. She's beautiful and you're, well, you. Might as well tell me what's going on."

"What the hell is that supposed to mean? I'm me? Are you calling me a player?"

"Calm down. I just meant you two have been spending quite a bit of time together over the past several weeks."

Before Gabe could defend himself, Daniel Hunt walked in the door. Seeing Chelsea's brother, Gabe felt a momentary pang of guilt. But he shouldn't feel bad about whom he wanted...and whom he'd had. Chelsea was a big girl and she had come to him—then left in the middle of the night.

He wasn't sure if he was more upset about her silent

departure or relieved that she'd held up their agreement to keep things simple. Although he had to admit, just to himself, he wished she'd stuck around because there was nothing he would've liked better than to roll over and feel her by his side in the morning.

Which was precisely why it was good she had left. A woman like Chelsea could make a man forget all about reality. Gabe was growing his business, doing damage control where needed, and the last thing he had time for was a relationship.

"Hey, man," Shane called to Daniel. "Didn't know you were in Royal."

Daniel came up to the bar on the other side of Shane and nodded for the bartender. "Erin wanted to do some shopping for Christmas and insists on the local shops here rather than Seattle. She said she wants to stay through Christmas because she loves this small-town feel and wants to experience her first Christmas here. Plus, she didn't want to miss the wedding or the annual candlelight and caroling ceremony on Christmas Eve."

Gabe raked his thumb over the condensation on his glass of beer and wished he'd ordered something stronger and stayed home.

"How's the wedding coming?" Daniel asked then leaned around to glance at Gabe. "You and my sister have everything covered? Knowing her, she's taken control."

An image of Chelsea straddling him last night when they'd finally made it to his bed flooded his mind. She'd taken control, all right, and he'd been more than okay with relinquishing the reins.

"It's more like divide and conquer," Gabe replied, refusing to say much more.

Shane threw him a glance, but Gabe merely picked

up his beer and drained the glass. "I need to head out," he said, pushing away from the bar.

"Stay," Daniel said. "Next round is on me."

Tempting as another drink was, he didn't want to sit around with his best friend who knew too much and the overprotective brother of the woman he was sleeping with. He could think of a hundred other things that sounded more appealing.

"I still have some work to tend to this evening." Not a total lie. He was always checking on his clients and staff. "And tomorrow is an early day for me."

Actually he had nothing planned, but it sounded like a good excuse. Besides, there was always something to be done and he was always up early and hitting work hard.

"I wanted to ask you about the Maverick case."

Gabe stilled. "Sheriff Battle said there are no new leads as to who helped Dusty. I've had my team working on this, as well. The security cameras outside the gym locker room had been tampered with."

Daniel rubbed the back of his neck and shook his head. "This is absurd. I don't know what I'll do when I get hold of the person who made my sister's life a living hell."

Gabe was right there with him, but best not to say that or to express too much interest in Chelsea. Daniel was definitely the overprotective big brother. What Daniel didn't know was that Gabe had also appointed himself to that role.

"I'll be sure to keep you informed," Gabe assured Daniel. "I'm hoping this is wrapped up soon and we can all move on for good."

"I appreciate that, Walsh."

Gabe tossed some bills onto the bar and grabbed his black hat off the stool. "Shane, I'll talk to you later. Daniel, hope to see you at the bachelor/bachelorette party."

"Wouldn't miss it," he answered. "Oh, Gabe, if you see my sister soon, tell her to stop dodging my calls and texts. I have a feeling you're with her more than anyone lately."

Gabe didn't miss the narrowed gaze or the knowing tone. He smiled and couldn't resist replying, "I'll tell her tonight."

"I don't need to tell you to be careful with my sister."

Blowing out a sigh, Gabe tapped his hat against the side of his leg. "You don't need to tell me. I'm well aware of how raw her emotions are right now, but you also need to understand she's stronger than people give her credit for."

Turning away, Gabe whistled and headed for the exit. As he plopped his hat on his head, he heard Shane say something to Daniel, but couldn't quite make it out. Gabe didn't care. He wasn't trying to be purposefully rude, but he also wasn't going to have anyone, especially Chelsea's brother, try to wedge his way into whatever it was they had going on.

Daniel had every right to worry about Chelsea because of the photos and the scandal. But Gabe also wanted the man to be aware that Chelsea was a strong woman and getting stronger every day.

The chatter about the scandalous photos had died down. Now, the town had shifted its focus to the breaking news about Dusty and figuring out what had motivated him to lash out at so many.

The questions swirled around the small town and were discussed everywhere from beauty salons to bar stools. Nobody really knew why Dusty Walsh had opted to make such poor life choices that had affected so many. Perhaps he was upset because he hadn't been admitted into the TCC, or maybe he was jealous of so many new members. Maybe he was just a bitter, terminally ill man who wanted others to be miserable, as well. Nobody truly knew what had motivated him to be so evil and conniving.

Even Gabe didn't have a clue. But now that Dusty was gone, the healing had begun and the town of Royal was getting back to normal. There was no greater way to celebrate than with Shane and Brandee's Christmas wedding.

Gabe headed toward his loft downtown, but before his turnoff, he decided to take a slight detour. He had a message to deliver, after all.

Nine

Chelsea glanced over her spreadsheet again. Hope filled her as she realized that this spring her dream would become a reality. She'd wanted to do something to give back and help struggling teens for so long, but had never really known how or what to do.

Smiling, she closed out her computer program. She couldn't wait to get her counseling center for teens suffering from depression and suicidal tendencies up and running. And once the idea started to become more of a reality, she'd discuss partnering with Brandee and her camp for teens. Between the two of them, they could really do some good for a whole new generation. Nobody should ever have to feel isolated or hopeless the way she'd felt.

Chelsea had known that crippling fear and loneliness all too well. She'd experienced it twice in her life. The first time, after her father passed, Chelsea had had Daniel. But a brother wasn't the same as a father and he'd been dealing with his own grief.

She'd experienced it again just months ago when so many in this town had seen photos of her in various states of nakedness in the TCC locker room.

When the compromising photos emerged, she'd gotten angry. She'd felt like she'd been stranded on a deserted island, that no one understood her.

Then she'd realized that there were people out there who had been hurt like her and that's when she'd circled back to the idea of giving back and helping others. So, in a warped sort of way, the Maverick scandal had helped her come to the conclusion that it was time to step forward and reach out to others.

Chelsea wanted to open a place that would help young people realize that they weren't alone, that there was always hope. She'd already started vetting counselors and had just purchased an old office building outside of town. Soon she would start renovations and then the true work would begin. Souls and lives would be changed.

This was her baby, something she was keeping close to her chest until she was ready to reveal everything. She wanted all the plans in place before she made a big announcement. Besides, she hadn't wanted to detract attention from the wedding of the year.

The name of her new organization still eluded her. She'd racked her brain and still nothing came to mind. It needed to be meaningful, simple, something that would call out and make troubled people feel safe, comfortable. Everything hinged on the name: the reputation, the feel of the business, the marketing. There was so much to think about other than just helping those in need.

Chelsea came to her feet and stretched. She'd yet to

change from her running gear after her evening jog. Several more ideas for the counseling center had come to her while she'd been out pounding the pavement and she'd rushed home to enter them in the computer. Now, it was time for a shower and to get ready for bed.

Chelsea loved her lacey bras and panties to be delicate and sexy and utterly feminine, and much of her sleepwear was the same. But tonight she just wanted her old cut-off shorts and her well-worn tank.

If she put on anything silky or lacy, she'd instantly think of Gabe and she needed to not go there.

She'd snuck out of his bed at promptly eighteen minutes after one the other morning, and hadn't spoken to him since. He was long overdue to come charging back into her life. Someone like Gabe probably didn't like the fact that she'd walked away without a word. She'd say that sex was his area of expertise and she couldn't help but wonder if anyone had ever left him like that before.

Chelsea was surprised he hadn't stopped by unannounced with some lame wedding question since then. But knowing Gabe, it was only a matter of time.

She quickly showered and pulled her hair back into a messy bun at the nape of her neck. This in-between length was driving her crazy. She either needed to cut it short or to let it grow. But right now she had so many other pressing matters, she couldn't even make the time for an appointment.

With work at Hunt & Co., the wedding planning, her secret project, which wouldn't be a secret much longer, and Gabriel Walsh consuming her mind every waking minute, was it any wonder she was exhausted?

It was Friday night and she was home alone. That right there should have told her something about her nonexistent social life. She was literally all work and no play.

Well, she'd played, but she didn't figure playing with Gabe counted. He was more like work, when it came to how impossible he was. At least with Hunt & Co. and the upcoming counseling center she was in control, whereas with Gabe, she never had a clue what would happen next. They both wanted to take charge, which meant that control volleyed back and forth between them.

As she finished putting on her nightclothes, the chime of her doorbell echoed through her house. Chelsea stilled then smiled. Well, it had taken him longer to come to her than she'd first thought. Though the fact he was standing outside her door right now had her stomach doing all sorts of girl-crush flips, which was absurd considering they weren't a couple or dating or anything.

Padding barefoot toward the front door, Chelsea instantly made out his silhouette through the etched glass of the door. Some might have said Gabe was predictable, but he was far from it. More like determined. He knew what he wanted and apparently wasn't stopping until he had it. She knew he wanted her, but that was just physical. Besides, he'd gotten what he wanted, so shouldn't he be done?

Chelsea flicked the lock on her door and pulled it open. Without waiting for an invite, Gabe removed his hat and stepped in, placing a kiss on her forehead as if to smooth over his abruptness.

"Won't you come in?" she muttered with a wave of her hand.

He didn't stop in the foyer. No, he went on into the living room as if he had every right to barge into her personal space.

Chelsea closed the door and followed, not at all surprised that he thought he could just take charge like he owned the place. He took a seat on her sofa, casual as you please, but she remained in the wide doorway. Practicing restraint around Gabe Walsh was difficult on a good day. This being the first time seeing him since they'd slept together, she figured she deserved some type of award for her control.

"Are you staying long?" she asked as she crossed her arms and leaned against the doorjamb.

"Not long," he replied. "I ran into your brother at TCC. He said you're not answering his texts."

Chelsea snorted. "So you're his messenger boy now? Since when did you two become so chatty?"

Gabe stretched his arm along the back of the couch and shifted his focus to her. "He offered to buy me a drink and asked about the Maverick case."

Chelsea wasn't quite sure how she felt about her brother and the man she'd just slept with discussing her without her present. She could only imagine the two alphas going head to head, both trying to protect her.

She licked her lips and kept her focus on Gabe. She didn't want him to know just how much he affected her simply by being in her space, large and masculine, taking up a good portion of her couch. She hadn't had a man in here in so long, and definitely not a man as sexy as Gabe.

"So why did you stop by?" she asked, hoping her voice didn't come across as breathy as it sounded to her. "You could've texted or called."

"Maybe I wanted to see you." That Southern voice warmed her just the same as if he'd touched her.

His words were often just as potent as his touch. She shivered at the passion, the desire shining back at her from his gray eyes.

"You should probably go," she whispered. If he stayed, they'd tumble into bed—and then what? She didn't think Gabe was looking for more, and she certainly wasn't, either. But the more time they spent together, the more she trusted him and wanted to explore. Surely that would be a mistake. Right?

Gabe didn't move. He barely blinked. Yet somehow from across the room he captured her attention.

"You don't really want me to go," he stated. "Besides, I want to know why you snuck out of my bed without a goodbye."

Clearly, this was going to take some time and he wasn't going anywhere without answers. Pulling in a deep breath, Chelsea went to the front window where she'd created a perfect window seat with plush, colorful pillows. She got comfortable and leaned back.

"I didn't want to wake you and I told you I wasn't staying."

"You didn't want a confrontation," he corrected. "What are you afraid of, Chels? I won't hurt you, I won't exploit you and everything we do is private. I'm aware of your sensitivity and I'd never make you uncomfortable. Unless you're afraid that you might want more than one night?"

That was exactly what scared her. There was no *might* about it. She did want more, but wanting more would lead to emotions and that was one area she couldn't afford to go to with someone like Gabriel Walsh.

"I can hear your mind working from over here," he stated. "Don't make this any more complicated than it needs to be."

"Says the man who doesn't have a past that haunts him."

Something dark came over his face in an instant. "You have no idea what's in my past, so don't assume."

"I'm sorry." Chelsea clutched the floral pillow tighter to her chest. "I never thought—"

"I had a life before I came to Royal, Chels. I had a demanding job and was too naïve. I thought I could have it all, but it was just another lie I told myself."

Chelsea waited for him to go on, listening as his voice took on a lonely, sad tone. He glanced around her living room then came to his feet. Raking a hand through his hair, he pulled in a deep breath. She didn't want him to feel like he owed her anything. He paced like a caged animal and she got the feeling he actually wanted to let her in on this portion of his life.

"I don't know how much you know about my time in Dallas, but I was an agent for the FBI."

"I was aware of that," she told him. "Listen, you don't have to tell me anything—"

"I do." He tipped his head to the side, raking his hand over his scruffy jawline. "I consider you a friend, even though I'm not sure how much you trust me at this point. You need to know the reasons for my actions, for why I'm so adamant about putting strict limits on relationships."

Again she remained silent and waited on him to continue.

He paced through the room in a random pattern before coming to stand by the fireplace. Resting his elbow on the mantel, he examined the photos she had on display.

There were older ones of her and Daniel and their parents, a couple of her and Brandee, and one Chelsea had taken of the most amazing sunset from the time she went on vacation in the Bahamas. She liked to keep the happy memories on display to showcase just how blessed she was in her life and how far she'd come since her darker days.

"I found myself attracted to a woman," he finally went on. "That attraction grew into something more, something I'd never experienced before. But there was a case—I can't get into specifics—and my loyalties were torn."

A sliver of jealousy spiraled through Chelsea at the thought of another woman getting so close to Gabe. But why? It wasn't like she was in love with him or anything. The night they'd shared meant nothing. Right?

Actually, no. That night meant something, more than it should have, and that was precisely the reason she'd had to scurry out and save herself the walk of shame the next morning. She'd left in the dark of night, praying he didn't wake and question her. All he'd had to do was roll over and ask her to stay and she had a feeling she would've done just that.

Gabe was getting to her. Beneath that mysterious aura, the tattoos, the smoldering eyes, he was a man she couldn't ignore. She hadn't trusted him at first, had been convinced he'd had something to do with the leaked photos. She knew better now. Gabe had just been the obvious target for her rage. She'd needed someone to take her anger, her humiliation, out on. Considering they'd been working together and he was a Walsh, he'd been too convenient.

"My partner was killed over a woman who interfered with our investigation. I let it happen because, where she was concerned, I was naïve. And the result was fatal. I'd let my feelings for her cloud my judgment and she'd been playing me the entire time. She was working for the guys we were trying to take down."

Gabe's stunning declaration jerked her back to the moment. "Oh, Gabe. How awful."

He turned from her mantel and crossed to her, taking a seat at the other end of the long cushion. Even though he was only a few feet away, the manner in which he stared off into the distance indicated he was back in the past and not here with her at all. Whatever scene played through his mind gave his face a pinched, tormented expression, as if the pain was still fresh.

"I vowed never to get tangled up with a woman again," he said, glancing down at his hands resting on his knees. "I can control work. I can control how good I am at my job. But not when I get blindsided by someone I'm supposed to trust."

The final brick in the wall of her defenses crumbled. This man hadn't betrayed her with those photos. He was a man of worth and integrity and loyalty. Someone who had experienced such a tragic loss at the hands of someone he'd trusted couldn't have done such horrific things to her—or anyone else in this town, for that matter. Gabe was definitely a man to be trusted. He had a big heart and was loyal to a fault.

Gabe sought justice. He was a man who valued his career and making sure the truth was revealed. No doubt this whole scenario involving Maverick disturbed him on a level she hadn't even thought of.

"Is that really why you came here?" she asked. "Did you need me to know about that time so I'd see a different side of you?"

Gabe stared at her for a minute before shaking his head and glancing away. "No. Maybe. Hell, I don't know. You deserve to know the real me."

"The guy not many people see," she muttered mostly to herself.

"I'm the same guy everyone sees," he whispered, still not looking her way. "Maybe I just want you to view me differently."

Why did he have to be so noble? It had almost been easier when she'd believed him to be the accomplice of her betrayer. Then she could keep him at a distance, protecting her heart in the process. But now that wasn't an option. Not anymore.

Chelsea came to her feet. She took a couple steps and sank to her knees in front of him. Taking his hands in hers, she stared into those unique gray eyes that never failed to captivate her. Now, though, she had a glimpse into his soul and all the insecurities he kept so well hidden. Maybe they were alike in more ways than she'd ever considered.

"I do see you differently."

His eyes widened, with surprise, with arousal. The muscle in his jaw clenched, as did his grip on her hands.

"You changed your mind about me over what I just told you?" he asked. "That fast?"

Chelsea offered a smile. "Let's say my defenses have been crumbling before now."

Gabe leaned forward, briefly touching his lips to hers. When she started to ease back, he released her hands and framed her face, taking the kiss even deeper.

In an instant, he had them both on their feet and had swept her up into his arms. Looping her arms around his neck, she threaded her fingers through his hair and opened to him. Feeling him touch her, knowing exactly what was to come, had anticipation pulsing through her.

"I'm staying the night," he muttered against her lips.

She didn't reply, because he hadn't asked. Gabe was finally going to claim her and nothing was going to stand in their way.

Ten

Sunlight slashed through the windows, waking Gabe. He stirred, but stilled when he realized he was alone... and not in his bed.

He sat up, rubbing his hands over his face. Coarse hairs bristled against his palms. He was in desperate need of a razor, though Chelsea hadn't complained a bit last night when he'd raked his scruff along her bare skin. In fact, the way he recalled, she'd moaned and jerked her hips against him as if silently begging for more.

Gabe glanced toward the empty side of the bed, at the indention in the crisp, white pillowcase. The sweet jasmine scent still permeated the air as if she were still there. That was twice now she'd left him to wake up alone. He'd always thought himself to be a light sleeper, but apparently not with this woman.

And now that he sat there surrounded by everything that was Chelsea, he realized he didn't like being alone.

For now, he wanted to be with her—whatever the hell that meant. He'd gotten a taste of her and needed more, and that scared the hell out of him.

Part of him was glad he'd told her about his past. At least now she saw him in a different light; he wasn't the monster she'd taken him for. On the other hand, he hated being exposed and vulnerable. He'd hated opening that wound from his past and letting her see into his soul.

He'd kept the details vague. Even if he had been at liberty to discuss a federal case, he wouldn't have. The emotion over being betrayed by a woman he'd cared for, the pain of losing his partner and friend, was still too raw. So much had changed in his life in that instant when he'd realized he'd been played and he'd put the life of a man who trusted him on the line.

Gabe had been on the brink of a major breakdown when he'd come to the realization he needed to move on and leave Dallas for good. He'd forced himself to put the nightmare of that botched assignment behind him. The move hadn't been easy, but for the sake of his sanity, he'd had to remove himself from the life that was sucking away his soul. Coming to Royal and taking over his family's security company had only made sense.

Of course after coming here he'd had to face the entire Maverick scandal. Out of the frying pan and into the proverbial fire was not his idea of a good time, but he wasn't leaving. He was seeing this through and standing his ground because he had nothing to be ashamed of. He'd done nothing wrong.

Stifling a yawn, Gabe looked around for a clock but didn't see one. From the way the sun was shining through the curtains, he guessed it wasn't too early. He should be making calls, checking emails, making sure he wasn't on the brink of losing any clients. Because not only did he want to hold on to the ones he had, he also wanted to expand and possibly go global. Nothing screamed confidence like expansion, so now was the time for him to go all-in, proving to his clients that he was the most reputable name in the business.

Besides, he truly didn't want to have to start over again. Granted, he could retire and never work another day in his life, but he would go positively insane if he had nothing to do other than travel and live the high life. He'd made wise investments over the years, he'd cashed in at the right times and reinvested. He may have been a kickass agent, but he'd also been a brilliant businessman.

While Gabe did enjoy getting away to one of his homes either in Miami or in the mountains in Montana, he had to work. After what had happened in Dallas and the Maverick situation here in Royal, the pursuit of justice would remain his lifelong calling.

Tossing the covers aside, Gabe searched the floor for his boxer briefs and jeans and put them on. Shirtless, he padded down the hallway and heard the clanging of a pan in the kitchen. Well, at least she hadn't completely left him.

Gabe stood in the doorway and watched as Chelsea mumbled to herself and scrolled through her phone. She muttered something about casserole and eggs then scrolled again. A grin tugged at the corners of his mouth. She had quite the creative way to curse about breakfast foods.

Her hair was messy on one side and flat on the other, she still had a sheet mark on the side of her cheek, and her oversize T-shirt had slipped down to reveal one slender shoulder. Arousal pumped through him and it wasn't breakfast he was hungry for anymore.

"I've never had a woman make me breakfast."

Chelsea started, flattening her hands on the island in front of her and glancing up at him. "You scared me to death."

"Were you expecting another man to greet you this morning?"

"I never remember which one I've left in my bed."

Gabe growled as he closed the gap between them and wrapped his arms around her waist. "There's no other man in your bed but me for now."

With a quirk of a perfectly arched brow, Chelsea patted his cheek. "Then I guess you're the one I'm making breakfast for."

"You don't have to make me breakfast." He nipped at her ear. "I'll make breakfast while you sit here and keep me company."

Without asking, he circled her waist with his hands and lifted her to sit on the counter. She squealed and laughed, smacking him on the shoulder.

She paused and then her fingertips started tracing the pattern of his tattoos from his biceps up over his shoulder and down onto his chest. Just that light touch had him ready to throw her over his shoulder and take her right back to those rumpled sheets he'd just left.

"I never thought tattoos were attractive before," she murmured almost to herself. "Now, I'm not sure I'll ever want a man without them."

The egotistical side of Gabe was thrilled he was ruining her for other men, but the other side, the one he didn't want to think too much about, couldn't stand the idea of her with someone else. For now, she was his and he damn well planned to take advantage of the situation.

Gabe kissed her chin then worked his way down the column of her throat. "Sit here while I cook."

Her body arched against his touch. "I'm not sitting here."

Gabe's hands covered the tops of her bare thighs, giving a gentle squeeze as he lifted his gaze to meet hers. "You are," he commanded. "Right here, wearing my shirt, while I make our food. You're going to need your strength."

Her eyes widened with shock, arousal. "Don't you have work to do today?"

He did. He'd gotten an email late last night about a client that was threatening to pull out and go elsewhere because they'd heard of the scandal surrounding the Walsh name. Gabe had already put his best man on the job and planned to follow up himself later today. That client wasn't going anywhere and neither was Chelsea.

"Right now I have a sexy woman wearing my clothes and I plan on stripping her and showing her how very thankful I am that she believes in me." He covered her lips with his for a quick kiss, a kiss that promised more. "But first, we're eating."

"I won't argue with you about that." She raked her hand through the top of his hair. "My cooking skills aren't what they should be."

Gabe jerked back. "The heiress of a steak empire can't cook?"

She lifted one slender shoulder, causing his shirt to slide down farther, exposing creamy skin he couldn't resist touching. Gabe curled his fingers around her shoulder and stroked his thumb over her collarbone.

"I mean, I can cook steak," she amended. "But most other things terrify me. Mixing ingredients, that's the hard part. Steak is simple."

"Your restaurants have the best steaks, so don't say

it's easy," he retorted. "Nobody even compares to what you guys do to a hunk of beef."

Her smiled widened. "That's the nicest thing you've ever said to me."

"I call you sexy and gorgeous, but I compliment your family's meat and you get all soft."

Chelsea tipped her head to the side. "I'm a simple girl."

Gabe laughed and shook his head as he turned away to look in her fridge. Chelsea Hunt was not simple, not by any stretch. She was as complex as his jumbled feelings for her.

There was no room for feelings, not unless they stayed superficial. Chelsea was fun, she was sexy and she wasn't looking for anything long-term, either. In short, they were perfect together, at least for now.

"So how long is this going to last?"

Her question threw him off, but he remembered Chelsea was nothing if not logical. He thought about his response as he cracked the eggs over the edge of a bowl and then whisked them to a nice froth.

"Done with me already?" he asked, purposely dodging the question.

"I'll at least let you feed me before I kick you out. But I may keep this comfy shirt."

Gabe threw her a glance and a wink. "You're all heart."

And he didn't even want the shirt back because it looked a hell of a lot better on her than him.

"I don't think our hearts are getting involved here."

Good answer. Because their hearts *couldn't* get involved here.

"I'd say last night was…fun," she continued.

"Fun?" he repeated, whisking the hell out of the eggs.

"It was spectacular and you know it. And your scream-ing and the scratches on my back prove you had more than fun."

"Fine," she amended. "It was fabulous and I wouldn't mind doing it again. So long as we're still on the same page about this not getting too serious."

Her words grated on his last nerve and annoyed the hell out of him. Gabe wanted to do the whole this-isn't-a-serious-relationship talk and she'd totally beat him to it. At least they were on the same page, though. Wasn't that what mattered? Shouldn't he be thanking every last star that she wasn't clingy and wanting more?

"There's no reason we can't go on seeing each other in this capacity," she added.

"Capacity? You mean having sex?"

"Yes. Just until the wedding."

His hand stilled on the whisk and the bowl as he turned to face her. "You're putting a deadline on sex?"

With a simple shrug, she met his gaze. "I think that's best considering neither of us want more. Besides, once the wedding passes, we won't have a reason to see each other. Right?"

Gabe swallowed, not liking the way his heart kicked up. But he wasn't allowing his heart to be involved. He'd just scolded himself about that very rule.

"Right," he agreed, turning back to breakfast. "We'll enjoy each other's company, keep this private and, after the wedding, go our separate ways."

"Perfect."

Gabe worked on getting some filets going and then the eggs. "Steak and eggs are a great source of protein and good for energy. Which you will need. If we've only got two weeks left, then I'm taking full advantage."

He turned and wiggled his brows at her. Chelsea took

her time uncrossing and recrossing her legs, giving him a glimpse of exactly the goal he had for the morning.

"If you keep that up, these steaks will go to waste."

She groaned and leaned back on her hands on the counter, arching her back. Even though his shirt was large on her, her breasts strained against the fabric and the hem inched up even higher on her bare thighs.

Keeping his gaze locked on hers, Gabe reached behind him and flicked off the burners. In two short steps he was on her, gripping her hips and pulling her toward the edge of the counter.

"What about breakfast?" she asked, quirking one brow and offering him that sultry smile that went straight to his gut.

"Oh, I'm still having breakfast."

And with that, he jerked the shirt up and over her head before taking exactly what she'd taunted him with.

"What about this one?" Brandee held up a lacy number with a matching thong. "Red or black?"

"Both," Chelsea replied, searching for her size in a short, sheer gown she knew would have Gabe's eyes rolling back in his head. She so enjoyed being the one who made him lose control.

"You didn't even look," Brandee complained.

Chelsea glanced up. "Again, both. It's lingerie. Men can never get enough and they rip it off you, anyway, so color doesn't matter."

"True. But what's Gabe's favorite color?"

Brandee's teasing tone and mocking grin had Chelsea biting the inside of her cheek. "You think you're so smart."

"Oh, I'm brilliant," Brandee stated, full-on smiling now. Her diamond ring glistened as she waved a hand toward Chelsea. "You two have spent quite a bit of time together and the kind of bickering and heated looks I've witnessed between you always leads to the bedroom."

And the kitchen. Mercy sakes, Chelsea would never look at her center kitchen island the same again. The things that man had done to her right there on her marble countertop should be illegal.

Chelsea hadn't intended to shop for lingerie, but since she was here with her friend, why not? Just because she and Gabe were only physical didn't mean she couldn't put a little flair into their time together.

"I actually haven't seen Gabe in two days," she returned defensively.

Granted, she'd only missed seeing him because he had some important business to attend to in Dallas with a new client and she had her own workload to take care of. She actually did have to work, as much as she'd rather spend her time between the sheets—or on the island—with her new lover.

Even though he was gone, Gabe had most definitely left her with a glorious goodbye and the promise of an even better return.

Actually, he'd advised her to rest up because he fully planned on making up for those two days, especially since their time together was limited anyway.

Which was why she was all too eager to find something in this little lingerie boutique that would drive him out of his mind. Her body heated up just thinking of all the things they'd get into when he returned.

But if they didn't slow down somewhat, Chelsea knew full well she'd fall head over-boots and be a lost cause. Her heart had already taken a tumble after his soulful admission about his past and if things between them dragged on, the end would only be more difficult. At least this way she could prepare herself for the end…and enjoy the ride all the way to their final day.

"I thought you only came with me to help me choose honeymoon wear and get some Christmas shopping done."

Chelsea ignored her best friend's questioning stare and returned to searching for her size. "I am Christmas shopping—my purchases just happen to be for selfish reasons."

Well, maybe they weren't totally selfish because Gabe would absolutely love unwrapping her. Oh, maybe she should just get a silky piece of fabric and tie herself up in a big bow. Just the thought of him jerking the knot and having the fabric wisp across her body as it floated down to puddle at her feet…

"This must be serious if you're dodging my questions."

Chelsea's hand stilled on the satin hanger. "Honestly, I don't know what's going on between us. We're keeping things private, but I do know that my feelings are stronger than I want to admit."

"Yet you just did."

Brandee came and stood on the other side of the rack, offering a sympathetic smile. "I know how you feel. I was there with Shane, remember? I went through a scandal of my own with Maverick and Shane pulled me through. We finally found our happily-ever-after."

Chelsea recalled all too well the emotional ride her friends had gone through before finally finding their destiny. Chelsea wasn't looking for a ring on her finger or the promise of a lifetime, but she couldn't stop the desire for Gabe that had settled deep in her soul. And this wasn't sexual desire, though there was an abundance of that. No, this was the desire to know more, to learn more, to have more with Gabe.

So where did that leave her? She still wasn't convinced she was looking long-term, but she wanted more than a romp while they were planning the wedding.

Damn it. She never should've put an expiration date on their interlude, but she sure as hell hadn't wanted to be on the receiving end of his conditions, either. This way, she'd set the terms and held all the power. At least she was well aware of how and when things would end. That was the only way she could cope because heartache was not something she wanted to experience again.

Chelsea knew she'd knocked Gabe off his game when she'd brought up an end date. But he'd gone along with her plan like he thought it was brilliant. It just proved he wasn't looking for anything more than a few nights together.

"The sex is amazing, but I'm to the point I want a real date."

Brandee's mouth dropped. "You've already had sex and you're just now telling me?"

Chelsea hated keeping secrets from her best friend, but everything had happened so fast. And then things had kept happening, so Chelsea had been a bit busy. Plus, they were supposed to be keeping it a secret. *Oops.*

"He'd been pursuing me for a while," Chelsea admitted.

Giving up on finding her size, she crossed the store and went to the back where a wall of drawers held other sultry treasures. Brandee, of course, followed. They were the only ones shopping and the clerks were always great in giving customers privacy and only assisting if asked.

"First he drove me out of my mind in the dressing room when my dress was stuck."

"Wait, what?"

"Then there was horseback riding." Chelsea went

on, ignoring her friend's shocked look because she just wanted to get all this out there. "Then he had to go and give you that extravagant wedding present and I totally melted at his selflessness."

"Back up for a second." Brandee held her hands up. "We'll get to all the details of the dressing room and the riding in a minute. I thought you were skeptical of him, that you believed he was in cahoots with his uncle."

"I did. But the more time I've spent with him, I've seen a side I never thought existed."

"Gabe wouldn't purposely hurt anyone, especially in such a callous way."

Chelsea nodded. "I know that now. I see the man he is."

"Oh, Chels. Are you in love with him?"

"What? No." She wasn't. She *wasn't*. "It's complicated."

"That's the exact way love is described."

Love. What a preposterous word for a relationship that wasn't even a *real* relationship.

Chelsea's father had thought himself in love, but in the end, that myth had shattered him. Chelsea wasn't going to follow the same path.

"Trust me. This isn't love." Great sex and a healthy dose of desire, absolutely. "And don't say anything to anyone. We really want to keep this private. Once we're done seeing each other, we don't want to answer a bunch of questions from people who thought we were a couple. You can see that would get confusing, not to mention annoying."

She thought no-strings sex was supposed to be uncomplicated. Yet there were suddenly so many rules with Gabe, including this whole term-limit thing and the secrecy.

She'd never actually had no-strings sex before be-

cause she'd been in solid relationships with all her partners. Those encounters actually hadn't had rules, so how
was this any easier?

Brandee's skeptical gaze held hers, mirroring the exact
doubts Chelsea had in her own mind. Brandee pursed her
lips and crossed her arms over her chest. Chelsea didn't
like the scrutiny, so she tugged open one of the wide
drawers and started checking the merchandise inside.

There were peacock-colored bra and panty sets, peach
teddies, so many choices all delicately displayed. Each
one she could imagine wearing for Gabe, but then, would
he wonder what her intentions were...other than the obvious? Would he wonder if she wanted more?

On a groan, Chelsea slid the drawer shut. "What am
I going to do?"

Brandee wrapped her arm around Chelsea's shoulder.
"We're going to pick out some killer lingerie that will
have our men begging. Then we're going to go get some
ice cream drenched in hot fudge and whipped cream.
After that, who knows what we'll get into. Maybe wine.
We definitely need some wine."

Chelsea laughed. "At some point I need to actually
Christmas shop. I have nothing for you yet."

Her friend gave her a slight squeeze before letting go.
"You're planning my bachelorette party and my wedding.
I'd say that's more than present enough."

"Speaking of the party, what are you wearing tomorrow?" Chelsea asked.

Brandee blew out a sigh. "I have no clue. I was thinking a cute dress and my boots, but then I think maybe I
should be dressier since I'm the bride. What about you?"

"I bought a white, off-the-shoulder dress and I'm pair-
ing it with my new cowgirl boots. I need some jewelry
to go with it."

Brandee's face lit up. "Then let's finish up here. I'll buy your jewelry for your Christmas present and you can buy me a dress for mine."

Chelsea drew her friend into a hug. "You've got a deal."

Now, all that was left before the promised ice cream and wine was to select the killer lingerie. Chelsea had no clue what turned Gabe on in the way of lace or silk so she opted to buy herself a few different options. Maybe after the bachelorette party, he'd get a little surprise.

Eleven

Gabe saw a flash of white turn the corner and he looked around to make sure nobody saw him follow. That damn dress had driven him crazy for the past three hours and he was done letting this temptress seduce him from afar. He wanted his hands on her. Now.

The coed bachelor/bachelorette party was in full swing at the club and everyone was having a great time. Brandee and Shane wanted all their friends to celebrate and have one last bash before the big day. Everyone loved gathering at TCC, especially since women were such a big part of the club now. Having a joint party here just made sense.

They'd gone with classic mason jars with candles for the center of the tables. Rope was used as cording around the edge of the tablecloths. On the food table was a large S and B wrapped in raffia and propped up with small, twinkling lights surrounding them.

Chelsea had seriously outdone herself on working with the in-house decorator. Brandee and Shane had been so thrilled with the results when they'd arrived.

But right now Gabe was twitching to see Chelsea. Alone.

When he'd arrived before the party officially started and seen Chelsea, he'd nearly swallowed his tongue. She was wearing a short, tight dress and those new cowboy boots, leaving a portion of her legs exposed. He wanted to feel those legs wrapped around his waist and he wanted to hike the skirt of her dress up to see what she wore beneath.

The last few days had been hell in terms of all the ass-kissing he'd had to do to appease his clients. One had threatened to pull all of his business, which would have been a significant loss. But Gabe had assured him that no other scandals would tarnish the company. Gabe knew he was riding a fine line and one more issue would be the end of this working relationship.

Gabe didn't intend to let anything happen again. He was in complete control now. But some of the clients handled by his staff weren't yet convinced. Gabe planned to keep a close eye on the situation and to reassure everyone that they were in the safest hands with the Walsh Group.

Now that he'd handled the damage control, Gabe was more than ready to get back to Chelsea.

When Gabe got to the hall she'd disappeared into, there was no sign of her. There were a couple offices and restrooms along the corridor but he had no idea where she'd gone.

A faint sound of sniffling had Gabe going still. He turned his attention toward one of the offices and crossed the hallway. He knocked on the door, but no answer.

That's when he heard colorful cursing from behind the closed door.

Gabe let himself in and found Chelsea. Her back was to him, her shoulders hunched as she pulled in a shaky breath. She pounded her fist on the desk with each curse word as if the inanimate object had offended her.

"Chels?"

She flinched and turned, her hand over her chest. "Sorry, I just needed a minute."

"To cry?"

"I'm not crying."

Maybe not, but she was on the verge of angry tears if that quivering chin was any indicator.

Gabe moved into the room, closing the door at his back and flicking on the light since he'd shut out the glow from the hall. Something at the party had bothered her because just moments ago he'd seen her laughing with guests and playing darts with some other ladies.

"What is it?"

Shaking her head, she attempted a smile. Did she truly think he'd just let her lie to his face and suffer alone? He wanted to know who the hell had hurt her so much that her cheeks were tinged pink and her eyes were practically shooting fire.

"It's nothing. I just needed to get away from the chaos out there for a second." Chelsea slid her palms over his chest and cocked her head. "I've missed you."

Gripping her wrists before she could distract him, he leaned forward. "Don't change the subject. Tell me what happened."

"Just some jerk thinking he can make crude comments about the photos." She slid her hands up around his neck and ran her fingers through his hair. "I didn't want to make a scene so I just walked out."

Rage pumped through him. "Tell me who."

Chelsea shook her head. "He's not ruining this night. That's why I didn't say anything. Daniel would go all big brother on me if he knew and Shane and Brandee would feel guilty for inviting someone here who was so ill-mannered."

To hell with Daniel or what anyone else would do. Gabe wanted his hands around the bastard's throat right this second. Nobody would ever make Chelsea feel inferior or knock her self-esteem down…not as long as he was around. Hell, even after they were through, he'd still consider her a friend and he'd never stand for anyone being cruel to her.

Gabe gritted his teeth and attempted to rein in his anger. He would find the bastard and make sure he understood never to mention Chelsea's name again or even to glance her way. If Shane knew about this, he'd haul the guy out of the party, but Gabe wouldn't let this dark cloud hang over the night and he sure as hell wasn't going to let it hang over Chelsea.

Daniel and Shane didn't need to know anything had happened. Gabe knew and he would damn well take care of things.

Forcing himself to remain calm, he nipped at her lips. "You look so damn sexy," he murmured against her mouth. "Did you wear this to drive me crazy? Because I'm ready to make our excuses and find someplace where we can be alone so I can see what you're wearing under this."

With that bright smile that never failed to pack a punch of lust, Chelsea tickled the nape of his neck with her fingertips. "Maybe I had someone in mind when I put this on."

"Is that right?" he growled.

She nodded and met his gaze beneath her heavy lids. "I may have also had that same person in mind when I made a special purchase yesterday. Maybe something lacy."

His entire body tightened as he plunged his hands into her hair and covered her mouth with his. Damn this party. He wanted her right now. It had been too long—days—since he'd had her and each second that ticked by brought them closer to the end. The need had grown stronger and stronger and, right at this moment, he was hanging on by a thread.

Chelsea pulled away. "We can't do this here."

"We can," he argued, reaching down to haul her hips flush with his. "I can clear off that desk and have you bent over in a second."

Her moan vibrated through her chest. "If we got caught here, Shane and Brandee would kill us. Besides, just think of all this as foreplay."

He'd been in foreplay mode all night. Seeing her hips in motion beneath that flimsy material had been like watching a slow-motion strip tease and he was damn tired of waiting for his prize.

"I want to know what's under this dress."

She gripped his jaw, wiping her thumb over his bottom lip. "I assure you, it will be worth the wait once we get back to my place."

"My place is closer. We'll go there."

Before Chelsea, he'd never taken a woman back to his place, but he'd never had a need like this. Chelsea was different in every respect. She'd already been to his loft and, he had to admit, having her there hadn't freaked him out. He'd actually enjoyed it.

He'd also exposed a part of himself, of his past, that he never would've divulged had Chelsea not gotten to him deeper on some level. Those were thoughts he wasn't ready to dive into right now.

The second this party was over, he wanted that dress off and he suddenly had the all-consuming desire to see her spread across his sheets. Any meaningful thoughts or questioning why he'd opened up to her had no place here.

"So impatient," she mocked. Dropping a quick kiss on his lips, she pulled away from his arms and adjusted her dress. "We better get back out there or people will wonder where we went."

Nobody knew about their current situation and Gabe wanted to keep things that way. Whatever was going on between Chelsea and him didn't concern anyone else. She was his and he wasn't too keen on sharing. And he was determined to track down the jerk who'd upset her. The party was large, but Gabe knew most everyone in attendance. It wouldn't be too difficult to figure it out.

"You go," he told her. "I'll be out in a minute."

She slipped out the door and Gabe needed more than a minute to gather his thoughts. Between the desire pumping through him and the fury over some guy who didn't have any manners, Gabe needed to rein it in before he went out there in a fit of rage.

Gabe let a good five-minute gap pass before he headed back out. The party was still in full swing. The drinks were flowing, laughter and conversation filled the open area, and couples were dancing to a slow country song by the hired band.

Standing back, Gabe surveyed the room, trying to pinpoint guests he didn't know. There was no way a friend of theirs would make snide remarks to Chelsea, so this guy had to be someone outside of their inner circle. Maybe a business associate of Shane's or Brandee's.

Within minutes Gabe had narrowed the options to

three guys. Gabe shoved his hands in his jeans and watched each of them for a few minutes. He needed to have absolutely no doubt which one he needed to rip apart.

Chelsea and Brandee were throwing darts in the corner. Erin stood near them, sipping on a glass of water and chatting with her friends. Shane and Daniel were at the other dartboard. Gabe figured he should mingle so he didn't look like he wanted to commit murder, but if any of those three guys said something to Chelsea again, Gabe wouldn't be responsible for his actions.

"Looks like you owe me a bourbon," Daniel stated, slapping Shane on the back as Gabe joined them near the dartboards.

"Considering it's an open bar, I'm paying for it anyway," Shane replied.

"Actually, Chelsea and I paid for it," Gabe interjected. "But feel free to drink all you want. We also have drivers to make sure everyone gets home safely."

"You guys really thought of everything," Shane said. "Thanks, man."

Gabe didn't want the accolades. Shane was his best buddy and there wasn't anything he wouldn't do for him. Besides, working with Chelsea was worth all the money and time he'd spent. She trusted him now. She believed in him. And he couldn't wait to get back to his place and make good on his promise to rip that dress off her body.

"I'll go get drinks," Shane offered. "What do you guys want?"

Daniel and Gabe gave their orders and Shane headed toward the bar. Risking a glance at the women, Gabe smiled when Chelsea threw the last dart in her hand and it hit the bull's-eye. She threw her arms in the air and spun toward her friends with a huge smile on her face. That punch of lust to his gut always caught him off guard—though it was something he really should have been used to by now.

"I'll go get us some drinks," she told them.

Gabe forced himself to look away, but when he turned back, Daniel was eyeing him.

"Something you want to tell me?" Chelsea's brother asked.

"No."

"You dodged that question before, Walsh."

Gabe shrugged. He'd continue dodging it until Chelsea wanted her brother in on what was going on…if she ever did.

Even if he and Chelsea hadn't agreed to keep things private, he wouldn't be chatting with her brother about this. Chelsea was Gabe's business. Simple as that.

"This is none of your concern."

Daniel lifted his brows. "Is that right? Because you were looking at my sister like… I can't even finish that without getting graphic. What the hell is going on with you guys?"

Gabe crossed to the board and plucked out the darts. "We're planning a wedding. You want to know anything else, you'd have to ask her."

"I'm asking you."

Gabe handed Daniel the red-tipped darts. "Winner gets the final say-so in this argument."

Taking the darts from Gabe, Daniel nodded. "I'll want the truth when I win."

Like Gabe would ever lose.

The crash of breaking glass had Gabe and Daniel spinning around. Chelsea stood in the midst of the mess, and some guy Gabe didn't know was clutching her elbow.

Oh, hell no. Gabe was across the room before he could

even think twice. Rage bubbled within him and all he saw
was Chelsea's shocked face, her mouth open, her eyes
wide. And fear. He saw fear and he damn well didn't like
it one bit because his Chelsea never cowered from anything. She was a fighter.

"C'mon, baby. Everyone has already seen everything
you have. Why don't you give me a private show?"

The guy slurred his words as the reek of alcohol
wafted off him. Before Gabe could make a move, Chelsea rammed her elbow into the man's stomach, causing
him to grunt and double over.

"You don't have to be a b—"

Gabe reached down, grabbing the guy by the throat
and pulling up so he could look him in the eye. He wanted
this jerk to know exactly who was threatening him.

"Get the hell out of here and don't come back. If I see
you near Chelsea—if I even think you've spoken her
name—you will find out just how difficult your life can
be. Are we clear?"

Daniel came up beside Chelsea, wrapping an arm
around her. Gabe knew she was fine, but he wanted the
trash taken out.

Yanking the guy by the back of the neck, Gabe es-
corted him to the door and made sure he headed toward
the parking lot. No way in hell was he going to allow
Chelsea to continue living with this black mark over her.
Everything that had happened to her wasn't her fault, but
the fault of his uncle.

Gabe wished the old bastard wasn't gone because he'd
go kick his ass and knock some sense into him. How did
one even get revenge on a dead man? Rage was a difficult
emotion to control, but Gabe forced himself to breath in
and out and get back to Chelsea without ripping someone's head off.

Chels was a strong woman, but there were only so many times someone could be knocked down, and in public, no less. Damn it all. Even though none of this was his fault, it was his family member who had set this ball in motion, ruining lives.

That was all in the past now and Gabe was hell-bent on making sure the whole nightmare stayed that way. The town was moving on. These people were moving on. Until that jerk made a scene, this party was proof that every one of his friends had found their own happiness despite Dusty's antics.

Gabe stepped back into the main room and made a beeline for Chelsea, who sat on a bar stool beneath a large bundle of mistletoe. It was almost as if he was being given the green light.

Several friends surrounded her: Erin, Brandee, Shane and her brother Daniel. Gabe didn't care how rude he was or what others thought. The whole secrecy thing be damned. He wanted her to know she wasn't alone and he wasn't just consoling her as a pal. No, he planned on consoling her like her lover.

Pushing past Shane, Gabe reached for Chelsea. Her eyes went wide when she spotted him and he wondered exactly what she saw written all over his face. Most likely, she saw every blasted thought racing through his head. Every instinct in him wanted to haul her out of there, but throwing her over his shoulder would only piss her off more.

Gabe said nothing as he framed her face and captured her mouth. He swallowed her shocked gasp and eased her to her feet. Cheers and music surrounded them, but he blocked everything out except Chelsea's sweet taste.

When he feathered the kiss and released her lips, her

lids took an extra moment to open. Desire and surprise stared back at him.

"Well, that was unexpected," she muttered. "Guess we're not keeping this private anymore."

Gabe grabbed her hand. "We're leaving."

"Don't be absurd, Gabe. We—"

He shot her a look that shut her up immediately.

"Go," Brandee stated from behind him. "The party is almost over, anyway."

"And we paid for people to clean up," he reminded her, never taking his eyes from Chelsea.

Her lips thinned as she nodded and gripped his hand.

Gabe turned to find Daniel with his arms crossed, his eyes narrowed.

"That dart game is going to have to wait," Gabe stated as he pushed by.

Daniel's eyes went to his sister. "Chels."

"I'll call you later," she told him.

Later? Maybe tomorrow. Right now they were going to be alone, away from people, phones. The world. Gabe wasn't in a sharing mood.

Something about having another man put his hands on his woman and terrorize her made Gabe even more protective, even more territorial, than ever.

Hadn't he wanted to keep this purely physical? Hadn't he wanted to keep things private?

Well, apparently manhandling the jerk who'd approached her and then kissing Chelsea beneath the mistletoe had blown that plan all to hell. But he'd answer everyone's questions another time.

Chelsea was his for another week and he damn well planned to take every opportunity to show her just how a woman should be treated. She deserved everything and, for now, he was going to be her everything. Once

JULES BENNETT   119

the wedding was over, well, he'd worry about that when the time came.

The valet brought Gabe's truck around and Gabe gave him a hefty tip before helping Chelsea get in. There were so many emotions pumping through him right now, he needed a minute. If she touched him, if she said anything, he was afraid his control would snap. He was that desperate to be with her and to prove that she was not defined by the scandal that continued to plague her. Gabe had never felt the need to prove something to someone and he'd never had this desperation before.

But this wasn't about him. Everything about this moment, about these emotions, was about Chelsea.

Being with this woman was like walking a tightrope. One wrong step and he could plummet into a territory he wasn't ready for. Gabe was already teetering as it was and he had a sinking feeling he wasn't going to be able to hang on much longer.

The second he settled in behind the wheel and put the truck into Drive, Chelsea turned in her seat. "Gabe—"

"Not now," he growled, gripping the wheel tightly.

Once they got to his place, they would talk. Or not. He'd much rather work his tension and stress out another way. He had a sinking feeling if he started opening up about his emotions now, he'd say things he'd vowed never to say to another woman and the last thing he wanted was for Chelsea to get hurt again.

Twelve

Anger rolled off Gabe in waves. She'd never seen him like this, had never thought someone so reserved could dole out such rage. But the man was practically shaking.

He'd been pissed back at the party. The way he'd handled that drunk guy, Chelsea wasn't so sure what would've happened had the room not been full of family and friends. Would Gabe have been so controlled or would he have pounded on the man? She'd been scared, not that Gabe would hurt her in his anger, but of what he'd do to the other guy and how she couldn't prevent it.

If she thought Daniel had been protective growing up, that was nothing compared to Gabe right now. How would Gabe react if he knew her past? Would he look at her differently? Would he see her as weak?

It didn't matter, though. Their time was drawing to a close and no matter how much her heart kept trying to get involved, Chelsea had to hold back at least some part of herself. If she gave him everything…well, she'd suffer even more heartache in the end.

Gabe ushered her into his penthouse loft apartment. She'd briefly been there before and hadn't paid much attention, but now that she was back, she could easily see this was his domain. The industrial yet country vibe surrounded her. The exposed brick walls were masculine, the chrome finishes and high-tech electronics taking up one entire end of the loft screamed money and power. There were closed-circuit TVs showing the outside of the apartment building, the parking garage beneath, the street in both directions.

Being so paranoid must be an occupational hazard for a former FBI agent turned security analyst.

"You sure do have quite a bit of surveillance," she casually commented.

"I own the building."

Chelsea didn't even bother hiding her surprise. "Seriously? How did I not know that?"

Gabe gave a shrug. "It's not something I talk about. I actually own several properties in Royal, but most are held under my company names."

Yet again, the man of mystery had more up his sleeve. He tended to keep her guessing on who the real Gabriel Walsh was. Just when she thought she'd uncovered the final layer, he revealed another.

Chelsea continued to peruse the open living area. There was a black metal outline of the state of Texas hanging on the wall at the other end of the room. The simple wall art was tasteful yet very Gabe. There was a pair of old cowboy boots over in the corner and several hats that hung on pegs near the front door. While the loft was neat and tidy, Gabe's presence was everywhere.

The gleaming kitchen with a long, concrete island

lined by eight bar stools just begged for a party. But she didn't think Gabe was too much of a partier, let alone a host. Still, she saw herself getting steaks ready, him serving up sides and handing out bourbon.

Wait, no. This wasn't some fantasy that would come to life. He'd brought her here for sex. Isn't that what they'd discussed in the office back at the club? But then he'd gone and gotten angry and now she wasn't so sure why she was there because there was still fury pouring from him.

This final week was going to be full of Gabe and the wedding. Gabe in private was going to be vastly different than Gabe as a cohost of the nuptials and a best man. The idea of walking down the aisle with him on her arm gave her heart a little extra beat. She absolutely couldn't get caught up in that image or that fantasy.

Gabe stalked to the living area and stared out the floor-to-ceiling windows. With jerky movements, he unbuttoned the cuffs on his sleeves and rolled them up his forearms. He'd hung his black hat by the others near the door and hadn't spoken a word.

"If you're just going to be angry, I'm not sure why I'm here."

She remained near the entryway, crossing her arms over her chest and waiting for him to respond. But he kept looking out onto the city, his hands shoved into the pockets of his perfectly fitted jeans.

"I'll just call someone to pick me up."

"Stay."

That one word settled between them and Chelsea softened just a bit. What the hell was he so angry about? It wasn't like this was his life that kept getting thrown back in his face. She had a feeling there would be jerks for some time to come who were all too eager to bring up those nude photos, thinking she was easy and willing to give them a private showing. It was humiliating, but right now all she could do was keep her head high and move on.

"You didn't see your face," Gabe said, still keeping his back to her. "When you dropped those glasses and I turned to see what happened… Chels, your face was pure terror. You'd gone white and I saw that guy's hand on you and I wanted to kill him right there."

The hurt in his tone had her moving toward him. She'd been so worried about what type of scene she'd caused and if she'd ruined the party to even think about how all of that had affected Gabe. Obviously he'd been angry with the guy. Someone like Gabe, so powerful and prominent, would see it as a setback, an embarrassment. They were just a fling, anyway, so why should he have to put up with her scandal?

"I completely understand if you want to call this quits between us." She stood only a few feet away now. Even though she wanted to reach out and touch him, she clasped her hands in front of her dress. "I know the scandal surrounding me is embarrassing. I wouldn't want someone else to have to bear the burden of the crass jokes or the mocking."

Gabe whirled around. "You think I'm trying to tell you…what? That I'm leaving you alone to deal with this mess? That I don't want to be associated with you because of it? Do you honestly think I'm that big of a jerk?"

Chelsea swallowed the burn in her throat. Why did love have to be complicated?

Wait. Love?

Well now was not the time for her to realize she'd completely fallen head-over-boots with this man. Not only was she completely unsure about where he stood, she knew he didn't do relationships. Fantastic. There was nothing like this feeling of despair when she was already battered and bruised.

"I don't think you're a jerk," she whispered, ignoring the extra thump of her heart. "I just wouldn't blame you for wanting to bring this to an end now instead of after the wedding."

She wouldn't blame him; she would be devastated. But the end was inevitable. Next week or now, did it really matter? Both ways she'd be alone, which she was used to. But being with Gabe had changed her into someone who didn't want to be alone, not when she knew how amazing he could be.

Damn it. When had she fallen in love? Somewhere between not trusting him and seeing him come to her defense tonight. She'd known for a few days that she was sinking deeper into territory she knew nothing about. She'd fought every step, but she couldn't lie to herself anymore.

Gabe reached out and hooked an arm around her waist. "I'm not ending a day sooner than we planned," he growled. "I'm angry you had to deal with that guy. I'm angry because you should never be afraid of what my family did and there's not a damn thing I can do to go back and change what happened to you."

Wait. Gabe was blaming himself for Dusty's actions?

Chelsea reached up, smoothing his unruly blond hair back from his forehead. Framing his face, she leaned in and briefly touched his lips.

"You aren't to blame," she assured him. "And you can't control what others say."

"Maybe not, but I can try to shield you from the hurt."

Her heart tumbled in her chest, but she knew he didn't want any part of her heart or her love. Which was such a shame, because she would give them both so freely to her knight in shining armor.

"I've never been so angry in my life," he murmured. "When my partner was killed, I was hurt and broken, yes. Angry? Yes. But I was able to stop the killer and bring him to justice. But all of this? I have no idea how to stop it completely and it rips me apart."

Chelsea eased back from his arms. "Well, for now I know something you can control. I believe you said something about wanting to see what I have on beneath my dress."

The darkness in his eyes mixed with arousal. Chelsea reached for the hem and eased it up and over her head. She tossed the dress onto the back of the sofa only a few feet away. When she turned her focus back to Gabe, the arousal in his eyes had turned to hunger and she knew she'd made the right decision in terms of lingerie tonight.

The white, lacy, strapless bustier and matching thong indeed had Gabe speechless. Most women trying to seduce a man would pair the outfit with heels, but she was all about her cowgirl boots.

"You bought this for me?" he asked, slowly making his way toward her.

"You know I did."

Because there was no one else.

Gabe muttered a curse beneath his breath. "I've never wanted someone more than you right now. You're breathtaking and sexy and…damn, Chels. You're killing me."

She couldn't help but smile because she'd finally managed to make him a stuttering mess. Feeling a tad saucy, she propped her hands on her hips and tipped her head.

"Maybe if you're good, I'll show you some other items I purchased."

His eyes snapped to hers. "You bought others?"

"Something in green to match my eyes and then there was this racy black number that I simply couldn't pass up."

With a growl, Gabe was on her. His arms circled her waist, his mouth crashed down onto hers, and he backed her against the window. The cool glass did nothing to calm the heat racing through her.

Gabe nipped at her lips before roaming over her jaw, down her neck, to the swell of her breasts. Her entire body felt as if she was lit up from within. As his hands seemed to touch her everywhere, his mouth was doing wonders driving her mad.

"I want you in my bed," he murmured against her skin. "I've envisioned you there all spread out, reaching for me."

The image in her mind had her arching against him. She'd take him anywhere he wanted.

"But the bed is too far away," he stated. "And my need for you is too great."

She thrust her fingers through his hair and held him as he yanked the top of her bustier down and covered her flesh with his mouth. She cried out, but then he started ridding her of the rest of her clothes and Chelsea could only hang on.

Once she was bare—except for her boots—Gabe took a half step back and raked his heavy-lidded gaze over her.

"Take off your clothes," she demanded.

His grin kicked up, wrinkling the corners of his eyes and making him seem all the more menacing. "You take them off."

In her next breath, she was making frantic work of his buttons and when she was down to the last two, she just jerked the shirt open. Gabe's laugh had his abs clenching, as if he was showing off just how spectacular his build truly was.

Chelsea's hands shook as she removed his pants. He toed off his boots and finally stood before her wearing nothing but desire.

He reached into his pants' pocket, pulled out protection and slipped it on. Chelsea's blood pumped faster, her nerves dancing with anticipation, and when he finally turned those gray eyes back to her, she didn't hesitate to reach for him.

Gabe lifted her off the floor. She toed off her boots and let them clunk to the floor before locking her ankles behind his back.

Gabe closed his mouth over hers at the same time he plunged into her. Then he stood still, right there in the middle of the room. Their bodies were joined, but he didn't move, and the erotic sensation was driving her absolutely out of her mind.

"I have no control with you," he murmured against the side of her neck. "I need you, Chels."

He spun around, sending them tumbling to the sofa. He cradled her face as his weight settled her deeper against the cushions.

Chelsea opened to him as he covered her mouth with his. He trailed one of his hands down her side and held tight to her hip, his fingertips gripping her skin.

This wasn't enough. She wanted more, needed more. Beyond the sex—though it was the best she'd ever had—she needed Gabe for everything.

He muttered something in her ear she didn't understand at the same time he tipped his hips just right to send her over the edge. She tightened around him, arched her back and dug her heels into his backside.

When Gabe's body shuddered against hers, he whispered something else, something she still didn't quite catch. She clung to him, though, taking his release as hers ebbed. He held his weight just off her, but she wanted all of him.

Chelsea circled his shoulders with her arms and pulled him closer as his body ceased trembling. His head rested in the crook of her neck. Darkness had fallen across the apartment. Only the glow of a small desk lamp across the room gave any light. She wanted this moment to carry on; she didn't want words or movement to break the spell of their time together.

Closing her eyes, Chelsea willed time to stop. If she held on tighter maybe he'd stay.

Fortunately, though, she wasn't a clinging woman. She'd never begged for a man and she wasn't going to start now. If there was ever a time or a man, though, Gabe was definitely worthy of her begging.

When he started to move, she trailed her fingertips up through his hair.

"What did you whisper in my ear earlier?"

Gabe froze, cringed actually. "I don't recall."

He was lying. It had been mere moments ago and he'd said it twice.

"Don't move," she murmured. "Let's just lie like this for another minute."

His hand softened on her hip as his hips shifted. "If I stay here too long, I'm going to want you again and the rest of my protection is in the bedroom."

Chelsea smiled up at him. "Then maybe we should make our way there."

Thirteen

The wedding was only four days away now. Chelsea couldn't believe the time had almost come for her best friend to say "I do." She'd be lying if she didn't admit, just to herself, that she was jealous. Chelsea hadn't thought she wanted romance and forever, but getting swept away in this real-life, fairy-tale ending had her wishes shifting.

Suddenly Hunt & Co. wasn't her only focus. If Gabe knew how much real estate he took up in her mind, her *heart*, he'd likely run fast and far. She had to keep this to herself. She knew deep in her soul that there was no future for them, not together, anyway. He'd made it abundantly clear from the start that he couldn't trust his heart that way again.

Trust. Hadn't that been the entire theme of their relationship? No matter if they were enemies, then friends, then lovers, everything surrounding them always circled back to trust.

He'd pursued her and she'd backed away, but now that she was fully on board, he was backing away. The dance they continued to perform was confusing, frustrating, and she wished like hell they were doing the same steps.

Chelsea pulled up her spreadsheet and attempted to get the new system up and running for the accounting department. That was her goal today, not to focus on the fact she'd enjoyed two days at Gabe's loft. The weekend had flown by in a blur of sex and time spent doing nothing but enjoying each other.

Monday was even harsher to handle after such an amazing few days with the man she loved.

She seriously needed to stop using that word. Love wasn't a good idea. Admitting her feelings this close to the end game...damn it. None of this was a game. Every single moment she'd spent with him had been real, had been amazing, and something she wanted forever.

A gentle tap on her door had Chelsea glancing across her office. Before she could mutter a reply, the door eased open and Daniel stepped in. She figured he'd be making his presence known. She'd known he was spending the holidays in Royal as opposed to Dallas, especially with the wedding coming up. Erin wanted to be at Crescent Moon, the Hunt family ranch, for Christmas. Chelsea made a mental note to swing by to see her soon-to-be sister-in-law and take her Christmas present. Well, she'd take the present just as soon as it was delivered, because she'd purchased nearly everything online.

Chelsea offered her brother a smile. Surprisingly he hadn't contacted her since she and Gabe had left the party abruptly the other night. Well, he'd texted her, but she'd been preoccupied.

"Your assistant said you don't have a meeting for another hour." Daniel closed the distance between them and took a seat opposite her desk. He crossed one ankle over his knee and settled in. "Hope this isn't a bad time."

"You wouldn't care if it was," she replied, turning her chair to fully face him. "You're here to question me about Gabe, so let's have it."

Daniel blew out a breath as he removed his cowboy hat and placed it over the arm of the chair. "What are you thinking, Chels? The guy is a loner and you're going to get your heart broken."

She'd expected nothing less from her big brother. "Did you rehearse that or just decide to wing it?"

"I'm winging it, so have pity on me when I'm trying to play the concerned older brother."

"You're not playing anything. You *are* the concerned older brother." Chelsea offered him a smile as she folded her arms across her desktop and carefully thought of what to say next. "Listen, I know you care about me and I get that you don't want me hurt. I'm not a fan of heartache myself, but Gabe and I know what we're doing. We have no preconceived notion that this is long-term."

No notions, but wishes…definitely.

"That's not like you."

She couldn't help but laugh. "And you know about my sex life? Is that really where you want to go?"

Daniel cringed. "Definitely not, but you're going to get hurt."

Most likely, but she couldn't live her life worrying about the future. If things were going to end with Gabe— no, *when* they ended—she at least wanted to enjoy the here and now. And she'd enjoyed the hell out of their weekend together.

"Daniel, I realize over this past year Royal has been overrun with happily-ever-afters and you and Erin want everyone to be as blissful as you guys, but right now I'm not looking for love."

Yet it had found her, anyway. She'd have to worry about that later. She vowed that she'd enjoy Gabe until the very last minute, and then she'd stock her fridge with her favorite ice cream and allow herself the pity party she would no doubt deserve. What a way to ring in the New Year.

"I swear, Gabe and I are fine, and at the end of the day, we're just friends."

Who give each other toe-curling orgasms and spend weekends together.

"Friends, huh?" Daniel asked with a grunt. "The man looked like he wanted to strangle that guy the other night and then he kissed you like he was staking his claim."

"Maybe he was," she replied simply. This was not a conversation she wanted to have with Daniel. And the truth was, he wouldn't want her honest opinion or feelings on the matter. It was best to keep him as far away from this as possible. "Was there something else you wanted to discuss?"

Daniel pursed his lips as if he were contemplating his next move.

Chelsea arched her brow, silently daring him to circle back to the topic she'd just closed.

"Erin and I wanted to have you over for dinner."

"That sounds great. When were you thinking?"

Daniel came to his feet and tapped his fingers on the edge of her desk. "Tonight, actually. We have something we want to discuss with you."

Chelsea stood, as well. "That sounds serious. Is everything okay?"

"We're fine," he assured her with his smile, one that matched their father's. "Does seven work for you?"

"I'll be there."

When he blew out a breath and looked into her eyes, she knew they weren't done with their heart-to-heart.

"You know I love you and just want what's best, right?"

Chelsea circled her desk and wrapped her arms around her great protector. She'd always looked up to him, always admired his opinion, and loved how he continually put her first.

"I feel the same about you," she told him then eased back. "Now, get out of here so I can finish this program for the accounting department or we're going to have a whole host of angry employees when their checks are messed up."

Daniel kissed her on the cheek and left her office, closing the door behind him. That talk had gone better than she'd thought. She wasn't quite sure how he'd react to Gabe's very public display of affection. Hadn't Gabe been the one to want to keep things under wraps? Yet when she was threatened, he hadn't cared one bit. He had to have some feelings for her...didn't he?

Regardless of what Daniel thought, or anyone else for that matter, Chelsea was going to enjoy this time with Gabe. Once the wedding was over and they were done working together, they wouldn't see each other as often. Maybe she'd get lucky and the desire would fizzle out.

The likelihood of that happening was about as great as her getting Gabe to fall in love with her—and that was never going to be a reality. He didn't do love, didn't do long-term, and even though she didn't know the full details of the case involving his partner's death, she had to respect his desires.

That didn't mean she had to like them.

Blowing out a breath, Chelsea went back to her computer. There was no sense in worrying about this now.

She had so much work to get done, surely she could block Gabe and focus.

The second she pulled up the program she'd been working on, her cell vibrated on her desktop. She glanced at the screen only to find a simple message from Gabe: Tonight you're mine.

So much for focusing on work.

Chelsea let herself into the main house at Crescent Moon. She'd grown up here, and returning as an adult always felt like coming home. She loved her house in Pine Valley, but Crescent Moon held such a special place in her heart.

She made her way through the open foyer. Erin's laughter filtered through the first floor and Chelsea could tell her brother and his fiancée were in the back of the house. When she got to the enclosed four-seasons room with three walls of windows overlooking the stables, she smiled. She'd always loved this room. She'd spent hour upon hour reading her favorite books in the corner chaise, which had since been replaced with another in a pretty pale yellow.

Erin slid her legs over the side of the chair and offered a bright smile. "Hey, glad you could make it." Coming to her feet, Erin closed the gap between them and wrapped her arms around Chelsea.

"A dinner that I didn't have to prepare?" Chelsea said, easing back. "I'm always up for that."

Daniel crossed to the minibar in the opposite corner. "Can I get you a drink? Dinner should be ready in about fifteen minutes."

"I'd love a glass of wine. White, please." While Daniel busied himself getting her wine, Chelsea glanced at Erin. "I'm sorry I've been so scarce lately. This wedding planning, plus work, has taken up a good bit of my time."

"And Gabe Walsh?" Erin asked, her brows rising as her smile widened.

Why deny it? The man had kissed her in front of nearly the entire town at that party. Her brother had already speculated about their connection and Brandee knew the truth. There wasn't much of a thread of secrecy to hold on to at this point.

"He has occupied a good portion of my time." Mainly the nights, but there was no need to get into that. "So what did you guys need to see me about?"

Daniel handed her the glass and clutched his own tumbler, most likely filled with bourbon. "We're pregnant."

Chelsea gripped the stem of her glass. "'Scuse me?"

"Way to go, Daniel." Erin shook her head and rested a hand over her stomach. "We are expecting, but I'd hoped to deliver the news in a little more of an exciting manner."

Chelsea sat her glass on the table and pulled Erin into another hug. "I'm so thrilled for you guys! I'm going to be an aunt."

She eased back and glanced down at Erin's flat belly. "How far along? Are you feeling okay? What can I do to help?"

Erin laughed and patted Chelsea's shoulder. "I'm fine. I went to the doctor today and I am six weeks."

Chelsea squealed and turned to her brother. "You guys are going to be such awesome parents. I can't wait to see Baby Hunt."

Daniel wrapped an arm around her. "We were hoping you'd agree to be the godmother. I know not many people do that anymore, but we want you to be a big part of our kids' lives."

"Of course," she answered then froze. "'Kids'?"

Erin beamed. "Twins."

Chelsea jerked her attention back to her brother. "Two babies? I'm going to need something stronger than wine."

Erin laughed and nodded. "I know, it's a shock. Believe me. We were stunned, but we knew we wanted a large family and I guess we're just getting a jump start. I'd been having some pain and they just did an ultrasound to make sure things looked okay. Apparently the pain is my uterus stretching faster than normal."

Two babies? Chelsea couldn't even imagine being a mother to one, let alone two. But Erin and Daniel were beaming and Chelsea couldn't be happier for them.

Tears pricked her eyes. "I don't even know what to say."

"Well, damn. Don't cry." Daniel picked up her wineglass. "I can't handle tears."

"I'm happy," Chelsea insisted. "Really. I'm just overwhelmed and excited and I can't even imagine how you guys feel."

"All of that and more," Erin assured her. "I've gotten used to the ups and downs of my emotions lately, but I know you're still taking it all in. Dinner should be ready. What do you say we go eat and discuss baby registries and nursery décor?"

"Maybe I should eat in the kitchen," Daniel groaned.

Chelsea smacked his chest. "You're eating with us, and we're going to have a nice family dinner. And we need to figure out which room to put the nursery in, and colors, and names. We need names."

Daniel groaned as he turned and headed toward the kitchen where his chef had no doubt prepared something fabulous. "We have a long time still to go," he growled as he walked away. "Why do I have a feeling my credit card is going to take a hard hit?"

Chelsea smiled as she looped her arm through Erin's. "Because it is."

* * *

He'd told her to be at his place at seven, yet it was now nearing eight and there was no sign of Chelsea. No call, no text. Absolutely nothing.

Gabe didn't like to be kept waiting, especially by the woman warming his bed.

The doorman buzzed him, letting him know Chelsea was on her way up. Had something happened that had prevented her from getting in touch to tell him she'd be late? Had she been delayed by some jerk harassing her again when she was out?

Everything in him stirred, churning toward anger. He wanted to shield her from all the flack she was taking. Even beyond that, he wanted to be her…what? They only had a few more days left together before their agreed-upon date to end things. And she'd never given any indication she wanted more.

Why the hell was he now choosing to think of something beyond sex? He'd done that once. His partner had been killed because Gabe had trusted the wrong woman. He'd let her into his personal life, thinking she loved him, only to find out she had actually been playing him all along to feed information to the drug cartel Gabe had been working to bring down.

He'd been such a damn fool.

But Chelsea was different. She'd dodged him and he'd continued to chase her. Gabe always got what he wanted, but now he wasn't so sure what that was. He knew for certain he didn't want things to end, yet at the same time he wasn't looking for a relationship.

Maybe all these wedding plans and seating charts and dress fittings were getting to him. He was just surrounded by the prospect of "forever" and "I do" and clearly getting caught up in the moment.

And most troubling was how he'd whispered his need to her the other night. He'd slipped and whispered how much he needed her, how much he cared for her. Not once but twice. Those words bordered on a confession he certainly wasn't ready to make now...if ever.

Here a quiet knock on his door, Gabe turned from the view of downtown and glanced toward the entryway. Chelsea let herself in, but the moment he spotted her, Gabe was crossing the room in long strides.

"What happened?" he asked, gripping her arms and studying her tear-streaked face. "Are you hurt?"

She smiled and shook her head, her eyes bright with unshed tears. "These are happy tears."

Happy tears? That always sounded like an oxymoron to him, just one more thing he would never understand.

"You're an hour late and you come in crying," he persisted. "What's going on?"

"Daniel and Erin are having twins."

Her declaration was made on another burst of tears. Gabe wasn't quite sure what to do, so he pulled her into his arms. "And you're sure these are happy tears?" he asked again.

She nodded against his shoulder. "I'm so excited for them. My best friend is getting married. My brother is having babies. I mean, it's all so life-changing and makes me think about my own life goals and—"

She jerked back, eyes wide. "I'm not saying that to scare you," she quickly amended. "I don't mean us. I'm just happy and excited, and I want that in my life. I want to have a family and a husband, and I never thought I did, but..."

Yeah, all this talk was making his gut tighten. Seeing Chelsea having an epiphany like this had him wondering about his own future. Hell, he'd just admitted to himself he may want more with her, but marriage and kids?

Let's not get too out of control here.

He framed her face in his hands, using the pads of his thumbs to wipe her tears. "Have you eaten dinner? I can call and have something brought to us."

"I ate at Daniel's." Her gaze held his; moisture glistened on her lashes. "Sorry I'm late. Erin and I got carried away with looking at baby things online. I may have already bought nursery furniture for them."

Gabe could see her getting so involved and wanting to play the doting aunt. How would she be with her own children? Would she want a large family?

The idea of her starting a life with some nameless, faceless, man had jealousy curling low in his gut. But who was Gabe to put a stop to this new goal she'd created? He was merely passing through her life.

"Want to help put up my Christmas tree?"

Chelsea jerked back and her eyes widened. "Tonight?"

"Might as well."

"It's only a few days until Christmas," she reminded him as if he didn't know the date. "Why do anything at this point?"

Because, surprisingly, he wanted to spend time with her, and not just in the bed. As crazy and absurd as that sounded, he found it to be true. He wanted to do something with Chelsea that was normal, something that would create memories.

Damn it. He was getting in deep here. Deeper than he'd anticipated. And he knew full well that in a few days, after the wedding was over, he wasn't going to want to let her go.

Hell, maybe he couldn't let her go.

Fourteen

"I can't believe those are the only ornaments you have."

Gabe glanced over at her, his brows drawn. "What's wrong with them?"

Chelsea didn't even attempt to hide her laughter. "You used one of your hats as the tree topper and the rest of your ornaments are shot glasses from around the world and plastic horseshoes. Don't you have any beads or ribbon or even a star for the top?"

Crossing his arms over his broad chest, Gabe glanced from the tree back to her. "I suppose your tree has all of that and is weighed down with glittery ornaments?"

Chelsea shrugged. So he'd described her tree perfectly. Well, the tree she'd always put up. This year she'd been so preoccupied with so many other things and she'd rarely been home.

"I may like a little glitter in my Christmas decorations," she admitted. "It's festive and happy. Besides,

most of my stuff belonged to my father. They're ornaments we hung when I was little."

She remembered her dad letting her pick out most of
the decorations. Even though she'd been young, she'd
chosen all the sparkles and, still as an adult, she loved
the shiny stuff.

"Do the holidays upset you?" he asked, glancing over
his shoulder to meet her eyes. "I imagine it's difficult
without your parents at times like this."

Chelsea wasn't quite sure what to say. Yes, it was hard,
but she couldn't quite focus on her response. Was Gabe
trying to get to know her more? Did he want to take this
relationship somewhere they hadn't discussed? Because
placing her past front and center in the conversation was
most definitely putting them on another level.

"Losing my father was the worst," she admitted,
staring at the tree because it was easier than looking
into those caring gray eyes. "I know he died of a broken heart. He gave up his will when the only woman he
loved walked out and was never heard from since."

Chelsea bit her lower lip, willing the burn in her throat
and the threat of more tears to cease. "I actually know
where my mother is. I have for years."

"Chels." Gabe crossed to her, sliding his hands up her
arms, curling his fingers over her shoulders. "Have you
contacted her?"

"No. Why would I?" Now, she did meet that mesmerizing gaze. "She made her choice. At first I just wanted
to see if I could use my skills to find her, and I did. She
doesn't live that far from here. She has a new life, and is
clearly not concerned with what she left behind."

"Baby, I'm sorry."

Baby. He'd not called her such an endearing term before. Well, he'd drawn out darlin' once or twice, but al-

ways in that devil-may-care attitude. The way he spoke to her now, the way he *looked* at her, was completely different.

She found she wanted to open up more now that she'd started. Never before had she felt like this, like she could trust a man with more than her body. Gabe was worth the risk.

"When she left and then Dad passed, I didn't handle things very well. I was on the verge of a breakdown and I broke."

Shame filled her. She'd never actually said the words out loud. When everything had happened, Daniel and Brandee were well aware of the situation and had gotten her the help she needed. She'd never had to fully tell the story. Even when she spoke with counselors, Chelsea had glossed over details or kept her feelings veiled.

"Hey." Gabe slid his finger beneath her chin and tipped her face up. "Whatever it is, you don't have to tell me. I want to help, but don't torture yourself."

She pulled in a breath and reached up to grip his wrist, as if drawing strength from him. "I tried to end my life."

Gabe's gasp had her cringing. "Chelsea." Her name came out somewhere between pain and fear as Gabe pulled her into his arms. He encircled her in a vise-like grip. "I don't even know what to say."

He held her another moment, the silence settling heavily around them. She knew by the way he held her that he was stunned, struggling with how to react.

"I felt so alone," she went on, clinging to him. "I know I had Daniel and Brandee, but my foundation was gone. My trust had been shattered when my mom left. I didn't know how to approach my dad to talk because he was so distraught. Then once he was gone…"

Gabe eased her back and framed her face, forcing her

to hold his attention. "I hate that you had to go through all of that. I hate that you felt alone and that there was no choice but to… Damn it, I can't even think it, let alone say it."

There was so much affection in his tone, so much, dare she hope love? Had his feelings changed toward her? It certainly hadn't been her intent to influence him when she'd decided to open up about her past. She'd grown to love and trust him, and decided that if she was going to go after what she truly wanted, then he needed to know the full story.

"Needless to say, that's why Daniel has always been so protective." Chelsea pulled in a breath, thankful the story was out and off her chest. "I guess I wanted you to know."

"You trust me."

There was almost a relief in his voice. Chelsea smiled through her tears and nodded. "I do trust you, Gabe."

She went up onto her toes and kissed him. She wanted to feel him, to taste him. She wanted to ignore the pain from her past and concentrate on what she hoped was her future.

Gabe flattened his hands on her back, urging her closer. From mouths to hips, they were joined. Chelsea knew she could never get enough. She only hoped he was starting to feel the same way.

When Gabe eased back, she had to stifle a groan. She wanted him to take her to the bedroom—or here on the floor would be fine—and finish what that kiss promised. She wanted to feel alive after the anguish of her admission.

"Want to go put your Christmas stuff up?" he asked, his brows drawn in.

Seriously? He was worried about her tree?

But the closer she looked at him, the more she realized he was out of his element here. He was unsure of how to approach her now, of how to handle her. There was so much affection in his eyes. She was used to the desire, the passion and fire. But seeing this side of Gabe warmed every single part of her and only added to the growing hope she had for them.

"It's late and we're so close to Christmas." Chelsea waved a hand in a silent gesture to just forget it. "Besides, is that really how you want to spend our time together? I mean, I could probably procure some mistletoe and we could toy with that. You can even decorate me if you want."

Longing instantly filled his eyes. "I can think of several ways for us to spend the rest of the night and you won't need to go get mistletoe. I'll have you unwrapped and begging in no time." He nipped once again at her lips. "You're staying, by the way."

Little did he know she'd never had any intention of leaving.

As he lay in the dark with Chelsea sleeping in the crook of his arm, Gabe couldn't stop replaying their conversation. The idea that this strong, independent woman had thought there was no way out of her stressful life, well, it absolutely crushed him. A world without Chelsea would be dull and lifeless.

Gabe realized now that he didn't want a world without her. She'd become part of him, part of everything he did and every thought he had. Somehow she'd managed to consume more space in his mind than work and that had never happened. Ever.

Chelsea made his days brighter. As silly and adolescent as that sounded, it was true. When he knew they were going to see each other, he found himself counting down the hours. Yes, the sex was amazing, better than he'd ever had, actually, but there was more. So much more.

He trailed his fingers up her arm and over the curve of her shoulder. They were supposed to end things in a couple of days but he wasn't planning on letting her go. She'd exposed too much of herself, of her troubled past, and he knew his Chelsea wouldn't have done that if she weren't having strong feelings for him.

Between the wedding and Christmas, Gabe figured this was about as magical as the timing could get. He wanted Chelsea to know that she was it for him. He wanted her to know that she would never feel alone again, not as long as he was in her life.

But he wanted her to know he meant it. He wanted her to see that he wasn't just in this for their time between the sheets. He wasn't sure when he'd started falling for her, but he'd done it just the same.

Their quick, whirlwind affair had forced him to realize that she was so much more than just a sexy woman who challenged him. She'd overcome so much in her past, yet she'd come out on top in her career and her life.

Still, the guilt hadn't subsided. She'd suffered even more than he ever suspected and hadn't said a word to anyone except her brother, her best friend, and now him.

That in and of itself told him all he needed to know about her feelings.

Gabe smiled into the darkness and rolled over to face her. Even though she continued to sleep, he couldn't let himself relax. He wanted to formulate the perfect plan to show Chelsea just how much he wanted her in his life, just how much he cared for her and, yes, just how much he loved her.

This would be the greatest Christmas yet.

* * *

Chelsea ended up going into Hunt & Co., after she'd gone home, showered and changed her clothes. After their emotional night, she'd woken with a smile on her face and Gabe had promptly given her something else to smile about.

Gabe couldn't wait until this evening. They planned on taking more decorations to the church for the wedding, which was closing in on them. That meant the deadline to achieve his goal of keeping Chelsea in his life was also closing in on him.

They hadn't spoken about it since before her heartfelt admission last night. He hoped she'd forget all about it, that she'd ignore the end date they'd set.

As much as he wanted to be with her, he was glad to have this time alone because he needed to plan. As soon as the wedding was over, he intended to bring her back to his place and tell her everything. That he didn't want to be without her, that he was so proud of her for learning to trust, and that he trusted her, too…with his heart.

Gabe headed down to the first floor to check his mail. He planned on swinging by the TCC to make sure everything was in place for the outdoor reception. He'd promised Chelsea he would and she'd even sent him a text of her notes so he didn't forget anything. Which was fine, considering he didn't have the first clue about wedding receptions.

Fortunately, he'd discovered quite a bit on this journey, though, and if Chelsea wanted a large wedding, he'd damn well give her one. Anything she wanted, so long as he was in her life.

Once upon a time the thought of a wedding with him as the groom would've scared the hell out of him, but not anymore. Having Chelsea all to himself forever had quickly become a dream he wanted to make a reality.

Gabe exited the elevator on the first floor and nodded to the daytime doorman standing at his post. Sunshine flooded the floor of the old building, highlighting the gleaming black-and-white-checkered flooring.

When Gabe checked his mailbox, he was surprised to only have one piece of mail. He hadn't checked it for nearly a week. But considering that most everything he did was online, and with the holidays fast approaching, it probably made sense there wasn't much mail.

He flipped the envelope over and noticed a note taped to the front.

This letter was placed in my box by mistake. I was out of town so I wasn't able to get it back to you until now.
Your Neighbor in 2C.

So the elderly lady who lived below him had received his mail. That rarely happened. She'd been out of town for the past several weeks visiting her kids across the state.

Gabe tore off the note and stilled. The letter was postmarked four weeks ago, but that wasn't the part that chilled him.

The return address was Dusty's. Seeing his uncle's handwriting, receiving this from him after his death, was a bit eerie.

Gabe had no clue what Dusty could've sent out only one day before his death, so he sure as hell didn't want to open this without privacy. He couldn't get back to his loft fast enough. Gabe had a sinking feeling whatever Maverick had started almost a year ago was about to come back to life in this piece of mail.

Once Gabe finally made it to his apartment, he barely got his door closed before he was tearing into the over-size envelope. He pulled out the contents, cursing under his breath when black-and-white glossies spilled out onto the floor at his feet. Glossies of the woman he loved.

Gabe crouched down and sifted through the images, one after another after another. His heart sank, his stomach turned.

He searched through each photo, but they all had the same theme. She was naked or partially dressed, in the locker room of her gym. From the angle, Gabe could tell someone had planted the camera in a vent or a light fixture. Each photo brought a new wave of rage. She'd had no clue these were taken. Were these just copies of the others that were out there? Because he'd deliberately never looked at those.

Or were these completely new?

Dread coiled in his gut as he gathered the photos and stalked to his kitchen. He tossed the images on the counter and started reading the letter.

Gabriel,

I don't know how much longer I have, so I'm reaching out to my only living relative.

By now, you may have figured everything out. Yes, I'm Maverick. I have my reasons for doing what I did, which I'll lay out below. But I also have some unfinished business and need your help.

As you know I was shunned at the Texas Cattleman's Club. My attempts to gain membership were constantly turned down. They let women in a man's club and kept me out? Well, I had to take matters into my own hands and, once I explain why, you'll understand. I hope you carry on where I had to leave off.

Years ago I had an affair with Colleen Humphreys. Her husband was a longtime president of the TCC and on the board until his death just a year ago. When he found out about the affair, he threatened to ruin me. But blacklisting me only backfired on his precious club. I mean, who had the last laugh? The revenge I took on the members was so sweet. I do feel a tad guilty for the lives I ruined, but they were merely pawns caught in the game. I had no choice.

Gabe gritted his teeth at his uncle's words. So Dusty had done all of this, terrorizing Royal for months on end, to get back at a man who'd been his victim to begin with? What kind of sick person had his uncle been?

Disgust filled Gabe as he focused on the rest of the letter.

Here are some final photos of Chelsea Hunt. I never shared these and I know you'll help me out by finishing this. You always were so loyal. I'm counting on you, Gabriel. Do what you see fit to ruin the TCC and all those who were allowed in when I was not. Women like Chelsea and so many others think they're too good, walking around all high and mighty. It's not right, but we'll make sure they suffer.

Gabe gripped the paper so tightly that it crinkled in his hand. Then he tossed it onto the counter, unable to even touch it another second. He had no clue what to do. He had to think. He'd believed this situation was behind them but it had just reared its ugly head once again. Now, he was in control…whether he wanted to be or not.

At least Dusty had mailed the photos and letter to him. Gabe hated to think what would've happened had they gotten into the wrong hands.

Disgusted, Gabe turned away from the heap of photos on the counter. He didn't want to see them anymore, didn't want *anyone* to see them. Gabe would have to turn them over to Sheriff Nathan Battle to be processed with the rest of the items. They were still trying to figure out who could've helped Dusty because obviously the man couldn't have planted a camera in a women's locker room by himself. Not with his poor health.

Gabe would get to the bottom of this. He'd find out who was helping his uncle, he'd make sure this was all in the past, and then he and Chelsea could move forward with their future.

Fifteen

"Can you believe tomorrow is the day?" Chelsea resisted a girlish squeal, but she hugged her best friend tight. "Everything is going to be perfect."

The rehearsal dinner was going exactly as planned. The food was perfect, the décor similar to what would be used in the actual wedding. Chelsea couldn't be more excited for her best friend.

"Everything is going to be perfect," Chelsea exclaimed.

Brandee eased back and nodded. "You and Gabe have gone above and beyond. I can't thank you guys enough."

"We were happy to help."

Brandee's brows rose as her smile widened. "Maybe we'll be planning your wedding next?"

As much as the idea gave Chelsea the warm fuzzies, she wasn't sure Gabe was ready for that. She wasn't even sure he was ready to hear her say how she truly felt. But, after the wedding tomorrow, she was going to tell him.

This was their last night together and she had every intention of making it unforgettable. She would love to open herself up to him tonight and tell him every emotion she'd kept bottled up, but if he turned her down, she didn't want the awkward tension at the wedding, especially since they were walking down the aisle together.

"We're just…" Chelsea wasn't quite sure how to describe the current situation. "Taking this one day at a time."

"You love him."

The chatter around them, the music from the DJ, the soft breeze, everything faded away at those three words. There was no use denying them, not to Brandee. The girl knew Chelsea better than she knew herself.

"I just hope he feels the same."

Brandee tipped her head. "If the way he's staring at you right now is any indicator, I'd say he feels more than lust."

A thrill shot through Chelsea. She so wanted Gabe to be on the same emotional page as she was. They'd had a breakthrough moment when she'd fully opened herself to him. He'd taken her to his bed and made love to her like she was the most fragile, most precious thing in his life. She only prayed that was true.

"Just be honest," Brandee urged. "I almost lost Shane, but we both fought for what we wanted. You're going to have to do the same."

Chelsea opened her mouth to reply, but Brandee squeezed her hands and shot a look over Chelsea's shoulder.

"I better go talk to the other guests," Brandee stated. "I'll see you in the morning at the church."

Chelsea watched as her friend went to talk to a couple of the other bridesmaids. The outdoor rehearsal dinner at

Hope Springs Ranch was perfect. With the temperatures hovering around fifty, they were able to have the event outside in comfort thanks to the heated tents.

This laid-back atmosphere was perfect before the rush and drama of tomorrow. The caterers had done a phenomenal job; of course, they'd used some beef tips from Hunt & Co. for the main course.

Strong hands curled around Chelsea's shoulders and she didn't even hesitate when Gabe eased her back against his chest.

"These little dresses of yours drive me out of my mind," he growled into her ear. "I think you enjoy teasing me."

Chelsea smiled and reached up to cup her hands over his. "I love wearing dresses with boots when the occasion calls for it. Driving you out of your mind is just a bonus."

"What are you wearing under this? Something else new?"

"Perhaps."

She'd put on the slinky teddy with him in mind, and had been counting down the time until they could leave so he could take it off.

"We practiced coming down the aisle and going back up, plus we've eaten." He nipped at her earlobe. "Are we done here yet?"

Chelsea turned in his arms. "You know, if we keep leaving parties early, people are going to know what we're up to."

His hands settled easily on her waist. Those gray eyes she'd come to love sought her from beneath the rim of his black hat.

"I don't care what people think," he told her. "I care about you and that's it."

He cared about her. Not quite a declaration of love,

but it was more than what they'd originally started with. Hope blossomed.

"We should at least say goodbye to our friends," she told him.

"Fine. Say your goodbyes. Be quick." He smacked a kiss on her mouth and stepped back. "Be at my place in fifteen minutes."

Chelsea laughed. "It takes me fifteen minutes to get there from here."

"Then you better just wave goodbye instead of saying it."

He turned and headed toward Shane. Chelsea watched as they did the one-armed man hug and then Gabe headed off toward the field where they'd all parked their cars.

"I imagine you'll be leaving, too."

Chelsea turned to see her brother eyeing her with concern. "I am," she confirmed.

"You're going to get hurt, Chels. I know guys like Walsh. Hell, I know Gabe. I can see the hearts in your eyes."

She attempted to tamp down her anger as she crossed her arms over her chest. "You've tried to warn me before. Do I look like I'm hurt? Don't interfere, Daniel. I've got this under control."

When she started to turn away, he grabbed her elbow and forced her to focus on him. "I hope your eyes are wide-open here. And I hope that he feels the same way as you do because you're in deep."

She hoped Gabe was on the same page with her feelings, too.

With a simple nod, Chelsea pulled her arm from Daniel's grasp. She knew he was just looking out for her, but this was ridiculous. No one was going to come between her and what she wanted—and she wanted Gabe Walsh in her life.

By the time she made it to his loft, her entire body was humming. Chelsea smiled at the doorman as she entered the building. The elevator ride seemed to take forever, then finally she was at Gabe's door. She didn't bother knocking as she turned the knob beneath her palm and eased the door open.

The only light in the loft was the sparkle from the Christmas tree and the city lights streaming through the wall of windows.

She'd barely gotten the door closed when Gabe's arms banded around her. Chelsea melted against him, more than ready to spend the night here.

"You're three minutes late."

Chelsea pushed away from him and crossed the apartment. She wasn't quite done driving him out of his mind.

"I had to talk to my brother," she explained. "And say goodbye to Brandee and Shane. Then I thanked the caterers."

"Take off your dress."

Chelsea turned back to face him. The large loft seemed to close in on her as Gabe took one slow step after another toward her. His eyes never left hers, giving her all the thrills. How could a look make her feel like he was touching her all over? How did he have so much control over not just her body but her mind?

"Come take it off me," she countered.

A low growl emanated from him as he closed the distance between them. In a flash move, he gripped the hem of her dress and jerked it up and over her head. The second he tossed it aside, his swift intake of breath had her confidence soaring. She propped her hands on her hips, thrusting her chest out and cocking her head to the side.

"Was it worth the wait, cowboy?"

"Damn," he whispered. "Had I known you were wearing that, we never would've made it to the dinner."

Chelsea couldn't help but laugh. "I'm pretty sure there's a rule against that."

"Maybe, but nobody would blame me."

She reached out, jerking on his silver buckle. "Why don't you just take me here? This is technically the last night in our agreement, right?"

As soon as the words were out of her mouth, she wanted to take them back. But seeing the flicker of annoyance in his eyes told her he wasn't ready to see this end.

Maybe she should tell him now. Maybe she should just throw it all out there and take the risk now.

But, no. Because if she'd read him wrong, she would never forgive herself for the resulting awkwardness at Brandee and Shane's wedding.

Gabe lifted her into his arms. With one arm behind her back, one arm behind her knees, he nipped at her lips as he walked through the loft. Romance had entered their relationship. This had all started with frenzied, passionate sex. Somewhere along the way love had settled in deep.

Chelsea wrapped her arms around his neck and nestled her head against his shoulder. "I expected you to take me against the window again," she murmured into his ear.

"Maybe tonight is different."

Maybe it was. As Gabe kicked the door shut to his bedroom, Chelsea finally felt like things were going her way. She'd found her happily-ever-after.

Early the following morning, Chelsea slid from bed. The sun still hadn't come up, but she couldn't sleep. Between the wedding, the fantastic night in Gabe's arms, and the talk she wanted to have with him later today about their future, there was just too much going on and her mind simply wouldn't shut down.

Chelsea glanced back to the bed where Gabe lay sprawled on his stomach, his light hair in disarray after she'd run her fingers through it. Her body still hummed as she snagged his T-shirt and put it on. She eased the door closed behind her as she made her way to the kitchen. Gabe was every bit the bachelor, but hopefully he had something she could make for their breakfast. She didn't have to be at the church for a few hours, so maybe breakfast in bed was a great way to start the day.

Humming as she started searching through his cabinets, Chelsea figured if all else failed, she could do coffee, eggs and toast. He at least had those on hand.

She pulled out a pan and the eggs. Once she had them cracked into a bowl, she tugged on a drawer for a whisk. Of course his utensils weren't in a drawer she would put them in. She tried another, only to find a junk drawer. She started to shut it when something caught her eye.

It was a black-and-white photograph. Chelsea focused on it, her heart hammering in her throat. No. That couldn't be. Gabe wasn't the accomplice. Was he? The sheriff had said they were searching for a female.

With a shaky hand she pulled the picture from the drawer, only to find more underneath it. She pulled them all out, then she saw a letter with Gabe's name on it.

Nausea settled in the pit of her stomach as she shuffled through each picture. These weren't the same ones that had circulated months back. These were actually newer, maybe a couple of months old. She knew that because she remembered the exact day at the gym. She recognized the outfit; she'd tried racquetball for the first time. Pretty soon after that, the first nude photos had been leaked and she hadn't been back to that gym since.

Pulling in a deep breath, she set the pictures on the counter, facing down. Her attention went to the letter; she quickly saw it was from Dusty. Did she really want to read this? Did she want to know what he and Gabe had discussed?

Her eyes scanned the scratchy penmanship first before she went back to the top and absorbed every single word.

She couldn't be reading this right. She just...she couldn't. This was important evidence that had been sent to Gabe weeks ago. Why was he hiding these photos in a drawer? Shouldn't he have turned these over to the sheriff by now? Was Gabe covering something up?

Dropping the letter on top of the pictures, Chelsea took a step back and stared at the pile. Such damning evidence of Gabe's involvement with his uncle mocked her and the future she'd been foolish enough to believe in.

Trust hadn't come easy and now she knew why. She should've trusted her instincts to begin with where Gabe was concerned.

The tears came before she even realized it. All the hurt, all the anger, and so much resentment flooded her. She should've listened to her initial suspicions. Hell, she should've listened to Daniel. Hadn't he been trying to warn her she'd get hurt?

She wasn't just hurt, she was utterly, completely, destroyed.

The glow from the Christmas tree in the living room mocked her, trying to pull her back to that night when they'd put it up. He'd completely played her for a naïve fool.

At least she hadn't told Gabe how she felt. He'd probably get a great kick out of knowing he'd duped her.

Chelsea blinked the tears away and went to the living room where her clothes were. She quickly changed, trying to figure out exactly what her next move should be. Did she really want to confront him? Did she want to hear more lies?

And that's what all of this had been. A relationship built on lies.

Once she was dressed, Chelsea tucked her hair behind her ears and glanced at the closed bedroom door. As much as she didn't want to even look at him and hear his excuses, she deserved answers. She deserved to know the real man…not just the one she'd fallen in love with. That man didn't exist.

Sixteen

The sound of the bedroom door creaking woke him. But it was the lights flashing on and the papers that were tossed onto the bed that had Gabe sitting straight up.

No. Not papers. Pictures.

His gut tightened as he glanced up at Chelsea. The brokenness and pain staring back at him told him all he needed to know. She believed he had deceived and betrayed her.

He now regretted that he hadn't done a better job securing the papers. He had intended to turn them over to the sheriff as soon as the wedding was over; he just hadn't wanted to risk more press attention to ruin Brandee and Shane's—not to mention Chelsea's—special day. She had worked so hard on this wedding and he didn't want it ruined for her. He'd had every intention of doing things the right way—or what he thought was right—but now he just looked like he'd been deceiving her all along.

"I don't even want you to defend yourself," she said, crossing her arms over her dress.

Damn it. She'd put her clothes back on, which meant he had about two seconds to get her to listen to the truth. Mentally, she'd already left.

"I just want to know what your motivation is," she went on. "What could you get from having these pictures just lying around your house? Were you planning on humiliating me further? Is this just family loyalty?"

Gabe came to his feet, jerking on a pair of shorts lying by the bed. "I have never set out to hurt you, Chels. I had nothing to do with these pictures being taken."

"Maybe not," she agreed then let out a harsh laugh. "But you know what? Dusty's letter spells things out pretty clearly. You were to take over since he was too sick. You could've destroyed these or turned them over to the sheriff, or hell, given them to me. Yet here you are with them tucked away in your apartment."

He started to take a step forward, but she held up a hand. "No. All this time you were with me, you made me believe you cared, but under the same roof you were hiding these pictures. I was a fool to trust you."

"You can trust me," he insisted. Gabe crossed the room, ignoring her when she shook her head and held her hands out to keep him back. "Look at me. Damn it, I was going to take them to Nathan, but not until after the wedding. I put them away so nobody would see them."

Chelsea kept her head turned away, refusing to look at him. "Convenient," she muttered.

Nothing he said now would make her believe. She'd seen the pictures and the letter, and had decided he'd been lying all along. He hated her thinking he would ever be involved in something like this, but most of all, he hated that she was hurting and he couldn't comfort her.

"What can I say to make you believe me?" he asked.

He wanted to reach out and hold her, but she would never allow that. Her red-rimmed eyes tore him apart. How long had she been in the other room tormenting herself with this?

The automatic bedroom shades rolled up right on time, the soft hum breaking the tension in the room. The sun was starting to rise, but the day that should've been one of the happiest for them had turned into anything but.

"There's nothing you can say," she whispered, her voice thick with tears. "I trusted you with a piece of me I've never given to another man. I thought…"

Her words died off as she bit her lower lip to compose herself. Gabe did reach for her now. He didn't give a damn what she wanted because he knew he hadn't done a thing wrong and he just wanted to hold her, to comfort her. She was absolutely breaking his heart and he'd promised her she'd never feel alone again.

Damn it. He *promised*.

Now, she stared up at him, unshed tears swimming in her eyes. "I thought after the wedding I'd tell you that I didn't want to end things. Stupid, right? I mean, all this time you've chosen to side with your uncle."

"No." He gently took her by the shoulders. "I never sided with him. I got all of that in the mail after he died. Just two days ago."

Chelsea broke free of his grip. "I'm not convinced that you had nothing to do with the first set of pictures, but let's pretend I do believe you. These pictures should never have been here. You should've turned them over. If you care for me at all, if you truly wanted me to believe you were innocent, you wouldn't have kept them."

"I was going to give them to Nathan," he insisted.

Stepping back, Chelsea wiped at her damp cheeks.

"Then you should've told me the second you got them. You have no excuse for that."

She was right. He didn't, other than the fact he didn't want to cause her any more pain.

When she turned away, Gabe's heart clenched. "Don't go. Don't leave this upset. Stay. We can talk this out and then I'll take you to the church."

Chelsea's shoulders straightened, but she didn't face him again. "I'm leaving and I'll get myself to the church. Brandee and Shane deserve this day to be perfect and I'll not let you ruin it for them. After the wedding and our duties are done, I never want to see or speak to you again."

It was difficult, but Gabe let her go.

Right now she needed space, and he needed to figure out how the hell he could fix this. Because he would fix it and he would make her realize that he was never that guy. He could never purposely cause her so much pain.

Though he had to admit beneath his denial and defensiveness, hurt started spreading through him. She actually thought he'd been capable of doing such heinous things. Maybe she'd never fully trusted him. Maybe in the back of her mind she'd always kept those suspicions in reserve.

He would have to put on a front for the wedding because Chelsea was right. This day belonged to Brandee and Shane. But if she thought for a second that he was just going to let her go and never hear from him again... well, she would be in for a surprise.

Gabe gathered the pictures and the letter and went out into the living room. Once he had them secured in an envelope, he laid them on the sofa table. Tomorrow he'd take them to the sheriff and be done with the likes of his uncle. Even dead, the man was ruining lives. Then he'd find out who the hell had assisted Dusty in obtaining the photos to begin with.

Padding barefoot to the kitchen, Gabe noticed the eggs on the counter, the pan on the stove, the bowl. His heart flipped and he gripped the edge of the countertop. She'd been prepared to make him breakfast. She'd found the pictures shoved in the drawer.

Damn it. He was a fool. He should've told her but, in his defense, he just hadn't wanted her to have to deal with that mess any longer. He'd been trying to protect her, but all he'd managed to do was to crush her hopes further and to destroy the trust they'd built.

He had to find a way to get her back. Gabe had never given up before and he sure as hell didn't intend to start now—not when this was the most important moment of his life.

Chelsea smoothed a hand down her gold dress and tried to forget the last time she'd had this on. She flashed back on the dressing room, on Gabe, his clever hands and magical touch.

Pain squeezed like a vise around her chest and she pushed the memory aside. She'd doubled up on concealer and powder, hoping to hide her puffy red eyes. Her waterproof mascara was definitely going to be put to the test.

When Chelsea had first arrived at the church, Brandee had questioned her, but Chelsea had just played it off as wedding tears.

Chelsea spun away from the mirror, not wanting to see herself in this dress. She could practically feel Gabe's hands at the side zipper.

Would his memory fade over time or would she be forced to battle him in her mind forever?

Chelsea crossed to the adjoining room where Brandee

was getting ready. It was time to get into full maid-of-honor mode. Pulling in a deep breath, Chelsea let herself into the room and gasped.

Brandee stood in front of the floor-length mirror, her gaze meeting Chelsea's in the reflection. Chelsea had seen the dress, but now it seemed different. With Brandee's long hair falling in simple waves down her back and the subtle makeup, she looked angelic.

"Can you help me with my veil?" Brandee asked, a wide smile on her face. "My hands are shaking."

Chelsea offered her best friend a smile and crossed to where the veil hung on the back of a closet door. Carefully, she removed it from the plastic wrap and hanger.

"Squat down just a tad," Chelsea told Brandee as she came to stand behind her. "Tip your head back a bit."

After adjusting the pins to be hidden in the soft curls, Chelsea stepped back. "There. How does that look?"

Seeing her best friend smile in the mirror—no, she wasn't just smiling, she was glowing—helped heal a portion of Chelsea's wounded heart. Love did exist, she was absolutely certain of that. She'd just misplaced hers.

"Everything okay?"

Chelsea focused her attention on Brandee's reflection and nodded. "Couldn't be better. You're the most beautiful bride I've ever seen. And this Christmas wedding is going to be magical."

Brandee turned and reached for Chelsea's hands. "I'm more focused on my happily-ever-after. Too many people focus on the wedding details and making a big show of things. I just want to spend my life with Shane."

"He's a lucky man."

"I'm the lucky one." Brandee tipped her head down and narrowed her eyes. "What's up, Chels? Something is off with you today."

There was no sense in lying again. Brandee wasn't buying it. "Just a mishap with Gabe. Nothing for you to worry about on your special day."

Brandee's brows drew in as she squeezed Chelsea's hands. "Oh, honey, what happened?"

The threat of tears burned the back of her throat. "He's not the man I thought he was."

"Did he hurt you?"

Chelsea dabbed beneath her eyes, already knowing she was going to have to have a makeup redo. "I found more pictures at his place. Pictures of me from the gym locker room."

Brandee jerked back. "What did he say?"

"He denied any involvement with his uncle. Dusty sent the photos with a letter—I read it. He wanted Gabe to carry on with what he'd started."

Brandee pursed her lips. "But Gabe didn't do anything with them, right?"

"Not yet. But he didn't tell me he had them," Chelsea replied. "He kept them hidden when he could've destroyed them or just explained what happened and why he had them in the first place."

Brandee reached up and wiped a tear from Chelsea's cheek before squeezing her hands once again. "Gabe wouldn't hurt you. Did you ever think that's the reason he didn't tell you? Maybe he's protecting you."

Or maybe he was still being loyal to his uncle.

There were just so many questions, and she was an emotional wreck. Now wasn't the time to try to solve all of her problems. She had a wedding to partake in…and a man waiting to walk down the aisle with her.

"Forget it," Chelsea said, squaring her shoulders and sniffling back the tears. "This is your day and whatever Gabe and I have going on, I swear it won't interfere with this."

"Of course it won't." Brandee smiled and dropped her hands to smooth down her gown. "I know how Gabe feels, though. Remember the way he manhandled that jerk who was mistreating you? And the way Gabe looks at you when you don't know is enough to set panties on fire. He cares for you and, if I'm not mistaken, he loves you."

Chelsea closed her eyes, willing those words to be true, but his actions said different...didn't they? Had she jumped to conclusions?

"We've all been through so much." Chelsea reached out to adjust her friend's veil around her face. "Let's just focus on the happiness of today. It's two days before Christmas and everything is finally settling back down after a year of scandal. This is going to be the best day and a new beginning."

Brandee nodded. "Let's fix your makeup and get ready for the pictures. But I want you to keep in mind, Gabe is exactly the man he claims to be. I'd stake my life on it."

Chelsea wasn't so sure she could say the same, but she'd laid her heart on the line, which was pretty much the same. She needed some space to think. Unfortunately, she'd be walking arm in arm with the only man she'd ever loved in a very short time.

Right now she needed to put on her happy face and coat of armor. This day was about to test every bit of her strength.

Seventeen

"You look stunning."

Gabe whispered the compliment as Chelsea slid her arm over his elbow. She clutched her gold ribbon that secured a ball of mistletoe. In lieu of bouquets, Chelsea and Brandee had gone with mistletoe…and now he was being mocked by the classic flower.

The late afternoon wedding at the TCC was perfect. As he glanced around, Gabe saw every detail that he and Chelsea had a hand in. He had to focus on things like that because the woman at his side was driving him out of his mind with want and need.

The way Chelsea's body shifted beneath the material of her dress, the way she delicately brushed against his body, had his mind pumping into overdrive.

The last time he'd seen her in that dress…

Gabe focused on making it down the aisle, his hand securing hers over his arm. He needed to touch her, needed to feel her. Regardless of whether this was just for the sake of appearances, he'd take what he could get at this point.

The way she'd left so hurt and angry only hours ago— yeah, he had to have some sort of contact. He'd sat in his apartment and slowly driven himself insane with what he should have done differently and how he could have avoided hurting her.

But he honestly didn't know that he would have done things differently. Yes, he could have informed her that he'd received the mail from his uncle, but he'd planned on doing that when he turned them over to the authorities.

She was understandably upset, but just as she had at the start of their relationship, she would come to see that she was wrong. His actions would speak for themselves. He just had to figure out how the hell to get her to understand that he had been protecting her.

Chelsea remained silent as they reached the end of the aisle and parted ways. His arm and hand instantly chilled. Holding this winter wedding outdoors had nothing to do with it, either. The tent where Brandee and Shane were about to exchange their vows was heated.

No, his chill came from the fact that the one woman he'd allowed himself to truly love, the one woman who'd entered his life like a whirlwind and settled deep into his heart, had pushed him away.

In her defense, she had good reasons for being wary. But where he was concerned, her fears and suspicions were misplaced.

Canon in D chimed through the very well hidden speakers and everyone in attendance came to their feet. Gabe glanced to the end of the aisle as Brandee came around the corner. Shane tipped his head down and rubbed his eyes. Gabe reached up and squeezed his shoulder in silent encouragement.

He couldn't imagine what was going through his best friend's mind. What would it be like to find the one you wanted to spend your life with? What would it be like to have her coming toward you, ready to take a risk together like nothing else in the entire world mattered?

Gabe turned his attention to Chelsea. Her eyes were locked on the bride, but her shoulders were stiff and she held tight to the ribbon of mistletoe. There was a hint of a smile on her face, but Gabe saw the hurt in her eyes and knew she was anything but relaxed.

Gabe paid little attention to the vows and ring exchange. He didn't take his eyes off Chelsea and when she met his gaze, he didn't look away. Neither did she.

He had no idea what was going through her mind, or what was even going on around them. He didn't care. All that mattered was Chelsea. Damn it. His heart flipped in his chest. She'd gone and worked her way right into the deepest part of him—and he realized that's exactly where he wanted her.

This wasn't just him wanting to prove his innocence to her and make sure she wasn't hurting. Yes, he did want both of those things, but the obvious reason was literally staring right back at him. He wanted Chelsea in his life, now, tomorrow, forever.

He wanted what Brandee and Shane had; he wanted what so many of their friends had found. There had never been another to grab his heart the way Chelsea had and he wasn't about to just let her walk out of his life.

As soon as the ceremony was over, Gabe waited for the newly married couple to turn to the guests and make their way back down the aisle. The music started up in celebration of the milestone moment.

Gabe stepped up, extending his elbow for Chelsea to take. She didn't meet his eyes as she did so.

"We need to talk," he murmured out the side of his mouth as they made their way off the elevated platform.

"Not yet."

Well, at least she'd replied and hadn't completely shot him down. That was a step in the right direction.

As they joined the party lining up in the back to greet guests, Chelsea quickly let go of him and went to stand next to Brandee.

The evening seemed to drag on for him, but he was positive the newly married couple was having the time of their lives. Chelsea always seemed busy or missing when he went to find her. Most likely she was avoiding him, and that was okay, but it was only so long before he caught up with her. He had no idea what he planned to say, no idea how to make this all go away, but he would.

Gabe caught a flash of gold in the distance, but by the time he crossed the patio area just off the TCC ballroom, he realized it wasn't Chelsea but another guest.

Cursing, Gabe turned and nearly tripped a waiter carrying a tray of drinks.

"'Scuse me," he said, holding his arms out to make sure the tray stayed level.

"Care for a bourbon?" the waiter asked.

Gabe grabbed one of the tumblers and muttered his thanks before moving on. He wasn't in the mood to mingle or dance; he only wanted to talk to Chelsea. As he rounded the back of the building near the walking trails and stables, he found Daniel and Chelsea in an embrace.

Clearly he'd stumbled upon something private. As he started to turn away, Chelsea's words stopped him.

"You warned me," she said, her voice slightly trembling. "You told me I'd get hurt and I didn't want to hear it."

Gabe slid behind some landscaping near the corner of the building so as not to be seen. He'd just listen for a minute, then he'd give them their privacy. He knew he should walk away now, but damn it, this was the woman he loved and he wanted to know what he was up against in this fight.

"I never wanted to be right about this," Daniel said. "I want you to find happiness, Chels. I just didn't think Gabe was the guy for you."

What the hell? Her brother had warned her off? Anger bubbled within Gabe and he started to step away from his hiding place, but Chelsea's cry stopped him in his tracks.

"But I love him."

Hope quickly replaced the anger. She loved him? So all the hurt he'd seen in her eyes was about thinking the man she loved had betrayed her trust. As much as he wanted to be angry over this whole situation—with his uncle and with himself for hurting Chelsea—all he could focus on was the fact that she loved him.

It was almost like a weight had been lifted from his chest. Those words were all he needed to know he'd get her back. Between his determination and her declaration, that was all the ammunition he needed to secure Chelsea in his life. Forever.

Chelsea pulled back from Daniel's embrace and dabbed beneath her eyes. "I didn't want to have a melt-down, but I wanted to let you know what was going on."

"You weren't acting like yourself," he replied, pulling a handkerchief from his pocket.

Chelsea smiled as she took it. "You always were a gentleman."

"So what are you going to do?" he asked. "You don't trust him, but you love him."

That about summed up this complex situation. Seeing Gabe in his tux, having him hold on to her for the briefest of moments before the wedding vows, had been almost too much to take. She'd tried to focus on the ceremony but keeping her eyes away from Gabe had been near impossible. He'd caught her looking at him once and she'd been unable to turn away. When those gray eyes had locked onto hers, Chelsea swore he was looking into her soul.

"I want to believe him." She looked up at her brother, knowing she'd find concern in his expression. "My heart and my head are saying two different things. I just need to talk to him, but I need time first."

"What can I do?"

Chelsea smoothed a hand down her gown and shook her head. "Nothing at all. Take care of Erin and those babies. I'll handle my love life."

Daniel's lips thinned as he shoved his hands into his suit pockets. "I know you're smart, but I just don't want you to be taken advantage of or to be wrapped up in another scandal."

"I won't be," she assured him. "We're all moving on now that Maverick has been pinpointed. I won't let anyone hurt me like that again. Whoever the accomplice is, they're likely lying low right now."

The words were for her brother's peace of mind, but they were a vow to herself. She refused to ever be the victim again.

"I should get back to the reception." Chelsea wrapped her arms around her brother once more. "Thanks for always listening."

"I wouldn't be anywhere else when you need me."

Chelsea turned away and made her way back to the reception. Thankfully it was wrapping up and Brandee and Shane would head off on their honeymoon soon. They were escaping to someplace tropical and private, so private they hadn't disclosed their destination to friends and family.

Now that the excitement and the hustle and bustle were over, Chelsea planned to take the next two days and do nothing but enjoy the Christmas season. She'd drink hot chocolate topped with whipped cream and peppermint flakes, she'd watch classic movies that were sure to take her mind off her current issues, and she'd not have any contact with Gabriel Walsh until she knew exactly what she wanted to say to him.

And until she could get her emotions under control because damn if she still didn't want the man.

Eighteen

It was Christmas Eve morning and he still hadn't heard a word from Chelsea. She'd slipped from the reception shortly after the bride and groom. In the few minutes Gabe had stayed beyond that, he'd been greeted with a glare from Daniel. Just when Chelsea's brother had started to make his way over to Gabe, Erin had intervened and they had left.

As much as Gabe wanted to stand his ground and talk to Daniel, the most important person he needed to see wasn't returning his texts. He got that she needed space, but her timeframe was about to expire.

Gabe had already taken steps to secure their future. He'd already made sure that nothing else incriminating or embarrassing would crop up out of nowhere down the road. Above all else, he had made sure she was protected. Even if she didn't accept his love, his commitment to her, Gabe still wanted to put a shield of protection around her.

Tonight would be the perfect time to approach her. The annual candlelight and caroling event around the twenty-foot tree in Royal's town square couldn't provide a better setting. He knew Chelsea would be there. Everyone went to the event to light candles, join family and friends, and sing carols. Then they'd all fellowship together afterward as the area businesses provided hot chocolate and baked goods and the shops that lined the square stayed open late. Everyone, no matter their background, their financial status or their age came to celebrate the season.

Chelsea would feel comfortable there. They'd be surrounded by people, so there would be no pressure, but there would also be nowhere for her to run.

Considering he had several more hours to worry about her response, Gabe decided to fill the time making calls and checking on his clients. The swift damage control he'd run in the last couple weeks had paid off. The reputation of his company was strong as ever and more potential clients were pouring in. His career couldn't be better and his global prospects seemed to be a great possibility.

He'd turned the photos over to Nathan, but Gabe wasn't relinquishing control of everything. The hunt for Dusty's accomplice would be over and done with soon and Chelsea could truly move on…hopefully with him. But Gabe was keeping his men on this search. He wanted to find the person who had helped his uncle.

Once Chelsea was back in his life, in his home, he would truly have it all. And Gabe always got what he wanted.

Chelsea went with her favorite emerald-green sweater, dark jeans, and her cowgirl boots. She did her hair in loose curls and applied a thin layer of gloss. There was no way she'd avoid Gabe tonight and she wanted to look good but not overly made up.

He'd texted over the past two days, but every time she'd started to reply, she simply hadn't found the right words. How did she get into such a dramatic conversation via text? What she needed to say to him had to be said in person.

Royal's candlelight and caroling was one of her favorite events of the entire year. When everyone gathered together, it almost seemed as if the outside world didn't exist, as if there were no problems, and peace on earth was indeed the reality. She wanted peace, not just for herself, but the town. The past year had been trying for so many, but this seemed to be a new hope and a new day to start over and move forward.

Dare she hope the same was true for her own life? She wasn't so much worried about the gossip regarding her photos anymore. Those who loved and cared for her had already forgotten and those who made rude remarks... well, she wasn't going to concern herself with them.

Her heart warmed as she thought back to how protective Gabe had been that night he'd handled one such jerk. Even though they'd agreed to keep their relationship private, he hadn't cared one bit about his secrecy because he'd been set on defending her. Shouldn't that tell her all she needed to know about the man she'd fallen for?

Sometimes what seemed to be the truth was just a haze covering up the reality. Those pictures in his loft were damning, yes, but what motive would he have had to put them out there? Just because Dusty asked him to? Chelsea didn't see Gabe doing such a thing. He had been angry about the scandal that had ensnared so many members of the TCC. And Gabe had been furious and mortified when Maverick's identity had been revealed.

Chelsea parked several blocks away from the town square and used the walk to clear her head. This was the first year she hadn't come with Brandee, but she knew her friend was having a much better time on her honeymoon.

The shops were all set up with their tables of last-minute Christmas items, baked goods, and hot chocolate and hot cider at the ready. Chelsea couldn't resist getting a cup of cider on her way to the tree. Each table also had candles, so she grabbed one of those, as well.

When she glanced at the white taper in her hand, she couldn't help but inwardly roll her eyes. There was a sprig of mistletoe tied around the base, just below the clear disc to catch any wax drippings.

Mistletoe seemed to be mocking her lately. She was having a difficult time dodging it—and dodging the man who stood only a few feet in front of her holding his own candle.

Chelsea's heart kicked up as she made her way toward Gabe. He'd spotted her already and his eyes held hers as she drew closer.

"I've been watching for you."

She'd missed his voice, missed looking into his face and seeing…everything. The desire, the concern, the love.

Could their relationship be so simple? Could she believe everything he told her and let down her guard again?

"I don't know what to say," she admitted, toying with the tie holding her mistletoe to the taper. "I want so much, Gabe. But I'm afraid."

Kids squealed and ran by; a mother chased them demanding that they stop. Gabe took hold of Chelsea's elbow and steered her toward the side of a building, away from the chaos.

"You think I'm not afraid?" he asked. With her back against the brick building, he shifted so his body blocked out the festivities behind them. "Having you walk out, thinking even for a second that I could hurt you in such a way, put more fear in me than I'd ever known."

Chelsea stared up into his eyes, her heart beating so fast. Gabe wasn't lying; he wasn't just saying pretty words. Everything he told her was from his heart.

"I didn't know what to think." She still didn't, but she couldn't ignore the pull of emotions steering her toward him. "I didn't want to believe the worst, but I panicked when I saw the letter. I know Dusty was all the family you had, so I got scared that your loyalty would override anything you felt for me."

Gabe dropped his candlestick to the ground and instantly framed her face, forcing her to hold his gaze. "Override love? Nothing and no one can replace what I feel for you."

Chelsea's breath caught in her throat. "Love?"

"Damn it, you know I love you." He closed his lips over hers briefly before easing back and resting his forehead against hers. "I can't live without you, Chels. I don't want to even try."

"I—"

"Wait." He shifted back to look at her once again, but he didn't let go. "You need to know that I've turned everything over to Nathan. I've also launched my own investigation into who could've helped Dusty because I agree he didn't act alone."

Tears pricked her eyes. She tried to blink them away, but they spilled over. Gabe gathered her against his chest, rubbing his hand up and down her back. He took the candle from her hand as she clutched his shirt and attempted to pull herself together. How could she, though, when everything she wanted was right here? The risk she was about to take would change her entire life.

"You really love me," she murmured.

She felt the soft rumble of laughter reverberate through his chest. "I really do. There's nothing I wouldn't do for you."

Chelsea slid her arms up and wrapped them around his neck. Pressing her lips to his, she held him tight, never wanting to let this moment go. The moment when he confessed his love, the moment when she decided to let it all go and trust in what they'd built.

"Tell me again," she muttered against his mouth. "Tell me you love me."

Gabe slid the pads of his thumbs over her damp cheeks. "No one will ever love you more. I ached when you left. That's how I knew what we had was real. The pain was too strong to be just casual. I want to build a life with you, Chelsea. No matter what we're doing or where we live, I want it with you."

"I want my life with you, too." Chelsea smiled. "But you should probably know I'm going to be opening a counseling center for young adults."

Gabe's eyes widened then he smiled. "That's a great idea."

"No. It's not just an idea. I bought the building, I'm searching for counselors now, and I want this up and running by spring. The focus will be on teens suffering from depression, anxiety, and suicidal tendencies."

Gabe kissed her hard, fast. "You're so damn remarkable, darlin'. Of course, you're already on the ball with this. Tell me what to do to help and I'm there."

Chelsea threaded her fingers through his hair. "Love me. That's all I need to get through."

The singing started up behind them. The cheerful chorus quickly spread through the street. The magical evening had begun and she stood in her lover's arms. Right now, nothing could destroy her happiness.

"I'll always love you, Chelsea. Always."

She went up onto her toes and kissed him. "I love you more."

Epilogue

"What are you thinking?"

Chelsea lay beside him, her head on the pillow. Soft moonlight filtered in through the blinds he'd left open because he'd wanted to make love to her by the pale light.

After a month of bouncing from her house in Pine Valley to his loft, he'd finally asked her to move in with him. But he knew they'd eventually get their own place and start fresh. Actually he didn't want to wait much longer.

"Gabe?"

He smiled at her, reaching up to stroke her hair away from her face. Touching her, watching her while she slept, just the mundane things they did together, made him anxious, and he was done waiting to ask.

Gabe leaned back and reached into his nightstand, pulling out the small velvet box. He tapped the remote on the nightstand one time, to add the softest light in the room. He wanted to see her face, but he didn't want harsh light to ruin the moment.

Chelsea gasped when he rolled back over and she saw what he was holding.

"I had something elaborate and romantic planned for next week, but—"

"Yes," she squealed.

Gabe laughed. "Will you let me at least ask?"

Chelsea shot up in bed, the sheets pooling around her waist as she took it from him. "No. I want to marry you, now. This minute."

Shaking his head, he took the box back. "We'll get to that, but let me be somewhat of a gentleman here."

He lifted the lid, keeping his eyes on hers. "Since you already answered, I guess I should tell you that your brother already approved this."

Her eyes darted from the ring to him. "You talked to Daniel?"

"Considering he had his doubts about us a month ago, yes. Besides, I always thought a man should ask permission from the father of the woman he wants to marry. For you, I knew I should go through Daniel."

Chelsea's eyes misted as she looked back at the ring. "It's a pearl. It's lovely, Gabe."

He felt a little silly now since he hadn't gone the traditional route with a diamond.

"I saw the pearl and immediately thought of how they're made. How they're the toughest, yet come from something so soft. It just reminded me of you."

She took the ring, but he tossed the box onto the covers and plucked the ring from her hand. "I'm at least putting this on you."

When he slid it onto her finger, she held it up and admired the way it looked on her hand.

In the last month so much had happened in their lives. Gabe had worked closely with Nathan and discovered that Dusty's once lover, whose husband had been on the TCC board, had indeed been the one to help plant the cameras. She apparently had divorced her husband some time back and was still secretly involved with Dusty, claiming her love until his death.

Her home had since been searched and all hard drives and any computers taken. Charges were pending and Gabe was confident Nathan would handle matters from here on out.

Maverick's reign of terror was indeed over. The town had moved on. Chelsea was gearing up to open her counseling center by late March and Brandee was completely on board with joining forces in the project, as well.

"I don't want a big wedding," Chelsea told him, reaching over to join their hands. "Something simple at the Crescent Moon is perfect for me. For us."

Gabe leaned forward and kissed her, sending them tumbling back to the pillows. "We can discuss wedding plans later. I want to celebrate."

Chelsea laughed as he jerked the covers up and proceeded to show her just how happy he was that she'd said yes.

* * * * *

"So, Mr. Novak. Have you ever thought about donating your sperm to a good cause?"

"Excuse me?" Yaeger asked.

"Your sperm," Hannah said, enunciating the word more clearly this time. "Have you ever thought about donating it?"

"Uh…no."

"I mean, if you would consider it—donating it to me, I mean—I'd sign any kind of legal documents you want to relieve you of all obligations for any offspring that might, um, you know, spring off me. I'd really appreciate it."

"Hannah, I…I'm flattered, but it's not a good idea for me to do something like that."

She looked crestfallen. "Why not?"

"Because I'm not good father material."

At this, she looked aghast. Almost comically so. "Are you kidding me? You're incredible father material. You're smart and interesting and brave and funny and well traveled and smart and, holy cow, you're *gorgeous*."

He bit back a smile at that. "Thanks. But those aren't things that necessarily make a good father."

"Maybe not, but they make an *excellent* breeder."

* * *

Baby in the Making
is part of the Accidental Heirs series:
First they find their fortunes, then they find love

BABY IN
THE MAKING

BY
ELIZABETH BEVARLY

First Published in Great Britain 2017
By Mills & Boon, an imprint of HarperCollins*Publishers*
1 London Bridge Street, London, SE1 9GF

© 2017 Elizabeth Bevarly

ISBN: 978-0-263-92847-1

51-1217

MIX
Paper from
responsible sources
FSC™ C007454

This book is produced from independently certified FSC™ paper to ensure responsible forest management.

For more information visit: www.harpercollins.co.uk/green

Printed and bound in Spain
by CPI, Barcelona

Elizabeth Bevarly is the award-winning, *New York Times* bestselling author of more than seventy books, novellas and screenplays. Although she has called home exotic places like San Juan, Puerto Rico and Haddonfield, New Jersey, she's now happily settled back in her native Kentucky with her husband and son. When she's not writing, she's binge-watching documentaries on Netflix, spending too much time on Reddit or making soup out of whatever she finds in the freezer. Visit her at www.elizabethbevarly.com for news about current and upcoming projects, for book, music and film recommendations, for recipes, and for lots of other fun stuff.

For Eli,
My greatest creation ever.

Love you, Peanut.

One

Really, it wasn't the gaping hole in the shirt and pants that troubled Hannah Robinson most. It wasn't the bloodstain, either. She'd seen worse. No, what troubled her most was how little Yeager Novak seemed to be bothered by the six tidy stitches binding his flesh just north of the waistband of his silk boxers. Then again, as far as Yeager's garments were concerned, this was par for the course. Such was life sewing for a tailor whose most profitable client made his living at cheating death—and planning similar travel adventures for others—then brought in what was left of his clothing after the most recent near miss to have them mended. Or, in the case of the shirt, completely recreated from scratch.

Yeager towered over her from her current position kneeling before him, tape measure in hand. But then, he towered over her when she was standing, too. Shoving a handful of coal-black hair off his forehead, he gazed down at her with eyes the color of sapphires and said, "I'll never let a bull get that close to me again." He darted his gaze from the stitches on his torso to the ruined clothing on the floor. "That was just a little too close for comfort."

Hannah blew a dark blond curl out of her eyes and pushed her reading glasses higher on her nose. "That's what you said last year when you ran with the bulls."

He looked puzzled. "I did?"

"Yes. It was the first time you came to see us here at Cathcart and Quinn, because your previous tailor told you to take a hike when you brought in one too many of his masterpieces to be mended." She arched a brow in meaningful reminder. "Except when you were in Pamplona last July, you escaped into a cantina before the bull was able to do more than tear the leg of your trousers."

"Right," he said, remembering. "That was where I met Jimena. Who came back to my hotel with me while I changed my clothes. And didn't get back into them for hours." His expression turned sublime. "I probably should have sent that bull a thank-you note."

Even after knowing him for a year, Hannah was still sometimes surprised by the frankness with which Yeager talked about his sex life. Then again, his personal life sounded like it was almost as adventurous as his professional life, so maybe he had trouble distinguishing between the two on occasion.

"Or at least sent Jimena a text that said adios," Hannah said, striving for the same matter-of-factness and not sure if she quite managed it.

He grinned. "Hey, don't worry about Jimena. She got what she wanted, too."

I'll bet, Hannah thought, her gaze traveling to the elegant bumps of muscle and sinew on his torso. Yeager Novak might well have been sculpted by the hands of the gods. But the scar left behind by his latest stitches would be in good company, what with the jagged pink line marring the flesh above his navel and the puckered arc to their left. He had scars all over his body, thanks to his extreme adventurer ways. And thanks to his total lack of inhibition when it came to being fitted for clothes, Hannah had seen all of them.

"So you think you can fix the shirt and pants?" he asked.

"The pants will be fine," she told him. "They just need a good washing. But the shirt is a goner." Before he could open his mouth to protest, she added, "Don't worry, Mr. Novak. I can make a new one that will look just like it."

He threw her an exasperated look. "How many times have I told you to call me Yeager?"

"Lots," she replied. "And, just like I told you all those other times, it's Mr. Cathcart's and Mr. Quinn's policy to use 'Mr.' or 'Ms.' with all of our clients."

Just like it was Cathcart and Quinn policy that Hannah wear the ugly little smock she had to wear while working and always keep her hair confined, as if the shop's sole female employee was a throwback to the Industrial Revolution.

"Anyway," she continued, "I learned pretty quickly to keep all of your patterns and cut enough fabric for two garments whenever I make one."

He smiled in a way that was nothing short of devastating. "And I love you for it," he told her.

She smiled back. "I know."

Yeager told Hannah he loved her all the time. He loved her for making him clothes that fit like a glove. He loved her for mending them when he thought he'd ruined them. He loved her for being able to remove bloodstains, oil stains, pampas stains, baba ghanoush stains, walrus stains...stains from more sources than any normal human being saw in a lifetime. And, hey, she loved Yeager, too. The same way she loved cannoli and luna moths and sunsets—with a certain sense of awe that such things even existed in the world.

She went back to measuring his inseam, pretending the action commanded every scrap of her attention when, by now, she had Yeager's measurements memorized. There was no reason he had to know that, was there? Sometimes a girl had to do what a girl had to do. Especially when said girl was between boyfriends. Like eight months between boyfriends. None of whom had torsos roped with muscle or smelled like a rugged, windswept canyon.

"Have you ever been to Spain, Hannah?" Yeager asked.

"I lived for a while in what used to be Spanish Harlem," she told him as she penned his inseam measurement onto the back of her hand. She lifted the tape measure to his waist. "Does that count?"

He chuckled. "No. You should go to Spain. It's an incredible country. Definitely in my top five favorite places to visit."

Hannah would have told him her top five were Queens, Manhattan, Brooklyn, the Bronx and Staten

Island, since she'd never ventured outside the five boroughs of New York. For fifteen of her first eighteen years, it was because she'd been a ward of the state, and even though she'd been shuffled around *a lot* during that time, she'd never landed outside the city's jurisdiction. For the last nine years, she hadn't had the funds to pay for something as frivolous as travel. What didn't go to keeping herself housed and fed went toward funding the business she'd started out of her Sunnyside apartment. Things like travel could wait until *after* she was the toast of the New York fashion industry.

"What are your other top four favorite places?" she asked.

She was going to go out on a limb and say that, to a man who'd built a billion-dollar company out of creating extreme adventure vacations for other alpha types, Sunnyside and what used to be Spanish Harlem probably weren't going to make the cut.

He didn't even have to think about his response. "New Zealand, Slovenia, Chile and Iceland. But ask me tomorrow and it could be a whole different list."

Hannah jotted the last of his measurements onto the back of her hand with the others, returned the pen to its perennial place in the bun she always wore for work and stood. Yep, Yeager still towered over her. Then again, since she stood five-two, most people did.

"All done," she told him. Reluctantly she added, "You can get dressed now."

He nodded toward the clothes on the floor. "Thanks for taking care of this."

"No problem. But you know, you could save a lot

of money on tailoring if you stayed in New York for more than a few weeks at a time."

"There's no way I can stay anywhere for more than a few weeks at a time," he said. "And I won't apologize for being an adventurer."

Hannah would never ask him to. She couldn't imagine Yeager sitting behind a desk punching a keyboard or standing on an assembly line screwing in machine parts. It would be like asking Superman to work as a parking attendant.

"All I'm saying is be careful."

He flinched. "Those are the last two words somebody like me wants to hear."

And they were the two words Hannah lived by. Not that she was a fearful person by any stretch of the imagination. You didn't survive a childhood and adolescence as a ward of the state by being timid. But after nearly a decade on her own, she'd carved out a life for herself that was quiet, steady and secure, and she was careful not to jeopardize that. Oh, blissful predictability. Oh, exalted stability. Oh, revered security. She'd never had any of those things growing up. No way would she risk losing them now.

"Your pants and new shirt will be ready a week from today," she told Yeager.

He thrust his arms through the sleeves of a gray linen shirt Hannah had made for him and began to button it. "Great. That'll be just in time for my trip to Gansbaai. South Africa," he clarified before she could ask. "I'm taking a group to go cage diving with great white sharks."

"Of course you are. Because after nearly being gored to death by a gigantic bull, why wouldn't you risk being bitten in two by a gigantic shark? It makes perfect sense."

He grinned again. "After that, it's off to Nunavut with a couple of buddies to climb Mount Thor."

"I would love to see your passport, Mr. Novak. It must be as thick as a novel."

"Yeah, it is. Like *Harry Potter and the Order of the Phoenix* size."

And the stories it could tell were probably every bit as fantastic.

"Well, have a good time," she told him. "I'll be at home, inventorying my swatches and organizing my bobbins."

He threw her one last smile as he reached for his charcoal trousers—also fashioned by Hannah. "And you say I live dangerously."

The bell above the shop entrance jingled, making her turn in that direction. "Excuse me," she said as she backed toward the fitting room entrance. "Your claim check will be at the register when you're ready."

The minute Hannah disappeared through the fitting room door, Yeager Novak's mind turned to other, more pressing, topics. When your life's work was creating extreme adventures for wealthy clients, you had to make plans, sometimes years in advance. In putting together vacation packages, he had a million things to consider—a country's culture and politics, its potential safety, its seasonal climate, how many people needed to be bribed for all the requisite permissions... The list was endless. And he always tried out the travel packages he designed for his clients first, to be sure they were doable without risk to life or limb.

Well, without *too* much risk to life or limb. *No* risk kind of defeated the purpose.

He knotted his tie, grabbed his suit jacket and headed for the register. Hannah's blond head was bent over her receipt pad as she wrote in her slow, precise hand, a few errant curls springing free of the prim little bun she always wore. Nice to know there was at least some part of her that wanted to break free of her buttoned-up, battened-down self. He'd never met anyone more straitlaced than Hannah…whatever her last name was.

As if she'd heard him say that out loud, she suddenly glanced up, her silver-gray eyes peering over the tops of her black half-glasses. She did have some beautiful eyes, though, he'd give her that. He'd never seen the color on another human being. But the rest of her… The shapeless jacket-thing she wore completely hid her gender, and if she was wearing any makeup, he sure couldn't see it. He guessed she was kind of cute in a wholesome, girl-next-door type of way, if you went for the wholesome, girl-next-door type—which he didn't. He liked talking to her, though. She was smart and funny. And, man, did her clothes make him look good. He knew nothing about sewing or fashion, but he knew excellent work when he saw it. And Hannah Whatshername definitely did excellent work.

"A week from today," she reiterated as she tore the receipt from the pad and extended it toward him.

"Thanks," he replied as he took it from her. "Any chance you could make a second shirt like it by then? Just in case?" Before she could object—because he could tell she was going to—he added, "There could be an extra hundred bucks in it for you."

She bit her lip thoughtfully, a gesture that was slightly—surprisingly—erotic. "I'm not allowed to take tips."

"Oh, c'mon. I don't see Leo or Monty around."

"Mr. Cathcart is on a buying trip to London," she said. "And Mr. Quinn is at lunch."

"Then they'll never know."

She expelled the kind of sigh someone makes when they know they're breaking the rules but they badly need cash for something. Yeager was intrigued. What could Ms. Goody Two-shoes Hannah need money for that would make her break the rules?

With clear reluctance she said, "I can't. I'm sorry. I just don't have time to do it here—we're so backlogged." Before he could protest, she hurried on. "However, I happen to know a seamstress who does freelance work at home. She's very good."

Yeager shook his head. "No way. I don't trust anyone with my clothes but you."

"No, you don't understand, Mr. Novak. I guarantee you'll like this woman's work. I know her *intimately.*"

"But—"

"You could even say that she and I are *one of a kind.* If you know what I mean."

She eyed him pointedly. And after a moment, Yeager understood. Hannah was the one who did freelance work at home. "Gotcha."

"If you happened to do a search on Craigslist for, say, 'Sunnyside seamstress,' she'd be the first listing that pops up. Ask if she can make you a shirt by next week for the same price you'd pay here, and I guarantee she'll be able to do it."

Yeager grabbed his phone from his pocket and

pulled up Craigslist. He should have known Hannah
would live in Sunnyside. It was the closest thing New
York had to Small Town America.

"Found you," he said.

She frowned at him.

"I mean…found *her*."

"Send her an email from that listing. I'm sure she'll
reply when she gets home from work tonight."

He was already typing when he said, "Great.
Thanks."

"But you'll have to pick it up at my—I mean, her
place," she told him. "She can't bring it here, and she
doesn't deliver."

"No problem."

He sent the email then returned his phone to one
pocket as he tugged his wallet from another. He withdrew five twenties from the ten he always had on him
and placed them on the counter. Hannah's eyes widened at the gesture, but she discreetly palmed the bills
and tucked them into her pocket.

Even so, she asked, "Don't you want to wait until
you have the extra shirt?"

He shook his head. "I trust you."

"Thanks."

"No, thank *you*. That was my favorite shirt. It will
be nice to have a spare. Not that I'll be letting any
sharks near my clothes, but you never know when
you'll meet another Jimena."

She nodded, but he was pretty sure it wasn't in un-
derstanding. Someone like her probably wouldn't let
a lover that spontaneous and temporary get anywhere
near her. She was way too buttoned-up, battened-down
and straitlaced for idle encounters, regardless of how

beautiful her eyes were or how erotically she bit her lip. Hannah, he was certain, only dated the same kind of upright, forthright, do-right person she was. To Yeager, that would be a fate worse than death.

"I'll see you in a week," he said, lifting a hand in farewell.

As he made his way to the door, he heard her call after him, "Have a great day, Mr. Novak! And remember to look both ways before you cross the street!"

A week later—the day Yeager was scheduled to pick up his new shirt at her apartment, in fact—Hannah was in the back room of Cathcart and Quinn, collecting fabric remnants to take home with her. Everyone else had gone for the day, and she was counting the minutes until she could begin closing up shop, when the store's entrance bell rang to announce a customer. Hoping it would just be someone picking up an alteration, she headed out front.

She didn't recognize the man at the register, but he had the potential to become a client, judging by his bespoke suit from… Aponte's, she decided. It looked like Paolo's work. The man's blond hair was cut with razor-precision, his eyes were cool and keen, and his smile was this just side of dispassionate.

"Hello," Hannah greeted him as she approached. "May I help you?"

"Hannah Robinson?" he asked. Her surprise that he knew her must have been obvious, because he quickly added, "My name is Gus Fiver. I'm an attorney with Tarrant, Fiver and Twigg. We're a probate law firm here in Manhattan."

His response only surprised her more. She didn't

have a will herself, and she knew no one who might
have included her in one. Her lack of connections was
what had landed her in the foster care system as a
three-year-old, after her mother died with no surviv-
ing relatives or friends to care for her. And although
Hannah hadn't had any especially horrible experiences in the system, she could safely say she'd never
met anyone there who would remember her in their
last wishes. There was no reason a probate attorney
should know her name or where she worked.

"Yes," she said cautiously. "I'm Hannah Robinson."

Gus Fiver's smile grew more genuine at her response. In a matter of seconds he went from being
a high-powered Manhattan attorney to an affable
boy next door. The change made Hannah feel a little better.

"Excellent," he said. Even his voice was warmer
now.

"I'm sorry, but how do you know me?" she asked.

"My firm has been looking for you since the beginning of the year. And one of our clients was looking
for you long before then."

"I don't understand. Why would anyone be looking
for me? Especially when I'm not that hard to find?"

Instead of answering her directly he said, "You
did most of your growing up in the foster care system, yes?"

Hannah was so stunned he would know that about
her—few of her friends even knew—that she could
only nod.

"You entered the program when you were three,
I believe, after your mother, Mary Robinson, died."

Her stomach knotted at the realization that he

would know about her past so precisely. But she automatically replied, "Yes."

"And do you remember what your life was like prior to that?"

"Mr. Fiver, what's this about?"

Instead of explaining he said, "Please, just bear with me for a moment, Ms. Robinson."

Hannah didn't normally share herself with other people until she'd known them for some time, and even then, there were barriers it took a while for most people to breach. But there was something about Gus Fiver that told her it was okay to trust him. To a point.

So she told him, "I only have a few vague memories. I know my mother was a bookkeeper for a welding company on Staten Island and that that's where she and I were living when she died. But I only know that because that's what I've been told. I don't have any mementos or anything. Everything she owned was sold after her death, and what was left in her estate after it was settled was put into trust for me until I turned eighteen and was booted out of the system."

Not that there had been much, but it had allowed Hannah to start life on her own without a lot of the stress she would have had otherwise, and she'd been enormously grateful for it.

"Is your mother the one you inherited your eyes from?" Mr. Fiver asked. "I don't mean to be forward, but they're such an unusual color."

Hannah had fielded enough remarks about her singularly colored eyes—even from total strangers—that she no longer considered them forward. "No," she said. "My mother had blue eyes."

"So you at least remember what she looked like?"

Hannah shook her head. "No. But I take back what I said about mementos. I do have one. A photograph of my mother that one of the social workers was kind enough to frame and give to me before I went into the system. Somehow, I always managed to keep it with me whenever they moved me to a new place."

This interested Mr. Fiver a lot. "Is there any chance you have this photograph with you?"

"I do, actually." Hannah had taken it out of the frame when she was old enough to have a wallet, because she'd always wanted to carry the photo with her. It was the only evidence of her mother she'd ever had.

"May I see it?" Mr. Fiver asked.

Hannah was about to tell him no, that this had gone on long enough. But her damnable curiosity now had the better of her, and she was kind of interested to see where this was going.

"It's in my wallet," she said.

He smiled again, notching another chink in her armor that weakened her mettle. "I don't mind waiting."

She retrieved her purse from beneath the counter and withdrew the photo, now creased and battered, from its plastic sheath to hand to Mr. Fiver. It had been cropped from what must have been a studio portrait, and showed her mother from the chest up, along with the shoulder of someone sitting next to her.

"And your father?" he asked as he studied the picture.

"I didn't know him," Hannah said. "He's listed as a Robert Williams on my birth certificate, but do you know how many Robert Williamses there are in New

York alone? No one ever found him. I never had any family but my mother."

Mr. Fiver returned the photo to her. "The reason we've been looking for you, Ms. Robinson, is because we have a client whose estate we've been managing since his death while we search for his next of kin. That's sort of our specialty at Tarrant, Fiver and Twigg. We locate heirs whose whereabouts or identities are unknown. We believe you may be this client's sole heir."

"I'm sorry to disappoint you, Mr. Fiver, but that's impossible. If my mother had had any family, the state would have found them twenty-five years ago."

He opened his portfolio and sifted through its contents, finally withdrawing an eight-by-ten photo he held up for Hannah to see. It was the same picture of her mother she had been carrying her entire life, but it included the person who'd been cropped from her copy—a man with blond hair and silver-gray eyes. Even more startling, a baby with the exact same coloring was sitting in her mother's lap.

Her gaze flew to Mr. Fiver's. But she had no idea what to say.

"This is a photograph of Stephen and Alicia Linden of Scarsdale, New York," he said. "The baby is their daughter, Amanda. Mrs. Linden and Amanda disappeared not long after this picture was taken."

A strange buzzing erupted in Hannah's head. How could Gus Fiver have a photo of her mother identical to hers? Was the baby in her mother's lap Hannah? Was the man her father? What the hell was going on?

All she could say, though, was, "I don't understand."

"One day, while Stephen Linden was at work in the city," Mr. Fiver continued, "Alicia bundled up ten-month-old Amanda and, with nothing but the clothes on their backs, left him." He paused for a moment, as if he were trying to choose his next words carefully. "Stephen Linden was, from all accounts, a…difficult man to live with. He…mistreated his wife. Badly. Alicia feared for her and her daughter's safety, but her husband's family was a very powerful one and she worried they would hinder her in her efforts to leave him. So she turned to an underground group active in aiding battered women, providing them with new identities and forged documents and small amounts of cash. With the assistance of this group, Alicia and Amanda Linden of Scarsdale were able to start a new life as Mary and Hannah Robinson of Staten Island."

By now, Hannah was reeling. She heard what Mr. Fiver was saying, but none of it quite registered. "I… I'm sorry, Mr. Fiver, but this… You're telling me I'm not the person I've always thought I was? That my whole life should have been different from the one I've lived? That's just… It's…"

Then another thought struck her and the air rushed from her lungs in a quick whoosh. Very softly, she asked, "Is my father still alive?"

At this, Mr. Fiver sobered. "No, I'm sorry. He died almost twenty years ago. Our client, who initially launched the search for you, was your paternal grandfather." He paused a telling beat before concluding, "Chandler Linden."

Had there been any breath left in Hannah, she would have gasped. Everyone in New York knew the name Chandler Linden. His ancestors had practically built this city, and, at the time of his death, he'd still owned a huge chunk of it.

Although she had no idea how she managed it, Hannah said, "Chandler Linden was a billionaire."

Mr. Fiver nodded. "Yes, he was. Ms. Robinson, you might want to close up shop early today. You and I have *a lot* to talk about."

Two

Yeager Novak didn't find himself in Queens very often. Or, for that matter, ever. And he wasn't supposed to be here now. His assistant, Amira, was supposed to be picking up his shirt at Hannah's. But she'd needed to take the afternoon off for a family emergency, so he'd told her he would deal with whatever was left on his agenda today himself—not realizing at the time that that would include going to Queens. By train. Which was another place he didn't find himself very often. Or, for that matter, ever. This time of day, though, the train was fastest and easiest, and he needed to be back in Manhattan ASAP.

But as he walked down Greenpoint Avenue toward 44th Street, he couldn't quite make himself hurry. Queens was different from Manhattan—less frantic, more relaxed. Especially now, at the end of the workday. The sun was hanging low in the sky, bathing the stunted brick buildings in gold and amber. Employees in storefronts were turning over Closed signs as waiters at cafés unfolded sandwich boards with nightly specials scrawled in bright-colored chalk. People on the street actually smiled and said hello to him as he passed. With every step he took, Yeager felt like he was moving backward in time, and somehow, that made him want to go slower. Hannah's neighborhood was even more quaint than he'd imagined.

He hated quaint. At least, he usually did. Somehow the quaintness of Sunnyside was less off-putting than most.

Whatever. To each his own. Yeager would suffocate in a place like this. Quiet. Cozy. Family friendly. Why was a healthy, red-blooded young woman with beautiful silver-gray eyes and a surprisingly erotic lip nibble living somewhere like this? Not that anything Hannah did was Yeager's business. But he did kind of wonder.

Her apartment was on the third and uppermost floor of one of those tawny brick buildings, above a Guatemalan *mercado*. He rang her bell and identified himself, and she buzzed him in. At the top of the stairs were three apartments. Hannah had said hers was B, but before he even knocked on the door, she opened it.

At least, he thought it was Hannah who opened it. She didn't look much like the woman he knew from Cathcart and Quinn. The little black half-glasses were gone and the normally bunned-up hair danced around her shoulders in loose, dark gold curls. In place of her shapeless work jacket, she had on a pair of striped shorts and a sleeveless red shirt knotted at her waist. As small as she was, she had surprisingly long legs and they ended in feet whose toenails were an even brighter red than her shirt.

But what really made him think someone else had taken Hannah's place was her expression. He'd never seen her be anything but cool and collected. This version looked agitated and anxious.

"Hannah?" he asked, just to be sure.

"Yeah, hi," she said. She sounded even more on edge than she looked. "I'm sorry. I totally forgot about your pickup tonight."

"Didn't my assistant email you yesterday to confirm?"

"She did, actually. But today was…" She shook her head as if trying to physically clear it of something. But that didn't seem to work, because she still looked distracted. "I got some, um, very weird news today. But it's okay, your shirt is finished." She hurried on. "I just…" She inhaled a deep breath, released it in a ragged sigh…and still looked as if she were a million miles away. "I forgot about the pickup," she said again. Almost as an afterthought, she added, "Come on in."

She opened the door wider and stepped back to get out of his way. Good thing, too, since the room he walked into was actually an alcove that was barely big enough to hold both of them. As he moved forward, Hannah wedged herself behind him to close the door, brushing against him—with all that naked skin—as she did. It was then he noticed something about her he'd never noticed before. She smelled like raspberries. Really ripe, really succulent, raspberries.

Another step forward took him into her apartment proper, but it wasn't much bigger than the alcove and seemed to consist of only one room. Yeager looked

ELIZABETH BEVARLY   27

for doors that would lead to others, but saw only one,
which had to be for the bathroom. The "kitchen" was
a couple of appliances tucked into another alcove adja-
cent to the single window in the place, one that offered
a view of a building on the next street. The apartment
was furnished with the bare essentials for living and
the tools of a seamstress's trade—a sewing machine
and ironing board, a trio of torso stands for works-in-
progress, stacks of fabric and a rack of plastic-covered garments.

"I guess my place is a little smaller than yours,
huh?" Hannah asked, obviously sensing his thoughts.

Smaller than his *place*? Her apartment was smaller
than his bedroom. But all he said was, "A bit."

She squeezed out of the alcove, past him—leaving
that tantalizing scent of raspberries in her wake—and
strode to the rolling rack, from which she withdrew
one of the plastic-covered garments. As he followed,
he noted a half-empty bottle of wine on one of the
end tables by the love seat. He thought maybe he'd interrupted a romantic evening she was spending with
someone else—the bathroom door was closed—then
noted that the near-empty glass sitting behind the bottle was alone.

"Do you want to try it on before you take it?" she
asked. "Just to be sure it fits?"

Yeager figured it probably wasn't a bad idea, since
he was leaving in two days for South Africa and there
wouldn't be time for Amira to come back for it if it
needed alterations. Truth be told, he also wasn't sure
he should leave Hannah alone just yet, what with the
wine, the distraction and the anxious look…and, okay,
all that naked skin.

"Yeah, I guess I should, just in case," he replied.

As she removed the plastic from the shirt, he tossed his suit jacket onto the love seat, tugged free his tie and unbuttoned the shirt he was wearing. By the time he shed it, she was holding up his new one for him to slip on. She looked a little steadier now and seemed more like herself. His concern began to ease a bit. Until he drew near and saw that her eyes housed a healthy bit of panic.

It was obvious there was something bothering her. A lot. Yeager told himself that whatever it was, it was none of his business. But that didn't keep him from wondering. Boyfriend troubles? Family conflicts? Problems at work? He knew nothing about her outside her job. Because there was no reason for him to know anything about her outside her job. There was no reason for him to care, either. That wasn't to be cold or unfeeling. That was just how he was. He didn't care about much of anything outside his immediate sphere of existence. Somehow, though, he suddenly kind of cared about Hannah.

"I'm sorry," she said as he thrust his arm through the shirt's sleeve, "but the fabric isn't exactly the same as the original. Since I was moonlighting, I couldn't use what we have at work, and that came from Portugal. But I found a beautiful dobby in nearly the same color. I hope it's okay. It brought the price down a bit."

Yeager couldn't have cared less about the price. He cared about quality and style. Maybe it was superficial, but a man who was the face of a Fortune 500 company had to look good. And, thanks to Hannah, he always did.

"No, this is good," he said. "It's got a great texture. I actually like this one better than the one you made for me at Cathcart and Quinn. Why aren't you the one they're sending on buying trips to London and Portugal?"

"You'll have to ask Mr. Cathcart that question," she said in a way that made him think she'd already broached the topic with her employer and been shot down. Probably more than once.

"Maybe I will," he said, wondering about his sudden desire to act as her champion. "Or maybe you should just open your own business."

As she studied the fit of his shirt, she gestured to the rack of clothes against the wall. "I'm trying."

Out of curiosity, Yeager walked over to look at what she'd made for her other clients. He was surprised to see that the majority of items hanging there were children's clothes.

"You mostly make stuff for kids?" he asked.

Instead of replying, Hannah moved to her sewing machine to withdraw a business card from a stack and handed it to Yeager. It was pale lavender, imprinted with the words, Joey & Kit, and decorated with a logo of a kangaroo and fox touching noses. Below them was the slogan, "Glad rags for happy kids." At the bottom were addresses for a website, an email and a PO box.

"This is your business?" Yeager asked, holding up the card.

She nodded. "I'm an S-corporation. I trademarked the name and logo and everything."

"Why kids' clothes? Seems like other areas of fashion would be more profitable."

"They would be," she said. He waited for her to elaborate. She didn't. He was about to ask her to when

she told him, "Turn around, so I can make sure the
back darts are aligned."

He did as she instructed, something that left him
looking out the apartment's solitary window. He didn't
know why, but it really bothered him that Hannah only
had one window from which to view the world. His
West Chelsea penthouse had panoramic views of Manhattan and the Hudson from floor-to-ceiling windows
in most rooms—including two of the three-and-a-half
baths. Not that he spent much time at home, but his
office in the Flatiron District had pretty breathtaking
views of the city, too. No matter where Yeager went in
the world, he always made sure he had a lot to look at.
Mountain ranges that disappeared into clouds, savan-
nas that dissolved into the horizon, oceans that met the
stars in the distant night sky. Some of the best parts
of adventure travel were just looking at things. But
Hannah lived her life in a square little room with one
window that opened onto a building across the way.

"You know, I don't usually have to put darts in a
man's shirt," she said. "But the way you're built…
broad shoulders, tapered waist…"

Yeager told himself he only imagined the sigh of
approval he heard.

"Anyway," she went on, "I think this looks good."

She ran her hand down the length of his back on
one side, then up again on the other, smoothing out
the seams in question. The gesture was in no way pro-
tracted or flirtatious. Her touch was deft and professional. Yet, somehow, it made his pulse twitch.

She stepped in front of him, gave him a final once-
over with eyes that still looked a little haunted, and
told him, "You're good to go."

It was one of his favorite statements to hear. Yeager loved going. Anywhere. Everywhere. Whenever he could. Strangely, though, in that moment, he didn't want to go. He told himself it was because, in spite of the relative ease of the last few minutes, there was still something about Hannah that was…off. He'd never seen her be anything but upbeat. This evening, she was subdued. And that just didn't sit well with him.

Before he realized what he was doing, he asked, "Hannah, is everything okay?"

Her eyes widened in now unmistakable panic. She opened her mouth to reply but no words emerged. Which may have been his biggest tip-off yet that there was something seriously wrong. Hannah was never at a loss for words. On the contrary, she was generally one of those people who had a snappy reply for everything.

He tried again. "You just don't seem like yourself tonight."

For a moment she looked as if she was going to deny anything was wrong. Then she made a defeated sound and her whole body seemed to slump forward.

"Is this about the weird news you got today?" he asked.

She nodded, but instead of looking at him, she lowered her gaze to the floor. Hannah never did that. She was one of the most direct people he knew, always making eye contact. It was one of the things he loved about her. So few people did that.

"What kind of news was it?"

She hesitated again, still not looking at him. Finally she said, "The kind that could not only completely change my future, but also confirmed that my past could have—should have—been a lot better than it was."

"I'm not sure I understand."

At this, she emitted a strangled chuckle completely devoid of humor. "Yeah, I know the feeling."

Maybe the wine had affected her more than he thought. Probably, he ought to just drop it and pay her for his shirt. Definitely, he should be getting the hell out of there.

Instead he heard himself ask, "Do you want to talk about it?"

At that, she finally pulled her gaze from the floor and met his squarely…for all of a nanosecond. Then she lifted both hands to cover her beautiful silver-gray eyes. Then her lips began to tremble. Then she sniffled. Twice. And that was when Yeager knew he was in trouble. Because Hannah crying was way worse than Hannah panicking. Panic eventually subsided. But sadness… Sadness could go on forever. No one knew that better than he did.

She didn't start crying, though. Not really. After a moment she wiped both eyes with the backs of her hands and dropped them to hug herself tight. But that gesture just made her look even more lost. Especially since her eyes were still damp. Something in Yeager's chest twisted tight at seeing her this way. He had no idea why. He barely knew her. He just hated seeing anyone this distraught.

"Holy crap, do I want to talk about it," she said softly. "I just don't have anyone to talk about it with."

That should have been his cue to get out while he still had the chance. The last thing he had time for—

hell, the last thing he wanted—was to listen to someone whose last name he didn't even know talk about her life-altering problems. He should be heading for the front door stat. And he would. Any minute now. Any second now. In five, four, three, two...

"Give me one minute to change my shirt," he told her, wondering what the hell had possessed him. "Then you can tell me about it."

While Yeager changed his shirt, Hannah moved to the love seat, perching herself on the very edge of the cushion and wondering what just happened. One minute, she'd been double-checking the fit of his shirt and had been almost—*almost*—able to forget, if only for a moment, everything she'd learned today from Gus Fiver. The next minute, Yeager had been offering a sympathetic shoulder to cry on.

Not that she would cry on him. Well, probably not. She didn't want to ruin his shirt. But she appreciated his offer to hang around for a little while. She hadn't felt more alone in her life than she had over the last few hours.

She'd taken Gus Fiver's advice to close Cathcart and Quinn early, then had sat with him in the empty shop for nearly an hour as he'd given her all the specifics about her situation. A situation that included the most stunning good news/bad news scenario she'd ever heard. Since then she'd been here in her apartment, combing the internet for information about her newly discovered family and mulling everything she'd learned, in the hope that it would help her make sense of the choice she had to make. Maybe someone like Yeager, who didn't have any personal involvement, would have a clearer perspective and some decent advice.

She watched as he changed his shirt, doing her best not to stare at the cords of muscle and sinew roping his arms, shoulders and torso. But in an apartment the size of hers, there wasn't much else to stare at. Then again, even if she'd had the frescoes of the Sistine Chapel surrounding her, it would still be Yeager that drew her eye. So she busied herself with filling her wineglass a third time, since the two glasses she'd already consumed had done nothing to take the edge off.

"You want a glass of wine?" she asked Yeager, belatedly realizing how negligent a hostess she'd been.

Also belatedly, she remembered she'd picked up the wine at Duane Reade on her way home from work. She reread the label as she placed it back on the table. Chateau Yvette claimed to be a "wine product" that paired well with pizza and beef stew. It probably wasn't a brand Yeager normally bought for himself. But it was too late to retract the offer now.

"Yeah, that'd be great," he said as he finished buttoning his shirt.

She retrieved another glass from the kitchen and poured the wine. By then, Yeager had draped the plastic back over his new shirt and was sitting on the love seat—taking up most of it. So much so that his thigh aligned with hers when she sat and handed him his glass. She enjoyed another healthy swig from her own and grimaced. She honestly hadn't realized until then how, uh, not-particularly-good it was. Probably because her head had been too full of *Omigod, omigod, omigod, what am I going to do?*

"So what's up?" he asked.

She inhaled a deep breath and released it slowly. It still came out shaky and uneven. Not surprising, since shaky and uneven was how she'd been feeling since Gus Fiver had dropped his Chandler Linden bombshell. There was nothing like the prospect of inheriting billions of dollars to send a person's pulse and brain synapses into overdrive.

If Hannah actually inherited it.

She took another breath and this time when she released it, it was a little less ragged. "Have you heard of a law firm called Tarrant, Fiver and Twigg?" she asked.

Yeager nodded. "Yeah. They're pretty high-profile. A lot of old money—big money—clients."

"Well, I had a meeting with one of their partners this afternoon."

Yeager couldn't quite hide his surprise that someone like her would be in touch with such a financial powerhouse, though he was obviously trying to. Hannah appreciated his attempt to be polite, but it was unnecessary. She wasn't bothered by being working class, nor was she ashamed of her upbringing. Even if she didn't talk freely about her past, she'd never tried to hide it, and she wasn't apologetic about the way she lived now. She'd done pretty well for herself and lived the best life she could. She was proud of that.

Still, she replied, "I know. They're not exactly my social stratum. But I didn't contact them. They contacted me."

"About?" he asked.

"About the fact that I'm apparently New York's equivalent to the Grand Duchess Anastasia of Russia."

Now Yeager looked puzzled. So she did her best to

explain. Except she ended up not so much explaining as just pouring out her guts into his lap.

Without naming names, and glossing over many of the details, she told him about her discovery that she'd been born to a family she never knew she had in a town she would have sworn she'd never visited. She told him about her father's addiction and abuse and about her mother's custodial kidnapping of her. She told him about their false identities and their move from Scarsdale to Staten Island. She told him about her mother's death when she was three and her entry into the foster care system, where she'd spent the next fifteen years. And she told him about how, in a matter of minutes today, she went from living the ordinary life of a seamstress to becoming one of those long-lost heirs to a fortune who seemed only to exist in over-the-top fiction.

Through it all, Yeager said not a word. When she finally paused—not that she was finished talking by a long shot, because there was still *so much more* to tell him—he only studied her in silence. Then he lifted the glass of wine he had been holding through her entire story and, in one long quaff, drained it.

And then he grimaced, too. Hard. "That," he finally said, "was unbelievable."

"I know," Hannah told him. "But it's all true."

He shook his head. "No, I mean the wine. It was unbelievably bad."

"Oh."

"Your life is… Wow."

For a moment he only looked out at her little apartment without speaking. Then he looked at Hannah again.

And he said, "This isn't the kind of conversation to be having over unbelievably bad wine."

"It isn't?"

He shook his head. "No. This is the kind of conversation that needs to be had over extremely good Scotch."

"I don't have any Scotch." And even if she did, it wouldn't be extremely good.

He roused a smile. "Then we'll just have to go find some, won't we?"

Three

Instead of extremely good Scotch, they found a sufficiently good Irish whiskey at a pub up the street from Hannah's apartment. She'd ducked into the bathroom to change before they'd left, trading her shorts for a printed skirt that matched her shirt and dipping her feet into a pair of flat sandals. By the time the bartender brought their drinks to them at a two-seater cocktail table tucked into the corner of the dimly lit bar, she was beginning to feel a little more like herself.

Until she looked at Yeager and found him eyeing her with a scrutiny unlike any she'd ever had from him before. Normally he showed her no more interest than he would…well, a seamstress who was sewing some clothes for him. Sure, the two of them bantered back and forth whenever he was in the shop, but it was the kind of exchange everybody shared with people they saw in passing on any given day—baristas, cashiers, doormen, that kind of thing. In the shop, his attention passed with the moments. But now...

Now, Yeager Novak's undivided attention was an awesome thing. His sapphire eyes glinted like the gems they resembled, and if she'd fancied he could see straight into her soul before, now she was certain of it. Her heart began to hammer hard in her chest, her blood began to zip through her veins and her breathing became more shallow than it had been all day. This time, though, the reactions had little to do with the news of her massive potential inheritance and a lot to do with Yeager.

He must have sensed her reaction—hyperventilation was generally a dead giveaway—because he nudged her glass closer to her hand and said, "Take a couple sips of your drink. Then tell me again about how you ended up in Staten Island."

She wanted to start talking now, but she did as he instructed and enjoyed a few slow sips of her whiskey. She wasn't much of a drinker, usually sticking to wine or some sissy, fruit-sprouting drink. The liquor was smooth going down, warming her mouth and throat and chest. She closed her eyes to let it do its thing, then opened them again to find Yeager still studying her. She was grateful for the dim lighting of the bar. Not just because it helped soothe her rattled nerves but because it might mask the effect he was having on her.

"According to Mr. Fiver," she said, "my mother got help from a group of women who aided other women in escaping their abusers. They paid counterfeiters to forge new identities for both of us—fake social security numbers, fake birth certificates, the works. I don't know how my mother found them, but she needed them because my father's family was super powerful and probably could have kept her from leaving him or, at least, made sure she couldn't take me with her."

"And just who was your father's family?"

Hannah hesitated. During her internet search of her birth name, she had come across a number of items about her and her mother's disappearance from Scarsdale a quarter century ago. Some of them had been articles that appeared in newspapers and magazines shortly after the fact, but many of them were fairly current on "unsolved mystery" type blogs and websites. It had been singularly creepy to read posts about herself from strangers speculating on her fate. Some people were convinced Stephen Linden had beaten his wife and daughter to death and disposed of their bodies, getting away with murder, thanks to his social standing. Some thought baby Amanda had been kidnapped by strangers for ransom and that her mother had interrupted the crime and been killed by the perpetrators, her body dumped in Long Island Sound. Other guesses were closer to the truth: that Alicia escaped her abusive marriage with Amanda in tow and both were living now in the safety of a foreign country.

What would Yeager make of all this?

Since Hannah had already told him so much—and still had a lot more to reveal—she said, "My father's name was Stephen Linden. He died about twenty years ago. It was my recently deceased grandfather, Chandler Linden, who was looking for me and wanted to leave me the family fortune."

Yeager studied her in silence for a moment. Then he said, "You're Amanda Linden."

She had thought he would remark on her grandfather's identity, not hers. But she guessed she shouldn't be surprised by his knowing about Amanda's disappearance, too, since so many others did.

"You know about that," she said.

He chuckled. "Hannah, everyone knows about that. Any kid who was ever curious about unsolved crimes has read about the disappearance of Amanda Linden and her mother." He lifted a shoulder and let it drop. "When I was in middle school, I wanted to be a private investigator. I was totally into that stuff."

"Yeah, well, I wasn't," she said. "I had no idea any of this happened. Let alone that it happened to me."

She took another sip of her drink and was surprised by how much she liked the taste. Since Yeager had ordered it, it was doubtless the best this place had. Maybe her Linden genes just had a natural affinity for the finer things in life. She sipped her drink again.

"So you were destined for a life of wealth and privilege," Yeager said, "and instead, you grew up in the New York foster care system."

"Yep."

"And how was that experience?"

Hannah dropped her gaze to her drink, dragging her finger up and down the side of the glass. "It wasn't as terrible as what some kids go through," she said. "But it wasn't terrific, either. I mean a couple of times I landed in a really good place, with really good people. But just when I started to think maybe I'd found a spot where I fit in and could be reasonably happy for a while, I always got yanked out and put somewhere else where I didn't fit in and wasn't particularly happy."

She glanced up to find that he was looking at her

as if she were some interesting specimen under a microscope. A specimen he couldn't quite figure out. So she returned her attention to her glass.

"That was the worst part, you know?" she continued. "Never feeling like I belonged anywhere. Never feeling like I had a real home or a real family. Now I know that I could have and should have—that I actually *did* have—both. The irony is that if I'd grown up as Amanda Linden, with all her wealth and privilege, I would have had a terrifying father who beat up my mother and very well could have come after me. Foster care was no picnic, but I was never physically abused. Dismissed and belittled, yeah. Neglected, sure. But never harmed. As Amanda, though…"

She didn't finish the statement. She didn't dare. She didn't even want to think about what kind of life she might have lived if her mother hadn't rescued her from it. What kind of life her mother had endured for years before her daughter's safety had compelled her to run.

"Some people would argue that neglect and belittlement *are* harm," Yeager said softly.

"Maybe," she conceded. "But I'd rather be neglected and belittled and shuffled around and have nothing to my name than live in the lap of luxury and go through what my mother must have gone through to make her escape the way she did. I just wish she'd had more time to enjoy her life once she got it back."

And Hannah wished she'd had more time herself to get to know her mother. Mary Robinson, formerly Alicia Linden, might very well have saved her daughter's life—both figuratively and literally. Yet Hannah had no way to thank her.

"Your grandfather, Chandler Linden, was a billionaire," Yeager said in the same matter-of-fact tone he'd been using all night.

Hannah's stomach pitched to have the knowledge she'd been carrying around in her head all evening spoken aloud. Somehow, having it out in the open like that made it so much more real. Her heart began to thunder again and her vision began to swim. Hyperventilation would come next, so she enjoyed another, larger, taste of her drink in an effort to stave it off.

"Yeah," she said quietly when she set her glass on the table. "He was."

"Which means that now you're a billionaire," Yeager said in the same casual tone.

Oh, boy. There went her stomach again. "Well, I *could* be a billionaire," she told him.

"*Could* be?" he echoed. "You said your grandfather bequeathed his entire estate to you. What are they waiting on? A DNA test?"

"Mr. Fiver took a sample of my saliva while we were talking," she said. "But that's just a formality for the courts. There's no question I'm Amanda. I didn't just inherit my father's unique eye color. I also have a crescent-shaped birthmark on my right shoulder blade that shows up with some regularity in the Linden line. And, yes, my grandfather wants his entire estate to go to me. But there are certain…terms…of his will that need to be met before I can inherit."

"What kind of terms?"

Hannah threw back the rest of her drink in one long gulp. Before her glass even hit the table, Yeager was lifting a hand to alert the bartender that they wanted another round. He even pointed at Hannah and added, "Make hers a double."

Hannah started to tell him that wouldn't be necessary. Then she remembered her grandfather's demands again and grabbed Yeager's drink, downing what was left of it, too. She would need all the false courage she could get if she was going to actually talk about this. Especially with someone like Yeager.

Once the whiskey settled in her stomach—woo, that warmth was starting to feel really good—she did her best to gather her thoughts, even though they all suddenly wanted to go wandering off in different directions. And she did her best to explain.

"Okay, so, as rich as the Lindens have always been," she said, "they weren't particularly, um, fruitful. I'm the last of the line. My father was an only child, and he didn't remarry before his death. My grandfather's sister never married or had children. Their father had twin brothers, but they both died from influenza before they were even teenagers. The Linden family tree prior to that had been growing sparser and sparser with each ensuing generation, so I'm all that's left of them."

Her thoughts were starting to get a little fuzzy, so Hannah drew in another long breath and let it go. There. That was better. Kind of. Where was she? Besides about to have a panic attack? Oh, right. The dried-up Linden family tree.

"*Any*way…" She started again. "I guess my grandfather was sort of horrified by the idea that the world would no longer be graced with the Linden family presence—we were, I have learned, some of the best fat cats and exploiters of the proletariat out there—so he tied some strings to my inheritance."

"What kind of strings?" Yeager asked.

"Well, actually it's only one string," she told him.

"A string that's more like a rope. A rope that's tied into a noose."

He was starting to look confused. She felt his pain.

"Hannah, I think I can safely say that I have no idea what you're talking about."

She tried again. "My grandfather included a condition I'll have to meet before I can inherit the family fortune. He wanted to make sure that I, um, further the Linden line."

"Further the line?"

She nodded. Then nodded some more. And then some more. Why couldn't she stop nodding? And why did her head feel like it was beginning to disconnect from her body? With great effort, she stilled and tried to think of the most tactful way to tell Yeager how her grandfather had stipulated that, before she could inherit the piles and piles and *piles* of Linden moolah, she'd have to become a Linden baby factory.

Finally she decided on, "My grandfather has stipulated that, before I can inherit the piles and piles and *piles* of Linden moolah, I have to become a Linden baby factory."

Yeager's eyebrows shot up to nearly his hairline. "He wants you to procreate in order to inherit?"

Yeah, that would have been a much more tactful way to say it. Oh, well. "That's exactly what he wants," she said. "It's what he demands. In order to inherit the family fortune, I have to either already be a mother or on my way to becoming one."

"Can he do that?"

"Apparently so. The wording of his will was something along the lines of, if, when I was located after his death, I had a child or children, then no problem, here's more money than you could have ever imagined having, don't spend it all in one place."

"But you don't have a child or children," Yeager pointed out.

"Nope."

"So what happens in that case?"

"In that case, I have six months to get pregnant."

Yeager's eyebrows shot back up. "And what happens if you don't get pregnant in six months?"

"Then *aaaallllll* the Linden money will go to charity and I'll get a small severance package of fifty grand for my troubles, thanks so much for playing. Which, don't get me wrong, would be great, and I'd be most appreciative, but…"

"It's not billions."

"Right."

He opened his mouth to say something then closed it again. For another moment he studied her in silence. Then he said, "Well, that sucks."

"Yeah."

The bartender arrived with their drinks and Hannah immediately enjoyed a healthy swallow of hers.

"See, though," she said afterward, "the problem isn't with me having children. I've always planned on having kids someday. I want to have kids. I love kids. I wouldn't even mind being a single mother, as long as I had the time and money to make sure I could do it right. Which, of course, I would, with billions of dollars. But to only have six months to make the decision and put it into action?"

"Actually, you don't even have six months, if that's the deadline," Yeager said oh, so helpfully. "I mean, I'm no expert in baby-making—and thank God for that—but even I know it doesn't always happen the first time. Or the second. Or the third. You're going to need all the time you can get."

Hannah closed her eyes at the reminder of what she already knew. "Thanks a lot, Grandpa. There's nothing like the pressure of a ticking clock to bring a girl's egg delivery to a crawl."

She snapped her eyes open again. Oh, God, did she actually just say that out loud? When she heard Yeager chuckle, she realized she had. Then again, this whole situation was kind of comical. In an over-the-top, stranger-than-fiction, absolutely surreal kind of way.

She leaned forward and banged her head lightly against the table. In some part of her brain, she'd already realized that, if she wanted to inherit this money—and she very much wanted to inherit this money, since it would enable her to realize every dream she'd ever dreamed—she was going to have to make a decision fast and get herself in the family way as soon as possible.

But now that the rest of her brain was getting in on the action, she knew the prospects weren't looking great. She had nothing remotely resembling a boyfriend. She didn't even have a boy who was her friend. And only one attempt at in vitro was way beyond her financial means. She'd already checked that out, too.

Which left visits to a sperm bank, something she'd also been researching online tonight. If necessary, she could afford a few of those—barely—but if none of the efforts took, and she didn't conceive by the six-month deadline, she would have drained what little savings she had. And fifty grand, although an impressive sum, wasn't going to go far in New York City.

These things came with no guarantees, especially if her anxiety about everything really did turn her eggs into the same kind of shrinking violets she was.

What Hannah needed was something that could counter her potentially diminished fertility. A super-tricked-out, ultra-souped-up, hypermasculine testosterone machine that could fairly guarantee to knock her up. And where the hell was she supposed to find a guy like—

She sat back up and looked at Yeager—and the super-tricked-out, ultra-souped-up, hypermasculine body that housed him. Talk about testosterone overload. The guy flew MiG 29s over the Russian tundra for kicks. He'd climbed Mt. Everest. Twice. He served himself up as shark bait *on purpose*, for God's sake. The man probably produced enough testosterone for ten men. If he couldn't put a woman in the family way, nobody could.

Maybe it was the wine. Maybe it was the whiskey. Maybe it was the wine followed by the whiskey. Or maybe it was just the unmitigated terror of having finally discovered who she was and where she belonged and everything she could attain. It wasn't just the reclaiming of a life that had been denied her, but the promise of a happiness she never thought she would have—and realizing she could lose it all in the blink of an eye or the shrink of an egg.

And she heard herself saying, "So, Mr. Novak. Have you ever thought about donating your sperm to a good cause?"

Before he could stop himself, Yeager spat back into his glass a mouthful of whiskey, something that had never happened to him before. Then again, no one had ever asked him about his intentions for his sperm before, either, so he guessed he was entitled to this one social lapse.

As he wiped his chin with his napkin, he tried to tell himself he'd mishcard Hannah's question. "Excuse me?" he asked.

"Your sperm," she said, enunciating the word more clearly this time. "Have you ever thought about donating it?"

So much for having misheard her. "Uh…no," he said decisively.

She eyed him intently, her gaze never wavering from his. For a minute he thought she was going to drop it. Then she asked, "Well, would you think about it now?"

"No," he said even more decisively.

Still, she wouldn't let it go. "I mean, if you would consider it—donating it to me, I mean—I'd sign any kind of documents you want me to, to relieve you of all legal and financial obligations for any offspring that might, um, you know, spring off me. And I'd really, really, really, really, really…"

Her voice trailed off and her brows knitted, as if she'd lost track of what she was going to say. Then her expression cleared. A little.

"I'd really appreciate it," she finally finished. "A lot."

He was about to tell her she was delusional. But another look at her expression, especially her piercing silver-gray eyes—which were a lot less piercing at the moment than they usually were—told him what she really was was drunk. Hell, of course she was drunk.

No woman in her right mind would ask a man she barely knew to father her child.

He never should have encouraged her to drink whiskey on top of bad wine. Hannah wasn't the kind of woman who could drink a man under the table, the way women he dated generally were. The only reason she was asking him such a ridiculous question was because her judgment was clouded. He should just let her down gently, explain why what she was asking him to do was a terrible idea, then make sure she got home safely.

He should also, as inconspicuously as possible, scoot both of their drinks out of her reach. Which he did. She didn't even notice, because she was hanging so heavily on his reply.

"Hannah, I... I'm flattered," he finally said. "But it's not a good idea for me to do something like that."

She looked crestfallen. "Why not?"

"Because I'm not good father material."

At this, she looked aghast. "Are you kidding? You're incredible father material. You're smart and interesting and brave and funny and, holy cow, you're *gorgeous*."

He bit back a smile. "Thanks. But those aren't things that necessarily make a good father."

"Maybe not, but they make an *ex*cellent breeder."

He wasn't sure how to respond to that. Part of him was inordinately proud of the suggestion. Another part felt kind of tawdry. Strange—no woman had ever made him feel cheap before.

He pushed the thought away. "Well, I appreciate you considering me that way—" *I think* "—but it's still not a good idea."

"Why not?" she insisted.

There were so many reasons he could give her. There was just no way Yeager was going to be a father at all. Ever. Not in any universe, known or unknown. Not in her dreams or in his. Children were a constant reminder of a person's mortality—nothing marked the passage of time and the steady march to old age better than a child growing by leaps and bounds. The last thing he wanted to be reminded of was that, someday, he would be too old—or too dead—to enjoy life to its fullest. Not to mention that if he knew there was a kid in the world he was responsible for, it might make him more cautious, something that would put a major crimp in his extreme-adventure, thumbing-his-nose-at-death lifestyle. And there was nothing Yeager loved more than his lifestyle.

There was just no way he was going to become a father. Period. No—exclamation point. No—double exclamation point. Triple. Quadruple. Quintuple. Whatever the "uple" was that came after infinity. But, how to make that clear to Hannah?

"It's not a good idea," he said again, more gently this time.

For some reason his softer tone had a greater impact in conveying his opposition than his decisive one. She slumped back in her seat and covered her face with her hands the way she had earlier in her apartment.

He felt that weird tightening in his chest again. But what was he supposed to do? Hannah definitely had a major problem on her hands. But it was *her* problem, not his. She was a resourceful person. She'd figure out what she needed to do. Tomorrow, after the shock had worn off some, she could assess with

a clearer head. If she didn't have a boyfriend—and
since she'd just asked Yeager to be her sperm donor,
it was clear she didn't have a boyfriend—then maybe
some other friend with a, um, Y-chromosome would,
ah, rise to the occasion. To put it crassly. Or there had
to be dozens of sperm banks in New York she could
use. Women did that all the time. It was no big deal.

Even if, somehow, Hannah doing that felt like kind
of a big deal.

"Come on," he said, "let's get you home."

He withdrew his wallet and threw a handful of bills
down on the table. Then, as gently as he could, he
pulled her hands away from her face. There were tears
in her eyes again, but he did his best to make himself immune to them. He almost succeeded. Then he
led her through the bar and out onto the street. It was
fully dark now, but there were still plenty of pedestri-
ans. Muted music filtered through the open doors of
the bars they passed, and the air was heavy with the
aroma of summer in the city.

Hannah said not a word as they made their way
back to her apartment. Absently, she withdrew her
keys from her purse and promptly dropped them, so
Yeager scooped them up and did the honors. It wasn't
that hard. She only had three keys on her ring and he
lucked into the correct one right off the bat. One of the
others opened her front door at the top of the stairs.
The third was probably for Cathcart and Quinn.

His own key ring held a dozen keys that he needed
to get through a typical week. Hannah only needed
three for the whole of her life. But then Hannah lived
in one room with one window, too. He pushed her
front door open and stood back for her to enter. A

family fortune would certainly make her life better. *If* she was able to inherit.

She would be, he assured himself as he followed her into her apartment. She was a smart, capable person. She'd figure out how to make it happen. Eventually.

"Are you going to be okay?" he asked.

She headed to the love seat and folded herself onto it. "Yeah," she assured him in a way that wasn't at all reassuring.

"You sure?"

She nodded. "Don't forget your shirt."

Damn. Good thing she'd reminded him. He actually had forgotten about it. And it was the whole reason he'd come there tonight. He crossed to the rack to retrieve it.

He'd already paid her the extra hundred he'd promised, but he hadn't paid for the shirt itself. So he asked, "How much do I owe you?"

She cited a price significantly lower than he would have paid had she made the shirt under the auspices of her employer, presumably because of the different fabric. So he pulled out all the bills that remained in his wallet, which was actually more than what the shirt would have cost him at Cathcart and Quinn, and handed them to her.

"That's too much," she said, handing a few bills back.

He started to insist she take them anyway, but something in her voice made him stop. She sounded almost offended that he was giving her more than she asked for. So he returned the bills to his wallet. She stretched out on the love seat, tucked a throw pillow under her head and closed her eyes. He wondered where she slept at night and then noted that the wall behind the love seat looked like it housed a Murphy bed. Lying there the way she was now, she looked even smaller than she usually did, swallowed by the tiny room in which she lived.

Business concluded, it was time for Yeager to go. His flight to the other side of the world left in thirty-six hours. He had a million things to do between now and then. So why was he hesitant to leave Hannah's cramped little apartment that looked at the back of a building across the way?

"I'm not leaving for South Africa until the day after tomorrow," he said. "If you need to talk between now and then, just…"

Just what? he asked himself. If she needed to talk, she should just call him and he'd come right over? Hell, on days as busy as tomorrow was promising to be, he didn't even answer his phone, let alone take on any activities that weren't absolutely essential.

"If you need to talk, you can call me," he told her.

"That's okay," she replied softly, not opening her eyes. "I'll be fine. Thanks."

"You're sure?"

She nodded.

"Okay," he said. And still didn't leave.

She opened her eyes and he felt better when he saw that some of the life had returned to their silvery depths. "Bon voyage," she told him. "Try not to bleed on anything this time, okay?"

He grinned. "I'll see you when I get back."

Because he always saw her when he got back. He invariably had something that needed mending or cleaning. Funny, though, how that was the last thing he was thinking about at the moment. She really did have beautiful eyes.

"Be careful," she told him.

"I told you those are the last words—"

"Break a leg," she amended.

"Actually, that's probably not the best thing to say to an extreme adventurer, either."

"Have fun."

"That's more like it."

Even though he didn't want to, Yeager made himself cross to the front door and open it. Hannah lifted a hand in farewell then he stepped across the threshold and closed the door behind him. Leaving him to focus on all the other things he needed to do before he left town. Instead, as he made his way down Greenpoint Avenue toward the train, Yeager found himself wondering what two eye colors had to mix in a set of parents to make such an interesting combination of gray and silver in their child.

And he wondered if, when Hannah had her baby— and he was sure that somehow, some way, that would definitely happen—her child would have silver-gray eyes, too.

Four

Three weeks after Hannah asked Yeager if he would consider donating his sperm for a worthy cause, she still couldn't believe she'd done it. Every time she remembered that conversation, she was mortified all over again. And she promised herself she would never mix acceptably good Irish whiskey and bad wine products again.

Not that she would be doing that anyway, since she'd taken the plunge and contacted a Manhattan sperm bank to begin the process of artificial insemination. With any luck, she'd be pregnant soon, something that would put an end to imbibing for a while. It would put an end to a lot of things, actually. If—no, when—Hannah became pregnant, she would enter an entirely new phase of her life, one from which she would never be able to backpedal.

She'd spent the entire week following her first conversation with Gus Fiver sorting out her thoughts, weighing the pros and cons and ins and outs of her prospects. And in the end she hadn't been all that surprised to realize that, even more than inheriting a fortune, she wanted to get pregnant because she was ready to start a family—and probably had been for some time.

She'd wanted to be a part of a family her entire life, after all. She'd just always assumed she would need to have a life partner to achieve that. Not only because of the biological requirements, but because of the financial ones, as well. As much as Hannah wanted to have kids, there was no way she could afford to do that on her own with the life she led now. But if she'd had the financial means to raise a child, she would have started a family years ago.

If things worked out the way she now hoped—and they would work out…she hoped—she would not only have the funds to establish Joey & Kit as a driving force in the children's fashion business, she'd also be surrounded by family as she did it. Because if she inherited the funds to raise a child right, then no way was she stopping at one. Hannah wanted a houseful of children. Children who would never, ever, be told they had to leave.

Thank goodness for twenty-first-century medical progress and social mores, enabling women who wanted a family to start one, with or without a life partner.

Which was how Hannah came to be sitting on her love seat three weeks after her first meeting with Gus Fiver, laptop open, chamomile steeping, as she pe-

rused all the online forms and documents provided
by the sperm bank she would be using. And, wow,
there were a lot of them. In addition to the regis-
tration form, there was the Agreement to Purchase
Donor Sperm form, the Authorization to Release Frozen Sperm form, and the Authorization to Transport
Frozen Specimen form. Also, the Sperm Cryopreser-
vation form, the Sperm Storage form, and the Egg/
Embryo/Ovarian Tissue Storage form.

And then there was all the stuff she had to read and
sign off on. Articles about andrology and semen analy-
sis and sperm-washing techniques. More articles about
infectious disease screening and genetic testing and
karyotyping. It was all so scientific. So clinical. So…

She sighed. So sterile.

She'd had no idea how much time, work and ex-
pense went into baby-making when a person wasn't
doing it the old-fashioned way. Still, if this was what
it took, she would persevere. What was a little carpal
tunnel if it meant there was a family at the end of it?
Family was what she'd wanted all her life. Family and
security. Now both were within her reach. Of course
she would do whatever she had to do to win both.

Even if it did feel kind of cold, impersonal and dispassionate, which was the last way a child should be
conceived.

It didn't matter, she told herself again. All that mattered was that she would be able to start a family and
a business and support them both. All that mattered
was that she would never be separated from a family—her family—again. All that mattered was that her
children would be loved to distraction and grow up in
a secure, stable, permanent environment.

Okay. Pep talk over. Hannah had things to do. She had forms to fill out, a donor to choose, an egg to release… Her evening was full. Cracking her knuckles, she went to the Donor Search tab to fill in her specifications. Unfortunately, when she input her preferred traits of Caucasian, blue eyes, black hair, six-feet-plus and postgraduate degree—she knew Yeager had a master's in Geopolitics, not that she was trying to recreate Yeager or anything like that—the search resulted in *No donors available at this time.*

She tried again, leaving out the part about six-feet-plus. Still nothing. Okay, fine. The donor didn't *have* to have a master's degree. Again, no results. Ultimately the closest she could get to her original preferences was a five-foot-eleven, green-eyed brunet with a BA in philosophy.

She had nearly finished filling out the initial application form when her intercom buzzer rang. Since she wasn't expecting anyone for a pickup from Joey & Kit, she figured it was someone looking for her across-the-hall neighbor Jeannette, who seemed to know everyone in New York, though no one in New York could seem to remember that Jeannette was in unit A, not B.

Hannah went to press the buzzer, ready to tell whoever it was that they had the wrong apartment. Before she had the chance, she heard a familiar voice coming over the intercom. "Hannah? It's Yeager. Are you home?"

After a moment of stunned surprise she replied, "Yeah, come on up," and buzzed him in.

She knew a moment's chagrin when she remembered she was already in her pajamas. Or, at least, what passed for pajamas on her—cotton pants decorated with fat cartoon sheep and a purple T-shirt whose sleeves she'd cut off to use for trim on one of her Joey & Kit creations. But she didn't have time to change, so she opened her front door and stepped into the hallway at the top of the stairs to wait for Yeager.

He climbed them sluggishly, his left hand dragging along the rail beside him. She immediately knew something was wrong. That was hammered home when he finally reached the landing and looked at her. His blue eyes, usually so animated and laughing, were flat and empty. His hair was unkempt. He was unshaved. He looked as if he'd slept in his khaki trousers and white shirt, which he hadn't even tucked in.

"Hey," she said gently by way of a greeting when he topped the last step.

"Hi," he said softly.

She was about to ask him what he was doing there, but something about his demeanor prevented her. Whatever his reason for coming to her place tonight, he would get to it eventually. Right now, he didn't seem inclined to talk.

"Come on in."

She entered first, waiting for him to pass her before closing the door behind him. He strode slowly to the love seat and heavily sat, staring straight ahead but not seeming to see anything.

Hannah sat beside him, closing her laptop and moving it to the floor to make room. "I'm sorry. I'm all out of bad wine," she said, hoping to lighten his mood. "Would you like something else? Coffee? Tea?"

He shook his head, not even smiling at her attempt at levity. "No, that's okay. Thanks."

Finally he turned to look at her. She waited for him to start talking, but he remained silent. So she asked the same question he'd asked three weeks ago, the one that had led to her spilling her troubles out to him.

"Is everything okay?"

He was silent for another moment. Then he said, "Not really." His dark brows arrowed downward and he met her gaze levelly. "I need to ask you a question."

Heat pooled in her belly at the seriousness of his tone. Even so, she told him, "Sure."

There was another bout of silence as he studied her face with great interest. And then, out of nowhere, he asked, "Is that offer to father your child still on the table?"

Yeager really hadn't meant to just blurt out the question the way he had. He'd intended to preface it with all the other things he had to tell Hannah first, so it wouldn't come as such a shock to her when he finally asked it. Then again, after what had happened in Nunavut—and how he'd felt since—the realization that he wanted to ask the question still came as a shock to him. Even more of a shock was how much he hoped she wouldn't tell him he was too late.

It had just been a hell of a few weeks, that was all. The trip to South Africa had been everything he'd hoped for and then some, one rush of adrenaline after another, an intoxicating brew of exuberance and euphoria. But the trip to Nunavut, the one that was supposed to have been no business and all pleasure...

"Yeah, the offer is still good," Hannah said, interrupting his thoughts, something for which he was grateful. "I mean, if you're the one who's interested, it is."

"I am," he replied immediately.

Although he could see surprise reflected in her silvery eyes, her voice was level and matter-of-fact when she replied.

"O-o-okay."

Well, except for the nervous stammer.

She wanted to know why he'd changed his mind—the look in her eyes made that clear, too. He waited for her to ask, but the question that came out instead was, "Are you, um, sober at the moment?"

For the first time in weeks he smiled. Not a big smile, but it was good to know he could still manage one. "Stone cold," he assured her.

"Okay," she said again, more steadily this time. "Just wanted to make sure."

"You want to know what's brought about this one-eighty, don't you?"

She nodded. He sighed. In spite of having gone over it in his head a million times, he still didn't know how to explain it. Ultimately he decided to begin with what had reawakened the idea of fathering a child with Hannah in his head.

"I lost a good friend a couple of weeks ago," he said.

"And by 'lost,' you mean…"

"He died."

"Oh, Mr. Novak. I am so sorry."

"Yeager," he corrected her, since this wasn't going to be the kind of conversation a person had with someone who only knew him on a last name basis. "Call me Yeager, Hannah. What's your last name?" he added, since this wasn't the kind of conversation a person had with someone he only knew on a first-name basis, either.

Surprise flashed in her eyes again but she recovered quickly and told him. "Robinson."

Hannah Robinson. The name suited her. Sturdy, no-nonsense.

She tried again. "I'm so sorry for your loss... Yeager."

"Thanks," he replied, marveling at the curl of pleasure that wound through him when she spoke his name. Where had that come from?

He waited for her to ask what had happened, but she didn't. Hannah Robinson was evidently the sort of person who didn't pry. Normally it would have been something else he loved about her. But it would help to have her guide him through what he had to say.

"You remember how I told you I was going to Nunavut to climb Mount Thor with friends?" he began.

She nodded.

"While we were there, one of those friends... One of them had a... There was an accident," he finally said. "We're still not sure how it happened. I mean, I guess it doesn't matter how it happened. But he...he fell to his death."

"Oh, no..."

"One minute he was there and the next..."

"Oh, Yeager."

Something in his chest grew tight and cold, a sensation that was becoming too familiar. So he did what he always did when that feeling threatened to overwhelm him. He pushed it away.

And he made himself continue. "He and I met in

college. We started Ends of the Earth together. I had
the head for business and he was the tech whiz. After
we incorporated, I became President and CEO, and he
was VP and Chief Technology Officer." He grinned.
"He was the only VP Chief Officer of anything for the
first three years. He was a great guy. A good friend.
Full of life. I still can't believe he's—"

Yeager felt himself starting to blather, so he shut
himself up. Hannah seemed to understand, because
she scooted closer to him on the love seat. She extended a hand toward him, hesitated, then settled it
gently on his forearm. It was a careful, innocent touch,
but he felt it to the depths of his soul. Maybe because
it was the first comforting gesture someone had made
to him since he'd returned to the States.

Hell, even before then. No one ever tried to comfort Yeager. For one thing, he had the kind of life that
didn't invite comforting, since it included everything
a human being could ever want. For another thing,
he had barriers in place that kept people far enough
away from him to prevent them from doing things
like offer comfort. At least, he'd always thought he
had barriers like that in place. Hannah, however, evidently couldn't see them.

"Did he have a family?" she asked.

Yeager shook his head. But her question was the
perfect segue for where he needed to steer the conversation. Maybe she'd be able to guide him through
this, after all.

"His dad died when he was still a baby and he lost
his mom a couple of years ago. He didn't have any
brothers or sisters. It was another thing that bonded
us when we first met, since I was an only child, too."

"Sounds like you two were a couple of lone wolves who made your own pack," Hannah said.

She lightly squeezed his arm and smiled a gentle smile. That was nice of her. Not many people tried that with Yeager, either.

"Yeah," he said. "Back in the day, being lone wolves suited us. Hell, last month, being lone wolves suited us. He was no more the marrying kind than I am. But suddenly…" Yeager hesitated again. "Suddenly, being a lone wolf has its drawbacks. I mean, there's nothing left of him in the world now, you know? Nothing left behind after his death that might bring comfort to the people who knew him and cared about him in life."

"But you must have some wonderful memories," Hannah said.

"I do. But that's just it. All any of us who knew him has is memories. Memories that will gradually fade then die when we do. After that, there won't be anything left of him at all. No indication that he ever even existed. He was such a larger-than-life person. He lived with such passion and exhilaration. For there to be nothing left now that was a part of him… That just seems wrong, you know?"

Hannah loosened her hold on Yeager's arm but didn't let go. There was something in her eyes now that told him she wasn't following him. Then again, she wasn't the kind of person who wanted to make her mark on the world. She'd said as much herself that time she'd told him what a prudent life she led.

But Yeager did want to make his mark on the world. He wanted to be remembered—and remembered well—long after he was gone. He wanted to leave behind a legacy of some kind. He'd never been sure exactly what kind of legacy, but it had to be something that people could point to and say, "Yeager Novak was here." Something that would keep his name and his spirit alive for years. For generations. Hell, forever. He'd always assumed he had plenty of time to figure out the particulars. But now he understood, too well, that life was fleeting, and he'd damned well better make the best of it because it could be snatched away anytime, without any kind of warning.

"I guess I just always thought he was immortal." Yeager tried again to explain. "That he'd go on forever. I thought both of us would. But now I know the clock is ticking on the immortality thing, and I realize that, if I died tomorrow, the same thing would happen to me that's happened to him. There'd be nothing of me in the world anymore."

"You want to leave behind a legacy after you're gone," she said.

He nodded, stunned that she'd used the same word he'd been thinking. "Yeah."

"And you think a child would be a good legacy."

"Yes."

She hesitated a moment, her gaze never leaving his. "There are other kinds of legacies that would—"

"No, there aren't," he interrupted, fearful she might be reconsidering her offer. "Other legacies can deteriorate or fall apart or be stored somewhere and forgotten about. But a child to carry on after I'm gone will be a literal part of me. And then his—or her—children will be a literal part of me. And their children will be, too. And then their children, and their children, and their children…" He forced a smile then was surprised to realize it wasn't forced at all. "When you get right down to it, Hannah, having a kid to carry on after you're gone damned near makes you immortal."

She smiled back. And something in that smile made Yeager feel better than he'd felt in a very long time. "I guess you're right."

"So I started thinking about that," he continued. "And I started warming to the idea of fathering a child." He might as well admit the rest, since that part had been as surprising as anything else. "I started warming to the idea of fathering *your* child."

Because he'd thought about all the other women he knew who might be amenable to that—there were actually more than a few—and realized Hannah was the only one he could honestly imagine doing the job right.

"If," he concluded, "like I said, the offer is still open."

"It's still open," she assured him again, even more quickly than she had the first time.

"Then I'd like to humbly offer my chromosomes to your cause," he told her.

He hesitated again, not sure how she was going to feel about the next part since it included conditions. He was sure she'd already had enough of those placed on her by her grandfather.

So, being careful for the first time he could remember, he said tentatively, "I have three conditions for my offer, though."

She released his arm. She didn't drop it like a hot potato or anything, but she did withdraw her hand. She also scooted a little bit away from him on the love seat and straightened her spine—a couple more telling gestures.

"What conditions?" she asked a little warily.

He didn't blame her for her caution. But he wasn't going to go into this thing lightly any more than she was.

"Number one," he began, "I'd like you to name the child after the friend I lost."

Her posture eased some. "Okay."

"Don't you want to make sure he didn't have a weird name, or one that's gender-specific?"

She smiled again; a softer smile that changed her whole demeanor. For the first time Yeager was seeing that she wasn't all diligence and pragmatism. There was a lot of gentleness and warmth there, too.

"It doesn't matter," she said. "It's a sweet, loving gesture you want to make, Yeager, and I would never say no to a sweet, loving gesture. There are too few of them in the world."

"His name was Thomas Brennan," Yeager said. "Tommy Brennan. I figure Brennan would suit a boy or girl."

She let it settle in then nodded. "Brennan Novak. That's a good name."

"You don't have to give your baby my last name," Yeager said. Even though, for some reason, he suddenly kind of liked the idea.

"Yeah. I kinda think I do," she said with a smile that was cryptic this time. "He or she will be Brennan Robinson Novak. That's a very good name."

"That is a very good name, now that you mention it," he agreed, feeling strangely gentle and warm himself.

"Okay, so that's settled," she said. "What else?"

His second condition wasn't going to be quite as easy to put on the table as the first. Even so, there was no reason to gloss over it. He might be seeing a softer side of Hannah this evening, but she was still the most practical woman he knew—something he suddenly kind of loved about her—and he knew she would appreciate his forthrightness.

"The second condition is that you and I have to make your baby the old-fashioned way, not with vials and test tubes and syringes. Having an adventurer's legacy come about by syringe just isn't very... I don't know. Adventurous."

"I guess I can see that."

"I'd just prefer to ensure my legacy—and honor Tommy's name—by having this baby come about through natural means and during an epic adventure. That just feels right for some reason. So you and I are going to have to have sex, Hannah. And we're going to have do it in epic proportions on some kind of epic adventure. I hope your passport is up to date."

He was relieved when she didn't look like she wanted to negotiate on the matter. In fact, from her expression, it kind of looked as though she wanted to get started right away.

She blinked a few times then said, pretty amenably, "Okay. If we *have* to."

"We do."

She was silent for another moment. "What's the third condition?"

The third condition was the only one he feared Hannah wouldn't agree to, and it was the most important one. At least, to Yeager. But where her refusal of the first condition would have been disappointing, but not a deal-breaker, and her refusal of the second was never really in doubt—all modesty aside, since he didn't have any, and he'd seen the way she looked at him in the shop when he was half-dressed—his third condition was sacrosanct. If she didn't go along with this one, then he would pull out of the deal.

"I want to be…" he began then changed his mind. "No, I *have* to be a part of the child's life." He hurried to clarify before she could object. "I won't be an intrusion in your life, Hannah. Hell, I don't want to alter my life very much, either. I'll definitely keep adventuring. You'll call the shots when it comes to child rearing. But I want my son or daughter to know me, and I want to know my son or daughter. Yes, you will be the child's primary parent. But I want regular visitation, and when the child is old enough, I want to include him or her in my travels whenever and wherever possible."

He thought she would tell him she'd need time to think about that. Ask if she could she sleep on it and get back to him tomorrow. Instead she told him without hesitation, "No problem."

His surprise that she conceded so easily must have been obvious, because she quickly explained.

"Yeager, I'm the last person to deny a child the right to know his or her parents, since I never knew my own and would have loved nothing more than to have had them in my life. I mean, yeah, it sounds like my father left a lot to be desired as a human being, but I would have still liked the opportunity to know him. Or at least know who he was when I was growing up. Good or bad, a lot of our identity is linked to our parents and where they come from. I never had a chance to know that part of my identity. And I never will. Of course I won't deny you the chance to be a part of your child's life. And I won't deny your child a chance to be a part of your life."

Yeager didn't know what to say. So he only said, "Thanks."

For a long time they sat on the love seat, staring at each other, as if neither knew what to do next. Then again, speaking for himself, Yeager had no idea what to do next. Naturally, he knew the mechanics that went into making a baby. But he also knew there were other things to consider beyond the act itself. Things like timing and opportunity, for instance. He had a pretty hectic schedule mapped out for the next six months. Not that he thought they'd need the full six months to conceive, since they were both young and healthy, but he did need to make some arrangements for the foreseeable future where the workings of Hannah's biological clock were concerned. He'd be there for her whenever she needed him, but, as was the case with living life, he needed some kind of timetable to work with for generating life, too.

"So," he finally said, "what do we do next?"

She lifted her shoulders a little self-consciously then let them drop. When she did, her shirt shifted enough to drop over one shoulder, exposing the delectable skin of her collarbone and the faint upper curve of one breast. In addition to having beautiful eyes, Hannah had some beautiful skin. Even if some of it was, at the moment, clothed in cartoon sheep.

"Well, you said we have to have sex," she replied softly, "so I guess we have sex."

Yeager was still pondering the creaminess of her breast when her words finally registered and, bizarrely, he knew a moment's panic. "Wait, what? You mean right now?"

Why was he panicking? He should have been— and normally would have been—standing up to go to work on his fly by now. But he could tell he wasn't the only one responding uncharacteristically. Hannah was blushing furiously. And seeing that made something inside him that hadn't been warm in a very long time go absolutely incandescent. He'd never seen a woman blush before. Certainly not with the adeptness with which Hannah managed it. And where before a woman blushing would have been off-putting, with her, it was...not. On the contrary...

"No, not right now," she said. "I'm not... I won't be..." She expelled a restless sigh. "My body has a schedule for this kind of thing," she finally said.

"Yeah, I know that much," he assured her. "But I need to know if I should book an extra ticket for my trip to Argentina next week or if we'll be...you know... before then."

You know? he echoed incredulously to himself. Had he just referred to sex as *you know*? What, was he twelve years old? Hell, he hadn't even referred to sex as *you know* when he was twelve.

Hannah blushed again. And that hot place inside him grew hotter still. What was going on with his body tonight? She was the one who was supposed to be experiencing physiological changes, not him.

"It won't be before next week," she told him. "I've mapped out my cycle for the next three months as best I can, and although there's going to be some give-and-take there, because I'm not exactly regular, I can say that the middle of next week will be prime time. But

I can't go to Argentina with you," she added. "I don't have a passport."

She didn't have a passport? Yeager marveled. What kind of person didn't have a passport? Oh, right. A seamstress in Sunnyside, New York, who had to work two jobs to make ends meet.

"Okay, we can get around that," he said. "I can send one of my senior agents on the Argentina trip in my place and stay here in the States. But you need to get a passport ASAP in case this first time doesn't work. Like I said, I really think, to honor Tommy's spirit and make this a legacy in the truest sense, the child should be conceived on an epic adventure."

"And I think that's a gallant and honorable gesture," Hannah told him. "But you need to find something epic to do here in New York. Because I can't take time off from Cathcart and Quinn."

"We have to go someplace other than New York. There's no epic adventure to be had here."

She gaped at him. "Are you out of your mind? New York is nothing but epic adventures. Have you taken the subway lately? Walked through the Garment District after dark? Eaten one of those chimi-churro-changa-chiladas from Taco Taberna? Nobody gets out alive after ingesting one of those things."

"Look, I'll figure out something. But you're going to have to take some time off from work next week, because we're going on an adventure, and that means getting out of New York. Do you have a specific day for us to…?" He would *not* say *you know* again. "A specific day for us to, um…"

"Wednesday," she hurriedly replied.

"Great," he said. "That gives me a few days to figure out where we'll be going."

"But I can't afford to take any days off from work," she insisted. "I barely save anything from my paycheck as it is. Speaking of, I don't have enough money to travel anywhere, anyway. I'm not a billionaire's granddaughter yet. Not financially, at least. I need that paycheck, and I can't lose my job in case you and I aren't successful at—"

"Oh, we'll be successful," he stated in no uncertain terms.

"You'll excuse me if I'm not as full of bravado as you are," she said.

"It's not bravado I'm full of," he assured her.

She sighed. "Fine. You're a raging tower of testosterone."

"Damn straight."

For the first time that evening she looked a little defeated. "Maybe I'm not quite as confident about my own contribution to the venture as you are of yours."

He wanted to tell her she had nothing to worry about there. Hannah Robinson was more woman than most women he knew. Funny that he was only now noticing that. "If it will help, I could talk to your bosses for you. Tell them I need you to do some work for me out of town for a couple of days or something and that I'll make it worth their while."

She was shaking her head before he even finished. "I appreciate it, but I'll talk to Mr. Cathcart and Mr. Quinn myself. Maybe they'll let me work over next weekend to make up for being out a couple of days during the week."

"But you shouldn't have to—"

"It's okay, Yeager. I've made my own way in the world this long. I can take care of myself."

He remembered how she'd told him she'd grown up in New York's foster care system. She hadn't gone into detail about it. But anyone who'd gone through something like that and come out on the other side as happy and well-adjusted as Hannah seemed to be could definitely take care of herself. There was a part of Yeager, though, that really wanted to help her out. He was surprised at the depth of his disappointment that she wouldn't let him.

He pushed those thoughts away. For now. Something told him he'd be coming back to them in the not too distant future. "So I should make plans for us to be away for…how long?" he asked.

Her gaze deflected from his, moving to something over his right shoulder, and she bit her lip in the thoughtful way that had intrigued him so much at the shop that day. It had the same heated effect on him now, except stronger, making a part of him twitch that had never twitched in Hannah's presence before. Interesting.

"Well, according to my reading," she said, "There's a three-day window for me to be at peak, and it's best for you to wait twenty-four hours between attempts to, um, replenish your, uh, stock."

Yeah, right. Like that was going to be necessary for him. "Okay, so we'll need three nights." For some reason he suddenly kind of liked the idea of spending that much time with Hannah. "We can leave early Tuesday morning and come back Friday. Let me see what I can arrange."

"But—"

"Kauai is the obvious choice for domestic adventure," he decided immediately. "The twelve-hour flight to Hawaii makes that kind of difficult, under the circumstances, though."

"But, Yeager—"

"Maybe the Grand Canyon or Yosemite. Or there are a few places in Maine that would be closer. Hell, even the parts of the Adirondacks might work."

"But, Yeager, I—"

"Don't worry about it, Hannah. I'll take care of all the arrangements. It's what I do for a living."

"It's not the arrangements I'm worried about," she told him. "It's the expenses."

"Don't worry about that part, either. I'll cover those, too. I'll take care of everything."

At this, she looked angry. "The hell you will. This is my baby, too."

Why was she getting so mad? It was ridiculous to argue about this. Yeager had more money than he knew what to do with. He could afford this better than Hannah could, and he was the one who was insisting that the conception be an adventure in its own right.

Even so, he relented. "Fine. You can pay me back after you inherit."

"But what if I don't—"

"You will," he assured her. Because there was no question about that.

She thought about it for a moment and then finally nodded. "Keep an itemized list of what you spend for this," she said. "Every mile, every meal, every minute. And bill me for my half of everything after I conceive. I intend to pay my fair share."

Of course she did. Because even with the flashing

eyes, the erotic lip nibble and the luscious skin, she was still, at heart, practical, pragmatic Hannah.

"Agreed," he said. And then, before she could offer any more objections, he told her, "I'll pick you up here Tuesday morning and return you here Friday afternoon. Pack for being outdoors, for warm and cool weather both. Bring clothes and shoes for walking and climbing. And sunscreen. I'll take care of everything else."

Well, except for the second set of chromosomes that would be necessary for conceiving a child. He'd need Hannah for that. Weird. Yeager hadn't needed anyone for a long time. Since his parents' deaths, he'd come to rely only on himself and had figured it would be that way for the rest of his life. He'd gotten to a point where he almost resented relying on other people for something. But needing Hannah…and needing her for this… He wasn't resentful at all. Needing her felt oddly appropriate. Even natural.

Probably, it was some primal instinct making him react that way. Man's inherent need to carry on the species that dated back to the beginning of time. Yeah, that had to be it. Because, seriously, what else could it be?

Five

When Yeager had told Hannah to pack for walking and hiking, she figured that meant they would be walking and hiking. So what was she doing sitting in a four-seater inflatable raft, wrapped in a life jacket and staring down a river in North Carolina that would eventually become miles and miles of whitewater?

She looked at Yeager, who was still on the dock, double-checking whatever he needed to double-check before they hurtled headlong into self-destruction. Not that he seemed concerned about that. Then again, had it not been for the raging aquatic disaster ahead, she might have been just as Zen-like as he was, because North Carolina was the greenest, the bluest, the most gorgeous and peaceful place she'd ever seen.

The closest Hannah ever came to the Great Outdoors was Central Park, a place she didn't even have an opportunity to visit as often as she liked. And as beautiful as it was, it was often crowded with people and was still surrounded by towering skyscrapers and bumper-to-bumper buses and cabs, its sky crisscrossed with air traffic. This was her first taste of actual, honest-to-god nature. And it was incredible.

Evergreens sprouted along both sides of the river, a hundred feet high, stretching into a cloudless blue sky that was as clear and bright as a gemstone. And the air. Holy cow, it was amazing. Warm and languid, touched with just a hint of humidity and filled with the scent of pine and earth and something vaguely, but not unpleasantly, fishy. Although the water wasn't yet rough enough to be called whitewater, it whirled and gurgled past in a hurry, tugging at the raft and vying with the wind for whose rush of sound was most eloquent.

It was hard to believe fewer than six hours had passed since Yeager had picked her up in Queens in a shiny black car, complete with driver. They'd driven to a small airport in New Jersey where they'd boarded a private jet—because, of course, Ends of the Earth had its own private jet—then made the two-hour flight to Asheville, North Carolina. It was Hannah's first time on a plane and her first time outside New York.

They'd ventured into Asheville long enough to eat breakfast, and although the town was small by New York standards, it was still kind of urban and cosmopolitan, so it hadn't felt *too* different from Queens. Well, except for the great green bumps of mountain surrounding it. But as they'd driven away from the

city in the Land Rover that had been waiting for them
on arrival, everything—*everything*—had changed.

So much green. So much sky. So little traffic. So
few people. The farther they'd traveled, the more isolated they'd become, even on the highway. And once
they'd exited the interstate, they might as well have
been the only two people on the planet. Instinctively,
Hannah had rolled down her window and turned her
face to the breeze, closing her eyes to feel the warmth
of the sun on her face and inhaling great gulps of air
that was unlike anything she'd ever drawn into her
body.

Yeager had driven up, up, up into the mountains,
until they arrived at a secluded dock on the Chattanooga River, where they'd found the very raft in which
she now sat. It had been conjured, presumably, by
magic, along with its contents of life jackets, cooler
and oars, because there wasn't another soul in sight.
Just Hannah and Yeager and the primordial earth spir-
its she was sure still lived here.

She eyed the river again, battling a gnarl of fear
curling up in her belly. He'd told her he would go
easy on her this trip and make the outing low-risk,
since she was still new to the adventure thing. He'd
promised the danger to her would be nonexistent. She
wasn't sure she believed him. There was a bend in the
river not far ahead, and she was worried about what
lay around it. Where her idea of staying safe was not
climbing into a tiny inflatable raft on a raging river—
or, you know, *any* river—Yeager's idea of safety probably meant there was enough oxygen to last ten minutes
or fewer scorpions than usual.

Potato, potahto.

"Are you sure this is safe?" she asked him.

He was shrugging his dun-colored life jacket over a skintight black T-shirt and khaki cargo shorts. Well-worn hiking boots, a gimme cap emblazoned with the Ends of the Earth logo and aviator sunglasses completed the ensemble. He looked every inch the wealthy epic adventurer. She could almost smell the testosterone oozing from every pore. She gazed down at her attire—cut-offs and a T-shirt she'd received for making a donation to public radio. Coupled with her sneakers and retro cat-eye sunglasses, and with her unruly hair stuffed into an even more unruly ponytail, she was going to go out on a limb and say she did *not* look like a wealthy epic adventurer. Especially in a life jacket that was two sizes too big for her.

"Of course it's safe," he assured her. "The rapids here are only Class Two. They have camps for middle-schoolers along this stretch."

Hannah eyed the river again. Yeah, right, she thought. Feral middle schoolers, maybe. Who'd been raised by wolves. She couldn't imagine any halfway responsible parent allowing their child anywhere near a river like this. Maybe she'd been too hasty in agreeing to Yeager's condition that they leave New York. She'd rather their adventure involve eating sushi from a food truck or crossing Queens Boulevard against the light. Now *that* was living dangerously.

She tried to object again. "But—"

"It's fine, Hannah," Yeager interrupted before she had the chance, cinching the belt of his life jacket. Then he threw her one of those smiles that always kindled something inside her. "You'll have fun. I promise.

C'mon. Do you really think I'd endanger the mother of my child?"

The warmth inside her sparked hotter at that. The mother of Yeager Novak's child. That was what she would be for the rest of her life if everything went the way it was supposed to. What a weird concept. What they were planning would bond the two of them together forever. She'd realized that when she'd accepted his last condition, of course, but she was only now beginning to understand exactly what that meant. The man standing above her looking like some omnipotent earth god would be moving in and out of her life *forever*. Was she really, truly, sure she wanted that?

He hopped down into the raft with her, making it rock back and forth enough for her to seize the ropes on its sides nearest her. Her stomach pitched. If she had ever doubted that she wasn't the risk-taking type—and, actually, she had never doubted that at all—she was now certain. They hadn't even left the dock yet and she was already bracing for a spectacular death.

Yeager leaned across the raft, reaching past her to grab a strap she hadn't even noticed was there. He tugged it across her lap and latched it to another one on her other side, effectively securing her in place. She should have been grateful there were seat belts in the raft. Instead, all she could do was panic that now she would drown if the damned thing tipped over.

"What do I do if—"

"The raft won't invert," he interrupted, reading her mind. Again. "The way it's designed, that's impossible. Not to mention—in case I haven't already—this part of the river is in no way dangerous."

Ever the optimist—kind of—Hannah countered, "Nothing is impossible."

Yeager grinned again. "You getting hurt on this trip is."

"Then why do I have to wear a seat belt?" she asked. "If this is as safe as you say it is, then how come even you put on a life jacket?"

"I'm an adventurer, Hannah. I'm not stupid."

Before she could say anything more, he threw off the last line and the raft was moving away from the dock. Hannah opened her mouth to scream—it might be her last chance to draw breath, after all—then realized they were only going about five miles an hour. If that. The raft floated along the water serenely, hitting the occasional gentle bump before turning a bit and gliding forward again.

Yeager held one oar deftly in both hands, maneuvering it first on one side of the raft then the other, steering it simultaneously forward and toward the center of the river. As they gradually picked up speed, so did the wind, until it was buffeting her hair around her face in a way that was actually kind of pleasant. She shoved it aside and gripped the ropes on the sides of the raft, but more out of reflex than because she was actually frightened. They really weren't going very fast and their surroundings really were beautiful.

For long moments they simply glided along the river, the raft rising and falling gently with the swells, turning left, then right, as Yeager guided it forward. Eventually, though, the water did grow rough and the raft's movements became more irregular and jarring. But he handled it expertly, switching the oar from right to left to keep the raft on track. Water splashed up over the sides, wetting Hannah's feet and face, but instead of being alarmed, she thrilled at the sensation. Every new jolt of the raft or pull of the current sent a wave of adrenaline shooting through her, making her pulse dance and her heart race. By the time the water began to cascade over the side of the raft, soaking her legs and arms, her entire body was buzzing with sensations unlike any she had ever experienced before. She held on tighter, but instead of panic it was elation that bubbled up inside her.

And then the water grew very rough and the raft was pitching over rocks and shoals, spinning and leaping and crashing down again. Water splashed fully over both sides of the craft, dowsing both of them. But instead of fearful, Hannah felt joyful. Especially when she saw how Yeager reacted to what must have been a minor feat of derring-do for him. He was grinning in a way she'd never seen him grin before, with a mix of ecstasy and exhilaration and exuberance, as if being right here, in this moment, was the absolute pinnacle of experience—and she was a part of it. Such pure, unadulterated happiness was contagious, and she was swept up into it as fiercely as he was, until she was whooping with laughter.

The journey continued for miles; the river, by turns, as turbulent as a whirlpool and as smooth as glass. During the smooth times, Hannah marveled at the scenery and the wildlife—She saw her first deer! Three of them! Right there on the riverbank!—and asked Yeager what kind of bird that was flying above them and how big pine trees could grow, and did it snow here in the winter. During the turbulent times, he schooled her in how to use her oar and laughed with her whenever she turned the raft backward—which was often.

By the time they reached the end of the course two hours after starting it, Hannah felt more alive than she'd ever felt in her life. As Yeager steered them toward a dock much like the one from which they'd departed, she was keenly disappointed that the ride was coming to an end. So when he slung a rope over a wooden post to secure the raft and turned to look at her to gauge her reaction, she responded in the only way she knew how.

"Can we do it again?" she asked eagerly.

Yeager could hardly believe that the Hannah at the end of their ride was the same one who'd climbed so carefully into the raft upriver. He'd never seen her smile like she was now, with such spirit and wonderment and…something else, something he wasn't sure he could identify, something there probably wasn't even a word for because it was so uniquely Hannah. She just looked more animated than he'd ever seen her, more carefree, more full of life.

Happy. She just looked happy. And he thought it odd that, as many times as he'd seen her and had conversations with her, and she'd seemed contented enough, she'd never really looked happy until now.

Then her question finally registered and he shook the other thoughts out of his brain. Or, at least, tried to. There was something about Hannah's newly found happiness that wouldn't quite leave him.

"We can't go again," he told her. "At least, not from here. We have to hike back upriver first."

She looked a little dejected at that.

"But we can go again tomorrow, if you want to."

"I want to," she immediately replied. Her smile brightened again and something inside Yeager grew brighter, too.

He stood, extending a hand to her. "Come on," he said. "We can do a little exploring before lunch."

She unhooked her safety belt and settled her hand in his, and he pulled her to standing, too. When he did, the raft rolled toward the dock a bit, pitching Hannah forward, into him. Instinctively he settled his hands on her hips as hers splayed open over his chest. Her touch was gentle, but he felt it to the depths of his soul. His hands tightened on her hips and, not sure why he did it, he dipped his head to kiss her. She gasped when he did, and he took advantage of her reaction to deepen the kiss, tasting her leisurely, taking his time to enjoy it. And he did enjoy it. A lot.

Hannah seemed to enjoy it, too, because, without missing a beat, she kissed him back, curling her fingers into the fabric of his shirt to pull him closer. He felt her heart beating hard against his torso, heard the catch of her breath, inhaled the earthy scent of her, becoming more intoxicated by her with each passing second.

He would have taken her right there, right then, shedding their clothes in the raft and settling her naked in his lap astride him. He was already envisioning just how erotic the union would be, but she ended the kiss—with clear reluctance—and pushed herself away from him as far as she could in the small raft. Her face was flushed and her breathing came in rough, irregular gasps. What was weird was that Yeager's breathing was ragged and uneven, too. It was just a kiss, he reminded himself. No big deal. He'd kissed dozens of women. Kisses were nothing but a prelude. There was no reason for him to feel so breathless. So weightless. So senseless.

"We, um, we should probably wait until tonight," she said softly. "Just to keep things as close to Wednesday as possible."

Right. They were on a schedule here. Yeager understood schedules. His entire life was scheduled. Of course they should wait until tonight to ensure optimum results. Even if he suddenly didn't want to wait. His *body* didn't want to wait, he hastily corrected himself. What had just happened between him and Hannah was just a chemical reaction to a physical stimulus. He himself could wait just fine. It was only sex. No problem waiting until tonight.

Even if tonight seemed way too far away.

"You, uh, said something about exploring?" she asked tentatively, her breathing still a little frayed.

Yeager nodded. "Right. Then we can hike farther downstream to where we'll be camping."

"Which is how far?"

"About three miles."

Her mouth dropped open at that. "We're going to hike three miles?"

"Piece a cake," he told her. "It'll be a walk in the park."

She shook her head. "I've walked in the park lots of times. *That's* a walk in the park. Three miles over rugged terrain is—"

"A great way to build up an appetite," he finished

for her. He'd let her decide for herself what kind of appetite he was talking about.

Evidently she knew exactly what kind he meant, because color suffused her face again. He'd never seen a woman with such a propensity for blushing. It should have been a turnoff. Yeager liked women who were as audacious and intrepid as he was. But something about Hannah's seeming innocence tugged at a part of him where he wasn't used to feeling things.

Before she could object again, he cinched her waist tighter and lifted her easily up onto the dock, setting her down on her ass as she sputtered in surprise. Then he unfastened the cooler from its mooring in the raft and raised it to the dock, too, placing it beside her. After hoisting himself up effortlessly, he stood and extended a hand to her as he had before. This time, though, he was more careful when he pulled her up alongside him.

Careful, he echoed to himself. He was actually being careful with Hannah. He was never careful with anyone. Anything. Careful was the last thing he ever wanted to be. But then, Hannah was a careful person, and what the two of them were trying to do—create a life together—took care. That was all there was to his reaction. It wasn't like he'd actually begun to, well, *care* for her. No more than he had before, anyway.

The dock was attached to a clearing on the riverbank that disappeared into the forest a few hundred feet away. Yeager was familiar with the area and knew it was rife with common fossils and less common arrowheads, so they shed their shoes to dry in a patch of sunshine and spent some time looking around. When he pointed out a handful of brachiopods and trilobites to Hanna, he might as well have been pouring diamonds into her lap, so delighted was her reaction. He reminded himself again that, in spite of her rocky upbringing, she'd led a fairly sheltered life. It was hard to fathom the contradiction. Hannah just seemed like such an anomaly sometimes.

By the time they finished lunch, their clothes and shoes were dry. Yeager packed the remnants of their meal in the cooler and secured it back in the moored raft, then rejoined Hannah on the dock.

"Don't we need to take those with us?" she asked.

He shook his head. "Someone will be coming for them later."

"The same someone who dropped them off at the first dock?"

Now he nodded. "Ends of the Earth contracts with other travel professionals all over the world. I found one in Raleigh that got everything set up for us here, from where we started in the raft to where we'll be camping. They'll pick up the Land Rover, too, and deliver it to the campsite so we'll have it if we need it."

She eyed him thoughtfully. "You know, when you said we'd be having an epic adventure, I had a picture of us machete-ing our way through the Everglades while dodging alligators or hang gliding across the Grand Canyon. I wasn't planning on coolers full of lobster and San Pellegrino and Land Rovers at our disposal."

Yeager smiled. "Yeah, well, normally machete-ing among alligators *is* the kind of trip Ends of the Earth puts together. The hang gliding is more likely to happen over an active volcano."

She started to laugh, then realized he was serious.

"Anyway, I'm having to break you in gently," he pointed out. Not to mention he'd been trying to do something a little romantic, which rarely included machetes and often included lobster.

"I didn't say you had to break me in gently," she told him. "I just said I couldn't travel outside the US this first time."

"Fine. Next time, we can go someplace where there's a political coup happening during a tsunami."

"If there is a next time," she said.

Right. Because if her calculations were correct, and everything went according to plan, this would be the only time the two of them did this. For some reason the realization didn't sit well with Yeager. In spite of what he'd just said about political coups and tsunamis—as fun as that would have been—he already had their next time planned, and it would be a shame to have spent an entire week working on it for nothing. Hannah was going to love canyoneering in Morocco. Which reminded him...

"Just in case, did you apply for your passport?"

"Yes."

"And did you—"

"Yes, I paid the extra fee for expediting it," she answered before he could even put voice to the question. "I should have it in a couple of weeks."

"Good."

"If I need it."

Why was she harping on *if*? Was it such a hardship for her, sexing it up with him? Hell, she'd enjoyed that kiss as much as he had.

He decided to change the subject. "Ready to hike? We're burning daylight here."

He told himself he did not sound impatient. There were still a lot of hours to fill before bedtime and the hike to their campsite would only use up a few. But that was okay. Just because Hannah wanted to wait until nightfall for the main event didn't mean they couldn't enjoy themselves before they enjoyed each other.

Six

It was dusk by the time Hannah and Yeager arrived at their campsite, made even duskier by the trees that towered overhead, obscuring what little was left of the sunlight. She was more than ready to call it a day. A walk in the park. Ha! Maybe if it was Yellowstone Park and the walk involved all eight billion acres of it. She'd figured hiking and walking were two different things, but she'd assumed those differences lay mostly in hiking being more vertical and walking being more horizontal. She now knew that hiking was actually different from walking in that it was like dousing your legs and feet in gasoline and then setting them on fire.

When they finally reached their destination, however, her mood improved considerably. Because, as the hiking path emptied into a clearing surrounded by evergreens that disappeared into a purpling sky, she saw a campsite setup that was more reminiscent of a vintage Hollywood epic than a modern epic adventure.

A round, canvas tent stood in the center, its flaps thrown back to reveal a platform bed with a pile of pillows. There was a copper chandelier with a dozen candles flickering in its sconces—the kind that worked on batteries, not the kind that could, left unattended, leave the Smoky Mountains in ashes—and a few others twinkled on a bedside table. To the right of the tent was a copper fire pit ready for lighting and a love seat laden with more pillows. On the other side was a table and chairs—set with fine china and crystal—and an oversize copper ice chest brimming with bottles and other containers. Across it all zigzagged strings of tiny white lights that glimmered like stars. Hannah had never seen a sight more dazzling.

"You didn't tell me we'd be glamping," she said with much delight.

"Glamping?" Yeager echoed dubiously.

When she turned to look at him, she could see he wasn't as charmed by the tableau as she was. In fact, the expression on his face probably would have been the same if he were staring at the stuff in the back of the butcher shop that never made it into the case.

"Yeah, glamping," she repeated. "Part glamour, part camping. I saw it on *Project Runway*."

"There is no glamour in camping," he stated decisively. "I mean, I didn't expect us to kill and clean our own dinner or sleep out in the open, but this…" He shook his head. "Adventure travel should never include throw pillows and wineglasses. I knew it was a bad idea to hire a company called Vampin' 'n' Campin'. There are way too many apostrophes in that name for it to be taken seriously. Unfortunately they were the only ones available on short notice."

"Well, I'm glad you did," she told him. "This is wonderful."

He made his way toward the site. Still sounding disgusted, he muttered, "The privy is probably copper-plated, too."

"There, see? We will, too, be roughing it," she said. "I've never spent a day of my life without plumbing or electricity." Although a couple of her foster homes had come close. She kept that to herself. No need to spoil the beauty of the moment. "And there's no tech out here. Talk about primitive conditions."

He made his way to the ice chest, withdrew a bottle to inspect its label, then grinned. "I guess this glamping thing has its upside. We won't have to drink our *Clos du Mesnil* warm. Now *that* would be roughing it."

Hannah joined him. "That ice isn't going to last three days," she said.

"No, but the solar-powered fridge and freezer they set up behind the tent will."

"Ah. Is the privy solar-powered, too?" she asked hopefully.

"It is. And compostable."

"And I think that's all I want to know about the plumbing. Unless," she added even more hopefully, "you also arranged for a solar-powered shower."

He chuckled. "It's not solar-powered, but there is a shower."

Considering the amount of sweating she'd done in the last few hours, Hannah definitely wanted to hear about that. "Okay, you can tell me about the shower."

"Actually, I can do better than that. I can show it to you."

She sighed. "That would be wonderful. I'd love to get clean before dinner."

"There should be some towels in the tent," he said. "Our bags should be in there, too. Grab whatever else you need."

When she entered the tent, she did, indeed, find their overnight bags, so she opened hers to collect some clean underwear, a red tank top and striped pajama bottoms, all of which would doubtless be a far cry from what Yeager's usual girlfriends wore for a night with him. But it was the best she could do on short notice and short funds. Not that she was Yeager's girlfriend, so she couldn't be held to that standard, anyway. Even so, she was now wishing she'd had the foresight to cough up a few bucks for something that at least hinted at seduction. She tried to remind herself that she and Yeager weren't here for romance. But that didn't quite feel right, either.

She found the towels on a folding wooden chair, underneath a bar of soap and bottle of shampoo, both environmentally friendly. Hannah didn't care what Yeager thought about Vampin' 'n' Campin'. As far as she—a lover of the Great Indoors—was concerned, they did camping just fine.

She emerged from the tent to find him waiting for her near a break in the trees, looking almost otherworldly in the growing darkness. His black hair was silvered by the moonlight, his biceps strained against his T-shirt, and a shadow fell across his face, imbuing him with just enough of the sinister to send a ribbon of apprehension shimmying through her.

Was she really going to go through with this to-night? Could she? Even considering everything that was at stake, she was beginning to have her doubts. Yeager was just so…so… She battled a wave of apprehension. So intimidating. He was almost literally twice the man of any guy she'd ever dated. She normally went for guys who were born to be mild. The ones who carried a novel by some obscure author in their messenger bags and whose clothes were always adorably rumpled. Guys who spent the weekend working on their bicycles and whose dinner orders never included substitutions. Safe guys. Predictable guys. Uncomplicated guys. How was she going to react to guys like that after a few nights with Yeager? Especially if he would be popping in and out of her life *forever* once those nights were concluded?

Maybe she should go the sperm bank route. If she changed her mind right now and asked Yeager to take her back to New York tonight, she might still have time to get pregnant this month. Her baby's father would be anonymous and in no way a part of their lives. Then, someday, she'd meet a safe, predictable, uncomplicated guy she could have more children with. She and Safe Guy could spend the rest of their days raising their family among *Consumer Reports*—endorsed products in their picket-fenced, asbestos-and lead-free home that was landscaped with noninvasive, allergen-free plants, while they protected their children from perils like sugary breakfast cereal, dog breeds weighing more than seven pounds and team sports.

Yeah. That sounded like a *great* life. She couldn't

wait to get started on that. Then she'd never have to suffer the heart-racing dangers of Yeager again.

"Did you forget something?" he asked when she made no move to join him.

Yeah. Her sense of self-preservation. But that was way too big to pack in an overnight bag.

"No, I think I'm ready."

Overstatement of the century.

He tilted his head toward the opening in the trees, so she forced her feet to move forward until she came to a halt beside him. Up close, he looked a little less sinister and a lot more seductive, so she decided— *oh, all right*—she could go through with having sex with him if she *had* to. She didn't want to waste a perfectly good ovulation, after all. At least, she hoped it was perfect.

Yeager eyed her thoughtfully for a few seconds and Hannah was torn between wishing she knew what he was thinking and hoping she never found out.

All he said, though, was, "It's this way." Then he preceded her down the path.

Oh, joy. More hiking.

The trees swallowed them up again, but Hannah didn't mind so much this time. With the sun down, the night was growing cooler and a gentle breeze rocked the leaves in the trees. Soft bursts of light erupted here and there, and it took her a moment to realize they were fireflies. She'd never seen even one, let alone the dozens that suddenly surrounded them, and she couldn't help the laughter that rippled from inside her.

"What's so funny?" Yeager asked, glancing over his shoulder.

"Fireflies," she said. "I've never seen them in person."

He stopped abruptly, turning to look at her. "You're joking."

She halted, too, since his big body blocked the path. "No, I'm not. I told you—I've never been out of New York."

"There are fireflies in New York," he said.

"Not in the neighborhoods where I've lived."

"You've never been outside the *City* of New York?" he asked incredulously. "I thought you meant the state."

She shook her head. "No, I meant the five boroughs."

He studied her in silence for a moment, but his face was in shadow again, so she couldn't tell what he was thinking. Finally he said, "What, one of the families you lived with couldn't even take you to Jones Beach for the day?"

In response Hannah only shrugged. Of course none of the families she'd lived with took her to Jones Beach. For most of them, she'd just been a way to add some money to their bank accounts. And for the few who had genuinely cared for the children they took in, all the money they received went to feed and clothe those children. There had never been anything left for luxuries like day trips.

"But you've seen the ocean, right?" Yeager asked. "Surely you hit Coney Island or Rockaway Beach at some point when you were a teenager."

"I didn't, actually," she confessed. "My friends and I preferred prowling Manhattan whenever we had a little free time. And, truth be told, on those rare occasions I found myself with a little extra money to do stuff, I spent it on fabric instead."

He said nothing for another moment. "You've never seen the ocean?"

"No. I haven't. Or, if I did before I lost my mom, I don't remember it."

"How is that possible?"

Again she shrugged. Even as an adult freed from the confines of the foster care system, Hannah had never felt the need or desire to explore beyond the city. She just wasn't one to stray outside her comfort zone, even for small adventures. She liked knowing where she was and how to navigate her surroundings. The thought of taking a day trip someplace had just never appealed to her.

Yet here she was, hundreds of miles away from home—and for more than just a day—and she didn't feel unsettled at all. She hadn't even been nervous about boarding a plane or leaving New York. On the contrary, she'd been excited before they'd left, and she'd had a lot of fun today. Enough to make her think she should have tried something like this a long time ago.

But it was only because Yeager was with her, she told herself. He was familiar enough to her to offset the strangeness of this trip. She couldn't do this all the time, especially not alone. And, hey, she didn't *want* to do this all the time. Once she was settled back in New York, she'd return to being her usual complacent self again. She was sure of it.

Another sound suddenly joined the rustle of leaves overhead, drawing her attention away from her thoughts and back to the night surrounding them.

Because even though this was her first time in the Great Outdoors, she recognized the sound. A waterfall. The shower Yeager had promised her was a waterfall. She'd assumed they were finished with adventures for the day—well, except for the greatest adventure of all that was still looming—yet here he was, presenting her with another. His life really was one exploit after another.

They exited the trees onto the banks of the river they'd navigated earlier, though here, it wasn't wide and rough with rapids. Here, it was narrow and flowed like silk. The waterfall was only about eight feet high, spilling into the river with a gentle percussion that sent ripples gliding outward. The sun had well and truly set by now, and the moon hung overhead like a bright silver dollar, surrounded by hundreds of glittering stars. Hannah had never seen the moon so bright and had never seen more than a few stars in the sky above her. She made her way carefully toward where Yeager had stopped on the edge of a rock, but she was so busy staring at the sky, she nearly walked right past him and into the river. He stopped her with a gentle hand to her shoulder, turning her until she faced him.

"Easy there, Sacagawea," he said. "The trail you're about to blaze could be your last."

She laughed, still looking at the sky. "I can't help it. It's so beautiful here."

"It's just your run-of-the-mill woods, Hannah."

Now she looked at Yeager. "It's not run-of-the-mill for me."

As she toed off her sneakers, she thought about how she must seem like an absolute freak to him. Her world was so tiny in comparison to his, her life experience virtually nonexistent. He lived for risk and danger, two things she wanted no part of. They couldn't be more different or less suited to each other. But that was good, right? It meant there was no chance of any messy emotional stuff getting in the way of their, ah, enterprise.

For a moment they only gazed at each other in silence. Well, except for the chirping of the crickets and the whisper of the wind and the shuffle of the waterfall. And, okay, the beating of Hannah's heart, which seemed to be loudest of all.

Yeager, however, seemed not to notice any of it, because he reached behind him and grabbed a handful of his T-shirt, pulling it over his head. "Come on," he said. "Last one in's a rotten egg."

Hannah scarcely heard what he said, because she was too busy staring at a half-naked Yeager. And even though she'd seen him half-naked a dozen times before, she'd never seen him as he was now—gilded by starlight and moonbeams and fireflies, looking like a creature of the night, if not the night itself. And then he was going to work on his fly, and she remembered he hadn't brought any clothes to change into after their swim—or even *for* their swim. And then she realized his half-naked state was about to become a full-naked state. And then... And then...

And then she was jumping into the river fully clothed, turning her back on him to feign much interest in the waterfall that was suddenly way more interesting than it should be, even for someone who'd never seen a waterfall in person before. The river was shallow enough here that she could stand with her head out of the water—just barely—but that didn't keep her knees from shaking. Though she was pretty sure that had nothing to do with the chill of the water. Especially since the water was surprisingly warm.

When she heard a splash behind her, she knew Yeager had joined her. And when she turned to see hiking boots and a pile of garments on the rock where he had been, she knew he was naked. She also knew that by the way he was grinning at her when he broke the surface of the water, jerking his head to sling back his wet hair.

And by his tone of voice when he said, "Most people undress before they bathe."

She bit back a strangled sound. "I just didn't want to be a rotten egg."

"Right."

"And I figured it might be a good idea to rinse out my clothes."

"Uh-huh."

"I mean, they did get pretty dirty today."

He swam toward her, quickly enough that Hannah, growing more panicky by the moment, didn't have a chance to swim away before he reached her.

"Well, then, let me help you," he said.

She felt his hands at the hem of her T-shirt and, before she could stop him, he was pushing it up over her torso. He took his time, though, opening his palms over her naked skin under the wet fabric, sliding his hands up over her waist and rib cage, halting just below her bra, the L of his index finger and thumb brushing the lower curves of her breasts. Her heart hammered even harder in her chest and heat pooled deep in her belly. His expression remained teasing, though, so she knew he was feeling none of the tumult she did.

"Lift your arms," he said softly.

Automatically she did and he tugged her shirt over her head, tossing it behind him toward the rock, where it landed perfectly alongside his own.

"Now the shorts," he said, moving his hand to the button at her waist.

Deftly, he undid it and the zipper, then tucked his hands inside the garment, settling one on each of her hips. For a moment he only held her in place, the warmth of his palms permeating the cotton of her panties, a sensation that made the heat in her belly spiral outward, kindling fires in every part of her. Then he gripped her shorts and tugged them down, lifting first one leg then the other, until that piece of clothing, too, had been stripped from her and tossed to the riverbank.

Although she was still in her bra and panties, the equivalent of a bathing suit, the sensations coursing through her made Hannah feel like she was as naked as Yeager was. It didn't help that his teasing expression had gradually grown into something much more heated. And when he began to dip his head toward hers...

She quickly turned around and began swimming toward the waterfall with all her might. But she was no match for Yeager, who caught up to her immediately.

"There," he said as he drew up alongside her. "After that swim, everything you have on should be totally clean. Time to take it off."

Well, golly gee whiz. Nothing like getting right to it. Talk about a wham-bam-thank-you-ma'am.

"Are you always this pragmatic when it comes to sex?" she asked.

"I'm never pragmatic when it comes to sex," he assured her. "But I've never had sex on a timetable. It's always a lot more spontaneous than this. And the reason for it is never baby-making. It's always merry-making."

"You don't think sex for making a baby can be fun?" she asked. "You just want to get this thing over with as quickly and cleanly as possible? Am I that unappealing to you?"

His response was to pull her close and cover her mouth with his, kissing her in a way that assured her he found her very appealing indeed, that he didn't intend for this thing to be in any way quick—never mind clean—and that he planned to have quite a lot of fun making a baby with her. By the time he pulled away from her, they were both breathing raggedly.

"Well, okay, then," Hannah managed to say.

But she still didn't take off her underwear. She just wasn't ready yet. It was a nice night. She was in a beautiful place with a beautiful man. She didn't feel the need to rush. So she turned onto her back to float on the water and look at the night sky. She heard Yeager emit a sound of reluctant resignation and then turn onto his back, too.

"Hey, that's the Big Dipper," she said, pointing toward a group of stars to the left of the moon. It kept her from looking at a naked Yeager floating on his back, gilded in moonlight.

"It is," he told her. "And you can follow the arc—"

"Follow the arc to Arcturus," she chorused with then finished for him. "I remember that from ninth-grade science. Isn't that weird? I don't think I remember anything else from that class. I'm not sure I even remember much from the rest of ninth grade. I moved around a lot in high school. Even more than when I was in elementary school."

He paddled closer to Hannah, so she paddled away. She really wasn't ready yet for a naked Yeager.

He growled restlessly, clearly frustrated that she was going to draw this out as long as she could. Despite that, he asked, "Where did you live when you were in ninth grade?"

"For the first three months, I was in Mott Haven," she told him. "Then they moved me to Vinegar Hill. After school broke for summer vacation, I went to Bed-Stuy for a while."

He was silent for a moment. Then softly he said, "You lived in some pretty rough neighborhoods."

"Yeah, well, you don't find too many people taking in foster kids on the Upper East Side. Go figure."

He was silent again.

"It wasn't all bad, Yeager," she told him. "I lived with a handful of families who were truly good people, and I still have friends I made while I was in the system. You only hear the horror stories about foster care in the news. But a lot of kids ended up way better off there than they were with their birth families."

"Did you ever wonder about your real family?"

"Sure. There were times when I would fantasize that someone must have made a mistake somewhere, and I really did have a mom and dad out there somewhere. Like I was mistakenly switched with another baby at the hospital. Or the woman who died that they thought was my mom was actually misidentified and my mom was still out there in the world somewhere, looking for me." She sighed. "But I knew it wasn't true. I knew I was right where I was supposed to be. It's just a weird irony that I actually wasn't."

"Sounds like little-kid Hannah was as down-to-earth as grown-up Hannah," Yeager said.

She didn't know whether to take that as a compliment or not. From his tone of voice, he seemed to respect down-to-earth people. On the other hand, he didn't spend much time in one place on the earth himself.

"How about you?" she asked, still gazing up at the sky. "Where were you in ninth grade?"

He hesitated for a telling moment. Then he said, so quietly that Hannah almost didn't hear him, "Peoria, Illinois."

His response surprised her enough that she forgot about his nakedness and glanced over at him. Fortunately—or not—it was dark enough now that the water had turned inky, hiding most of him. Of all the places she could have imagined Yeager being from, Peoria, Illinois, would never have made the cut.

"You actually grew up in the city that's an icon of Midwestern conservatism?"

"I actually did."

It occurred to her then how little she really knew of Yeager. Sure, he'd revealed snippets of his life from time to time during their conversations at Cathcart and Quinn, but she knew nothing about what had made him Yeager Novak, global adventurer. And suddenly, for some reason, she wanted to know that very badly.

"Did you live your whole life there?" she asked.

"I did until I was eighteen."

"What brought you to New York?"

"A full-ride hockey scholarship to Clarkson University in Potsdam."

"You play hockey?"

"I used to."

"What do your mom and dad do for a living?"

He sighed in a way that made her think he really, really, *really* didn't want to talk about this. Despite that, he replied, "My mom managed a bookstore and my dad was an accountant."

The son of a bookstore manager and an accountant had grown up to be one of the world's greatest risk-takers? How the hell had that happened?

"So how did you wind up—"

Before she could finish her question, he righted himself in the water and strode toward her. Hannah straightened, too. She thought he just wanted to get closer to continue their conversation. Instead, the moment he was within reaching distance, he wrapped an arm around her waist, pulled her toward him until she was flush against him and kissed her.

As he did, he reached behind her to unfasten her bra, slipping it over her arms and releasing it into the flow of the river. Hannah started to object at the loss of the garment, but Yeager moved his hands to her breasts, covering both with sure fingers, and anything she might have said got caught in her throat. He brushed the pad of one thumb over her sensitive nipple. When she gasped, he took advantage of her reaction to taste her more deeply. She opened her mouth wider to accommodate him, splaying one hand wide over the ropes of muscle on his torso, threading the fingers of the other through his silky, wet hair.

He growled something unintelligible against her mouth, then dragged soft, butterfly kisses along her jaw, her neck and her shoulder. The hand at her waist moved to her back, skimming until he gripped the wet cotton of her panties and pulled them down. Then he was caressing her naked bottom, curving his fingers over the swells of her soft flesh, guiding his fingers into its elegant cleft, penetrating her with the tip of one.

When Hannah cried out loud at the sensation, he moved again, pulling down her panties in the front to push his hand between her legs. She felt his fingers against her, moving through the folds of flesh made damp by her reaction to him, furrowing slowly at first, teasing her with gentle pressure. Hastily, she shed her panties completely, then opened her legs wider, silently inviting more. But instead of escalating his attentions, Yeager only continued with his slow and steady cadence, gliding his fingers over her until she felt as though she would burst into flame.

"Please, Yeager," she whispered. But those two words were the only ones she could manage.

He seemed to understand, though, because he slipped a finger closer to the feminine core of her, drawing languid circles before venturing inside. He entered her with one long finger, once, twice, three times, four, each with a single, long stroke to her clitoris that sent tremors of need shuddering through her. Before she could climax, though, he moved his hand away. She was about to beg him to touch her again, but he circled her wrist and guided her hand toward him instead, wrapping her fingers around his long length.

She opened her eyes to find him watching her intently, his blue eyes dark with wanting. So she enclosed his shaft at its base and stroked upward, curving her palm over its head before moving back down again. This time Yeager was the one to close his eyes, and this time it was his breath that hitched in his chest. When Hannah pulled her hand up and down him again, he reached for her, aligning her body against his, covering her mouth with his, tucking his hand between her legs once more.

For a long time they only kissed and caressed, their gestures growing bolder and more invasive, until both were close to climax. Then Yeager lifted Hannah by her waist and wrapped her legs around his middle to enter her. Up and down he moved her body, going deeper inside her with every thrust. Gently he curved his hands under her bottom to lift her higher, bringing her down harder, entering her as deeply as he could.

The hot coil inside Hannah cinched tighter with every thrust, until she knew she was close to crashing. Then she felt his finger behind her again, pushing softly inside her, and she came apart at the seams.

Yeager held on for a few more moments then climaxed hard, spilling himself hot and deep inside her. He held her in place for a long time afterward, as if he wanted to ensure every drop of his essence found its way to her center.

Hannah lay her head against his shoulder and clung to him, shivering, though not from the soft circles of water eddying around them.

"Are you cold?" he whispered against her ear.

Somehow she managed to murmur, "No. I'm good."

She stopped herself before saying she was better than good, better than she'd ever been in her life, because she knew she must be imagining that. She'd just never had a lover like Yeager, that was all. He really was larger than life. A part of her was thrilled by that, but a part of her was sobered by it, too. She might never have another experience—another adventure—like Yeager Novak again. And she just wasn't sure if that was a good thing or not.

Seven

Yeager was working in his office in the Flatiron Building, his tie loosened, the top two buttons of his dress shirt unfastened, when his assistant, Amira, texted him from her desk in End of the Earth's reception area. She only did that when she was trying to be discreet about something. In this case, it was that there was a Hannah Robinson, who didn't have an appointment, here to see him. Should she just show her the door the way she usually did with the women who came to see Yeager at the office without an appointment, or should she tell her to wait until he had a free moment, which would probably be in a couple of hours—maybe—and hope Hannah left on her own after sitting in the waiting room for a while?

Instead of texting back that she should do neither, Yeager headed out to the reception area himself and ignored Amira's astonished expression when he got there.

Hannah was standing with her back to him, studying an enlarged photo of the Sinabung volcano on Sumatra that he'd taken five years ago. The first thing he noticed was that her clothes matched the photo, her shirt the same rich blue as the sky, her skirt printed in the same variegated yellows as the sulfur. The second thing he noticed was that she didn't look pregnant.

He mentally slapped himself. Of course she didn't look pregnant. She could only be a couple of weeks along, at most, since it had only been eleven days since he'd last seen her and twelve since he'd made love to her. But she must be pregnant. Otherwise, why would she have come to his office? If their first effort had failed, she could have just texted him to say, *Sorry, see you next month*.

"Hey," he said by way of a greeting, his heart racing at the prospect of good news, way more than he expected it would in these circumstances.

She spun around, her gaze connecting immediately with his. That was when something cool and unpleasant settled in Yeager's midsection. Because he could tell by the look on her face that she *wasn't* pregnant.

"Come on back to my office," he said. Then, to Amira, he added, "I'm unavailable for the rest of the morning. Maybe the afternoon, too."

"Sure thing, Yeager," Amira said, sounding even more shocked than she looked.

Hannah threw a soft but obviously manufactured smile at his assistant and murmured a quiet, "Thanks." Then she crossed her arms over her midsection and followed him silently to his office.

He closed the door behind them and directed her to one of two leather chairs in front of his massive

Victorian desk. His office, like the rest of Ends of the Earth, was cluttered with antique furniture and vintage maps and artifacts. A deliberate effort to replicate a time when world travel was full of intrigue and danger, attempted by only the most intrepid explorers. He pulled the second chair closer to Hannah's and sat.

"It didn't work, did it?" he asked. "You're not pregnant, are you?"

She shook her head.

Even though he'd already known that was what she was going to say, he was surprised by the depth of his disappointment. He really had thought they'd be successful the first time they tried. They were healthy adults with even healthier libidos, and when they'd made love in North Carolina, it had been with exuberance and passion and a *very* long finish. In the days in between, they'd bungee jumped from an abandoned train trestle and zip-lined through the mountains. He still smiled when he remembered Hannah's expression and half-baked objections both times as he cinched her safety harness to his, followed by her unmitigated elation at the end of each adventure.

But his disappointment wasn't just for a failed effort after his confidence that they would succeed. He felt genuine sadness that there wasn't a tiny Yeager or Hannah growing inside her at this very moment. And it wasn't until now that he understood how very much he wanted to have this child with her.

"It's okay," he said. Even if it didn't really feel okay at the moment. "We'll try again."

Hannah nodded but she didn't look convinced. Not sure why he did it, Yeager lifted a hand and cupped her cheek in his palm. Then he leaned forward and pressed his lips lightly to hers. It was a quick, chaste kiss. One intended to reassure. But the moment his mouth touched hers, desire erupted inside him. It was all he could do not to swoop in for a second, more demanding kiss. Instead he dropped his hand to hers and wove their fingers together.

"Are you all right?" he asked.

Very softly she replied, "I think so."

He could tell she wanted to say more, but no other words came out. "Do you want to talk about it?" he asked.

"No," she said. Then she quickly amended, "Yes." She expelled a frustrated sound. "I don't know. I feel so weird right now."

That made two of them.

"It's just…" She inhaled a deep breath and released it slowly, then met his gaze. Her beautiful silver-gray eyes seemed enormous and limitless, filled with something he had never seen in them before. Not just disappointment, but uncertainty. He'd never known Hannah to be a victim of either of those things. She was always so sunny and contented whenever he saw her. Even in her tiny apartment that offered so little to be sunny or contented with, she'd seemed to be both.

Hannah was one of those rare people who was satisfied with what life had brought her, even after life had brought her so little. Not that she didn't have aspirations or goals, but she wasn't blindsided by a single-minded, driven ambition that overshadowed everything else, the way most people were when they were going after what they wanted. She took life day by day and enjoyed what each of those days brought. At least, she had until now.

"It's not about the money, you know?" she said. "I mean, at first, it was. I did always plan on having kids someday, but my timetable was fluid where that was concerned, and I didn't really give it that much thought. Then, when I found out about my grandfather and all that money..." At this, she managed an almost earnest chuckle. "Well, hell, yeah, it was about the money. I could do everything I ever wanted if I inherited the Linden billions. But this morning, when I discovered I wasn't pregnant, it wasn't the money I thought about first. It was the baby. And how there wasn't going to be one. And I just felt so..."

She blinked and a single, fat tear spilled from one eye. Yeager brushed it away with the pad of his thumb before it even reached her cheek. Then he kissed her again. A little longer this time. Maybe because he needed reassuring as much as she did, which was the most surprising thing of all this morning.

"It's okay," he repeated. "I bet no one gets pregnant the first time they try." He smiled gently. "Really, when you think about all the logistics that go into procreating, it's amazing anyone ever gets pregnant at all."

He had meant for the comment to lighten the mood. Instead, Hannah looked horrified.

"I'm kidding," he said quickly. "It'll happen, Hannah. Don't worry. This just gives us the chance to go to Malta next time. I know this very isolated, extremely wild beach where there are some incredible caves for diving. You'll love it. I promise. A few days in the Mediterranean, lying on a sunny beach, eating all that great food..." He stopped himself from adding the part about the virile young stud she'd be

spending her nights with, since that part went without saying. "Who wouldn't get pregnant with all that
as a backdrop?"

She smiled again and, this time, it was a little more
convincing. "You're taking me to the beach," she said.

"I am."

"I'll finally get to see the ocean."

"You will."

"How long have you been planning this trip?"

Yeager had started planning it in North Carolina,
the minute she'd told him she'd never seen the ocean.
For some reason, though, he didn't want to admit that.
So he hedged. "I've had a few ideas for destinations
in my head all along. Malta was just one of them."

Which was true. He just didn't mention that Malta
had been at the bottom of the list, since beaches, even
the Mediterranean ones, were usually pretty lacking in
adventure, and besides, when you've seen one beach
and ocean, you've pretty much seen them all. Except,
of course, for Hannah. So Malta it was.

"That's sweet of you, Yeager."

It wasn't sweet of him. He just didn't think it was
fair that a perfectly nice person like Hannah had
never seen the ocean, that was all. And, hey, that
Mediterranean diet was supposed to be all kinds of
healthy.

"Will it be a problem for you to take the time off
from work?" he asked.

"I'm sure Mr. Cathcart and Mr. Quinn won't be too
crazy about me asking off again. But when I remind
them how, in the ten years I've worked for them, I
hadn't had a single vacation before last month, they'll
probably grudgingly concede. I'm not sure how many

more times I'll be able to play that card, though. And it really will eat into my paycheck."

Yeager started to offer to intercede on her behalf with her employers for her again and cover any of her lost wages. Then he remembered how adamant Hannah had been that she could make her own way. Besides, he really was sure the trip to Malta would be, ah, fruitful. There was a good chance Hannah wouldn't need to ask for any more time off, because she'd be able to quit that job and follow her dreams.

"It'll be okay, Hannah," he told her a third time. Because three was a charm, right?

Except in baby-making, he quickly amended. In baby-making, two was. They *would* be successful next time. Yeager was sure of it.

Hannah stood on the balcony of the breathtaking suite in the luxury hotel Yeager had booked for them in Valletta, gazing out at the Grand Harbour at night, waiting for him to finish his shower.

She was beginning to understand why he lived the way he did. This place was amazing. The city was awash with light against the black sky, practically glowing with a golden grandeur reflected in the water of the bay. The moon and stars, too, were gilded with an otherworldly radiance that made her feel as if she'd completely left the planet and arrived on some ethereal plane. She couldn't be farther removed from her life in New York than she would be if she were standing at the outer reaches of the universe.

The mere view from a European balcony wasn't enough to satisfy Yeager's idea of adventure, though. For him, the adventure for this trip had lain in the ocean caves where they'd spent yesterday diving. And that had certainly been fun. But to Hannah, the true adventure was simply being in a place that was so different from her own. There really was a lot more to the world than the neighborhoods she'd called home. And she'd only visited two places at this point. Maybe, if everything worked out the way it was supposed to, once her life settled down, she'd think about doing a little more globe-trotting with her child or children in the future.

A wave of apprehension spilled over her. Right now, that *child or children* was still a big *if.* Though she and Yeager were spending this trip at a more leisurely pace than their days in North Carolina. The cave diving yesterday had been peaceful—even the heart-racing moments of interacting with a real, live, albeit small, octopus—and today, they'd lain in the sun and strolled along the streets of Valletta and stuffed themselves with local cuisine. With any luck, Hannah would drop an egg at some point tomorrow—or the next day—that was ripe for fertilization. And tonight…

The thought stopped there. Yeah. Tonight. Tonight was… Tonight would be… She sighed. This time last month she'd been looking at the night ahead as a task necessary for her to complete to claim her legacy. Not that she hadn't liked the idea of having sex with Yeager—a lot—but, originally, that was all it was supposed to be: sex with Yeager. Something that would conveniently lead to her achieving her goal of starting a family. After actually having sex with Yeager, however, everything seemed to…shift. She still couldn't put her finger on what was different about this attempt to become pregnant from the last one, but there was definitely something. Something different about Yeager. Something different about her.

When she heard a door open in the suite behind her, she spun around to see him emerging from the bathroom wearing nothing but a pair of midnight blue boxers, scrubbing his black hair dry with a towel.

She watched as he crossed to the walk-in closet and stepped inside it. He then withdrew, wearing buff-colored trousers and buttoning up a chocolate-brown shirt. She recognized both as pieces she had made for him, and a ribbon of unexpected pleasure wound through her. She didn't know why. She'd probably made, or at least altered, half his wardrobe, the same way she had for many of Cathcart and Quinn's clients. His wearing of her clothes had never affected her any more than some other man's wearing of them. For some reason, though, she suddenly liked the idea of Yeager being wrapped in garments she had sewed for him.

She continued to watch him as he strode to a table where a bottle of champagne had been chilling since they'd returned from their day in town. Deftly, he popped the cork and poured two flutes, then nestled the bottle back into the ice. Hannah didn't think she could ever get tired of just looking at him. He moved with such ease and elegance, utterly assured in himself but completely unconscious of that confidence. She remembered how, in North Carolina, he'd revealed his seemingly quiet upbringing in the heart of the Midwest. Try as she might, he hadn't let her bring up the subject again. And she was dying to know how that little boy from Peoria had become such a raging scion of world adventure.

He made his way toward the French doors leading to the balcony, where Hannah awaited him in the
darkness. His eyes must not have adjusted from the
light of the room because he didn't seem to see her
at first. Then he smiled and headed toward her. He
halted just before reaching her, though, and gave her
a thorough once-over.

"Wow," he said. "You look incredible."

She warmed at the compliment. They had res-
ervations for a late dinner at some upscale seafood
place he'd told her was one of his favorite places in
the world. She'd had to scramble to find something to
bring with her that would be suitable, since *upscale*
didn't exist in her normal wardrobe—or her normal
life, for that matter. Fortunately she'd had a couple
of large enough fabric remnants to stitch together a
flowy, pale yellow halter dress and had found some
reasonably decent dressy sandals at her favorite thrift
shop.

She was also wearing the strapless bra and brief
panties Yeager had given her their first day in Valletta
to compensate for the ones he'd sent down the river
in North Carolina. Or so he'd said. Somehow, though,
the sheer ivory silk-and-lace confections bore no re-
semblance to the cotton Hanes Her Way that they'd
replaced. And she was reasonably certain they didn't
come in two-and five-packs.

"Thanks," she said, the word coming out more quietly and less confidently than she'd intended. "You
look pretty amazing yourself."

He smiled. "Thanks to you."

Another frisson of delight shuddered through her.
Why was his opinion suddenly more important to her

than it had been before? She knew she was good at her job—she didn't need the approval of others to reinforce that. But Yeager's approval suddenly meant a lot to her.

He handed her a glass of champagne then turned to look at the city lights she'd been marveling at. "I think this may be one of the most beautiful cities I've ever visited," he said.

There was a wistfulness in his voice she'd never heard before. She wouldn't have thought Yeager Novak could be wistful. She smiled. "You talk like there are actually cities you haven't visited."

He chuckled. "One or two."

She shook her head. "I can't imagine living the life you do. Are you ever in one place for any length of time?"

"I try to spend at least one week a month in New York," he said.

"One week is not a length of time," she told him.

"Maybe not to you. But even a week in one place can make me restless. Besides, I can pretty much run Ends of the Earth from anywhere. And there are times when I have to be out of the country for months."

"Have to be?" she echoed. "Or just want to be?"

He lifted one shoulder and let it drop. "Could be they're one and the same."

Interesting way to put it.

"So, what?" she asked. "You just live in hotels?"

"Sometimes. Or in tents. Or out in the open. Depends on where I am. I do own homes in the places I visit most often."

"Which are?"

He turned to look at her full-on. "I don't want to talk about me. Let's talk about you."

She shook her head adamantly. "Oh, no. No way. We talked about me the whole time in North Carolina. You know everything there is to know about me. This time, we're going to talk *aaalll* about you."

He bristled palpably at the comment. Hannah didn't care. The last time they were together, he'd avoided every effort she'd made to learn more about him, always turning the conversation back to her.

Yeager really did know everything there was to know about her. About how she'd nearly failed phys ed at her Harlem middle school because she was so bad at gymnastics. About the four stitches and tetanus shot she'd had to get when she was seven, after slicing open her knee in a vacant lot on Lexington Avenue. About how, to this day, she still missed the grumpy, one-eyed tabby named Bing Clawsby that had lived in one of her homes.

He knew her favorite color was purple, her favorite food was fettuccine Alfredo, her favorite movie was *Wall-E* and her favorite band was the Shins. He knew she was a Sagittarius, that she'd never learned how to drive, that she believed in ghosts and, how, if she could be any animal in the world, she'd be a fennec fox. All she knew about him was that he was the only child of a quiet-sounding couple from Peoria and that he'd played hockey for a college so far upstate he might as well have been in Canada. He wasn't going to avoid her this time.

"Oh, come on," she said. "How bad can your secrets be? You barely have two thousand hits on Google."

He arched his eyebrows at that. "You looked me up online?"

"Of course I looked you up online." Hell, she'd done it after the first time he'd come into Cathcart and Quinn. There was no reason he had to know that part, though. "You're going to be the father of my child." She hoped. "But all that turned up was your social media accounts, stuff about Ends of the Earth, and mentions in some extreme adventure blogs. Even that article about you in *Outside* magazine didn't reveal anything about the real Yeager Novak."

He enjoyed a healthy taste of his champagne and avoided her gaze. Hannah remained silent as she waited him out. She was surprised when she won the battle after a few seconds and he turned to gaze out at the bay again.

Quietly he said, "That article in *Outside* revealed everything you need to know about me."

"It didn't tell me you're from Peoria."

"That's because Peoria isn't a part of my life."

"But it's where you grew up," she objected. "Where and how a person grows up is a huge part of who they are."

"It's a huge part of who they *were*," he argued. "You can't go home again."

"Everyone goes home again at some point, Yeager, in some way. It's inescapable." When he said nothing she asked, "Do your folks still live in Peoria?"

He sighed that sigh of resignation she was beginning to recognize fairly well. "No," he told her. "They died within a year of each other when I was in college."

"Oh," she said soberly. "I'm sorry."

She was sorry for his loss, not sorry that she'd asked. This was exactly the sort of thing two people should be sharing when their lives were going to be linked—she hoped—by a child. The things that had impacted them, the things that had shaped and moved them.

"I was one of those late-life surprises," he said. "My mother was fifty-two when I was born. My father was nearly sixty. He had a fatal heart attack my junior year of college. My mom had a stroke ten months later."

Which could explain one of the reasons Yeager kept himself so physically fit. It didn't, however, explain why he kept traversing the globe over and over.

"I'm sorry," Hannah said again.

He gazed down into his glass. "It was a long time ago."

Maybe. But two losses like that, so close together, had to have taken a toll on a college kid hundreds of miles away from home.

Hannah changed the subject from his parents to his school. "So…hockey scholarship. You must have been pretty good."

He nodded. "I was, actually. I had interest from a couple of pro teams before I graduated."

"Why didn't you stay with it?"

He shrugged again, even more half-heartedly. "Hockey was something I shared with my dad. He was my coach when I started in a youth league at five. He took me to Blackhawk games once a month before I even started school, even though Chicago was a three-or four-hour drive one-way. We'd make a weekend of it—my mom would come, too—and we'd do touristy stuff while we were there. Hit Navy Pier or

the Shedd Aquarium or the Field Museum or something. And my dad never missed one of my games, all
the way through high school. He even hung around
the rink to watch me practice when he could. After he
died, it wasn't the same. Hockey didn't mean as much
to me as it did before. I just didn't have the heart for
it anymore, you know?"

Hannah didn't know, actually. She could no more
imagine what that had been like for Yeager than she
could swim from here to New York. She'd never had
a relationship like that—had never shared anything
like that—with anyone. So she didn't respond.

He didn't seem to expect an answer, anyway, because he continued. "That was when Tommy and I
started talking about going into business together.
He'd spent his childhood living all over the world,
thanks to his mom's job, and after my parents' deaths,
going someplace else in the world—anywhere else in
the world—sounded pretty damned good to me. So
that was where we put our efforts."

Hannah had thought it would take the entirety of
their trip this time—and then some—to uncover what
it was that made Yeager tick. But in less time than it
took to drink a glass of champagne, she was beginning
to understand exactly why he'd become the traveler
and risk-taker he was. It was clear he'd been very close
to his parents, and that they'd been a loving family.
A family he'd lost while he was still a kid and whom
he missed terribly. A part of him might even still be
looking for that family, in his own way.

Maybe, deep down, she and Yeager weren't quite so
different as she'd first thought. But where her way to
deal with that loss was to stay put in one place to try

to a build a life there, his was to escape any reminder
of what he'd once had.

He lifted his glass, drained its contents, then gazed
at the bay again. Hannah sipped her champagne carefully—the way she did everything—and studied him
in silence. After a moment he almost physically shook
off his sober mood and looked at her again. He even
smiled. Kind of.

Evidently heartened by having overcome the most
difficult hurdle she could throw in front of him, he
asked, "So what else do you want to know about me?"

She smiled back. "Favorite color?" Even though
she already knew it was blue.

"Blue."

"Favorite food?"

"Anything from the ocean that's been blackened
and grilled."

And on it went until she knew his favorite movie
was *High Noon* and his favorite band was whatever
happened to be streaming that didn't suck. That he
was, ironically, a Virgo. That he even knew how to
drive—and actually preferred—a stick shift. That he
thought ghosts were a lot of hooey and that, of all the
animals in the world, he'd choose to be not a lone wolf
but a Komodo dragon because, hey, dragon.

By the time Hannah finished her interrogation,
Yeager was pouring the last of the champagne into
their glasses, and she was feeling mellower than she'd
ever felt in her life. In North Carolina, they'd scarcely
had a single minute when they weren't doing something adventurous. Including the sex, which, even
though they'd had a perfectly good bed in their glamping tent, had happened that last time on a blanket in a

clearing in the woods, under the stars, surrounded by fireflies. They'd been stargazing at the time, then one thing had led to another and, suddenly, Hannah had been naked, and then Yeager had been naked, and then she'd been on all fours with him behind her, thrusting into her again and again and again, and, well... It had just been, you know, super, super adventurous the whole time.

Anyway.

This time felt a lot less demanding. A lot less needful. A lot less urgent.

Until she looked at Yeager again and realized that, somehow, he was thinking about the exact same things she'd just been thinking about. Right down to the nakedness, the all fours and the thrusting again and again and again.

"You know," he said softly, "we can always cancel our dinner reservation."

Heat erupted in Hannah's belly at the suggestion. "But I thought you said it was one of your favorite places to eat in the whole, wide world."

His gaze turned incandescent. "I can think of other places I like better."

"How do you always know what I'm thinking?" she asked, her voice scarcely a whisper.

"I don't," he told her. "Except when you're thinking about sex. It's your eyes. They get darker. And there's something there that's just...wild. You have the most expressive eyes I've ever seen in a human being. At least, they are when it comes to wanting something."

"Or someone," she said before she could stop herself.

He took her glass from her hand and set it with his

on the balcony railing. "We should definitely cancel our dinner reservation," he said decisively.

"Okay," Hannah agreed readily. Although she was certainly hungry, dinner was the last thing on her mind. "If we *have* to."

Yeager took her hand in his and tugged her to him. Then he dipped his head and kissed her. It was a gentle kiss, with none of the heat and urgency she knew was surging through both of them. He brushed his lips over hers, once, twice, three times, four, then covered her mouth completely with his, tasting her long and hard and deep.

Oh. Okay. There was the heat. There was the urgency. There was the...

He skimmed one hand over her bare shoulder and down her arm, settling it on her waist to pull her closer.

Hannah went willingly, looping her arms around his neck, tangling the fingers of one hand in his still-damp hair. His heat surrounded her, pulling her into him, until she wasn't sure where her body ended and his began. Slowly he began moving them backward, into their suite. He paused long enough to switch off the single lamp that had been illuminated, and then they were bathed in the pale light of the moon and the golden city outside.

Yeager continued to kiss her as he guided them toward the bed, his tongue tangling with hers, his mouth hot against her skin. He reached for the tie of her halter at the same moment she reached for the button of his trousers. As she unzipped his pants, he unzipped her dress, until the garment fell into a pool around her feet. She felt his member surge against her fingers, hard and heavy against the soft silk of his boxers. So she tucked her hand inside to cover him, bare skin to bare skin. He was so... *Oh*. And she could scarcely wait to have him inside her again.

As she stroked him, he bent his head and tasted her breast over the fabric of her bra, laving her with the flat of his tongue until her nipple strained against the damp fabric. His hand at her waist crept lower, his fingers dipping into the waistband of her panties, then lower still, between her legs. Somehow, Hannah managed to take a small step to the side to open herself wider to him, and he threaded his fingers into the damp folds of her flesh. She gasped at the contact, gripping his shoulder tight when her legs threatened to buckle beneath her, her caressing of his erection growing slower and more irregular.

Yeager didn't seem to mind. As he fingered her with one hand, he moved the other to her back, expertly unfastening her bra until it fell to the floor, too. Then he pulled as much of her breast as he could into his mouth, the pressure of his tongue against her nipple coupled with his hand between her legs bringing her near orgasm. When he realized how close she was, he moved his hand away, dragging his wet fingers up over her torso to cradle her breast in his palm.

He lifted his head again and covered her mouth with his, kissing her deeply. His member twitched beneath her hand, and she knew a keen desire to have him inside her *now*. With trembling fingers, she freed him long enough to unbutton his shirt and shove it from his shoulders. Then she tugged his trousers and his boxers down over his hips, kneeling before him to skim them off his legs completely. When he stood in front of her, towering over her, his member straight and stiff, Hannah couldn't help herself. She wrapped her fingers around him and guided him toward her mouth.

He groaned his approval at her gesture, tangling his fingers in her hair. She ran her tongue down the length of him, back up again, then covered the head of his shaft completely, pulling him deep inside. Eagerly, she consumed him, taking her time to pleasure them both until she knew he was close to his breaking point. Only then did she rise again, dragging her fingers up along his thighs and taut buttocks, over the ropes of sinew and muscle on his torso, pushing herself up on tiptoe to kiss him as hungrily as he had her.

He reached for her panties and pushed them down over her hips, and she pulled them the rest of the way off. Then he lifted her up off the floor and, after one more fierce kiss, threw her playfully to the center of the bed. She landed on her fanny with a laugh, until he joined her, spreading her legs wide to bury his head between them.

Now Hannah was the one to gasp—and moan and purr—as he devoured her, drawing circles with the tip of his tongue, nibbling the sensitive nub of her clitoris until she thought she would come apart at the seams. Then he was turning their bodies so that he was sitting on the edge of the mattress again, with her astride him, facing him. Gripping her hips, he lowered her over his shaft, bucking his hips upward as he entered her, long and hard and deep. Hannah did cry out then, so filled was she by him. He moved her up, then down, then up again, until she picked up his rhythm fluently. Over and over their bodies joined, until they seemed to become one. And then they were climaxing together, Yeager surging hotly inside her.

Immediately he turned them again, so that Hannah was on her back and he was atop her, bracing himself on his strong forearms. He murmured something about staying inside her until he was sure she was pregnant this time—because he was sure she would be pregnant this time—then kissed her again for a very long time.

All Hannah could do was open her hands over the hot, slick skin of his back and return the kiss, and hope like hell he was right.

Eight

It was raining in New York the second time Hannah came to see Yeager at his office. Since undertaking this...this...this whatever it was with her—since *deal* didn't seem like the right word anymore—he'd been trying to stay close to his home base as much as he could. That way, when Hannah had good news to tell him, she could do so in person.

But he knew the moment she stepped into his office—he'd told Amira weeks ago to send Hannah back anytime she showed up—that she didn't have good news. Her dark expression was completely at odds with the bright pink-and-orange dress she was wearing, and she didn't look as if she'd slept for days.

Something cold and unpleasant settled in Yeager's midsection. He'd been disappointed last month when she'd told him she wasn't pregnant, but this... What he was feeling now went beyond disappointment. It went beyond sadness. He wasn't even sure there was a word to cover the emotions swirling inside him at the moment.

Hannah, though, looked even worse than he felt. So he rose and rounded his desk, ushering her to the same chair she'd sat in before, drawing his up alongside hers. As he had before, he took her hand in his and wove their fingers together.

And he did his best to inject a lightness he didn't feel into his voice when he said, "Another miss, huh?"

She nodded silently.

"It's okay, Hannah," he told her, just as he had the first time. And, just like the first time, it didn't feel okay at all. "There's still plenty of time before the deadline." Even though he sincerely doubted it was the deadline she was worrying about right now.

Her reply was a heavy sigh, followed by a soft, "I know."

Still forcing his cheerfulness, trying not to choke on it, he added, "And, hey, bonus, we'll get to spend more time together."

It wasn't until he said it that he realized that actually would be a bonus. He'd enjoyed his two trips with Hannah more than he'd thought he would. He liked being around her. She brought an aspect to his travels he'd never had before—the newness of the experience. He'd forgotten how much fun going someplace for the first time could be. Hell, he couldn't even remember the last time he'd gone someplace for the first time. Watching Hannah's exuberance rafting down the Chattanooga River and seeing her euphoria in the underwater caves of Gozo, he'd felt like he was seeing it all for the first time, too.

He supposed, in a way, he had been. Because he didn't think he'd ever approached adventuring the way she did. For Yeager, going someplace else in the world felt like an escape. Hell, it was an escape. For Hannah, it was a discovery. Which, maybe, was what an adventure was supposed to be about in the first place.

He pushed the thought away. He pushed all his thoughts away and focused on Hannah. He hadn't been lying when he'd said she had the most expressive eyes he'd ever seen on a human being. He had been lying when he'd told her they were only expressive when it came to sex. He'd said that in Malta because he'd wanted sex at the moment, and so had she, and it had been the perfect segue to it—not that either of them had really needed one. Her eyes really were the proverbial window onto her soul. He always knew what Hannah was thinking lately, no matter what she was thinking about. Just by looking into her eyes.

And what she was thinking now was that she was never going to get pregnant. Yeager begged to differ. They'd tried twice. Big damn deal. He knew people who had tried for years to get pregnant, then had two or three rug rats in a row. Not that he and Hannah had years—although, he had to admit, the idea of that wasn't as off-putting to him as it might have been a couple of months ago—but they did still have time. The clock on her inheritance had started ticking in July. That meant she had until January to get pregnant. It was only October. Including this month, they had three more shots. So to speak. Was it crazy that Yeager was suddenly kind of hoping they'd have to use up them all?

Hannah still hadn't replied to his last comment about how getting to spend more time together would be a bonus. Maybe she didn't think of it that way. Maybe what no longer felt like a deal to him was still very much a deal to her. Maybe she wasn't enjoying this as much as he was. Maybe she was just going through the motions and—

Yeah, right. As though the way the two of them had come together in Valletta, and before that, in North Carolina, was going through the motions. Hannah Robinson might be circumspect and careful when it came to living her life, but when it came to sex, she'd been surprisingly, gratifyingly adventurous.

An idea suddenly struck him. "Hey," he said, "if you could go anywhere in the world you wanted, where would you go?"

She gazed at him questioningly. "What do you mean?"

"I mean the two trips we've taken so far have been ones I've put together. I'd still like to honor Tommy's spirit and leave my legacy through an adventure, but maybe the secret to this baby-making is to go someplace *you* want to go. Do something *you* want to do. What do you think?"

Although the question seemed to stump her, it also seemed to pull her out of her funk. "I don't know," she said. "I've never really thought about it." Then she braved a soft smile. "Jones Beach?"

He smiled back. But there was no way he was going to let her get away with a day trip she could take anytime she wanted to when he could take her anywhere in the world.

"Come on," he coaxed. "When you were a kid, there had to be someplace you dreamed about going. Something you dreamed about doing."

"Yeager, I've spent my whole life imagining being able to *stay* in one place and *not* move around."

He didn't buy it. "There's not a kid in the world who hasn't wanted to go someplace far away at some point and do something they've never done before. Think about it for a minute."

For a minute, she did. Then she smiled again. A better smile this time. One that did something to Yeager's insides he'd never felt before. Weird.

"Okay, so when I was about six or seven," she said, "I read this book. *Stellaluna*. Are you familiar with it?"

He shook his head. He'd never been a huge reader growing up and what little reading he had done was always about sports or superheroes.

She continued. "It's about a baby fruit bat named Stellaluna who gets separated from her mother and is taken in by a family of birds. She has to live by the birds' rules, which are totally counter to her own bat instincts, but they become a family. All the while, though, Stellaluna's mother is looking for her. In the end, she finds her and they live happily ever after. So you can see why I read the book a million times when I was a kid and why I identified so much with a fruit bat."

"I can absolutely see that," Yeager agreed. And he absolutely could.

"For a while," she went on, "I got onto this fruit

bat kick. I read a lot about them, and I decided that, even though the book never mentions where Stellaluna lives, she lived in a rainforest in Madagascar. And I thought Madagascar sounded like a really cool place."

"So you want to go to Madagascar," he said.

Hannah nodded. "Either that or Hogwarts."

He laughed. He was still disappointed that Hannah wasn't pregnant. But there was something about the prospect of trying again that made him feel better. He told himself it was because he hadn't been to Madagascar for a long time. But it was probably more because, this time, he'd be seeing it with Hannah.

"I can't help you with Hogwarts," he said. "But we can definitely go to Madagascar. Did you know there are treehouses there that you can rent?"

At this, Hannah lit up in a way he hadn't seen from her in months. Not since that night in North Carolina when she'd seen her first fireflies.

"We could really live like Stellaluna?" she asked.

"Yeah."

And if living out her childhood dream didn't put Hannah in the family way, Yeager didn't know what would.

Then another thought struck him. "Will it be a problem to take time off from work again?"

She sighed. "Yeah. But I'll handle it. I may have to finally explain to Mr. Cathcart and Mr. Quinn about my grandfather's will, which was something I really didn't want to share with anyone until I got pregnant, since I may nev—"

"Yes, you will," Yeager cut her off. And before she could say anything else, he added, "I'll have Amira

clear my morning. You and I can make the plans together."

The light in Hannah dimmed some at that. "I can't,"
she said. "I have to be at work in a half hour."

"Right," he said. "But you have an hour for lunch,
don't you?"

She nodded.

"So I'll meet you at one at Cathcart and Quinn. I'll
bring lunch and my tablet with me. We'll make the
arrangements then."

"Are you sure you have the time for all that?"

Was she nuts? Yeager Novak not have time for the
mother of his offspring?

"Of course I have time. I'll see you at one."

"Okay."

"A Madagascar treehouse, Hannah. That will do
the trick," he promised her. "This time next month,
you'll be pregnant. I'm sure of it."

But the Madagascar treehouse didn't do the trick.
And neither did the isolated castle in Scotland—the
closest thing Yeager and Hannah could find to Hogwarts—in November. By the middle of December,
she was so convinced there was something wrong that
made it impossible for them to conceive that they both
had their doctors do a second workup to see if that
was the case.

But the results were the same then as they'd been in
the summer, before they'd even started trying to conceive—they were both healthy, fertile adults for whom
conception should pose no problem. Hannah's doctor
tried to reassure her that it was perfectly normal for
some couples to take several months to conceive and

that, sometimes, the harder two people tried, the more elusive conception became. "Relax," her doctor told her. "Don't worry about it. It will happen."

Which was all well and good, Hannah thought a few evenings later in her apartment, if there weren't other factors at play. Billions of factors, in fact. If she wasn't able to inherit the Linden family fortune—her family fortune—she could be working for the rest of her life at a job that barely enabled her to take care of herself, never mind a child. Her fifty thousand dollar consolation prize would make the start of a nice nest egg, but it wasn't enough to start a business and keep it going here in New York. And without the funds to get Joey & Kit off the ground, there was no way she would ever be able to support a family. Yes, she might someday meet Mr. Right and get married and settle down. With two incomes coming in, she might be able to launch Joey & Kit and eventually turn it into a viable business.

Then again, she might not do any of those things. Nothing in life was guaranteed. Unless maybe you had billions of dollars.

And with or without the Linden fortune, Hannah knew now without question that she wanted to start a family. That had become clearer every time a pregnancy test came back negative and she was overcome by a sadness unlike any she'd ever known. Finding her Mr. Right would be beneficial in more than just a financial sense. But finding him was going to become more and more difficult the more time she spent with Yeager. The last five months with him had been the most enjoyable she'd ever spent. And not just because of the travels and adventures, either.

With every moment she spent with him, he crept further under her skin. She wasn't sure she'd ever be able to forget him once their time together came to an end—with or without a child. Before going into this venture with him, she'd considered him a frivolous, one-dimensional player. A guy who was fun to talk to and easy on the eyes, but who could never take anything in life seriously—especially a woman or a family. But she knew now that wasn't true. Yeager Novak was... He was...

She gazed out the only window in her apartment, at the back of the building on the next block. During the warm months, the backyards and fire escapes of both that building and hers were alive with activity, from Mr. Aizawa's tending of his bonsai trees to Mrs. Medina's courtyard flamenco lessons to the luscious smells wafting over from the Singhs' rooftop tandoor. In December, though, everything was still and quiet. Christmas lights twinkled from the Blomqvists' balcony, the Gorskis had lit the first candle in their window menorah and Lilah Windermere was revving up for Saturnalia, her share of the fire escape bedecked with suns and crescent moons.

Yeager Novak, Hannah continued with her thoughts, was the sort of man a woman could easily—oh, so easily—fall in love with. There was just something inside him that connected with something inside her—she didn't know any other way to put it. He was kind and smart and funny. And, for the last couple of months, he'd put her needs before his own.

She had always thought his incessant travels were due to some misplaced desire to prove he could live forever. He'd said as much himself, both that first night when he'd turned down her offer to father her child, and again the evening he'd agreed to. Now she understood, even if Yeager didn't, that he moved around so much to escape the loneliness of having lost his family when he was young. There were times when she even wondered if his agreement to donate a second set of chromosomes for her child might be the result not of his wish for a legacy, but of an unconscious desire to recreate the family he no longer had.

He was a good man. A complicated man. A multi-layered man. A man with more substance and appeal than anyone she knew. Not the kind of guy Hannah normally went for at all. Which, maybe, was why she was falling for him so much harder.

The buzz of her doorbell interrupted her thoughts and she was grateful. She somehow knew before she even crossed to the intercom and heard his voice that it would be Yeager. But she didn't know why he'd be dropping by on a wintry Wednesday evening. They weren't supposed to meet again until Saturday morning, New York time, when they would arrive separately in Fiji for their final adventure together—this one to camp near a volcano on Koro Island. Yeager had read it was the site of an ancient fertility ritual and he intended to recreate it, right down to the running naked across hot coals after ingesting copious amounts of kava from a coconut shell. He had to leave tomorrow for a trip to Vancouver, but would take a red-eye to Suva and meet her within an hour of her own arrival.

A few months ago Hannah would have been excited by the idea of an adventure in Fiji, especially with Yeager. Tonight the thought of another quick trip—the

most exotic one of all—only to return to her normal
life a week later held no appeal. Her normal life, period, didn't hold much appeal these days. Which was,
perhaps, the most troubling realization of all. Even if it
hadn't been remarkable, her life five months ago had
been perfectly acceptable to her. Then Gus Fiver of
Tarrant, Fiver & Twigg walked in and everything—
everything—changed. She wondered now if she would
ever be content again.

She buzzed Yeager in and opened her front door,
meeting him at the top of the stairs. He was still
dressed for work, in a tailored, black wool coat flap-
ping open over a charcoal suit—though he'd unbuttoned his shirt collar and loosened his tie. Hannah, too,
was still in her work clothes, a black pencil skirt paired
with a red sweater and red-and-black polka-dot tights.

As he topped the last stair, she started to take a step
back toward her apartment to give him room. Before
she could, though, he swept her up against him and
dropped a swift kiss on her lips. The gesture surprised
her. Especially when, after he completed it, he made
no move to release her.

Instead he gazed into her eyes and murmured, "Hi.
How you doing?"

"I… I'm good," she stammered. And then, because
she couldn't think of anything else to say, thanks to
the way the blood zipping through her veins made
her a little—okay, a lot—muddleheaded, she added,
"How are you?"

He grinned. "I'm good, too. I thought maybe we
could do something tonight."

Her eyebrows shot up at that. "Why?"

He chuckled. "Why not?"

"Because I'm not... I mean, it's not time for me to... I still have a couple of days before I..."

He laughed again. Something inside Hannah caught fire.

"I wasn't planning on getting you pregnant tonight," he told her. "I was in the neighborhood, meeting with a potential contractor, and I thought I'd drop by and see if we could grab some dinner together. Maybe go over our itinerary for Fiji one more time. I have a car waiting downstairs. We can go anywhere you want."

It wasn't that unusual of a request. Well, okay, the car waiting downstairs was a little outside her usual experiences, since Hannah normally bused or trained it everywhere. Even so, it took her a moment to reply.

"Anywhere?" she finally repeated. Because, if he was offering, she did have something kind of specific in mind.

"Anywhere," he promised.

"Okay," she said. "Dinner would be good. Just let me get my coat."

In retrospect, Yeager decided a couple of hours later, maybe he shouldn't have told Hannah they could go anywhere she wanted. Because she'd chosen the Russian Tea Room. Not that he had anything against it, but...it was the Russian Tea Room, which wasn't exactly his cup of tea. But Hannah had never been before and had always wanted to go, so here they were. And, truth be told, his cheese and cherry blintze had been pretty freaking amazing.

It wasn't even nine o'clock when they exited the restaurant, and Yeager didn't want the evening to end

just yet. He didn't have to be at the airport for his
flight to Vancouver until eleven tomorrow morning,
so it wasn't like he had to be in bed early. He started
to ask Hannah what else she wanted to do, but hesitated. She might tell him she wanted to go to the roof
of the Empire State Building. Or, worse, on one of
those cruises to see the Statue of Liberty. Or, worst of
all, go ice-skating under the Christmas tree at Rock-
efeller Center.

He risked it anyway. "What do you want to do
next?"

And heard an answer that was far, far worse.

"Can we take a carriage ride around Central Park?"

Yeager flinched as if she'd just hit him with a brick.
Seriously? What was this, Prom Night?

Then he remembered how she'd once told him she
hadn't gone to her prom because no one had asked her
and she'd been too scared to ask anyone herself. She'd
just transferred to a new school a few months before
all the senior events started happening. All the kids
had steered clear of her once they learned she was in
the system because they'd figured she was, at best, a
weirdo and, at worst, a psycho.

"Please, Yeager?" she asked, sounding very much
like a high school senior who'd just moved to a new
school and had no friends. "It'll be so much fun. The
Christmas lights will be up in Central Park, and it's
supposed to snow."

Oh, good. The only thing that would make a carriage ride through Central Park more fun would be
doing it in a snow globe they could buy later from
some guy in a trench coat in Times Square. But Hannah's heart was in her eyes again. Standing there in

her red coat with its multicolored buttons, her striped scarf wound around her neck what looked like a dozen times, her mittened hands before her in a way that made her look like she was praying he would say yes...

He sighed with resignation. "Yeah, okay. Why not?"

Her eyes went incandescent at that and, somehow, he minded a lot less that he was doing the crass tourist thing in New York with Hannah when he could have, quite literally, been anywhere in the world doing anything he wanted. He liked being here with Hannah. He liked being anywhere with her. It didn't matter what they were doing.

They found a free carriage at 7th Avenue and 59th Street. The driver introduced himself as Yuri and his horse as Arthur, the latter delighting Hannah since, as she told Yeager, she'd never been this close to a horse before. When Yuri heard that, he handed her a carrot to feed the animal and, by her reaction as she fed Arthur, she might as well have been donning the Crown Jewels. Then they climbed into the white carriage with red velvet seats and settled in for the ride, nestled under a red-and-black-plaid blanket to chase away the chill.

Central Park opened up before them like a Christmas card, surrounding them with a winter wonderland of lamplight and moonlight and twinkling white tree lights. All was calm, all was bright, with silver lanes aglow and kids jingle-belling and chestnut vendors roasting their fare on an open fire and passersby dressed up like Eskimos. Barely ten minutes in, snow began to swirl around them, giving everything an otherworldly glow and buffering the sounds of this

frosty symphony. Hannah looped her arm through
his as if it were the most natural thing in the world
to do, leaning her head on his shoulder. And Yeager
had to admit there were worse ways to spend an evening than inside a Christmas snow globe with Hannah Robinson.

They rode in silence for a little while then Hannah
sighed with much feeling. "I knew it would be like
this," she said.

"Like what?" Yeager asked.

She hesitated, sighed again and whispered, "Magical."

On any other night, with any other person, Yeager would have said that was ridiculous. There was
no such thing as magic. This was just Central Park,
a place they both must have visited dozens of times.
Lights ran on electricity. Snow was just frozen pieces
of water. There was an explanation for every single
thing around them.

Except, maybe, for why he wanted so badly to kiss
her when there was no reason to do it.

"When you were a kid," she said quietly, "did you
believe in Santa Claus?"

"Of course I believed in Santa Claus," he told
her. Hell, he'd held out on the Santa-being-real thing
way longer than his classmates, something that had
brought him no end of ribbing. He hadn't cared. He'd
been absolutely certain a white-bearded man dressed
in red came down their chimney every year to scat-
ter toys across every inch of the living room, leaving cookie crumbs and a half-empty glass of milk
behind. What other explanation could there be? Such
had been the innocence of his childhood. An inno-

cence that was shattered one night in upstate New York, when his mother called him from almost a thousand miles away to tell him he would never see his father alive again.

"How about you?" he asked Hannah, pushing the memory as far to the back of his brain as he could. He thought she would reply the same way. So he wasn't quite prepared for the answer she gave him.

"I don't think I ever had the chance to believe in him. I mean, maybe when I lived with my mom before she died, I did. I don't know. But I don't remember ever looking out the window, up at the sky, waiting for his arrival. Someone must have told me at one of my first homes that there was no such thing as Santa."

When he and Hannah had their baby, Yeager thought, no one was ever going to do that. Every child should have the opportunity to believe in magic for as long as they wanted to believe. Even if Yeager didn't believe in it anymore.

"Did you at least have presents to open on Christmas morning?" he asked.

"Usually."

Usually, he echoed to himself. Meaning there had been some Christmas mornings when Hannah had gone without the breathtaking exhilaration that came with ripping brightly colored paper off boxes to see what treasure was inside. That wasn't going to happen to their child, either.

"What kind of Christmas traditions did your family have?" she asked. Probably because she'd never been in one place long enough to establish traditions of her own.

There was a time when Yeager would have refused

to answer, since he generally hated talking about his parents and the life he'd had with them. That life just didn't feel like it was his anymore. In a way, it felt like it had happened to someone else. With Hannah, though, he didn't mind talking about it so much. With Hannah, that life didn't seem so alien. It didn't feel so far away.

"Every Christmas Eve," he said, "my mom made Cornish hens, with sweet potatoes and Brussels sprouts as a side."

None of which he'd eaten since her death.

"We had this Christmas china she got somewhere," he continued, "and she'd break it out for that meal and Christmas Day, then it would be boxed up again and stowed for another year."

Yeager still had that china. Somewhere. For some reason, he hadn't been able to part with it when it came to disposing of his parents' possessions after graduating from college. Maybe he'd look around for it this year. Break it out before Christmas. Maybe he and Hannah could—

But he wouldn't be in New York for Christmas, he reminded himself. He had long-standing plans to be skiing with friends in Vail.

"I got to open one gift on Christmas Eve," he continued for Hannah, "and I always took about an hour to pick out which one. Christmas morning, I wasn't allowed to get out of bed before eight, even though I was always awake by six. But at one second after eight, I'd run downstairs and behold the glory that was Christmas morning."

For the first time in a long, long time, he was able to smile at the recollections. Hell, it was surprising that he was even able to tolerate the memories in the first place. How the tree lights would be on when he awoke, even though his father was adamant they be turned off before he went to bed. How, somehow, there were already cinnamon rolls baking in the oven and hot chocolate heating on the stove and Christmas carols playing on the CD player. Back then, he'd put it all down to Santa. Santa and the magic of Christmas.

He told Hannah about all that and more, until the snow was falling furiously around them and he was dipping his head toward hers and she was lifting hers in return to meet him halfway. Their lips connected gently at first, the subtle brush of their mouths against each other a warm counterpoint to the night around them.

They chatted and canoodled for the rest of the ride around the park. When Yuri pulled Arthur to a halt where they had begun, Yeager was surprised by the depth of his disappointment. Part of him wanted to go around again. But another part of him—a bigger part—just wanted to be alone with Hannah.

As they drew up in front of her building in the car he'd hired for the day, he grew more disconcerted. Why did he feel so annoyed at having to say good-night to her? He'd be seeing her again in Fiji in a few days. For some reason, though, the days between now and then felt like an interminable—intolerable—period of time. But how to finagle an invitation to...oh, he didn't know...spend the night with her, without sounding like a jerk.

"So, Hannah, what would you think if maybe I—"

"So, Yeager, is there any chance you might want to—" she said at the same time.

They stopped talking as one, their gazes connecting. Then, as one, they both smiled.

"I think it's a great idea," she told him.

"I'd love to," he said at the same time.

He sent the driver on his way after that, emptying his wallet for the tip, not wanting to waste any more time doing something as mundane as keeping track of his cash flow.

Hand in hand, he and Hannah climbed the stairs to her apartment and entered. The moment they were inside with the door closed behind them, he kissed her. Strangely, it wasn't like the kisses that had preceded their couplings in other places. It wasn't hot and urgent, filled with need. It was slow and sweet, almost innocent, as if this were the first time for both of them, and neither was sure exactly what to do.

Later, Yeager wouldn't even remember moving the love seat to pull down the Murphy bed. Later, he wouldn't remember the two of them undressing each other and climbing into it. Later, he would only remember making love to Hannah in a way they hadn't made love before. With care and attention, and something else that hadn't been there earlier, either. Something he wasn't sure how to describe or what to call. But it felt as natural and necessary as breathing.

After they spent themselves, when he wrapped his arms around her and pulled her close, she nestled into him and tucked her head beneath his chin. As Hannah slept beside him, Yeager looked out the window—the only window she had onto the world—and watched the snow fall.

And he wondered what he was going to do if he and Hannah weren't successful with their final attempt at conception in Fiji. Worse, he wondered what he was going to do after their baby was born, when he would be moving in and out of their lives, and Hannah would never have a need for a night like this again.

Nine

Hannah was throwing the last of her toiletries into the suitcase she'd be carting to Fiji in an hour when her phone rang. She wasn't surprised to see Yeager on the Caller ID, since he always called just before she was due to leave to remind her to bring sunscreen—even to Scotland—which she'd always already packed.

She thumbed the answer button and lifted the phone to her ear. "Yes, I packed sunscreen, and yes, it's SPF thirty," she greeted him.

Silence met her from the other end for a moment. Then, in a quiet, too steady voice, Yeager replied, "Hannah, I have some bad news."

Something seized up in her chest at the absolute absence of emotion in his voice. She'd never heard him sound this way before. "Are you okay?"

"Yes," he told her quickly. "But I'm not in Vancouver."

He was supposed to have been in Vancouver yesterday afternoon, West Coast time. He'd planned to check out a site for some new mountain adventure today, then take a late-night flight that would put him in Suva before breakfast on Sunday morning, Fiji time, which would be Saturday afternoon New York time. That gave them plenty of time to get settled, since that would be the day before Hannah was set to ovulate. They'd planned everything down to the minute. At least, they had before Yeager turned up someplace he wasn't supposed to be.

"Where are you?" she asked.

He muttered an exasperated sound. "I'm in Alberta. Long story short, what was supposed to be an uneventful flight, both time-and weather-wise, got delayed a couple of hours, then a storm blew in out of nowhere just as we were approaching the Rockies. The jet I chartered had to make an emergency landing on a little airstrip at a research station in the middle of nowhere."

Hannah's tension increased with every word he spoke. "That happened yesterday?"

"Yeah."

"Why didn't you call me?"

"I didn't think it would be that big a deal. I figured the storm would blow over and we'd still make it to Vancouver today. Worst case scenario, I'd have to cancel my day trip to look at the property I'm interested in and just head right on to Fiji as planned."

"So you think you'll still be able to do that?"

His answer was way too quick for her liking. "No."

Okay, so they wouldn't be going to Fiji. That was all right. Hannah hadn't been all that keen on flying fifteen hours one way, anyway, with or without a fer-

tility volcano—and Yeager—at the end of the journey.
She was totally okay with their next attempt at conception being right here in New York. They could check
into a nice hotel, have dinner—maybe even take another carriage ride around Central Park, which, of all
the experiences she'd shared with Yeager, had been,
hands down, the most enjoyable. Well, except for all
their, um, attempts at conception.

"So I guess we're not going to Fiji then," she said.

"No," he told her. "I'm definitely not going to get
out of here in time for that."

He still sounded way too somber for her liking.
Way too serious. Way too worried.

"Well, when will you be able to leave?" she asked.

This time, there was a long pause followed by a
quiet, "I honestly don't know."

Now Hannah felt somber, serious and worried, too.
"Why not?"

"Because we're completely snowed in here. And
another storm is coming right at us."

She told herself not to panic. There was still plenty
of time for him to get back to New York, right? Sunday was still two days away. A flight from Alberta
couldn't take more than four or five hours, could it?
A third of the time it would have taken to fly to Fiji.

"But you'll be back in New York by Sunday, right?"
she asked.

There was another pause, longer this time. Then a
very weary-sounding Yeager told her, "I don't know,
Hannah."

"But—"

"The jet took a beating before we landed. My pilot
almost didn't get us to the ground in one piece."

Her nerves went barbed-wire sharp at that. "Yeager! You nearly died? And you didn't call me yesterday to tell me?"

What the hell was the matter with him? Okay, yeah, they weren't girlfriend and boyfriend, so he wasn't obligated to keep her apprised of everything that happened in his life, even when his life was threatened. But they were friends, weren't they? Kind of? Sort of? In a way? Okay, maybe they weren't friends, either—she wasn't sure what they were, actually. But they *were* trying to make a baby together, so the least he could do was keep her informed about things that put him in danger.

Then she remembered he made his living courting danger. He lived his life courting danger. Yeager wasn't happy unless he was thumbing his nose at death with some kind of crazy adventure. Nearly crashing into the side of a mountain in a private jet was probably nothing compared to some of the activities he undertook. How could she have thought it would be a good idea to have a baby with a guy like that? She was going to be worrying about the safety of her child's father for the rest of her life.

Or not. Because it was starting to sound like they might miss their last chance for her to conceive before the time ran out on the Linden fortune. If Yeager got stuck in Alberta much longer...

"The jet landed safely," he hurried to reassure her. "But not before it developed some mechanical problems that are going to keep it grounded until it can be repaired. And this place is totally closed off by road this time of year. The only way in and out is by plane, and there aren't any others here right now. Even if this new storm subsides soon, I'm going to be stuck until someone else can get in and fly us out. And I just don't know how long that will take. There must be three feet of snow on the ground."

With every word he spoke, Hannah's fears grew worse. Not just for Yeager's safety, but that the last chance she had to conceive a child with him—to start a family with him—was gone. Sunday was supposed to be her fertile day. She knew that an egg, once dropped, could be viable for, at best, twenty-four hours. If her calculations were correct—though, honestly, she had no idea these days if they were, and the fertility monitors and ovulation tests she'd tried to use hadn't been all that helpful—she could still become pregnant if Yeager made it back to New York by Monday night.

Maybe. Possibly. Perhaps.

But if he didn't make it back by then, that was it. No baby for Hannah. No Linden fortune that would have ensured the rest of her life was a happy, safe, secure one. Instead she'd be dogged forever by the specter of what might have been.

She tried not to think about the irony. Had she never discovered she was the missing Linden heir, the rest of her life would have been happy. Happy enough, anyway. She would have lived it as she always had, day by day, satisfied with what she had, working toward a future she hoped and dreamed would eventually happen. She would have had a vague idea about starting a family someday, but wouldn't have been in any big hurry. And if it never happened, well, that probably would have been okay, because she never would have known what she was missing. But now...

Now she would have to live with the very real knowledge that she wanted a family badly and might never have one. Worse, now she knew she wanted that family with Yeager, and she would never have him, either. Without him as the father of her child, there would be no reason for him to stay in her life. Not as anything other than one of her regulars at Cathcart and Quinn—though one she would now know quite a bit better than most. The only reason he would have continued to be a part of her life otherwise would have been because he was her baby's father. He wasn't the kind of man to settle down in one place with one woman—any woman. Sure, he was determined to be a father to their child, but only between trips to all four corners of the world. His idea of parenting would be swooping in with *Matryoshka* dolls and *Mozartkugel* and didgeridoos to regale his progeny with stories of his travels, then fly off again for another adventure— most likely with someone named Luydmila or Fritzi or Sheila.

Yes, Yeager Novak wanted to be a father. But he didn't want to be a *father*. Not the kind who dealt with the skinned knees and carpools and picket fences. Or with the hand-holding strolls and the Sunday-morning snuggles and the firefly-spattered evenings on the patio after the kids went to bed, the way Hannah wanted to be a mother. And the way she wanted to be—she might as well admit it—a wife.

So if Yeager didn't make it back to New York soon...

"Well, when do you think someone will be able to fly you out?" she asked.

There was another one of those uncomfortable silences. "I just don't know, Hannah. I'm sorry."

"It's okay," she told him. Even if it wasn't. Even if it kind of felt like she was stranded alone in an icy, isolated wilderness herself. "I'm sure you'll get out of there soon. I'm not supposed to ovulate until Sunday. Maybe it'll even happen Monday. As long as we can get together by Tuesday, we should be fine. You'll be back by Tuesday, right?"

The silence that met her for that reply was the worst one yet. So was the hopeless, defeated tone in Yeager's voice when he said, "Yeah. Sure. Sure, I will. It'll be fine. Look, I'm sorry, but I have to go. The power here is iffy, too, right now, and I'm not sure how long I'll have my battery. I'll call you again when I can, okay? Let you know what's going on."

"Okay," Hannah said. "Keep me posted. And, Yeager?"

"Yeah?"

She knew he hated to hear the words, but she was going to say them, anyway. "Be careful."

"I will," he said.

And that, more than anything, told her all she needed to know. He was worried, too.

She said goodbye and thumbed off the phone, then looked at the suitcase she hadn't yet closed. On top was the lacy underwear Yeager had given to her in Malta. She'd worn it every trip since, thinking it would bring them luck. And also because of the look in Yeager's eyes whenever he saw her wearing it. Automatically, she began removing everything she'd packed, piece by piece, putting it all back where it belonged. Then she gazed at the empty suitcase, feeling every bit as empty.

She told herself there was probably still time to go the sperm bank route. She'd finished the application process last summer and been cleared while she was waiting for Yeager to see a doctor about his health to ensure he was up to the task of conceiving a child. It was possible they might be able to accommodate her, especially if she explained the situation to them. She might still be able to conceive a baby this month with some anonymous donor.

But she didn't want to have a baby with some anonymous donor. She wanted Yeager to be the father of any child she might have. Having a baby wasn't about winning the Linden billions anymore. It hadn't been about that for a long time. Hannah didn't want to just start a family, not even for a family fortune. She wanted to start a family with Yeager. Because, somewhere along the line, Yeager had begun to feel like family.

Surely he'd make it home by Tuesday. Surely her egg would wait until he was there before it made an appearance. Surely this time—this last, final time—would be the one that worked.

Surely it would. Surely.

It took Yeager a full week after becoming stranded in Alberta to get back to New York, much too late for him and Hannah to even attempt conception. For the last couple of months she'd been using one of those prediction kits that indicated a surge in some hormone that happened prior to ovulation. By Wednesday afternoon, when Yeager finally called her to tell her he would be flying out the next day, that surge was non-existent. Hannah's egg had come and gone without him. They'd never stood a chance.

He'd told her on Sunday night to go to the sperm bank on Monday and get pregnant that way. But she'd said she would wait for him. He'd been surprised by her decision—she was almost certainly not going to get pregnant if she waited for him to get back to New York, and by the time they could try next month, it would be past the legal deadline for her to inherit. But a part of him had been delighted by her decision, too. He still liked the idea of having a child with Hannah. Now, though, there wouldn't be any financial benefit to her, so he couldn't see her wanting to continue the effort.

Even if he offered to pay for everything the child needed—and then some—he couldn't see her going along. Hannah wanted to make her own way in the world. She wanted to have a child on her terms, not his, which was perfectly understandable. But she wouldn't be able to do that until she was at a place in her life where having a child fit in. Now that she wouldn't be claiming her family fortune, who knew when she'd be able to swing it? And by the time she could, there would probably be some other guy in the picture who could provide the paternity. And maybe provide a life with her, too. She wouldn't need Yeager for any of it. Not that he wanted to spend a life with Hannah—or any woman. But the idea of her starting a family with someone else now was just…inconceivable. No pun intended.

He wished her grandfather was still alive. Not just so Yeager could tell the guy what an incredible granddaughter he had—so it was unfair to put some ridiculous condition on her inheritance like insisting she have a child—but also so he could strangle the guy with his bare hands. Seriously, what kind of jerk turned a woman into an incubator, just so he could ensure his family line remained intact?

Okay, so, in a way, maybe Yeager had kind of done that to Hannah, too. That was beside the point. The point was...

He sighed with much feeling as he gazed out the window of his office at the snow falling over New York. The point was that he and Hannah had both wanted a child for their own reasons, and now they wouldn't be having one. What could either of them say or do at this point that would make that better? It wasn't like either of them was at fault for what had happened, but that didn't make it any easier to bear.

So where did that leave them? What would they be to each other now? It wasn't like they could go back to just being seamstress and client. But they didn't feel like just friends, either. Sure, they were lovers—or maybe former lovers—but even that didn't feel like the right word to use. Yeager had had lots of lovers—and he had lots of former lovers—but he'd never felt for any of them the way he felt for Hannah.

He forced himself to turn away from the window and go back to his desk, where a mountain of work awaited him after his stay in Alberta. He told himself he was way overthinking this. He and Hannah *were* friends. Period. That was why he felt differently about her than he had other women he'd dated. Those women had been great, and he'd liked all of them, but they'd never been... Hannah. And he didn't kid himself that he'd ever meet another woman who was like her. Who would be a *friend* like her, he corrected himself. Women would come and go in his life the way they always had, but Hannah would be constant. The way friends were.

Yeah, that was it. They were friends. Friends who would stay friends, no matter what. Even if they didn't have a child to tie them together. Wouldn't they?

Surely they would. Surely.

Hannah awoke on New Year's Day with *the* weirdest feeling, after having some of *the* weirdest dreams she'd ever had. In one, she was underwater, but perfectly capable of breathing, and was suddenly surrounded by and swimming among dolphins. In another, she was tending to a garden full of lotuses and turtles kept coming up out of the soil. Yeager was in another, bringing her a basket of acorns that she upended and consumed in one gulp. Just...weird.

She also realized she'd slept way past the usual time she awoke on days when Cathcart and Quinn was closed. It was nearly eleven when she finally opened her eyes and looked at the clock.

Still feeling as if someone had wrapped her in cotton gauze, she rolled over and, for some reason, settled both hands over her lower abdomen, splaying her fingers wide. It shouldn't have been an unusual gesture. Except that she never did it. Usually, when she awoke and turned to lie on her back in bed, she tucked both hands behind her head. What the hell was up with those dreams, and why did she have her hands on her abdomen instead of—

Heat suddenly flared in her belly. She dared not hope...but did anyway. Was her body trying to tell her brain something it hadn't yet figured out? Like maybe...

She was supposed to have started her period yesterday or the day before, but she'd put down the lateness as a result of, number one, her cycle never being all that regular to begin with and, two, the stress of the last several months taking its toll. She shouldn't have been fertile the night she and Yeager made love in New York, and sperm normally weren't viable for more than three days after they launched. On the other hand, she'd read that it was possible for some of those little swimmers to hang around for five days after their release. And, hey, it *was* Yeager's little swimmers she was talking about.

It was also possible she'd dropped an egg before she thought she would. Those ovulation predictor kits were iffy. They only told you your hormones were in the right place for you to ovulate, but not exactly when you would. So maybe, *maybe*, that snowy night when they'd made love right here in her bed, the circumstances had been right.

She had a pregnancy kit in her bathroom she'd bought after their last attempt failed. Her hands were actually shaking as she withdrew it from the medicine cabinet. And she didn't think she took a single breath while she counted down the seconds it took for the indicator to produce the word *Yes* or *No*. Five times she had performed this ritual. Five times, it had ended with the word *No*. She waited a full minute longer than she needed to to check the results this morning. And she had one eye closed, and the other narrowed, when she finally picked up the indicator to look at it. So it was no wonder she was still doubtful when she saw that the answer this time was—

Yes.

Heat exploded inside her at those three little letters. She didn't believe it. Couldn't believe it. Wouldn't believe it until she took a second test. Which she didn't have. So she yanked on some pants and threw her coat on over her pajama shirt, tugged snow boots on over her bare feet, grabbed her wallet and ran downstairs to the *mercado* below her apartment…only to find it closed for the holiday.

She knew a moment of panic. Until she remembered the twenty-four-hour Duane Reade two blocks up. She knew it was closed on Thanksgiving and Christmas. Oh, *pleasepleaseplease*, Pregnancy Gods and Goddesses, don't let it be closed on New Year's, too.

The gods and goddesses were good to Hannah that day because a half hour later she was counting down to see the results of the second test. The sample wouldn't be nearly as strong as the first, because she'd been storing up that one all night, and this one was the result of two hastily consumed cups of coffee purchased along with the pregnancy test. But even with the weakened sample, when she picked up the wand, studying it with both eyes wide open this time, the word she saw was—

Yes.

No matter how many times Hannah looked at it, and no matter from what angle, the word she saw, again and again, was *Yes.*

Yes. *Yes.* YES. *Yessssss!*

Holy cow. She was going to have a baby. She and Yeager were going to have a baby. She was going to have a family. A real family. The way she'd always wanted. The way she'd never really thought she would.

She had to tell him. Immediately. In person. She could shower and change and be at his place by—

By never, because she realized in that moment that she didn't even know where he lived. There had never been a reason to visit him at his place, and other than one vague mention of his having a condo in West Chelsea, the topic of where he lived had never come up in their conversations. Why should it? There had never been a reason for her to visit him at home, and there never would be, unless—until—they had a child together. Which had seemed less and less likely with every passing month.

They weren't boyfriend and girlfriend, she reminded herself for perhaps the hundredth time since going into this venture with him. They weren't even lovers, at least not on Yeager's part. It didn't matter that Hannah was battling some weird emotions on that front herself. Maybe she had grown to love him over the last six months—maybe—but she would fall out of love again, once the two of them weren't so involved. Right? Of course.

They were partners. That was all. And they would always be partners, thanks to this baby. But it was more like a business arrangement than anything else. They'd even signed paperwork outlining their obligations to each other during the conception process and to the child once its conception was achieved. They had each gone into it with individual needs and goals, and this baby—they were going to have a baby!— would fulfill those needs and goals for each of them. Yes, that sounded kind of indifferent and calculating, but that was exactly what their agreement had been at first. Nothing personal. Everything planned. And now...

A wave of something that was in no way indifferent or calculating—or impersonal or unplanned—rolled through her midsection. Oh, God. Now it was so, *so* much more than any of those things. Now it was...it was...

She grabbed her phone to text Yeager, asking him only where he was. They hadn't spoken since his return to New York—probably because neither of them had known what to say. He might not even be in New York at the moment. How did billionaire adventurers celebrate New Year's Eve, anyway? For all she knew, he'd followed the holiday around the world, celebrating it a dozen times, starting in Samoa and ending in Pago Pago.

He texted back immediately, telling her he was at home. Why?

She didn't want to announce something like this with a text. Or even a phone call. So her text back to him was simple, if vague. Would it be okay if I came over for a little while?

He again replied immediately. Sure. Everything ok?

Fine, she returned. Just want to talk. Then she backspaced over the last part before hitting Send and amended it to Just need to talk.

Yeager texted back his address on West 21st and said he'd be working at home all day. Hannah told him she'd be there in an hour or so. The 7 train on holidays never ran very efficiently, after all. Fortunately for Hannah, though, her body finally was.

Ten

Damn the 7 train, anyway, Yeager thought as he waited for Hannah's arrival nearly two hours later. It never ran well on holidays.

He'd given up trying to work after she'd sent her last text, because he'd been too busy wondering what she needed to talk about. He'd at least showered and shaved and changed into a pair of jeans and an oatmeal-colored sweater, but that had only eaten up about thirty minutes. For the last—he glanced at the Bavarian clock on his mantel nestled between the Turkish *Iznik* bowl and a Puerto Rican *vejigante* mask—seventy-eight minutes, he'd done little more than pace from room to room trying to find something to occupy himself. He hadn't even eaten lunch because his stomach was too full of apprehension.

Two hours and sixteen minutes after Hannah's last

text, there was finally a knock at his front door—Yeager had already notified Baxter, the doorman, that he was expecting her and to send her right up. He couldn't believe how nervous he was when he went to answer the door. As he strode down the long gallery from the living room where he'd been pacing, it did that cinematic stretch thing where it seemed to quadruple in length.

It had just been too long since he'd seen her, that was all. Since July, they'd never gone more than a couple of weeks without contact. Then he realized it had only been a couple of weeks since he and Hannah had taken that carriage ride through Central Park. No different from most other months and hardly an eon. Even if it did feel like one.

He opened his front door to find her standing there in her red coat with the funny, different-colored buttons that she'd designed and made herself, her striped scarf tripled around her neck. Her hair was damp and glistening from the snow that had begun to fall not long after she'd texted. And her eyes...

Damn. Those eyes. Even after knowing her as long as he had, even after making love to her a dozen times, her eyes still seized something deep inside him and held fast. Yeager would always be startled by the clarity and depth of emotion in Hannah's eyes.

"Hi," she said.

Still feeling as nervous as a schoolboy at his first dance—even though he hadn't even been this nervous as a schoolboy at his first dance—he replied, "Hi."

He took a step backward and gestured her inside, and she strode past him slowly, almost cautiously, as if she weren't sure of her reception here. Why was this the first time she'd ever been in his home? He should have invited her over a long time ago.

He closed the door behind her and followed her down the gallery, Hannah unwinding her scarf as she went. By the time they reached his living room with its panoramic windows on both sides, she had shrugged it off, along with her coat. Beneath, she was wearing jeans and a fuzzy white sweater. She transferred her coat restlessly from one hand to the other.

"Let me take your coat," Yeager said, reaching toward it.

She looked a little confused by the gesture at first, as if her thoughts were a million miles away. Then she awkwardly extended her coat to him. He awkwardly took it from her. Then he shifted it from one hand to the other a couple of times before tossing it onto the chair nearest him.

"So," he began...then realized he had no idea what else to say. Finally he went with, "How've you been?"

And immediately regretted the question. How the hell did he think she'd been? She wasn't going to have the family or the fortune that had been dangled in front of her for six months then cruelly yanked away from her to leave her with neither. He was going to go out on a limb and say she hadn't been too great.

Instead of replying, she darted her gaze around his living room, from the travel trophies on his mantelpiece to the Russian mosaic on the wall above them to the Chilean pottery lining one windowsill to the Indonesian shadow puppets hanging above the door to his office. Her gaze seemed to light on every item he'd ever brought home with him from his adventures— and there were scores of them in this room alone.

Finally she looked at him again. "I didn't think you'd be home," she said softly.

"Why not?"

"I just figured you'd be somewhere else. I mean, look at this place, Yeager. It's incredible. How many people can live the way you do? I just thought you'd be celebrating New Year's somewhere besides New York, that's all."

He started to tell her he hadn't felt like celebrating. The New Year or anything else. Instead he told her, "I have a lot that needs attention here right now."

One of those things should have been Hannah. One of those things was Hannah. He just wasn't sure yet what kind of attention to direct her way. He wasn't sure he'd ever know.

"Hannah, is everything okay?" he asked.

She opened her mouth to reply then something over his shoulder caught her eye. She moved to the side of his living room that looked out onto the Hudson.

"You can see the Statue of Liberty from here," she said.

Yeager had forgotten about that. He'd lived here long enough that he guessed he took it for granted. And why the hell wasn't she answering his question?

She walked to the other side of the living room and looked out the windows there. "And you can see the Empire State Building from here," she said.

Yeah, he'd forgotten about that, too. He'd honestly stopped seeing the views as anything other than New York City in general and Manhattan in particular. Not that he didn't appreciate the view, he just hadn't really given it much thought in the last few years. To someone like Hannah, though, who'd spent who knew how long in her cramped Sunnyside studio with one window that looked at the apartment building on the next street, his view of the city was doubtless pretty incredible.

Why had he forgotten about that when it was what had impressed him about the place so much the first time he'd looked at it? The minute he'd seen the views Hannah had just seen, the little boy from Peoria had surged up inside him and hadn't been able to believe it was possible to see so much from one room. It was like looking at the whole, wide world in one swoop. And at night, when the city lights were on, it was like the world went on *forever*.

When Hannah turned to look at him again, she had tears in her eyes. The only other times Yeager had seen her cry were the night he'd initially turned down her request that he be the father of her child and that first time she'd come to his office to tell him she wasn't pregnant. Both times she'd been in a position where she thought she would miss out on inheriting her family's fortune—or, at least, that was why he'd thought she was crying at the time. He knew now that the money wasn't the primary reason Hannah had wanted to get pregnant—she genuinely wanted to start the family she'd never thought she might have. But, come on—who wouldn't cry at the prospect of losing billions of dollars? Yeager almost felt like crying himself.

Even so, it had been weeks since they'd realized they wouldn't make the deadline for the terms of her grandfather's will. Why was she crying now?

"Hannah?" He tried again. "Are you okay?"

She nodded, wiping at each eye. "Yeah, I am. It's

just that standing here, looking at your place... It's
just... It's *huge*, Yeager. And it's gorgeous. It embod-
ies everything good that money can make happen. All
morning, I've only been thinking about what it will be
like to finally have a family. I'm just now remembering I'll have enough money to live the way you do. I'd
actually forgotten about that. Isn't that weird? When I
realized this morning that I'm pregnant, I didn't even
think about the Linden fortune. All I could think about
was the baby and you."

Yeager had pretty much stopped hearing what she
said after the words *I'm pregnant*. Probably because
the roar of adrenaline that started rushing through him
made it impossible to register anything else.

"You're pregnant?" he asked, his breath shallow.

She nodded.

"You're sure?"

She nodded again. "I took two tests. They were
both positive. I mean, I need to see the doctor for a
blood test, too, I guess, but those home tests are pretty
freaking accurate."

Yeager still couldn't believe it. "But how? I was
in Alberta."

Hannah laughed. "It didn't happen when you were
in Alberta, obviously. It happened here in New York.
That night we went to the Russian Tea Room and took
the carriage ride through Central Park."

He shook his head. "So all those times we planned
down to the minute, all those adventures, all those exotic places..."

She shrugged. "Turns out I just needed some spon-
taneity in familiar surroundings to be at my most,
um, fertile."

Hey, whatever worked. That night at the Russian Tea Room and riding around Central Park with Hannah had still been an adventure, Yeager realized. He'd done things that night he'd never done before, and he'd felt as exhilarated by them as he had by any other risk he'd ever taken. Hell, any time he spent with Hannah was an adventure. They'd still be doing his legacy—and Tommy—proud.

"We're going to have a baby?" Yeager asked. Because he *still* couldn't believe he'd heard her correctly.

"Yeah, Yeager. We're going to have a baby."

They were going to have a baby. Even though they'd been working toward the goal for months, he had no idea what to say or how to act. He'd been so certain the first time they'd tried that it would happen immediately. He and Hannah could pat each other on the back and say, *Job well done.* Then they'd see each other again in a year or so—after she'd had a few months to get used to the whole motherhood thing—to arrange a visitation schedule. When he'd initially envisioned the arrangement, he hadn't seen much point in visiting the baby when he or she was still an infant, since babies couldn't communicate or interact or do much of anything but lie there and stare at you. They sure as hell couldn't travel or have adventures. But by the time the child was three or four, it would be a good time to get to know his progeny and gradually start introducing him or her to the world. Now, however...

He'd been such an idiot.

Because now, after months of disappointment and fear that he would never become a father, Yeager realized he wanted a lot more than to just put a miniature version of himself on the planet to be his legacy

after he was gone. He couldn't just settle for visiting
his child a couple of times a year and taking him or
her on age-appropriate adventures. Sending an exotic
gift and having a Skype conversation from the other
side of the world on birthdays and holidays wouldn't
be enough. Yeager wanted...

He wanted to be a father.

"So, pretty cool, huh?" Hannah said, her voice
sounding like it was coming through an echo cham-
ber on the other side of the planet.

Cool? Yeah, it was cool. Among other things. A
million, billion other things that Yeager would be able
to identify if his brain wasn't trying to light on every
single one of them at the same time.

When he still didn't say anything—because he honestly couldn't figure out yet what to say—Hannah
continued, less enthusiastically. "I mean, it's what we
both wanted, right?"

Yeager nodded. But he still couldn't find his voice.

"I'll get my family and my family fortune," she
said, "and you'll get your legacy to carry on after
you're gone."

He still couldn't believe it was that easy. Then
again, he knew it hadn't been easy. On either of them.
But it had probably been tougher on Hannah than on
him. With or without a child, his life—or, at least,
his lifestyle—wasn't going to change all that much.
But hers...

Now she could live her life any way she wanted to.
She would have everything she'd ever hoped for, everything she'd ever wanted. A family. Financial free-
dom. A business empire she built all by herself. Yeager
knew how gratifying all of those things could be. He

was happy for Hannah. He was. It just felt kind of weird that she'd have all those things without him.

She was still looking at him expectantly, her eyes full of joy and wonder and relief, but also apprehension and fear and a host of other emotions that cut right to his soul. And then he felt the joy and wonder, too, and he realized it didn't matter that he couldn't find the words. He didn't need words. He crossed the room to where she was standing and swept her into his arms.

"We're going to have a baby," he said in the same astonished, ecstatic way she had.

And then they were laughing and staring at each other in disbelief and both of them were groping for words.

"Wow, we're really..."

"And we're..."

"I know, right? It's just so..."

"Exactly. How can...?"

"I don't know. It's just so..."

"Yeah. It really is the most..."

"And it's..."

"Totally unbelievably..."

"Awesome," they finally said as one.

And that word, more than any other Yeager knew, captured everything that needed to be said. At least for now. The rest...

Well, he'd worry about the rest of it later. Once he had it all figured out. In a million years or so.

It was dark by the time it occurred to Hannah that she should be going home. She and Yeager had spent hours trying to get accustomed to the new life growing inside her and how it was going to change *everything*.

They fixed lunch together in his kitchen and ate it in his dining room, and talked some more about how the baby was going to change *everything*. Not so much for Yeager, since he would still be living his life the way he always had, arranging his schedule here and there to visit his son or daughter, but for Hannah.

She had called Gus Fiver at his home—as he'd told her to do, should there be any developments like this outside regular office hours—to tell the attorney the good news and had arranged to meet with him in a few days, after she'd had a chance to see her doctor to confirm what she already knew. She wasn't sure what kind of legal hurdles still lay ahead or what kind of time frame she was looking at for coming into her inheritance, but she figured it was probably safe at this point to give her two weeks' notice to Cathcart and Quinn. And then...

She had no idea. She had to find a bigger place to live, obviously, someplace with a yard that was close to good schools and lots of child-friendly places and activities. But she didn't want to move too far from where she lived now, since Queens was familiar and she liked it a lot. Maybe she could find a house with a nice yard in Astoria or Jackson Heights. Someplace that had a lot of families and things for families to do and places for families to go. Because once she had this baby, she would be part of a family. A family who could go anywhere and do anything and live any way they wanted.

Before the realization of that started making her woozy again, she told Yeager, "I should probably head home."

They were sitting on his sofa, gazing out the windows that faced the Empire State Building, the city sparkling like fairy lights against the black sky. When night had first fallen, Hannah thought the view breathtaking. Now, though, she marveled at how Yeager could see so much of New York from his place, but knew nothing about the people who were living out there. Maybe her tiny apartment didn't boast a spectacular view like this one, but she knew most of the people who populated it. That, she hoped, would never change, no matter where the future took her.

"Go?" Yeager echoed from beside her. He had his arm comfortably draped across the sofa behind her, his feet propped on the antique steamer trunk he used for a coffee table. His posture suggested this was something the two them did all the time instead of this being Hannah's first visit to his home. "But you just got here."

"We've been talking for hours," she said. "And it's getting late."

"Stay here tonight," he told her.

His tone of voice was as comfortable as the rest of him, but Hannah was surprised by the invitation. And she had mixed feelings about accepting it. On one hand, she absolutely wanted to spend the night with Yeager. She wanted to spend every night with him. She wanted to spend her life with him. On the other hand, their "business" together really was concluded, at least until after the baby was born. There was no reason for her to prolong her time with him. Especially since she knew that the more time she spent with him, the more difficult that parting was going to be.

"I can't," she said reluctantly. "I have to work tomorrow and I don't have any of my stuff with me."

"You can use my stuff."

The intimacy inherent in that statement made her toes curl. He was speaking as if the two of them shared this space all the time. He was probably accustomed to having his girlfriends spend the night on a regular basis—even though, Hannah reminded herself again, she wasn't his girlfriend. They weren't intimate, even if they had made love several times and were now expecting a baby. Intimacy was more than the sharing of bodies. It was the sharing of souls. It was the sharing of everything. And *everything* was the last thing Yeager wanted to share with anyone.

"I can't use your stuff," she told him. "Your clothes won't fit me."

He grinned lasciviously. "Who said anything about wearing clothes?"

Her heart raced. He still wanted to have sex with her, even without the goal of getting her pregnant. Maybe...

Maybe nothing, she told herself firmly. He was Yeager Novak. He wanted to have sex with every woman in North America. And South America. And Europe, Asia, Africa, Australia and Antarctica.

"I have to work tomorrow," she told him, hoping she only imagined the husky, sex-starved quality her voice seemed to suddenly have. "And Cathcart and Quinn has a strict dress code."

"Then don't go to work," he said.

"I have to go to work."

"Why? You're rich."

She started to tell him—again—that she wasn't rich yet, then remembered that, at this point, that was no longer true. It was merely a formality. She would be rich—her stomach pitched at the reminder. But she wouldn't breathe easy about that until everything was official. And she couldn't just quit her job impulsively. Maybe Misters Cathcart and Quinn hadn't been the most accommodating employers all the time, but they'd done her a solid favor ten years ago, giving her a job while she was still in high school with little work experience. And once she'd explained her situation with her grandfather's will, they'd granted her all the time off she needed. It would be ungrateful and mean to just walk away without warning.

"I have to give my two weeks' notice," she said. "I can't leave Cathcart and Quinn hanging without a seamstress. That would be irresponsible. Not to mention just a crappy thing to do."

She hesitated a moment, then made herself say the rest of what she had to say. Especially since she and Yeager both seemed to need to hear it spelled out. "Besides, you and I aren't... We won't be... It's not necessary for us to..." She sighed in frustration and tried again. "We don't...need each other anymore, Yeager."

Which, she told herself, was the truth. Although she needed him—although she loved him—he didn't need or love her. So the *each other* part of that statement kept it from being a lie.

His gaze locked with hers but he said nothing. Unable to tolerate the intensity of his blue, blue eyes, Hannah looked out at the city and said the rest. "I appreciate everything you've done. Oh, God, that was a terrible platitude." She hurried on when she realized what she was saying. "I just mean..." She muttered a ripe oath under her breath. "I'm honestly not sure what I can say that *won't* sound like a platitude, but I'll give it a shot."

She made herself look at him again. And wished she hadn't. Because there was something in his eyes she'd never seen before, something she couldn't identify, except to say that it wasn't good. In spite of that, she pressed on.

"Thank you for everything you've done for me over the last six months, Yeager. Not just in providing the biological essentials I needed to make a baby, but in showing me the world, too. I'm a different person, a better person now than I was five months ago, thanks to you. And not just because of the new life growing inside me. But because of other things inside me now, too."

Probably best not to dwell on those *other things*, since they included being in love for the first time in her life and the knowledge that she would never love anyone like this again.

"I know this…this venture…was time-consuming for you and I know it kept you tethered in one place for a lot longer than you're used to being confined. I understand you need to get back to business as usual. I need to get back to business as usual, too. Even if things are going to be a lot different for me now. So you don't have to invite me to spend the night because it's getting late. I'll be okay on my own. I promise. I've been okay on my own for a long time."

She deliberately used singular pronouns when she spoke, because she knew she and Yeager weren't a collective anymore. This baby was her baby, and it was his baby, but it wasn't *their* baby. In the agreement they'd signed, Hannah alone would be respon-

sible for her pregnancy, without any obligation on
Yeager's part. She would contact him after her baby
was born to see when he wanted to start visiting his
son or daughter and work from there.

That was how they'd both wanted it five-and-a-half
months ago. It was doubtless how Yeager still wanted
it. Just because Hannah had begun to wish he would
be there for her now...that he would be there for her
forever... It was irrelevant. *Their* time was at an end.
From here on out, Hannah would have her time, and
Yeager would have his time, and they would only interact whenever he could fit a visit to his child into
his schedule.

"So...thanks," she said again. "But I've got this."

Yeager studied her in silence for a long time. Then
he said, "And what if I want it, too?"

Heat suffused her, but not for the same reason it
usually did when Yeager looked at her the way he
sometimes did. This look was certainly heated. But it
was heated in a way she'd never seen before.

"What do you mean?" she asked.

He hesitated again then he said, "I mean, what if I
want to be a part of your pregnancy? What if I want
to be there when our baby is born?"

"I..." she began.

Then she halted. She really did want to get on with
her life without Yeager as quickly and cleanly as possible. It was going to become more and more difficult
to do that the longer he stayed a part of it. But her baby
was his baby, too. If he wanted to be there for its birth,
could she really deny him that?

"All right," she said reluctantly. "If you don't mind
sticking close to New York when the due date ap-

proaches, then I'll call you when I leave for the hospital and you can be there when the baby is born."

"I can definitely stay close to New York," he said. And there was something in his voice when he said it that made it seem like he was talking about more than just for the baby's due date. "And what if I want to be... What do you call it? Like a pregnancy coach or something? What if I want to be there for your pregnancy, too?"

"I don't think there's such a thing as a pregnancy coach." Hannah hedged, avoiding an answer. "But the person who coaches you through labor is a doula."

"Okay, so what if I want to be a doula?" he asked.

His request surprised her. "I don't know if a man can be a doula."

"It's the twenty-first century, Hannah. Gender roles are fluid."

Still stalling, she replied, "Oh, sure. Tell that to all the women making seventy-nine cents for every man's dollar."

He smiled at that. She felt a little better. Though she still felt plenty weird. Just what was Yeager asking, really?

"Then maybe I can be a dude-la," he said. "Be there for you during your pregnancy, whenever you need me. What would you think about that?"

She narrowed her eyes at him. "I think it would be tough for you to do that from places like Kyrgyzstan and Djibouti."

He lifted a shoulder and let it drop. "Like I said, I can stay close to New York."

Well, this was certainly news to Hannah. She could count on all her fingers and toes and then some the times he'd told her he could never stay in one place for too long. "Since when?" she asked.

This time Yeager didn't hesitate at all when he replied. "Since the minute you told me you're pregnant."

"You've always said you'd suffocate if you had to stay in one place for any length of time," she reminded him.

"That's what I used to think," he agreed. "Back when I was an idiot. But now..."

"Now what?"

He sat forward, removing his feet from the steamer trunk to place them firmly on the floor. As if he were trying to anchor himself here.

"Look, I won't lie," he said. "There's still a lot I need to figure out about this whole fatherhood thing. But that's just the point, Hannah. I want to figure it out. I don't just want a legacy. I'm beginning to wonder if that was what I really wanted in the first place. I don't know. I don't know a lot of things. But there's one thing I *do* know. I want more than to be a long-distance parent."

He turned to face her fully, then lifted a hand to cup her cheek. "And I know one other thing, too," he said softly. "I want *us* to be more than long-distance parents. I want us to be more than parents, period. I don't want us to be you and me. I want us to be...us."

Hannah covered his hand with hers, worried he might take it back. Worried he might take it all back. But she had no idea what to say.

Yeager didn't seem to be finished, though, because he continued. "I've spent my adult life circling the globe, trying to find the thing that will make my pulse pound hardest, my heart hammer fastest and my soul sing loudest. I've done things no normal human being has ever done, and I've had one adrenaline buzz after another. But today, when you told me you're pregnant… Hannah, I've never felt anything like that in my life. And I'm still reeling from it. It's intoxicating, this feeling of…of…"

"Joy," she finished for him. Because she'd had more time than he to identify it for what it was.

"Yeah," he agreed. "Joy. And, yes, it's partly because of the baby, but even more, it's because of you. Even before this baby happened, I knew I wanted more with you. Since I started spending time with you, Hannah, *everything* in my life has been different. No matter where I've been, as long as I've been with you, I've been…happy. Since my parents died, I was beginning to think I'd never feel that way again. Maybe that's why I keep circling the globe—I'm looking for that. But I don't need to keep running all over the world. I only need to be where you are. Where you and our baby are. Because starting a family with the woman I love? That's the ultimate adventure. One I want to live over and over again."

Now Hannah was the one experiencing the heart-hammering, pulse-pounding, soul-singing adrenaline rush. And all because of three little words. Very softly, she asked, "You love me?"

Yeager nodded. "It may have taken me a while to figure that out, too, but I finally did. I do love you. I've probably loved you since that first trip we took together. And I will love you for the rest of my days, no matter where I spend them."

"Just for the sake of clarification," she said, not sure why she was belaboring this, "you love me for more than being able to stitch up your clothes and clean out the walrus stains, right?"

He smiled. "Yeah. For more than that. A lot more."

He waited for Hannah's response and, when it didn't come—mostly because she was too stunned to say anything—he sobered some. And he said, "Please tell me this isn't a one-sided thing. I mean, I know you were doing your best to keep us separated with all the 'I' and 'you' talk a minute ago, but I can't help feeling maybe you at least like me more than you did when we first went into this thing."

"No, I don't like you more," she told him. "I love you. Always."

His smile turned dazzling. "So what do you say then? You want to hitch our stars together? See where it takes us?"

She thought about that for a moment. And after another moment, she smiled back. "I'll agree on two conditions," she told him.

"Conditions?" he asked, smiling at the echo of their conversation six months ago.

She smiled back, obviously remembering. "Number one, we *have* to have a home base here in New York where we can put down roots. A place where we can take hand-holding strolls and have Sunday-morning snuggles and enjoy firefly-spattered evenings on the patio after the kids go to bed."

"Kids," he repeated. "As in plural?"

She nodded. "That's the second condition. We *have* to keep traveling and having adventures in exotic places to get pregnant again. I want to have lots of kids, Yeager, which means we have to have lots of epic sex."

He eyed her speculatively. "Well, okay. If we *have* to."

They smiled as one and wove their hands together. Then they leaned back on the sofa and gazed at the lights of Manhattan, marveling at what their lives ahead held. Maybe Hannah could spend the night here tonight. And maybe she could call out from work tomorrow. It would only be one day. And, hey, she and Yeager were celebrating.

"Happy New Year, Yeager," she said softly.

"Happy New Life, Hannah," he replied.

And she knew in that moment, it would be. Because no matter where life took them, no matter what adventures awaited, they were a family. And they always would be.

* * * * *

WE'RE HAVING A MAKEOVER...

We'll still be bringing you the very best in romance from authors you love...all with a fabulous new look!

Look out for our stylish new logo, too

MILLS & BOON

COMING JANUARY 2018

MILLS & BOON®

Desire™

PASSIONATE AND DRAMATIC LOVE STORIES

sneak peek at next month's titles...

In stores from 14th December 2017:

Taming the Texan – Jules Bennett *and* **Little Secrets: Unexpectedly Pregnant** – Joss Wood

The Rancher's Baby – Maisey Yates *and* **Claiming His Secret Heir** – Joanne Rock

Contract Bride – Kat Cantrell *and* **Pregnant by the CEO** – HelenKay Dimon

Just can't wait?
Buy our books online before they hit the shops!
www.millsandboon.co.uk

Also available as eBooks.

YOU LOVE ROMANCE?

WE LOVE ROMANCE!